INDIGO ABYSS

John H. Cunningham

ISBN: 9780998796598

ALSO BY JOHN H. CUNNINGHAM

Buck Reilly Adventure Series

Red Right Return

Green to Go

Crystal Blue

Second Chance Gold

Maroon Rising

Free Fall to Black

Silver Goodbye

White Knight

Historical Fiction

The Last Raft

INDIGO
ABYSS

DEDICATION

For Chris, Sandi, Rick and Gemma
The Bonfire Bunch

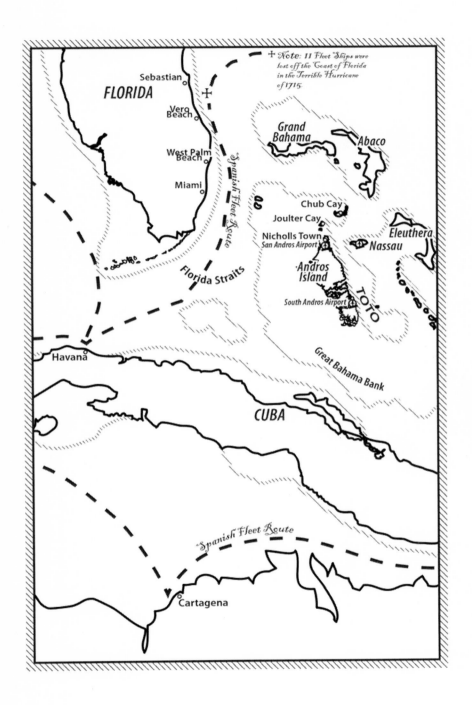

SECTION 1

TIMES

LIKE

THESE

1

A HUNDRED MILES OUT IN THE FLORIDA STRAITS, we sat in two circles under a large tropical almond tree on a moonless star-filled night, illuminated more closely by candle-light. Blue Heaven at nine o'clock on a Saturday night had never been so empty, but tonight, it was closed for special circumstances.

I watched the men in the larger circle as they played instruments and took turns singing a variety of songs. There wasn't much of an audience: me; town council member and part-time bartender Lenny Jackson; Bruiser Lewis and his brother Truck; Shawn Martin, the rum maker at Pilar; and Ray Floyd, my eccentric aviation mechanic and partner at Last Resort Charter and Salvage. And we were anything but festive.

"How old was Willy?" Shawn asked.

"Sixty-four, man," Lenny said. "Too damn young to die."

"Diabetic with heart problems," I said. "Same as a lot of others who've died from——"

"That and being a black man," Truck said. "Shit's killed more of us and Latinos than anyone else."

Truck was right about the stats from around the country. Thankfully, only a few dozen had died in the Keys.

I took a long pull on the dark and stormy Lenny had made me. Reverend Willy Peebles of the Church of the Redeemer had been a pillar of the Bahama Village community in Key West for most of his life. To those who knew him well, he'd been called the

Ruler because he'd used a wooden ruler to smack the hands—or occasionally the heads—of the wayward youth in his flock, steering them back onto the straight and narrow path of right-eousness. Lenny, Bruiser, Truck—hell, even I'd been nudged by Willy into doing the right thing on occasion, even if in some cases that meant doing the wrong thing to get there. Social justice didn't always conform to the legal system.

I exhaled a deep breath.

And here we were, on the day of his sudden passing, thanks to the damned pandemic, to honor him.

"I'll fly away, oh glory
I'll fly away, in the morning
When I dies, Hallelujah by and by
I'll fly away …"

David Wegman, the painter and raconteur, sang the words of the dirge in a voice much softer than you'd expect for a man of his physique. Broad shouldered, stout, with close-cropped hair under a straw hat and a braided silver beard that made him instantly recognizable. He strummed a tiny banjo as he tenderly whispered the words.

"Oh, how glad and happy when we meet
I'll fly away
No more cold iron shackles on my feet
I'll fly away …"

Truck shook his head. "Some wake this is, man. Iron shack-les? Willy wouldn't like that shit."

"Better than hanging out at the vestry with all them weeping old women," Lenny said.

Bruiser shifted his muscular bulk to stare at Lenny a long moment. "Gonna need to change your tune and get used to that, brotha."

"Shit."

Lenny poured himself a short shot of Patrón and slammed it down with a flourish. The tension between them was as palpable as the humidity after a tropical storm.

"What's that supposed to mean?" I said.

Lenny glanced at each of us, poured another shot—full this time—and downed it. He cleared his throat.

"This'll be my last night tending bar here, boys," he said. "Not to mention the end of my political career, too."

What the hell?

In the silence that followed—I realized Wegman had finished his song—Richard, the owner of Blue Heaven, began to tap his palms on a bongo drum. Wegman picked up the beat on his banjo, followed by Robin Smith-Martin on acoustic guitar.

"You gonna tell everybody the Ruler's dying command, Lenny?" Bruiser said.

Lenny poured another shot. A grimace twisted his mouth as he pushed the tequila toward Truck.

"Willy's dying request was for me to take over as pastor of the church," Lenny said.

I choked—then sprayed the cocktail from my mouth onto the bar.

"More like ordered you to," Truck said.

"What?" I said. "*Pastor* Lenny?" He may not have been present for the original sin, but Lenny had worked his entire thirty-plus years racking up as many as he could. "After all these years of Willy grooming you for politics?"

"I thought you were going to run for mayor," Shawn said.

"Was," Lenny said. "Not no more."

Dizziness or disbelief caused me to shake my head. "But Willy was the badass Ruler," I said. "No offense, but how're you going to fill those shoes?"

"I'll handle that part of the job," Bruiser said. The once-professional boxer had the look of Mike Tyson mixed with Aaron Neville, complete with tattoos on his neck, thick chiseled arms, and soft voice.

Shawn smiled. "You two gonna talk like a butterfly and sting like a .44 Magnum."

"Something like that," Lenny said.

"Damn, conch man," I said. "Hearts will be breaking all over town tonight."

Cayman Smith-Martin, Robin's brother, leaned into his stand-up bass guitar and began to pluck what I recognized as a song by Pink Floyd.

> "Long you live and high you fly,
> Smile's you'll give and tears you'll cry,
> And all you touch and all you see
> Is all your life will ever be ..."

The musicians were in their own heads, playing their instruments, following each other's leads. Paying homage to Willy in their own ways.

"We need to get the older people to take better care of themselves," Lenny said. "That's why they're dying from this crap."

"And get better jobs," Truck said. "They've been more exposed from front line bullshit at grocery stores, labor—"

"Being pastors," Ray Floyd said.

"Willy's flock always came first," Truck said. He glanced toward Lenny and narrowed his eyes. "Not about himself—"

"You want the job?" Lenny said. "It's yours."

"He raised you for this," Bruiser said. "It's what you were meant to do."

"Damn," I said.

Bruiser swiveled his thick neck to gaze at me. "What are you meant to do, Reilly? Fly people around in them old seaplanes of yours? Get your ass kicked in the boxing ring every now and then?"

"There it is." Truck laughed.

Bruiser loved to remind me of the time we boxed here at Blue Heaven years ago. I nearly had him—or he'd played possum— only to surprise me with an island-size paw to my chin that knocked me out.

"Good question, man," Lenny said. "Times like these, they make people think hard on their lives. With all you done, Buck, what do you believe in your heart you're *meant* to do?"

They all stared at me, waiting for an answer. As if I had one.

I felt my throat constrict as a wave of memories passed over me.

I coughed. "Still trying to figure that out."

Cayman belted out the next verse.

"Run, rabbit, run,

Dig that hole, forget the sun,

When at last the work is done

Don't sit down, it's time to dig another one ..."

A chill curled my shoulders forward. Richard tapped harder on the bongo, Robin strummed, and Wegman glanced over toward me. It was as if he could smell my discomfort.

Wegman tilted his head toward our circle. "Last thing Willy would want—any of us would want—would be some mopey gathering crying over his passing." He paused. "Celebrate his life, dammit."

I slid off my stool, as much to avoid their question about what my purpose was as to step into the music. I took a tambourine painted with a nude ebony island woman from Wegman's pile of instruments. I'd never learned to play guitar, much less banjo. I shook the tambourine slowly and tried to keep the beat.

But even through the music, Bruiser and Lenny's question played like a loop in my mind: What the hell *was* I meant to do?

2

I WAS THE ONLY PERSON LIVING at the La Concha Hotel during this most recent spike in the pandemic. I'd been here through hurricanes, floods, and the redecoration of lobbies, common spaces, and restaurants, but never a pandemic. The staff were all quarantined at their homes—or had left the Keys. Had I not lived here for several years, management would have kicked me out, too. It might be one of the oldest hotels in Key West and the tallest building in town, situated right in the middle of Duval Street, but for me, it was home. I owed that to Harry Greenbaum, the largest investor in my former company, e-Antiquity. A British gentleman of the highest order; an old family friend; and a billionaire, entrepreneur, mentor, and confidant. Had it not been for Harry, I could never have afforded to live here full time, on the top floor in a suite, no less.

A pang of guilt hit me that I hadn't checked with Harry since early in the pandemic. He'd left me a message that he was holed up in his country estate an hour outside of London and invited me to weather the storm with him, his five-thousand-bottle wine collection and private chef, and a year's supply of the finest foods and delicacies. I'd appreciated the offer, but tempting as it was, I'd declined. Key West was my home now, and whatever happened here, I wanted to stay and deal with it directly. "One Human Family" was the informal motto of those who lived here, which I believed in.

My cell phone rang. The caller ID showed *Ben Reilly*.

What would my dear brother Ben want?

Another pang hit me. I'd checked in with Ben a couple weeks ago and he had sounded happy as a clam. Yes, he was staying at home in what had been our parents' horse farm in Middleburg, Virginia, which he'd inherited along with all their cash and other assets when they died—killed by hit-and-run as they crossed a road in Geneva, Switzerland. I exhaled a long breath, as I did every time I thought of that.

The phone continued to ring.

My father had been on his way to Paris for high-level meetings as an undersecretary of state, but my world had been crashing down around me thanks to Jack Dodson, my former partner and CEO of e-Antiquity. Jack had been cooking our books and siphoning cash away, which caused the company to collapse. When it became clear that e-Antiquity was toast, I took all the research, letters, manifests, maps, and other clues to a number of missing treasures—stole them to keep them away from creditors—and had my parents divert to Geneva. The plan was for them to open a numbered account at Swiss Bank to deposit my plunder. They were killed minutes later.

The phone kept ringing.

Our parents' deaths had created a permanent chasm between my brother and me. For years, Interpol and the Feds had claimed I was involved, but it never made sense, especially since they'd left everything to Ben. At the time they wrote their last will and testament, my net worth was north of fifty million dollars on paper. Had they lived through my personal bankruptcy, divorce from supermodel Heather Drake, and international humiliation, I think they'd have changed their wills, but Ben wouldn't hear it. He said I'd proven myself capable of creating a fortune before, and I no doubt could again.

The phone stopped ringing.

A glance at my five-hundred-square-foot suite and a mental

highlight reel of the last ten years since my parents' deaths—more like lowlight reel—didn't speak well for Ben's bold prediction. But, truth be told, the hell I'd gone through had caused me to swear off success, social media, watching television—I'd just gotten a cell phone a year ago, and I only used that to coordinate charters (and for backup in case one of the antique planes in Last Resort Charter and Salvage's fleet crapped out and I needed to call Ray Floyd for help).

I glanced at the phone. "I'm sure you're doing fine, Ben."

He was the type to totally ignore all the social distancing responsibilities thrust upon the world. He was young and in good health, and he had millions of dollars for the best care possible.

But here in Key West, Willy Peebles had died. Stubborn to the end, he'd refused to close down the Church of the Redeemer. He'd said it was his mission to support the congregation, and if the Lord was going to take him, then that was His plan.

The year was drawing to a close and there had been over four thousand cases here in the Keys, but the loss of Willy Peebles hit very close to home.

The death of loved ones or close friends isn't something you ever get over—at least I never had. Whether they'd stuck with me as angels or guilty reminders for the life I'd led, their memories were always close. My brother had always joked that I was too sensitive, and when he and I went to Switzerland to collect what our parents had deposited at Swiss Bank, we had a surprise that partially explained our differences. We found a letter from my father explaining that they'd adopted me at birth. It blew my mind, but to Ben's point, it explained a lot. He never showed emotion, and for all I could tell, never grieved over our parents. Whether or not I was adopted, they were my family, and I loved them.

I stood up and went to the counter in my small kitchenette, took a glass, added a couple cubes of ice, and poured three fingers of a special Pilar Rum blend Shawn Martin had given me at Blue Heaven. I held the glass up.

"God bless you, Willy." I took a sip, then raised my glass again. "Mom and Dad."

The room phone now rang. What the heck? I only used that number for business, so I hesitated, but then sat on the bed and picked it up.

"Last Resort Charter and Salvage."

"It's Jesse McDermitt."

McDermitt? The last time I saw him, he had some rare jewels he was researching. "Find any bright shiny things lately?"

"Not really my thing," Jesse said. "I wondered if I could pick your brain about an airplane?"

"What plane and where?"

"Not any specific plane," he said. "I'm thinking of upgrading. You remember my little Beaver?"

"Great little puddle jumper," I said. "I know a lot of people who'd be glad to take it off your hands."

"Maybe upgrade was the wrong word. Add to might be better. Do you know of any Grummans for sale? Flying boats, specifically."

Business had been nonexistent, but I had no plans to sell either of Last Resort's planes if I didn't have to. Plus, Ray would kill me. Fortunately, between the two of us, we knew almost every other operable flying boat in the country.

"I might," I said. "That's a very small community. Any preference on size?"

"My Beaver and your Widgeon are comparable in range and passengers. I'm looking for something with greater range and room."

That left the Goose, Mallard, or Albatross. "I'll check with a few people and see what's out there. Do you care about what condition it's in?"

"Airworthy would be a plus," he said with a chuckle. "But dismantled and on a trailer would work if it's all there. Or fully restored. I just don't want to have to hunt for a specific wingnut on a strut."

Jesse would be a good guy to owe me a favor, so helping him now might come in handy someday. "I can get back to you at this number?"

"Yeah," he said.

"Give me a couple of days," I said. "I'll call you after Christmas."

We hung up, and my mind went back to tonight's gathering at Blue Heaven. Being stuck alone at the hotel in quarantine had not been good for my morale, so seeing my friends had been a nice break, even under the circumstances. I pictured what the scene must be like at Redeemer. A sudden image of Lenny a few years ago as we flew around in Betty—my 1946 Grumman Widgeon—searching for a missing boat made me smile. He'd been terrified of flying.

"And now it's Pastor Lenny Jackson. Good Lord."

I had music playing on my phone, and the Foo Fighters song "Times Like These" came on. The recollection of my conversation with Lenny and Bruiser pierced my moment of introspection.

"What am I meant to do?"

On the shelves by my front door amidst the books on art and history was a small Lucite block we'd had made for e-Antiquity's original investors after our initial public offering. For a big part of my life, treasure hunting had been what I was meant to do. Hell, I'd done it well.

"King Buck." I took a long pull on the dark rum. "Dammit, I was good at that."

After spending months alone at home, you get used to talking to yourself. I wasn't one to talk on the phone much, and my outings had been infrequent, especially when the town opened up and the number of cases spiked, so I was getting as stir-crazy as the rest of the world. Seeing those guys tonight—my closest friends—at our Blue Heaven rendezvous had stirred my soul and got my mind spinning. Archeology, research, treasure hunting, schmoozing governments and universities—all of it—that had been my purpose until Jack took it all away.

I pulled open my closet and unlocked the wall safe—I'd installed a real safe a few years ago, since the standard-issue hotel safe had been too small and insecure for the contents I kept here. I pulled out the fat waterproof pouch of research materials I'd recovered from the Swiss Bank vault—the original documents I'd stolen from e-Antiquity before the FBI, SEC, and creditors had descended upon our offices to seize everything we owned. I'd rationalized that I'd been the one who'd busted my ass to acquire all the research material in the armpits and crotches of the world, and Jack had stolen all the company's cash, so I deserved something. I later learned when he launched a new salvage company that he too had made copies of all these same materials, the sneaky bastard.

I laid the fragile contents out on my dining table, with overflow on the countertop. Each item had an acquisition tale of its own, and cumulatively, we'd paid over a million dollars for the lot. Each one told a story and had promise of riches. The El Mirador Mayan maps were here, along with missing Spanish galleons outside of Colombia, the Dominican Republic, Cuba, and the Treasure Coast of Florida—branded that because of the eleven ships that sank in 1715 due to a hurricane and weren't rediscovered until the early 1960s when gold and silver coins washed up on Florida's eastern beaches. I flipped through others off Porto Bello, the English Channel, Cairo, Katmandu, Ushuaia, and even the Great Lakes.

Could I have sold these documents piecemeal and lived more comfortably after going broke? Not without running the risk of attracting the attention of my old nemesis, T. Edward Booth, special agent of the Federal Bureau of Investigation, who had spent years monitoring my activities and forcing me to do deeds outside of his jurisdiction to help him climb the Bureau's ladder. Plus, I'd always harbored the idea that one day, just maybe, I'd reinvent myself as an archeologist and treasure hunter.

That had been my purpose.

My eyes locked on one of my charts of the Florida Keys. It covered the area out near Fort Jefferson and the Dry Tortugas. The chart was marked in different colors of ink and magic marker where I'd searched in a grid pattern for the *Esmeralda*, a seventeenth-century Spanish wreck that Ernest Hemingway had inadvertently found when he'd pulled anchor after a day of fishing and a long gold chain had come up with the anchor. I learned of his discovery after acquiring a letter he'd written to his editor, Max Perkins, where he noted the find amidst a description of fishing out near the Fort. After I moved to Key West in the wake of e-Antiquity's liquidation, I began to search for the wreck because it was close and easy, even though the location was in National Park waters, where it's illegal to disturb the reefs, do any type of salvage, or recover anything, since, technically, it all belongs to the Park Service.

Details, details ...

In light of Willy's passing and the question the guys had laid upon me tonight, which had hit with the force of a Bruiser Lewis uppercut, seeing this chart now relit the pilot light on my past life. If I wanted to go down that dusty trail again, it made sense to start with the *Esmeralda*.

"What's my purpose, Lenny and Bruiser?" I glanced from relic to relic, map to map, faded letters written in foreign tongues to a notebook with their translations transcribed by period experts, and finally back to the area chart of the Dry Tortugas.

I felt my lips go taut. "I'm looking at it."

3

"KIND OF LATE TO BE CALLING, ISN'T IT?"

"Sorry, Ray, but I had an epiphany after our wake for Willy."

"It couldn't wait until tomorrow?"

I could hear the sound of one of his shoot-'em-up video games in the background. Ray had put on twenty pounds from eating nothing but frozen dinners and sitting on his recliner during the quarantine. He needed a change as much as I did. "Want to go flying with me in the morning out to the Dry Tortugas?"

"Fort Jefferson? Why would we go out there?"

"We both need a change of scenery. Plus, while I'm diving, you can keep an eye on Betty."

"Diving?" Ray paused, and I could almost hear the wheels turning in his head. "You know it's illegal to remove anything from Park property—we're partners now, Buck. If you do something stupid, I could get incriminated. I'm not going to jail—"

"Relax, Ray. I'm just going to look around. There are no patrols out there these days, anyway. Being at Willy's tonight made me realize life's too short not to pursue your dreams."

A series of explosions and gunfire filled my phone's receiver. Ray didn't respond, either too engaged in his war game or hoping I'd leave him alone. I ran my palm over a week's worth of stubble on my cheek.

"You ever think about what your purpose is, Ray?"

"Told you a hundred times: to keep our old beauties flying

and keep you from polluting the ocean with their remains."

"That's good. 'Cause I'm thinking we might start flying more now."

"What's that supposed to mean?"

"Life *is* short. Fact is, I used to be pretty good at what I did back in the e-Antiquity days. Maybe it's time we make another run at it."

"Treasure hunting? Last Resort Charter and Salvage is getting into treasure hunting?"

"I'd like to think of it more as getting *back* into archeological research. Should there be beneficial discoveries beyond those for posterity, we'll collect that treasure when we come to it."

He exhaled loudly into the phone. "Sounds like you're ready to descend into Malebolge."

"Excuse me?" I said.

"The eighth circle of hell. Malebolge is the cavern that's divided into ten concentric circular ditches. There are long bridges that lead into its center, like spokes on a wheel. In the middle of Malebolge is the ninth and final circle of hell."

"Is this another of your philosophical constructs?"

"No, Buck. It's from Dante's *Inferno*—the conclusion of the journey into hell. That's what your idea to start treasure hunting again sounds like to me."

I let a beat pass before continuing. "There haven't been any cruise ships here since late March. A1A was blocked for months to all but residents, and inbound flights have been drastically reduced. The air is cleaner, the water clearer, and we need to get back to flying again, *partner*," I said.

"We haven't had any income in six months," Ray said. "I've kept our expenses to a minimum, but if you want to ramp up a search effort, our savings will dwindle fast."

"By the way, Jesse McDermitt called. He's looking for help to buy a flying boat, if you want to call some of your contacts in

Alaska."

"Guy with the Beaver? Sure, if we can get a commission." He paused. "My dream plane's still for sale in Tennessee."

"That Albatross?"

"She's spectacular. They spent four years restoring her back to absolute perfection—"

"Jesse didn't tell me his price range, but I didn't get the impression he'd want to spend a half-million dollars, and he said something larger than a Widgeon, but not necessarily the largest of the Grumman fleet," I said. "I suspect the Albatross is too big."

"I'll think about it," Ray said. "Back to treasure hunting, how are we going to afford this?"

"I don't know yet. It's too soon to reach out to potential investors yet, and we shouldn't do that without a hot lead and a solid business plan. But for tomorrow, I thought it would be good therapy to enjoy the clear sky, see the turtles dotting the surface, pods of porpoise dancing across mild seas, cormorants diving, pelicans floating, and frigate birds soaring." I paused. "And see if we can find the *Esmeralda*."

"Mother Nature is happy—now, at least," Ray said.

"What do you mean, *now*?"

"Feels to me like she's been using the pandemic to eradicate the human race for abusing her natural resources. Increased water temperatures have led to more intense storms, the ice caps are melting and threatening shorelines, wildfires have been burning uncontrollably in drought-ravaged western states, and now record snowstorms and racial-equality riots are raging around the globe," Ray said. "In fact, forget Mother Nature. This is getting biblical."

I'd learned not to engage Ray in his philosophical rants. There was no winning when he was on a roll, so I used it to my advantage.

"All the more reason for us to shit or get off the pot with all this historical research I've been sitting on for so long."

"So you finally got tired of being poor, huh?" Ray said.

"I'm not saying we should do this to get rich. More for the challenge, the hunt, and, well, ideally the redemption of recreating what nobody believes I could re-accomplish."

"Those guys really got to you with the 'what's your purpose' stuff, huh?"

"I realized how much I miss the adrenaline rush," I said.

"You've made some finds in the past few years."

"Yeah, but mostly helping other people. Now I'd be doing it for myself—"

"For us, you mean, *partner.*"

"That's what I meant, Ray."

"Didn't you have a lot of help back in the day?"

Rain on my parade much? "At the height of e-Antiquity, we had nearly a hundred employees—but that team helped propel our success. I had twenty or so people in my research department, including Scarlet Roberson."

"The mother of your child," Ray said.

He didn't mean to be malicious, but the thought of Scarlet caused me to shift in my seat. She'd been educated at Oxford, a Rhodes scholar, but she had an intuition for connecting clues unlike anyone I'd ever known, often including me. But it was the soft feel of her freckled skin against mine that I missed the most. We'd broken all the employer-employee rules, and she'd stayed with me in my tent on nearly every archeological dig we'd pursued. In hindsight, she'd been in love with me, but I had been too blind to see it. After we'd discovered the tomb of the Mayan Serpent King in Guatemala, my popularity and ego soared. That's when I met Heather Drake and dropped Scarlet without looking back. I never knew about my son, Charlie, until he was ten years old.

"I've made my share of mistakes, Ray, and I've sat on the

sidelines long enough. We're partners in Last Resort, and you're my best friend. If we made a little extra money, would that be so bad? After all, I can't live in the La Concha Hotel my entire life."

A loud explosion sounded and then the background noise fell silent. "Great," Ray said. "I just got killed in the game I've been playing for two weeks." He paused. "Fine, I'll go flying with you in the morning. I was planning to be at the airport early to work on Betty's port engine anyway, so I'll see you there."

I pumped my fist. "Great. See you bright and early."

"But one stipulation, okay, Buck?"

"What's that?"

"Pick a project that won't put us in jail."

4

RAY'S ADMONITION GNAWED AT ME.

Pick a project that won't put us in jail.

Access was always a consideration when treasure hunting, and getting it was one of the skills I'd mastered—negotiating permission, cutting a deal to share a portion of the find for the benefit of a designated museum, city, country, or other special interest. There could be no such deal with the National Park Service for the *Esmeralda*.

I went back to pick through my piles of maps, letters, clues, and documents and sorted them by geographic accessibility, lower costs to search (since we had little money), fewest number of legal hurdles, and how much intel I had or could get my hands on.

There were nearly seven hundred documented shipwrecks in the Caribbean and along Florida's east coast, and approximately two hundred and fifty of them were in Cuban waters and one hundred and fifty were in Florida's waters. Several of the valuable galleons that had sunk off Florida's coast had initially originated from England, France, and Spain, which is why we spent a lot of time there searching for clues that could lead us to wreck sites. That approach didn't yield a lot of leads, but those we dug up, I kept in a separate envelope within the files.

One such letter was from General Don Juan Esteban de Ubilla, who'd commanded the *flota de Nueva España*, or New Spain flotilla, which comprised five of the eleven ships that sank in a hurricane on July 31 in 1715, a week after leaving Cuba. Ubilla had been aboard the *Capitana*, which carried over thirteen hundred wooden chests containing three million silver coins and purportedly a trove of fine jewels for the new queen of Spain. Ubilla perished aboard the *Capitana* that fateful morning, somewhere near the Saint Sebastian River in Florida.

Prior to that, Ubilla had purchased a small frigate in Havana on July 15, 1715, called the *Santa Rita y Anima*, one of the documented eleven ships in the fleet. However, what I didn't think anybody but us had discovered was a letter Ubilla wrote to his wife back in Seville, dated the day of the fleet's departure. In the letter, he stated that he'd purchased yet another frigate, which he renamed *Señora Nuestra Elisabeth Farnese* after the new Spanish queen. The letter noted that along with the *Griffon*, also a frigate, the *Farnese* had set sail a half day before the rest of the fleet, with instructions to sail an easterly course toward the Bahamas on the most direct route possible to Spain (apparently King Philip V was impatient after waiting for his queen's dowry for two years).

Ubilla wrote that he was concerned about such a huge fleet being an easy target, so he had instructed the galleons to stick close to the Florida coast but had sent the frigates east. Galleons were notoriously slow, especially when stuffed to the gills with silver, gold, emeralds, and other valuables.

My educated guessing told me Ubilla acquired the two frigates because of their speed, wanting to hedge his bets against marauders, or even storms, in order to ensure that the queen's jewels made it back to Spain on the most direct course. No further information had ever been found on the *Farnese*, though, and Ubilla went to a watery grave aboard the *Capitana*, and to me, back in the e-Antiquity days, this had been a loose end. The *Griffon* was the only ship to survive the storm, and it arrived in Brest, France a month later.

Another pair of targets, the *Nuestra Señora del Rosario* and *Nues-*

tra Señora de la Victoria, sank in 1590 off Cape San Antonio, Cuba. Most of their cargo had been recovered after they sank, but while searching the Spanish archives in Seville, Spain, we learned that over one hundred cases of gold coins were still unaccounted for. That would be worth a nice chunk of change today. We uncovered similar information about the *Nuestra Señora de Loreto*, which had been sunk in a battle against the English outside the port of Havana and also had never been salvaged.

But per Ray's stipulation, mounting an expedition in Cuba would be impossible thanks to the never-ending embargo, and doing so under the radar would land us in a Cuban jail. So while these two might be options for the future, they and many like them would require a lot of sophisticated equipment, not to mention a ton of working capital. Last Resort Charter and Salvage had minimal cash, two antique aircraft, and no boat. Not exactly the ideal arsenal to pursue a protracted and complex nautical search.

Which is why the *Esmeralda* was low-hanging fruit.

With two fingers of El Dorado fifteen-year-old rum in a snifter, I sat back on my couch to ponder what I'd tell Ray in the morning.

"Pick something that won't put us in jail, huh?"

A pleasant burn in the back of my throat tingled as I polished off the rum, then killed the lights and crawled into my bed. I wanted to be fresh to dive in the Dry Tortugas in the morning.

I FLOATED OVER AZURE SEAS at low altitude. Morro

Castle could be seen in the distance at the mouth of Havana Harbor. I leaned down to push Betty's stick forward—but there was no stick—there was no Betty: I was aloft in the clouds. I lifted my arms to slow my descent, then pulled my arms back to my side and dove toward the Harbor. With laser-sharp vision, my eyes cut through the brown water in search of the *Nuestra Señora de Loreto*, knowing I was close. Could I get in and out without being detected?

Large ships passed below me as I dove—my speed increasing until my eyes watered so badly I could hardly see—I veered to the right to avoid a cruise ship littered with obese Europeans spread across the deck in Speedos and badly fitting bikinis. The water came quickly—I sliced in without a sound, my speed unabated. Now I kicked with the grace of a blue whale and covered vast distances with each repetition. The water was brown as coffee, but I could see the bottom clearly, covered with chunks of ships, bottles, a '57 Chevy convertible in pristine condition, blue marlin cruising with hammerhead sharks and a school of dorado flashing blue and gold.

Gold. A brilliant glow emanated from a pit ahead that was surrounded by wood timbers, cannons, an old mast, a stained sail fluttering in the current. I held my arms wide to slow my velocity until I came to a stop, just before the hole, where the golden light shined up like it was the womb of the second coming. I kicked slowly now, the light blinding me—

A loud snort—my own—caused me to lurch up in my bed.

I was alone. I'd been dreaming.

As I rolled over, a thought pierced my sleep-fogged mind. Was my dream guiding me toward the wreck of the *Nuestra Señora de Loreto*?

5

A STEADY POUNDING NOISE gradually penetrated my sleep. I cracked an eye open and saw the orange light of dawn peering beneath the blackout shades on my windows, which overlooked Duval Street, six floors below.

KNOCK, KNOCK, KNOCK.

I rolled over, away from the light and the incessant pounding.

KNOCK, KNOCK, KNOCK.

Whoever it was, they weren't going away. My eyes fluttered. Wait a minute. I was the only one staying in the La Concha, and nobody had worked here in weeks. I sat up in my bed. Who the hell could it—?

KNOCK, KNOCK, KNOCK.

"Coming! Give me a minute!"

I pulled on a Last Resort Charter and Salvage t-shirt and the shorts I'd dumped at the bottom of my bed last night. In a glance around the room, I saw my dinner dishes piled up, three empty beer bottles, and Styrofoam containers from El Siboney. The clock read 7:13 a.m.

"Son of a bitch," I said as I walked toward the door.

KNOCK, KNOCK—

I pulled the door open fast to eliminate any further knocking. The person standing outside made me wish I were still dreaming.

"Buck Reilly. How the hell are you?"

My breathing was so shallow I couldn't utter a word. I shook my head once and purposefully sucked in a deep breath.

"What the hell?" I finally said.

Richard Rostenkowski, aka Gunner, replete with mirrored blue sunglasses, watermelon-sized head, and a wide girth of muscle and brawn packed into a black fishing shirt, stood before me grinning like a long-lost friend.

"Flew in yesterday," he said. "Saw my old Widgeon on the tarmac when I got off the plane—"

"She was never *your* Widgeon, Gunner."

His grin widened, though that might've been a sneer. With his small square teeth, he looked like a wolverine ready to gnaw on roadkill.

"Sure it was. I collected it off the Cuban beach where you'd abandoned it and gave her new life."

"And I had to fix your butcher job to make it airworthy again."

"You know those Cuban mechanics, they can fix anything. May not have looked original, but it flew just fine."

Gunner sized me up. We hadn't seen each other since Jamaica a few years ago, when a judge awarded me and the Maroon people rights to a cache of treasure that had belonged to Captain Henry Morgan. I'd used my share to buy Betty back from Jack Dodson, my former partner—Gunner's current partner.

"You gonna invite me in?" He leaned forward as he spoke in what I could feel in my bones was a menacing posture.

I took a step back. "Why would I do that?"

"Because we have a proposal for you, Reilly."

"We? Like you and Jack?"

"That's right. Me and Jack."

A shiver shot up my spine. We'd crossed paths too many times to count, from Panama to St. Barths to Jamaica, and it had always been adversarial. Gunner suggesting a *proposal* made the hairs on the back of my neck stand up.

"Not interested."

"You will be."

"No chance—"

Gunner took a deep breath, then scratched his ample gut. As he did, he pulled up his untucked shirt just enough for me to see the gun in his belt. Gunner armed was like a leopard with a cobra as a sidekick. We'd wrestled on more than one occasion, and he'd bested me all but once.

"Okay, so it's not a proposal." The smile was gone. "It's a demand."

"Demand? What the hell makes you think—"

"We have your brother. Ben. Whiny little shit."

His eyes were fixed on mine as they narrowed, then widened. I stepped back and swung the door in his face—his pork loin of a forearm appeared at the last second as the door crashed into it— he shoved the door hard back at me and I stumbled backwards, nearly fell—but when I righted myself, he was standing inside.

He locked the handle and strung the chain.

I was 6'3" and 225 pounds of muscle. Gunner was the same height, but he was pushing 275 pounds of gristle and meanness. I stood tall to try and appear threatening, but having not emptied my bladder yet, it was more likely I'd piss my pants. I had no guns, and Gunner was between me and the knives I had in the kitchen. It was like coming face-to-face with a Cape buffalo on a walking safari. You had to stay cool, not look them in the eye, and hope they let you live.

"What would you want with Ben?"

"To use him as leverage against you."

"I don't believe you. How about I call him up?"

Gunner pulled a phone out of his pocket and extended his arm toward me.

"I'll call him from my own phone."

I used the opportunity to squeeze past him and head toward the bedside table, where my hotel/business phone sat rarely used.

The idea of dialing 911 passed fleetingly through the circuits of my cortex, but it would be a fool's effort. I dialed Ben's number from memory, it having been my own phone number for half my life until I left for college.

It rang once, then again. I glanced up at Gunner, who was texting on his phone.

"Hello?" A shaky voice answered. Was that …?

"Ben, that you?"

"Buck, oh, Buck, thank … God …"

His sniveling made me wince. Gunner smiled at me.

"What's going on there?" I said.

"You didn't answer my calls—they have guns—they say they'll ki-ki-kill me if you don't agree to help them! Buck, please! Do whatever they ask!"

"Satisfied, Reilly?" Gunner said.

I realized my hand that held the phone was shaking. "Relax, Ben, I'm here. I won't let anything happen to you." Gunner's smug smile sent battery acid through my veins. "Is Jack there? Is he the one holding you hostage?"

"Jack? As in Dodson? Why would he—is he behind this? That s-s-son of a bitch!"

"One of his partners is here in Key West. I'll see what they want. It'll be okay, I promise."

"Please, Buck! Please do what they ask—I don't … want … to … die …"

"I'll call you back once everything is straightened out."

With that I hung up. Rage pulsed through me with such force I could've picked Gunner up and flung him out my window regardless of his size. But they had Ben. Which meant they had me too.

"You know, if you'd answered your brother's calls, I wouldn't have had to drag my ass down here, Reilly." He paused. "We figure you owe us after Jamaica, but knowing how selfish you are, we needed leverage."

Jamaica. Heather had been there with Jack. Was she part of this too? "That was years ago, Gunner."

"We been busy."

"Dare I ask?"

"Don't need to. I'm gonna show you." The square teeth appeared. "We're even gonna cut you in."

I pressed my lips tightly together. As much as I wanted to argue with him, cuss him out, beat his brains in, it wasn't an option. I had to shift gears. Learn their game, then figure out how to turn the tables as soon as possible.

"Better pack a bag. We're leaving this shitty rock." He smiled again. He enjoyed the upper hand. "Bring some long pants, too. And your passport."

I hesitated. My passport was in the safe. Along with …

"Yep, bring that pouch of yours too. One with all the clues to the treasures you stole from Jack's old company—"

"My company. The one he put in bankruptcy by cooking the books."

"Semantics, Reilly. He has copies of all that crap, but partners need all our cards on the table, know what I'm saying?"

Partners. The word made me cringe. Gunner had been a killer for hire his entire adult life, a mercenary for Blackwater in the Middle East, then in Africa, and then as Jack's fixer. He'd kill a human no different than a gnat. And he hated my guts.

"Chop chop, Reilly. We got places to go and people to see. And your brother may just shit himself to death if we don't get a move on."

"You're not going to tell me about it?" I said.

"We got plenty of time." He smiled. "Partner."

His laugh made me feel like my skin was covered with cockroaches.

As I pulled a travel bag together, I wondered if this was some kind of ironic divine game for deciding that treasure hunting was again my purpose in life. If that was going to be the case, then I needed to play the game. To win.

6

GUNNER BARELY FIT INTO MY ROVER. Since the bench seat was fixed, his girth was pressed into the metal dashboard. The sliding side window and vent below the windshield did little to stem the flood of perspiration that poured from him like a dam ready to burst. I took my time.

"You going to tell me what you want?" I said.

"Already did."

"No, you said you needed help." I glanced at him out of the corner of my eye as I fought to turn the non-power steering wheel to the left. "With what?"

He tried to suck in a deep breath, but he was constrained by the dashboard. If they didn't have Ben, it would have been the perfect time to launch an attack. I took another left instead, driving as slowly as I could in second gear.

"The 1715 fleet."

Another quick glance revealed that his small teeth were again on display. "Those ships have been picked over for decades," I said. "Everyone from Kip Wagner to Mel Fisher and every amateur treasure hunter in the country has pawed their way through the shallows from Fort Pierce to Cape Canaveral. Not to mention the Spaniards who stuck around for fifteen years after the wrecks to gather up everything they could find."

If anything, Gunner's smile grew wider as I spoke. I pressed my lips together. I might be rusty, but one thing I learned back in the e-Antiquity days was to challenge supposed information, then await the seller's response. People loved to gloat, and I'd turned up a lot of tidbits that way. Too bad Gunner was anything but predictable.

"All that's true, Reilly. Mostly."

I now bit my lip to prevent appearing overanxious. None of that mattered given the situation, but whether by trying to sniff out the value of potential information or by making myself useful to save my brother's life, I had to play the game. I realized all over again that I hated playing games.

"Sooner you get us to the airport, the sooner you'll learn more," he said.

I pressed my foot on the gas and shifted into third gear, and a blast of salt air blew in from Smathers Beach as we drove past. We parked at the private aviation terminal, near the only other car parked there: Ray Floyd's sun-bleached Toyota Camry. With my bags in tow, I followed Gunner into the empty FBO.

"If we're flying international, I need to file a flight plan," I said.

"We'll have time for that later."

I followed Gunner onto the tarmac. The cowling on Betty's port engine was popped open. We walked toward my old Widgeon. Gunner moved swiftly and silently for a man of his size, skills he no doubt had perfected in the deserts and jungles of third-world nations as a gun for hire.

Ray was on a ladder, his back to us, and struggling with something on Betty's port engine. I glanced at Gunner and held my hands palm up as if to say, *Now what?* Gunner nodded toward Ray.

"Hey, Ray," I said.

Ray responded, but with his head inside the cowling of the engine, it was unintelligible.

"Ray," I said with another glance toward Gunner, who flared his nostrils. "Ray!"

"I said I'll be ready in a few minutes!" Ray peered around the outside of the cowling at an awkward angle. His eyes immediately registered on Gunner, and they opened wide without hesitation. "You! What are you doing—why are you with him, Buck?"

"Bad luck," I said.

Ray stood frozen. "I thought we were going out to Fort—ah—flying today," he said.

"Change of plans." I wasn't sure what Gunner wanted but intended to keep this brief in order to protect Ray. "I need the keys to the Beast."

"Which one's that?" Gunner said.

"The Goose."

"No, the Widgeon," he said.

"We won't fit," I said.

"It's unlocked," Ray said. "But I have the plugs pulled on this engine, so it won't run. I didn't know—"

"Are you the one who re-restored the Widgeon?" Gunner said.

"Ah, yeah," Ray said.

"I'll admit she looks better now." Gunner sneered at me. "Bitch was unstable. Kind of like your ex-wife, Reilly."

"Couldn't agree more," I said. "But don't talk bad about Betty. If we're going somewhere in her—"

"Nah," Gunner said. "I just need to get something out of her. Jack didn't tell me he was selling her before, so I never had the chance. I left something on board."

"We had her stripped all the way down," Ray said. "Didn't find anything—"

"Get inside, fat boy," Gunner said.

Ray sagged. "Why me?"

"Because you're a pussy, and pussies don't try things. Now get off the ladder and get inside."

Ray climbed slowly down the ladder. I could see hurt in his

eyes. All the shoot-'em-up video games he played made him feel like a warrior, but in most cases since I'd known him, he'd shrunk from confrontation. He slumped at the bottom of the ladder, and my heart ached for him.

"Anything happens to Ray, I'm out," I said.

"Relax, Reilly."

Once Ray popped the port hatch, he climbed inside, and Gunner followed. I watched them through the windows. Ray was a lot closer to me than Ben had ever been. I didn't want to abandon my brother, but bigger than me and armed or not, I wouldn't let Gunner hurt Ray.

Once inside the cockpit, Gunner pointed for Ray to sit in the right seat. Then Gunner bent down and grabbed the yoke. From where I was, it looked like he was twisting the handles—no, not the handles but the rubber handgrip.

Gunner ripped the handgrip off the yoke. He pointed toward it and said something to Ray, who tentatively put his index finger inside the hollow tube and felt around. I saw his eyes get wider, and they exchanged words, but I couldn't hear what they said. Ray lifted his finger out with a rolled-up piece of paper. Gunner took it from him, then shimmied back to the hatch and climbed out.

"Now let's get in the Goose," Gunner said.

"Where are we going?" Ray said.

"Not you. Reilly."

In Ray's momentary exhale of relief, his red Hawaiian shirt sagged, but he quickly stood erect again and glanced at me. All three of us walked over to the Beast. Ray's eyes lingered on my travel bag.

"Are you going to be back to take the Sheleskys out to Woman Key to renew their wedding vows tomorrow?" he said.

"No, he's not," Gunner said.

Ray stopped. "Buck," he said. "Do you need anything?"

"Yeah," Gunner says. "For you to butt out."

I popped the hatch on the plane and turned to assess Gunner's expression—cold and inscrutable. Then to Ray's, pale and worried. "I'll be okay, Ray. I, ah, have to help Gunner and Jack with something. I won't be gone long."

Gunner grunted.

"Jack as in Dodson? Your mortal enemy?" Ray said.

Gunner spun on him, and Ray flinched. "That's enough out of you, fat Magnum. Bucky-boy is coming with me of his own free will, so spare us the matronly concern and go finish cleaning the spark plugs."

Ray turned his now-angry eyes to me. I gave him a slight shake of my head. His eyebrows lifted. Definitely not free will.

"Let's go, Reilly," Gunner said.

"I'll call you, Ray," I said.

He held his palms up as if to ask what he should do, but I turned away.

Once inside the Beast, I stood aside so Gunner could enter and then turned to close the hatch. Ray's eyes and mine caught, and I gave him a slight shake of my head. His eyes narrowed. I wasn't going of my own free will, but I didn't want him to do anything about it.

Yet.

7

AS I FINISHED THE PRE-FLIGHT PREPARATION on the Beast, I watched the fuel truck pull away. With the Beast's twin radial engines fired up and no traffic in the pattern, I added throttle, and we rumbled up the taxiway to the head of the runway. Air traffic control gave me the all clear.

"Be a good time to tell me where we're going," I said.

"KVRB."

I only hesitated a moment. When Gunner had said it was the 1715 fleet they were pursuing, I immediately thought of the few private FBOs along the Treasure Coast. KVRB was Vero Beach Municipal Airport.

I pushed the throttles forward and lit out down runway 9. Alone with Gunner in the tight cockpit, I could smell his perspiration, and it raised the hair on the back of my neck. Our past run-ins had been vicious, and I'd unfortunately smelled him up close and personal more times than I cared to count, often at the receiving end of a sucker punch. Except for the time I clocked him and broke his ever-present reflective blue sunglasses. I'd learned with him that even when he had the upper hand, it was best to keep him off-balance.

"New shades, Gunner?"

He crossed his arms, shrugged, and continued to watch the upper Keys trail past from the starboard window.

"You said you had some information about the 1715 fleet. Might as well bring me up to speed while we have an hour to kill."

"Not the whole fleet," he said. "The queen's dowry. We have reason to believe people have been looking in the wrong place for the last three hundred years."

The queen's dowry—or jewels, as most treasure hunters referred to it—referred to the as-of-yet undiscovered cache of gold, silver, pearls, emeralds, and fine jewelry that King Philip V of Spain commissioned in 1714. His wife, Queen Maria Luisa Gabriella of Savoy, had passed away earlier that year. In need of a new queen, King Philip was married by proxy to the Duchess of Parma, Elisabeth Farnese, who demanded that she be given the most unique jewelry in the world as part of the deal. King Philip wanted to get off on the right foot with his new bride, so he sought to acquire the best jewels, gold, and fine workmanship from the New World. Unfortunately for him, those jewels vanished when the eleven ships in the 1715 fleet were ravaged and sunk in a hurricane four days after they sailed from Havana. To date, none of the queen's jewels had been found.

"Historians believe the queen's jewels were aboard General Ubilla's *Capitana*," I said. "Remains of that ship are believed to have been found near the others."

"We think not."

"And you have research to support that?"

His square teeth flashed, but he didn't answer.

"Then why do you need me?"

"You're the archeologist. Jack was the money man." His smile faded. "And I'm the enforcer."

"I haven't searched for treasure in ages." I didn't want to piss him off by mentioning the exception, when we competed to find Henry Morgan's treasure in Jamaica.

"If you want to see your brother again, you better shake the rust off."

WHOOSH!

A loud sound rocked the Beast—a jet flew just above us—jet wash!

The swirl of air caused us to roll hard to port. I glanced up—it was a private jet—G-IV by the look of it—bastard!

Our nose was pointed down toward the Everglades, and I could only pull on the yoke so hard to not overstress the wings. Fortunately, we had the altitude to recover. As I felt the pressure back on the elevators and yoke, I heard laughing in my headset.

It was Gunner. He pointed from me to the plane that was quickly becoming a dot on the horizon ahead. Was he so dulled to danger from a lifetime as a mercenary that he had no fear of near-death experiences? Sick bastard.

At four hundred feet of altitude, I finally got the Beast under full control and began our climb back to the altitude that ATC had been yelling in my ear.

"Glad you found that entertaining," I said. "You get the tail number on that asshole?"

"As a matter of fact, I did. NJET4. Cocky bastard, huh?"

I could see my angry expression in the reflection of his glasses. "I'm going to alert the NTSB when we land in Vero Beach, the son of a bitch."

Gunner's laugh was a shrill whine. It sent a chill down my arms.

"Are you going to tell me more about your queen's jewels theory?"

"Not yet, Reilly. We'll be there soon enough, so long as you don't crash this old jalopy."

"From what I know, this is a waste of time." I glanced back at Gunner. My close proximity to him caused a sudden pang of anxiety. "You been tested for COVID?"

Another shrill laugh as Gunner shook his head and patted his leg as if it were the funniest thing he'd ever heard. So much for social distancing.

For the remainder of the flight, I considered everything I knew about the 1715 fleet. Jack had all the same information, with the exception of the letter I'd reviewed last night from General Don Juan Esteban de Ubilla to his wife about the second frigate he'd bought in Havana. I didn't think there was any way Jack had a copy of that—not that it really mattered. This was his expedition, and I hadn't been bluffing when I told Gunner the Treasure Coast had been picked clean. Unless they had some as-of-yet undiscovered intel, this was a fool's errand.

And what new information could they have? And where would they have found it? Jack and Gunner were far from capable at doing research on something that happened hundreds of years ago. Gunner wasn't talking, but I had the feeling I'd find out soon enough.

8

"YOU'RE CLEARED TO LAND ON RUNWAY 3, GRUM-MAN."

"Roger, tower. Grumman on final approach."

Northerly winds rocked the Beast as our increased flaps reduced our speed.

"These old birds are too damn slow," Gunner said. "Hurry the hell up and put her down."

I took my time with the approach, keeping our speed just above stall. Down below, I saw several one- and two-engine propeller planes lined up in twin rows along the flight line. Just past them was a single row of a half dozen private jets. We touched down and glided to a slow taxi.

"We have a slot reserved at the end of the line," Gunner said. "Keep going past all this junk."

I spotted the open slot at the end before the jets—wait, was that—"What did you say the tail number was on that G-IV?"

Gunner smiled. "You mean that one right there?"

What the hell was going on? NJET4? Was that his plane?

"Yours, huh," I said. "Maybe the pilot was trying to kill us both with that near collision. Why did I need to fly my plane up here if you have that thing?"

"They were just playing games, Reilly. You need to relax and get in the right mindset."

I refrained from asking what would happen if I didn't. It would have been a rhetorical question. Play the game, Buck. Play the game.

After a quick shutdown, I started my post-flight checklist.

"Grab your bags and let's go," Gunner said.

"I need to—"

"Spare me. This plane's seventy-five years old. Nothing you're doing will change anything."

He scurried ahead of me through the fuselage, half bent over, then opened the hatch without waiting. I glanced around the cockpit one last time and followed after him, grabbing my bags from the back seats on the way. He stood outside wiping sweat from his brow.

"Flying an antique in the tropics like that with no air conditioning is barbaric."

"Where are we going, Gunner?"

He looked past me and smiled. I turned just in time to see the hatch mechanically lower on the G-IV. I held my breath as the stairs dropped into place. After a few seconds, a man in tan linen slacks and a light blue linen shirt trotted down into the sunlight. Tall with tattooed arms, stylish haircut, and aviator glasses, the man hesitated at the bottom, smiled, then continued toward us.

Jack Dodson.

I swallowed, hard. There was so much history between Jack and me it made me dizzy to see him here, the picture of success, a multi-millionaire. But to me, he was a lying snake who'd defraud-ed our investors and me of those same millions, an ex-con who abandoned his wife and children and ran off with my ex-wife. Now he'd added kidnapping to his curriculum vitae.

"Buck! Great to see you." He stepped up and tried to give me a hug. I stiffened, unable to play along.

"Yeah, sure, Jack. Likewise."

Behind him I saw the fuel truck rush up to his G-IV. I real-ized nobody else had climbed off. Had Jack received a commercial rating? Even if he had, the G-IV required two pilots.

He must have seen me staring at the plane.

"Sweet plane, isn't it? Just a rental though. For now."

I turned back to face him. "The 1715 fleet's been harvested for decades. Queen's jewels or not, do you really think you've found something worth kidnapping my brother?"

Jack smile grew wider. Gunner pumped his eyebrows.

"That's why you're here, Buck. You're going to have to be the judge of that," Jack said.

"Fine, where are we going? Vero? Sebastian Inlet? Let's get it over with."

Gunner's omniscient smile was really getting on my nerves.

"A little further, actually. Come on, they're finished refueling. Let's get back on board the jet."

I stood frozen. Gunner made me bring my passport. A second passed as the decision tree in my brain burned like it had been hit by lightning. My conclusion didn't change: it was still clear to me that the faster I pushed this process, the sooner I'd get Ben released and be done with these assholes. As many bad things as Jack had become, to my knowledge, he wasn't a murderer. Gunner, on the other hand, would kill his mother with no hesitation, as long as he was getting paid.

"Okay, whatever, let's go." Without waiting for them, I walked forward to the G-IV. Flashbacks of dozens of similar approaches to similar planes back in the e-Antiquity days flickered in my memory banks. Those flights had almost always been filled with anticipation and excitement, but now, it felt like I was walking the plank.

I took the steps two at a time and ducked into the leather and mahogany interior. To my left, two pilots wore headsets and dined on sandwiches. A flight attendant in a short black skirt walked forward from the rear of the plane.

"Welcome aboard!" Was her English accent a clue to our destination?

I walked past the tan leather couch on the left and chose the forward-facing leather seat just past a table that was replete with trays of fresh fruit, sushi, and a champagne bucket. The flight attendant took my duffel bag and backpack. "My name is Jenny. Let me know if there's anything you need."

"Thanks."

Jack and Gunner stepped inside. Gunner took up half the couch and Jack sat across from me, his back to the cockpit. The door closed behind him. Outside, I saw the fuel truck pulling away. Without hesitation, the plane began to taxi.

"Little different than the old Grummans, huh, Buck?" Jack said.

"Tell me about it," Gunner said. "I'm still sweating." He reached forward and grabbed the champagne. Jenny ran forward and took the bottle and poured three glasses.

"Little soon to be celebrating, wouldn't you say?" I said. "Where are we headed? London? Portsmouth?"

Jack smiled. "Right continent, wrong country. Brest, actually. France—"

"I know where it is." The destination immediately told me that their supposed intel must have something to do with the *Griffon*, the only ship to have survived the hurricane that sank the rest of the fleet. But I'd let Jack show his cards first.

"Which, given that Gunner told you we had information on the 1715 fleet, you must know that was the port of call of the French warship *Griffon*."

My move. I pulled a grape from the platter as the jet lifted off the runway and climbed sharply into the sky.

"*Le Griffon* was a French frigate captained by Antoine d'Aire," I said. "He'd been forced to sail with the Spanish ships out of Havana because the commander of the Plate Fleet was worried he'd alert pirates of their voyage."

Gunner nodded and took a slug of champagne.

"He arrived in Brest a month later and claimed not to know that the rest of the fleet had sunk in the storm," Jack said.

"Claimed?"

"The *Griffon* was the first ship to leave Havana." Jack took a sip of champagne. "The rest of the fleet hugged Florida's coast and foundered in the shallow reefs when the storm pressed in from the east, but the *Griffon*'s captain managed to avoid the storm."

"Every amateur treasure hunter and tourist who's visited the Treasure Coast knows that—"

"They don't know what we know," Gunner said—and this time he wasn't smiling.

"Which is?"

"We'll get to that," Jack said.

As the plane leveled off, Jenny appeared with bottles of water and provided options for dinner. All I could think of was my brother's hysteria on the phone, a prisoner in his own home in Virginia. One step at a time.

"You think the *Griffon* had the queen's jewels on board?"

Jack shook his head from side to side. "The Spanish commander would have never allowed a French ship to carry that, no, but I do have reason to believe that Captain d'Aire is the key to finding the ship that carried the jewels."

The sudden urge to dissuade them from this venture pressed me forward in my plush leather seat. "Remnants of the fleet have been found spread out over hundreds of miles of ocean bottom, and those eleven ships sank over three hundred years ago, Jack. Unless you have a Walt Disney treasure map with a big X marking the spot, this is a waste of time. I was the archeologist, remember? We never pursued the 1715 fleet because it was too sparse—"

"Don't forget Scarlet Roberson," Jack said.

I sat back and sank in the leather. "What?"

"You said you were the archeologist. I'm reminding you that Scarlet Roberson was a big part of our success, too." He paused, his smile gone. "*King* Buck."

The statement burned inside me. Our eyes were locked together, and Gunner was visible out of the corner of my eye, glancing back and forth between Jack and me.

"Maybe you should just hire her then," I said.

A sly grin returned to Jack's lips. "Hire may not be the right word, but she has been involved."

Sudden turbulence rocked the plane, but it did nothing to release my stare from Jack's face.

What the hell had they done with Scarlet?

9

"WHAT'S THAT SUPPOSED TO MEAN?"

"I know you and Scarlet were recently reunited—your vacation in the Virgin Islands was well publicized," Jack said.

"First Lady of France, Reilly?" Gunner said. "That was a major score."

"Fuck you, Gunner. It wasn't a score. And my reunion with Scarlet didn't go so well—"

"By the way, congrats on the kid," Jack said. "What's his name, Charlie? Bet you never saw that coming."

"Gotta wear protection, Reilly." Gunner still had on his silly blue reflective glasses, and his comment made me want to knock them off his smug face.

I had to take a deep breath to calm my escalating heart rate.

"Full disclosure," Jack said. "We retained Scarlet, and she helped us initially. Then she got cold feet."

"What the hell's that supposed to mean?"

"She used to be very good behind the scenes back in the day," he said. "She'd find the raw data, you'd connect the dots, and boom, next thing you know, e-Antiquity had another big find. It was a strong partnership."

I felt my lips quiver as Jack rambled on.

"So she found some information related to the *Griffon*, great. What do you mean she got cold feet?"

"She didn't like being away from the kid," Gunner said. "Got indignant. Said we should get you to do it and demanded we take her home."

I clutched the arms of the leather seat. Why hadn't she called me? Had Gunner showed up at her door too? Where had Charlie been?

"Where is she now?"

"Quarantined back at home. Pandemic and all, I have a man watching her to make sure she's safe, and—"

I lunged for him—Jack dove at me and shoved me aside—I hit the end of the couch and bounced to the floor. Jenny stood in the back of the plane watching us. Her expression betrayed no concern or surprise.

Welcome to Air Lunatic. Thanks for flying the crazy skies.

"He didn't hurt her—"

"You go near Scarlet or my son and I'll end you once and for all, Gunner!"

"Relax, partner." His steady smile sent chills of electricity through my limbs and my fists balled tight as hammers. "You do your job, everybody will be fine."

Standing over me, Jack lowered his hand to help me up. It hung in the air.

Play the goddamned game, Buck.

I took his hand and he pulled me forward. I brushed off my shirt and jeans, grabbed the champagne, guzzled the full glass, and sat back down. Jack sat too. Jenny appeared and refilled my glass. What the hell, I was a prisoner on board a premium private jet flying to Europe. I'd drink Jack's champagne all night just to rack up his bill.

"We promised to pay Scarlet handsomely, still will if you can finish what she started," Jack said.

"Where was Charlie when she was in France?"

"Safe at home," Gunner said. "My guy's a prince."

"She agreed to additional consultation if it helps you to put the pieces together," Jack said.

"Ben and Scarlet? Really?" I said.

"Leverage, Reilly. I say jump, you better fucking pole vault," Gunner said.

I squirmed in the chair, grabbed the flute and drank another mouthful of champagne—too fast—the bubbles burned my nose and throat. I held my glass up for Jenny without looking back.

"You want my help, you get his goon away from her and my son."

Gunner scooped up a mitt of sushi, which disappeared in his gullet before his back hit the couch. Champagne again brimmed at the top of my glass. I'd need something help me sleep to be sharp when the time came.

"We'll see how things go in Brest," Jack said. "But to get ready, I'll share with you the details of what Scarlet found while there."

I practiced deep breathing and did my best to keep a straight face. "I'm all ears."

"We have good reason to believe there was more to the *Griffon* getting away than just good luck," Jack said. "Scarlet found pages from a ship's log and confirmed it had belonged to Captain d'Aire."

Since it was the only ship to survive the fateful hurricane, conspiracy theories about the *Griffon* had raged for centuries, but nothing had ever been remotely substantiated. If Scarlet truly had found something, it had the potential to be illuminating.

"Where did she find the supposed pages to the ship's log?"

"In Brest, of course. You'll meet the same man she did, and he'll show you the same pages so you can take it from where she left off," Jack said.

"So it is a wild goose chase."

"The pertinent translation mentions the author as being aboard the *Griffon*, makes note of their departure from Havana shortly before the Spanish fleet, and—here's the hook—it mentions another mystery frigate the fleet commander had just purchased the day before."

I licked my lips. That actually matched up with the letter I had from General Ubilla to his wife about the frigate he'd purchased in Havana—the *Farnese*. We always wondered if he'd bought it to stash important cargo as a hedge against the fleet being discovered and plundered by buccaneers. Jack must have read my silence as disbelief, because he leaned forward and snapped me out of my introspection.

"The log goes on to say that this other mystery frigate was under Spanish control by one of the top captains in the Tierra Firme fleet, with orders to stick closely to the *Griffon* and to distance themselves from the treasure fleet."

"Why would they do that?"

Gunner leaned forward. "Frigates were faster ships," he said.

"I know that. What was the point of distancing themselves from the fleet?"

Jack smiled. "General Ubilla didn't share that with Captain d'Aire, but he surmised that the Spanish frigate was carrying very valuable cargo because they were ordered to depart before the fleet and take the most direct route. They must have sailed further east, which put them in a totally different location than where the balance of the fleet was when the hurricane hit."

Scarlet knew about my copy of Ubilla's letter. Had she told Jack? Is that why I was here? If what Jack was saying was true, my letter corroborated the supposed ship's log, but it also said Ubilla had instructed the ships to sail close to the Bahamas. Did they know that? It dawned on me that to protect Scarlet, Charlie, Ben, and myself, I needed to appear cooperative but hold back select details as bargaining chips later.

"All that's intriguing, Jack, but so what? Even if there was another frigate, and even if it was loaded to the gills with the queen's jewels, what's it matter if we don't know where to look for it?"

He raised his champagne flute and tilted it toward me. "Exactly," he said. "That's why you're here."

"I'm not a magician. If that's all the log said—"

He held has palm up. "There's more." Then he sat staring at me with his irritating smirk.

"I'm not a mind reader, either," I said.

"We'll save it for Brest."

I couldn't think of a time I had ever dreaded going to France. Until now.

SECTION 2

FRENCHMAN
FOR A
NIGHT

10

THE G-IV TOUCHED DOWN after a long night of flying that included a refueling stop in Reykjavik, Iceland. Jenny had fed us dinner, and after more champagne, my sleep was assured. Morning came with cottonmouth and that sticky sensation of sleeping in your clothes. I recovered my duffel bag from a storage hatch and went to the bathroom to brush my teeth and change into a fresh shirt. But more importantly, I retrieved my cell phone and tried to call Scarlet. No answer.

Damn.

I tried Ben too. "Hi, I can't come to the phone right now. Leave a message and I'll call you back."

Beep.

"It's me, Buck. Tell whoever is watching you to call or text me to let me know you're okay. I'm on my way to Brest, France with Dodson and his goon, Gunner, which will hopefully lead to information that will set you free." I paused. "Hang in there, brother."

Back in the main cabin, breakfast was served. Fresh coffee, croissants, and fruit, along with bacon and eggs. Jenny was ruffled, her hair askew, her shirt wrinkled, but we all looked the same.

Customs was perfunctory at Brest Bretagne Airport, and we were met by a spacious Mercedes van to take us wherever Jack had planned. Gunner pulled the side door open—Jack grabbed my arm—I turned to face him.

He held up his phone for me to read: "Buck tried calling Ben and told him you were in Brest. Keep him under control."

"Give me your phone," Jack said.

"How do I know he's okay?" I said.

He scrolled the text down to reveal a picture of Ben holding a copy of *USA Today*. He zoomed in and I saw it was dated from yesterday. "Today's paper hasn't come yet—it's 1:00 a.m. there. I told you we wouldn't hurt him if you cooperated." He paused and our eyes locked. "So far, so good."

"What about Scarlet?"

"Nobody's going to hurt Scarlet or Charlie."

Gunner cleared his throat, loudly.

Son of a bitch.

Brest was on the western tip of France, part of Brittany, and had been a strategic location for nearly a thousand years. We drove south in morning traffic toward the coast of the Élorn River and passed the Moulin Blanc beach, which was connected to a large aquarium called Océanopolis. There was a slight fog over the river, and the air was crisp. The road continued along the river past a large shipyard and the central port. Formal gardens were on the right side of the road as we drove west, and behind them was Brest's downtown commercial district. I cracked open my window, and the aromas of bakeries, cigarettes, and car exhaust were in the air.

Numerous naval and container ships were visible at the port. "The French Naval Academy is here," I said.

"Pretty ugly city except for that old castle up ahead," Gunner said.

"The Brest naval museum," Jack said. "It's the location of the French National Maritime Museum."

"Cardinal Richelieu turned the confluence of the Élorn and Penfeld Rivers into a naval base in the early 1600s," I said. "Brest was the port of embarkation for American soldiers during World

War I, and it was a German U-boat base in World War II."

"Save your showing off for the ship's log, Reilly," Gunner said.

The whole town was built into sharp hillsides, and we drove past dozens of long flights of pedestrian steps that connected the many terraced levels.

Gunner pulled a copy of *Le Monde*, the daily newspaper, out of the seatback in front of him. The cover caught my eye. I craned over to get a better look as he held it up to face me.

"Looky who's on the cover, Reilly. Giselle Huibert, the First Lady of France." He lifted his blue reflective sunglasses to get a better glance. "She's a hottie. Kudos."

I hadn't spoken to her since the pandemic swept the globe, but I'd kept my eye on French news and knew that she and her husband, François, the president, were both in good health and doing what they could to protect the French people.

The driver glanced into his rearview mirror to get a better glance of me. My rescuing Giselle and our subsequent run for our lives through the Caribbean had been world news, especially here in France. I was awarded the French Legion of Honour for rescuing the First Lady but refused to come to the ceremony to collect. Her husband knew we'd developed an intense relationship as we fled the would-be killers, but I had to hand it to him— the French in general—for their ability to look beyond marital indiscretions. I exhaled a long breath. Good or bad, it was part of their culture.

"Bet you'd like to snuggle up to her right now, huh, Reilly?" Gunner said. His smile turned to a scowl. "Don't even think about it."

I wanted to swat the paper out of his sweaty palms as he leered at her photo, but I turned to watch the passing city traffic instead. Gunner had a knack for getting under my skin, and if I was going to save my brother's and Scarlet's lives, not to mention my own, I needed to keep my cool and help add some value to this situation.

"Just up ahead," Jack said.

The road turned to cobblestone as the stone turrets of the Maritime Museum grew larger ahead. The seventeenth-century castle had been one of the few structures left standing after the Allied bombing that turned the majority of the city to rubble. The sheer gray walls of the fortress climbed skyward at an angle away from the parking lot where we left the van and driver, who craned his head to watch me as I passed. I nodded to him and hoped he might gossip about having driven me, which could potentially alert local authorities to my presence. I was certain the president would have had my name and passport number flagged upon entering the country, if for no other reason than to know I may be coming to see his wife. With any luck, the French police would connect the dots and find me here. I'd help Jack in order to get my family released safely, but it wouldn't break my heart to have French *gendarmes* covering my ass.

A dapper man in a tweed jacket with white tousled hair and a long white goatee stood in front of the museum's entrance. He smiled as we approached. He glanced at all our faces, nodded toward Gunner, then settled his gaze on me.

"*Monsieur* Dodson?"

I nodded toward Jack.

"Director Roth, it's a pleasure to meet you in person," Jack said. His big smile and firm handshake tripped another memory of Jack schmoozing bankers on behalf of e-Antiquity. He was good at that, but it hadn't been enough for his ego.

"*Bienvenue, messieurs.* I hope your flight was comfortable." He hesitated and glanced around at us again.

"Allow me to introduce you to my partner, Buck Reilly," Jack said. His smile was steely now as he glanced toward me.

"Monsieur Reilly, it is truly pleasure to meet you," Roth said.

"Your work around the globe as an archeologist unlocked so many secrets."

I glanced at Jack. "Indeed."

"When Monsieur Dodson told me you were coming out of retirement to help on this project, I was thrilled to have the chance to meet you."

We followed the director inside as he spoke, his eyes wide and his hands waving with animation. "I understand you met my research colleague, Scarlet Roberson," I said. I wanted to understand the lay of the land before we got too far along with the good director.

Jack turned his head sharply toward me.

"*Bien sûr.* A brilliant and lovely woman, I might add." He beamed. "She spent days here searching the journals and our collection of digitized books, plans, and sections of naval vessels from the late 1600s and early 1700s."

We passed by wood and marble statues of women and seafaring men, exhibits of ships, and glass-encased relics as we walked through the museum. We entered a door marked *Privée* that led into a long corridor with glass doors along one side. Each door led into large rooms of file cabinets, library shelves full of old books, and tables with computers and notepads. All appeared to be devoid of people. As if reading my mind, the director turned to me.

"We have been closed due to the pandemic, but I opened today to accommodate your and Monsieur Dodson's request to meet and view the materials Madame Roberson selected."

"Was she here alone during her visit?" I said.

"Her research assistant, Monsieur Rostenkowski, accompanied her." Director Roth smiled toward Gunner, who offered him a curt nod, followed by an eyebrow pump for me.

I stopped in my tracks. Jack bumped into me. "That reminds me," I said. "I forgot to ask Scarlet an important question related to our meeting this morning. Can you call her, *Mr.* Rostenkow-ski?"

All eyes turned to Gunner.

"I don't believe she's available," he said.

"It's really important that I speak with her," I said. "In fact, this entire trip depends on it." I clenched my teeth after I spoke and watched Gunner and Jack's expressions closely.

"It's the middle of the night in Florida, Buck," Jack said. "I'd hate to disturb her."

"It's imperative, Jack." My jaw quivered as I thought of Gunner's mercenary goon holding Scarlet against her will.

Director Roth stood watching us, and he clasped his hands in front of his chest. I recognized the fuck-you slant of Jack's eyes, which I'd provoked in him multiple times since our friendship began in high school. He slowly reached into his pocket, removed his cell phone, scrolled through, then pressed send and placed the call on speaker.

After three rings, a groggy voice answered.

"Scarlet, I'm so sorry to wake you," Jack said.

"What's going on, Jack? Did you talk to Buck? I want this man—"

"Yes, we just arrived in Brest. I'm here with Buck, Director Roth, and, ah, your assistant." He cleared his throat. "Buck has an urgent question for you."

"Yes—hi, Buck. I'm so happy you agreed to help—Charlie and I both are."

I took the phone from Jack, turned off the speaker, and turned my back to the others. "Are you okay?"

A sniffle made her pause. "So far, yes." Her voice cracked. "Please, Buck, I don't want anything more to do with this—just help them find what they want so they'll leave us alone."

My hands balled into fists. "I will, Scarlet. I promise."

"Okay, Buck?" Jack said.

I held a finger up. "Did, ah, your assistant, Rostenkowski, happen to mention my brother to you while you were here together?"

"Ben? Why would he have mentioned him?" She paused. "Have they done something to Ben? My God—"

"Everything's fine." I didn't want to upset her more. "I'm sure I'll have questions about your research; I'll call back, okay?"

Gunner scowled.

Jack took the phone from my sweaty hand and put it up to his ear. "Thanks, Scarlet," he said. "Sorry to have woken you. Let's hope Buck can pick up where you left off so we can move the next phase ahead." He glanced at all of us watching his every word. "After we review the documents, Buck will call back if he has questions." Jack pressed end and the line went quiet. "Happy, Buck?"

"Thrilled."

11

JACK'S PREDICITION WAS CORRECT. It took us several hours to parse through the material Scarlet had taken days to gather under duress within the museum's vaults. As I took copious notes on a pad provided by Director Roth, several facts swirled to create a series of observations, or at least interesting assumptions. However, none of them led to what I suspected Jack and Gunner hoped to hear, which was that the *Griffon* would lead us to the missing queen's jewels.

Director Roth had lunch delivered while I pored through the documents, copies of microfiche, and the select pages Scarlet had copied from the *Griffon*'s ship log. Gunner gnawing on a baguette and chewing with his mouth open finally broke my concentration. They'd been quiet for hours while I read through everything, but Jack now leaned forward like he was at a doctor's office awaiting news.

"What'd you find?" he said.

I pulled one of the plated sandwiches toward me, drank from my water glass, and wiped my mouth with a cloth napkin. "Lots of loose details."

His eyes narrowed slightly.

"Nothing definitive," I said. "But some thought-provoking observations."

"Like what?" Gunner said as he chewed.

"Mostly context."

"What the hell's that supposed to mean?" Gunner said.

"Maybe nothing, or maybe details that could have motivated Captain d'Aire's break from the rest of the fleet."

"What would his motivation tell us?" Jack said.

I took a bite of the ham and cheese sandwich and thought. Making them wait was fun, but mostly I was processing the information I'd pulled out of Scarlet's broader collection of data. I wished circumstances were different and she were here now to discuss my ideas. She'd been brilliant to work with back in the day, and together, we'd been able to draw leads from disparate circumstances that had on several occasions led to major victories. I had little to no confidence in Jack's or Gunner's abilities to assist the thought process, but then I glanced toward Director Roth. Perhaps he could help me.

"Okay, let's build a picture of that era to try and understand the captain's mindset." I sorted through my notes until I found a list of dates. "It's important to know that Europe was in constant turmoil in the decades that preceded 1715. Alliances were constantly shifting, and the expansionism and competition for resources make today's environment seem like a lovefest." All three men stared at me.

"I hope you're going somewhere with this, Reilly," Gunner said. Director Roth's eyebrows arched, and he turned his head sharply toward Gunner. A research assistant blatantly disrespecting an esteemed archeologist would be an affront to him. It was to me too, but treasure hunting is different than academic research, and I doubted Director Roth knew what our motivation was exactly.

"In 1688, the Nine Years' War began."

"What does this have to do with anything?" Gunner said.

I ignored him. "There was a Grand Alliance of the Dutch Republic, England, the Holy Roman Empire, Spain, and Scotland versus France, Ireland, and the Scottish Jacobites."

"France was continuously at war with her neighbors back

then," Director Roth said. "The Treaty of Ryswick ended the war between France and Spain in 1697."

"Right," I said. "But then came the War of the Spanish Succession, which again had almost everyone—including England and the Spanish loyal to recently deceased King Charles II—at war with the Spanish loyal to Philip V and the French Bourbons—"

"I'll need bourbon if you keep up with this," Gunner said.

Director Roth sat erect. "Dear God, man, let Monsieur Reilly finish."

"Be patient, Gunner," Jack said. "Ah, *Richard.*"

"You see, King Charles of Spain died without an heir, but before his death, he appointed Philip V, the grandson of Louis XIV of France as his successor. That really pissed off Leopold I, the Holy Roman emperor, as he wanted *his* son, Archduke Charles, to ascend the Spanish throne. And equally important, he wanted to prevent what would have become a major alliance between Spain and France."

"When the war broke out in 1701, everyone was against Spain and France," Director Roth said.

"And right off the bat, England was kicking Spain's ass and making Philip look bad. They lost naval battles in 1701, 1702, and 1708—" I turned the page quickly, caught up in the history. "Then they lost a treasure ship in another hurricane off the coast of Cuba in 1708."

Gunner took in a sharp breath, and Jack quickly raised a palm to him, then turned to me. "What does this all have to do with the *Griffon?*"

I smiled. "Captain d'Aire of the *Griffon* was French."

Gunner scowled. "So?"

Director Roth rubbed his palms together. "Then came the Peace of Utrecht."

I pointed to the director. "Exactly." Confusion was clear on

Jack and Gunner's faces. "Spain was bankrupt and couldn't continue the war, but Philip didn't want to give up the crown. William III of England wanted to prevent domination by France since Louis XIV's grandson was now king of Spain, so in negotiating the end of hostilities in 1713, they demanded that Philip renounce his claim to the French throne."

"Which he agreed to do," Director Roth said.

"Which meant the rest of Europe was now aligned with Spain, and France was left destitute. French king Louis XIV was heavily criticized at home due to massive tax increases, which led to famine and peasant uprisings that he brutally repressed. Bottom line is that France went from being at the pinnacle of power to penniless thanks to Spain abandoning them in the Peace of Utrecht."

Gunner finally jumped to his feet and circled around the table to stand behind me. I kept my eyes on the director, who stared aghast as the brute of the man hovered over my shoulder.

"So Captain d'Aire was French, got it. I understand how frustrating getting dumped by Spain must have been, but it's time to close the circle here. How does that impact our interests?"

"Let Buck finish," Jack said.

The director sat back in his chair. His eyes now registered something else, possibly recognition that all was not right with the situation. That recognition stirred an uneasy twist in my stomach that he could be at risk if he said the wrong thing, so I raised my hands.

"Allow me to connect the dots." I paused. "We need to understand the context of the time. That's important to understanding where Captain d'Aire's heart and thoughts would have been when the fleet sailed out of Havana on July 24th, 1715. Now that we do …"

I sorted through my pages of notes until I found what I was looking for. "I found the *Griffon*'s records in the history of French naval vessels." I pointed to one of the fat leather-bound volumes on the table. "She was a frigate of the first order, or a fourth-rank vessel."

"So it was a piece of shit?" Gunner said.

"Fourth rank doesn't mean poor quality. It was a succession of order and determined the number of decks and armament. They were usually two-deck vessels that carried twelve-pounder guns on the lower deck battery and six-pounder guns on the upper deck—which is a fairly light armament, so they weren't frontline battleships. Frigates were known for being fast, so their main function was cruising and protecting trade vessels."

"Sounds right," Jack said.

"The *Griffon* was launched on January 10th, 1705, and had forty-four guns. So think of the context we ran through a minute ago. The *Griffon* was built during the early part of the War of the Spanish Succession, when France and Spain were aligned. The ship, however, was captured by the British navy in August of 1712 and not released until the Peace of Utrecht in 1713," I said.

"Was Captain d'Aire held as a prisoner by the British until the war ended?" Jack asked.

"We can only presume that, since there's no crew list in the records," I said. "And when they were released after the war, the ship was immediately dispatched by King Philip to Veracruz, Mexico to collect monies owed to the Crown by the Duke of Liares, the Spanish governor in place in Veracruz."

"Wait, you said the French were cast aside like cheap whores by the Spanish king," Gunner said. "Why would the *Griffon* be sent on a mission for Spain?" Gunner said.

"Because Spain paid for the ship," Director Roth said, "and would have kept it and her crew as indentured servants as part of the Peace of Utrecht."

Gunner walked back around the table and sat next to Jack. "No soldier—Frog navy or not—likes being conscripted in a foreign force." He smiled. "Unless they're getting paid really well."

"That's it, Buck?" Jack said.

"For the context, yes, but I agree with Gunner that if d'Aire had been a prisoner of war and likely held under poor conditions, he would have been pissed that upon his release he was sent across the Atlantic to bid for a king who had renounced his French birthright."

"Most unpleasant," Director Roth said.

"What about the ship's log?" Jack said.

I reached over and pulled the pages Scarlet had printed from the microfiche copy of the log, which noted the *Griffon*'s name, and turned to the director. "Any chance we could see the original?"

"I have no idea where it is but can try and find out," he said. My stare lingered until his eyes opened wider. "Now?"

"We'll be leaving soon."

Director Roth stood and took one of the copies of the pages to search the microfiche code to connect it to the archives. After he left the room, I turned to Jack. "Based on the translation of the section of log she copied, we know the *Griffon* left Havana with another frigate—"

"Scarlet confirmed General Ubilla purchased another frigate in Havana. It was the *Santa Rita y Animas*, which was one of the eleven ships confirmed to have sunk," Jack said. "But Ubilla's second mystery frigate, which would be the thirteenth ship, sailed together with the *Griffon*."

I debated internally on how to play my knowledge of what Jack referred to as the "mystery frigate," which I knew was named the *Farnese*. I decided on playing ignorant. Jack didn't know about Ubilla's letter, which corroborated the reference in d'Aire's log of the second frigate and his instructions for them to take an easterly course.

"So wouldn't d'Aire have been pissed when part of his crew—his French crew—was taken by the Spanish captain on this unnamed thirteenth ship?"

"Good question," Jack said.

"The log noted that d'Aire's first mate was seconded to other ship since he was expert in sailing a boat of this same class. Also that Ubilla had commanded this other ship to stay close to the *Griffon*."

"That's it?" Gunner said.

"Yes, in the pages that had been translated from the microfiche," I said.

"Translated?" he said. "Let me see them."

I hesitated, but I took the three pages from the top of my pile and handed them over. I held my breath, wondering whether Gunner spoke French. The log was faded, the writing ornate and the language archaic, but it was still French—the one language I did speak aside from English. Scarlet hadn't referenced a line from the letter that mentioned the ships had been instructed to sail an easterly course toward the Bahamas and, like Ubilla's letter, to take the fastest route to Spain.

A burst of optimism lit in my heart, since I suspected she had done that for my benefit, knowing I'd have no choice but to come here but providing me leverage to use when necessary.

Gunner threw down the papers. "Gibberish."

I bit my lip to contain my smile. I hadn't seen much more because the entire log hadn't been copied—again, I was hoping on purpose—but what I did see and didn't share was that the other ship, the *Farnese*, had foundered. It didn't say where, but my hope was that more detail would be available in the balance of the log. I had another idea, too, that may might actually merit additional research here and could be helpful to better understanding d'Aire.

"Another reason the context is important is because there's

no documentation about the cargo from d'Aire's original mission to Veracruz—the entire reason the *Griffon* was in the Caribbean," I said.

"What about it?" Jack said.

"We know he was sent there to collect on a debt for the king. We have to assume that was accomplished."

"How much was the debt?" Gunner said.

"48,801 *piastres*, or silver pieces of eight," I said.

"How much is that worth?"

"At Mel Fisher's store in Key West, a top-quality piece of eight sells for $3,000. So multiply that by 48,801—"

"That's $146,000,000," Jack said.

"You've always been the numbers guy, Jack," I said. "The point is, he sailed east away from the fleet and survived but continued past Spain and came here to Brest." I paused and watched as their eyes slowly widened.

"So what happened to the pieces of eight?" Gunner said.

"Like I said, he was French and had every reason to hate the Spanish for selling them out in the Peace of Utrecht."

"I'll be damned," Jack said.

"One other thing I found—" I was interrupted when Director Roth reentered the room empty-handed.

"What?" Gunner said.

I held a finger up. "Any luck, Director?" I said.

"*Oui*, I found the log, but it is off-site, and I need to file the pertinent paperwork to have the document returned here, thanks to the pandemic."

"How long will that take?" Jack said.

"Two days, maybe three."

Gunner grunted. "Can't that be expedited? Our rental plane turns into a pumpkin tomorrow."

I took one of the pieces of paper and wrote my contact information on it. "Here's my email address. Can you copy the balance and send it to me once you find it?"

"Of course," he said.

"*Entre nous.*" I winked.

Director Roth glanced at Gunner out of the corner of his eye. "*Bien sûr.*"

"What's all that mean?" Gunner said.

"I said thank you in French." I'd really said "between us," which the director had clearly understood, given Gunner's rude behavior throughout.

As we walked out of the room and down the hallway, the director leaned closer to me. "Will you be seeing the First Lady while you're here?"

"I don't—"

"No time for romance this trip," Gunner said.

"Indeed," Director Roth said, then pursed his lips.

"If you know anybody at the Palais, please ask them to let her know I was here but, ah, too busy to reach out."

Our eyes held for a long second.

The director nodded.

12

WE LEFT DIRECTOR ROTH AT THE FRONT DOOR and walked toward our van.

"What was the one other thing, Reilly?" Gunner said.

I had debated whether to share this with them, but in the interest of getting this over with as fast as possible to get my brother freed and Gunner's goon away from Scarlet, I had no choice.

"There was an address in Scarlet's notes. She didn't copy the page, but I'm guessing it belonged to Captain d'Aire."

"His home address?" Jack said.

"I don't know."

"Is it here in Brest?" Gunner said.

No," I said. "But if my memory of Brittany is accurate, it's not far away."

Jack pulled out his phone and opened a map app. "What's the address?"

"Not an actual street address but a town. Saint-Renan."

After a minute's search, Jack looked up. "Ten miles as the crow flies."

"Let's fly," Gunner said.

Once we were in the van, our driver nodded at the inquiry of Saint-Renan's location. Jack continued to search his phone for details on the town. "It has history noted back to the fifth century. It developed simultaneously with Brest in the Middle Ages." He scrolled on his phone as we crossed the Penfeld River bridge. The

Tanguy Tower was on our left as we drove up a boulevard to the west through Brest. "Eight thousand people live in Saint-Renan now."

"Must have been tiny back in the 1700s," I said. "We just find the oldest part of town and see what we can learn."

The ten miles took over thirty minutes as we wove our way through suburban Brest and headed northwest between green fields, then past the outside perimeter of another town called Guilers.

"Saint-Renan is ahead," the driver said.

Much of the town looked far less than a hundred years old. "Is there a historic downtown or tourist office?" I asked.

He nodded and drove on. A few minutes later, we pulled up to what had to be the old city square: old row houses with peaked roofs, cafés, and shops that lined the open area where cars were prohibited. On the corner of a street that fed into the square was a sign for the *Office de Tourisme* in a four-story stone building with flower boxes on each window.

"Now what?" Gunner said.

"Excuse me, driver," I said. "Do you know if there's a history museum here?"

He grunted, then scratched his neck. "Only the Musée du Ponant around the corner there." He pointed to the next street over to the left of the tourism office.

"Let's start there," I said.

With that, we were on foot marching through the picturesque stone square. Even in the cool air, the café's outdoor tables were full with people drinking coffee and beer, smoking cigarettes, and laughing, some pressed in close, face-to-face, sharing lover's secrets. None had a visible care in the world.

The museum was mid-block and had a bright red façade. Through the glass, I could see an elderly man seated at a desk, asleep. Nobody else was inside the small space.

"This looks promising." Gunner rolled his eyes.

"Process of elimination and discovery are the same thing," I said. "We're trying to find information on a guy who lived over three hundred years ago in a town that's been here for fifteen hundred years. To say it's a needle in a haystack doesn't do it justice, but it's how this work is done."

Jack yawned.

"You always thought it was some kind of romantic hunt out on the research trail, didn't you?"

"It was between you and Scarlet," he said.

I pressed my lips together—hard—to prevent the retort that fought to be heard: *While you, Jack, cheated with my wife after I got married.* I pulled open the glass door instead—bells jingled, and the old man sat up abruptly.

"*Bonjour*," he croaked as his eyes blinked rapidly.

"You speak English?" Gunner said.

"Let me handle this, will you?" I said.

Jack put a hand on Gunner's chest as if to hold him back.

"Ah *oui*, yes, yes," the man said.

"My name's Buck Reilly and these are my, ah, colleagues." I held my hand wide toward Gunner, who looked like a pitbull, and Jack, a tall, slick, muscular creep. "I'm an archeologist. We've come from Brest, where we spent the day with Director Roth from the Maritime Museum."

His eyes blinked faster for a second and then grew wider. "Pleasure to meet you. Director Roth is a renowned historian. Did he, um, send you to me?"

"Yes," I lied.

The man stood more erect and pressed his hand down the front of his wrinkled shirt. "And how can I help you?"

"We are researching a seventeenth-century sailing vessel called *Le Griffon*. The boat itself is an unremarkable frigate of the time, but its captain is of interest to us. He lived here in Saint-

Renan?"

"Hmm, I see." He scratched his neck again. "*Le Griffon*, you say? Do you have any specific years?"

"Yes, it was launched in 1705 at Lorient and was in the New World on behalf of King Philip V of Spain beginning in 1713. It arrived back at Brest on August 31, 1715."

"Oh, *oui, Le Griffon*, the only ship from a fleet of twelve that survived a tempest in the Caribbean! It was considered a triumph of French seamanship." He nodded his head emphatically. "The captain, Antoine d'Aire, was from here."

Gunner rolled his eyes, but Jack's were glassy with expectation.

"That's right," I said. "Director Roth clearly sent us to the right man."

"Antoine d'Aire, Antoine d'Aire," he repeated.

"Does he have any surviving family members here?" Jack said.

The man looked at Jack as if for the first time. "Not that I'm aware of."

"Do you have a local phone book?" Gunner said.

The man paused. "They no longer print them."

As I was about to admonish Jack and Gunner, the man raised a finger. "But I keep an old one because nothing much changes here." His smile revealed tobacco-stained front teeth.

As the man stepped back to his desk and pulled open a top drawer, I glared at my traveling cohorts. The phone book was larger than expected, but I saw it had a map of the entirety of Brittany on its cover. He placed it on his desk, licked a finger, and began to fan slowly through pages.

"D'Aire, d'Aire, d'Aire," he repeated.

The three of us crowded in around his desk. Jack and Gunner's expressions were taut with expectation. Research rookies. What did they expect, one potential lead would—

"*Voilà!*" The man said.

Gunner nearly muscled me out of the way as he bent over to see what the man had discovered. "There's only three of them," he said.

"That's good. If there were a hundred, it would take us weeks to sort through them," I said. Then, to the man, "Would you do us a tremendous favor? Would you mind calling the three numbers and asking if they are related to the captain?"

"Well, I'm rather busy this afternoon—"

"You were sleeping!" Gunner said.

The man's eyes grew wide, and the corners of his mouth pointed sharply down. Jack dug into his pocket and produced a roll of euros.

"Of course, sir, allow me to compensate you for your time and effort." He peeled off two one hundred euro notes, and the man's eyes flickered momentarily. He palmed the cash.

"I will make time." He ambled back around to his chair and dropped in with a practiced thud. With glasses now perched on his nose, he pulled the phone book closer and craned forward to read the numbers. "This first one is in Lorient."

The others looked toward me, their eyebrows lifted. "About an hour and a half south," I said. Once the man dialed, I could hear the phone ringing from the earpiece.

"*Allô?*"

The man spoke quickly in a pompous tone. I heard the name of his museum, followed by "*Les américains*," and then he mentioned the captain's name and the year 1715.

There was a brief response on the other end. He asked another question, thanked the person, and hung up. "She asked if I was serious and how would she know if she was related to a man from three hundred years ago."

"That's it?" Gunner said.

"Two more."

The next call—this time to a number in Saint-Malo on the northern coast—resulted in curiosity but no connection. We were zero for two.

"The last one is from here in Saint-Renan," he said.

The three of us shared a *why didn't he start with that one first* glance. More pleasantries with the person who answered, and then he repeated his now-familiar statement about the museum. His eyes gradually widened, and I could tell by the conversation that the person knew the museum. He invited them to come visit and then finally got to the point, asking if the other person was related to the captain.

A long response kept him nodding, glancing up to meet my eyes, and nodding more. He said something about Spain, then Havana, and after the response on the other end, he rolled his eyes. "*Merci beaucoup, madame. Visitez-moi ici lundi a vendredi. Merci.*"

He hung up the phone and held our gazes with an amused smile. "That woman was a talker—"

"What did she say?" Gunner asked.

One thing I'd learned long ago was to let people talk: they would reveal more on their own accord than by being prodded. But Gunner was prone to interrogation.

"She is very old and has lived in this village her entire life. She claims to be related to the captain, but then she said things that don't match up, so I suspect she is lying or has dementia."

"What details didn't match?" I said.

"She said her family heritage was very wealthy and that it was a distant relative named Antoine who was a sea captain that was the source of their wealth."

The air sucked from the room. I heard the other two men shuffle in place behind me. "It may have been him," I said. "What else did she say?"

"He is buried at *l'église* Notre Dame de Liesse."

"Where's that?" I said.

"One block over."

"You mentioned she was from here in Saint-Renan. Does the phone book have her address?" I said.

"She will talk your ear off if you go see her." He placed the glasses back on the tip of his nose and hunkered down. "Yes, 13 Rue Casse la Foi. Same street as the church, a block closer to here."

I loved small towns of this vintage. The older parts were condensed, and if there was anything to be found, it was usually concentrated—like here.

We thanked the director of the mini-museum and stepped back outside. The afternoon was now casting long shadows of chimneys and television dishes over the cobblestoned street.

"Was that good news or bad news?" Gunner said.

"If it's our boy, then he came back from the Americas a very wealthy man," Jack said.

"Why do we care where he was buried or where the old motormouth lived?" Gunner said.

"If he was buried here, that means he probably never left."

"Again, so what?"

"Let's go assess his stature."

"How?" The blue reflective sunglasses blocked Gunner's eyes, but I guessed they were squinted.

"By the quality of the home and the size of the headstone at the church."

13

THE HOUSE WAS IN THE MIDDLE OF A BLOCK of stone row homes. It was narrow: two stories with two windows on the front of each level.

"Doesn't look like much," Gunner said.

"We can always count on you to state the obvious," I said.

I turned slowly around to check out the other buildings on the block. All were fairly similar, stone, some with dormers on the roofs, and the homes on the ends of the blocks were slightly larger—three windows on the front. Didn't look like the house of a man who'd stashed away millions in stolen silver coins.

"Maybe he lived somewhere else in town," I said.

"I'll get her to tell us everything she knows," Gunner said.

"Don't be ridiculous," I said. "Why don't you two wait out here—"

"Not happening, Buck," Jack said.

"Fine, but he'll terrify the poor woman. Just let me handle it, all right?"

Gunner's expression never changed, and he didn't respond. After a second, he waved his hand toward the house as if to tell us to get on with it.

We walked up to the door and I knocked. A moment later, an elderly woman opened the door. Her eyes were alert, and she wore a colorful dress and her hair was done. My immediate impression was that she lived on her own and was self-reliant and quick-witted.

"*Bonjour, madame. Je m'appelle* Buck Reilly—"

"From the museum?" she said in English. "The director said you were American."

"That's right. I'm an archeologist, and we're researching Captain Antoine d'Aire."

"As I told him, he was my distant grandfather."

Jack put on a big Wall Street smile. "Can we come inside to talk?"

"No, that's not possible. I'm leaving soon for dinner." Her cordial smile faded and was replaced with arched eyebrows and crossed arms. If she was eighty, she had the attitude and presence of someone half her age.

"We're very sorry to interrupt you, and I promise not to take more than a couple minutes," I said. "You mentioned Captain d'Aire was buried at the church up the street. Was this his home?"

A smirk bent the corners of her lips up. "He owned all of the homes on this side of the street." Her chin lifted higher. "He lived in the largest one on the end. The rest were used by family members and servants."

"Impressive," I said.

"How did he make his money?" Jack said.

The corners of her lips quickly turned down. "Shipping."

"Of course," I said. A cold glance at Jack out of the corner of my eye would hopefully stem any further brutish inquiry. "He must have been quite famous for surviving the hurricane that sank so many other ships."

"The Spanish ships." She spat out the country's name as if the Peace of Utrecht was still a fresh point of irritation.

"And as a sailor who'd traveled to and from the New World successfully, I'm sure he was able to build upon that with, ah, his shipping business."

She glanced at her wristwatch, the face of which was so small

I couldn't see the hands to read the time. "He only ran the shipping business for five years after returning from the Americas. He passed in 1720—was killed, in fact—but yes, he was quite successful given the challenges here in France at the time."

"Killed?" I said.

"Murdered by a crewman—someone who had sailed with him on *Le Griffon*. No details exist, probably jealousy, but it's ancient history now." She glanced from Jack to me. "Was there something specific you wanted to ask me?"

"Yes." I blurted out the word so Jack wouldn't answer first but then had vapor lock on what to say. Then inspiration hit. "Do you know if there are any biographies or family history with details about the captain?"

"None that I've seen."

"Are there any other family members still alive?"

"Sadly, no. My husband passed ten years ago, so I'm the last of the family. I'm sorry, but I really must—"

"One last question, madame, and thank you again for speaking with us. Do you recall the name of Captain d'Aire's shipping company?"

"Of course. His success in those brief years paid for generations that followed. Compagnie Maritime Andros was the name."

The name caused a spark in my head, but I tried to keep a straight face. Jack's expression changed too—was he smiling?

"Now, *excusez-moi*, but I really must go." She took a step back inside, then paused and leaned her head out. "But if you learn anything of interest, I'd appreciate you telling me too." She closed the door quietly.

I turned to face Jack, who still had an irritating grin on his face. "Something she say resonate with you?"

"Compagnie Maritime Andros. The name of d'Aire's company."

"What about it?"

"Andros, like in the Bahamas."

Gunner appeared from behind a shrub where he'd been lurking. "Did you say Bahamas?"

Jack nodded. "The good captain started a company upon his return, which he apparently monetized quite successfully for five years before being murdered by a former *Griffon* crewman. His company was called Compagnie Maritime Andros."

Gunner's pumpkin-sized head swelled in a smile.

Irritated at what I could easily see was an epiphany between Jack and Gunner, I held my hands up. There was no mention in Scarlet's notes about d'Aire being instructed to sail an easterly course to the Bahamas—that was only in Ubilla's letter, so they couldn't know that.

"What's so interesting about Andros?"

Just then, the front door reopened and Madame d'Aire emerged, her hair up in a scarf. She did a double take on us and scowled, probably at the sight of Gunner.

"Let's keep moving up to the church," I said.

"Where's that?" Jack said.

I pointed up the block to a steeple that rose above the rooftops. I glanced back, and Madame d'Aire had turned the opposite direction and was headed toward the old square.

"So, partners, are you going to fill me in on why Andros has you both grinning like schoolboys with their first *Playboy*?"

"In due time, Buck. In due time," Jack said.

Whether it was because he was repeating himself or because I'd followed my hunches to get us here, only for these jerks to connect dots they now wouldn't explain, I wasn't sure. And it didn't really matter. A deep breath was all it took to remember that I was here against my will, that Ben, Scarlet, and Charlie were all being held captive, and that our collective survival depended upon helping these assholes.

Maybe I should have felt relieved, happy at making progress, but I didn't.

I was pissed.

14

THE ÉGLISE NOTRE DAME DE LIESSE was a simple church constructed of the same light gray stone as most of the other buildings from the same period in town, but according to a small sign out front, Notre Dame was newer. It was consecrated in 1772 as a substitute for a chapel that had been struck by lightning in the same location in 1768. Originally a site of worship for druids who held pilgrimages here, the chapel was named Notre Dame in 1747.

I walked forward and up the steps to the arched stone entrance and its pair of heavy green doors. Inside, the nave extended forward, and the vaulted room was dark except for the muted light filtering through the tall stained glass windows on the sides and surrounding the apse ahead. There was a single aisle with pews on each side, making the church less than half the size of the typical French cathedral found in major cities.

"What are we looking for?" Jack said.

"Any clues related to Captain d'Aire."

"Churches give me the creeps," Gunner said.

Gunner looked foolish in his reflective blue sunglasses inside the dark church. I was going to make a quip that given the crimes against humanity he'd no doubt perpetrated, he could be turned into a pillar of salt at any moment, but I didn't bother. His nervous expression spoke for itself.

"Small chapels on the sides or in the corners of larger church-es are often dedicated to wealthy patrons who contributed to their construction or made substantial gifts," I said. "Since the original chapel must have burned down after being struck by lightning, and Captain d'Aire died twenty-seven years prior to that, it's unlikely he's memorialized here, but it's still worth a look."

"I'll check the right side." Jack walked to the far wall.

"And I'll keep my eye on you," Gunner said.

He followed after me as I studied every name under every painting. The church wasn't big, and there were only a couple side chapels, one on each side. The one on our side had a painting of an old man whose name was Gautier. As I walked forward toward the apse, I studied the subjects on the stained glass. They weren't portraying classical religious symbols or scenes but images of buildings—ones whose architecture was the same as here in Saint-Renan. On the last one before the transept, I spotted a sailing ship. The background was of light blue water, and it had a palm tree–lined island behind it. Standing next to the ship was a man. I leaned in close and saw a name etched at the base of the glass: Capitaine Antoine d'Aire.

"Holy crap," I whispered.

"What have you got?" Gunner said.

"Check it out."

"No shit?" Gunner studied the images built into the glass. The tropical island; the Caribbean-blue water; the captain standing boldly with his foot resting on what I thought was a rock but, as I studied it closer, realized were crates; and behind him, the ship—a seventeenth-century frigate.

"That, Gunner, is most likely the *Griffon*."

"No shit."

Jack walked up behind us. "Is that our man?" he said.

"Looks that way," I said. "And given the tropical setting, I'm guessing that's either Florida or the Bahamas. Buts since his company's called Andros, makes sense to assume the Bahamas."

"Unbelievable," Jack said.

I studied the crates under the captain's foot. Could they have held treasure? Next to the *Griffon*, something odd caught my attention: it looked like the top of a ship's mast sticking up out of the water.

"Look at that," I said. "There must have been a wreck there. Maybe he salvaged it."

The sharp intake of Jack's breath caused me to turn toward him. The schoolboy grin was back, and he was pumping his eyebrows toward Gunner. He too again had the silly smile. They knew something I didn't, but I had to work it out fast, or I'd become unnecessary.

Ubilla's letter from the day they left Havana came to mind. Could the tip of the mast depicted in the window belong to the frigate Ubilla bought in Havana, the *Farnese*? And if it was, had the ship been carrying treasure as insurance against the main fleet being attacked? Ubilla wouldn't have been worried about hurricanes—they had no way to know they were sailing straight into a storm that would sink the entire fleet—but he'd been cagey enough to offset their risk by sending the two frigates east through the Bahamas.

It was starting to feel clear that Captain d'Aire knew the *Farnese* held treasure—not to mention the forty-eight thousand *piastres* he'd picked up in Veracruz. Maybe they'd divided it between the ships to protect it. Or had d'Aire salvaged the contents of the *Farnese*? Were Jack and Gunner giddy because they knew that somehow?

A small group of people walked past us down the center aisle. I looked to see where they'd come from and saw a docent watching them depart. I waved to him, and he came toward us. He was a small, portly man with red hair and a matching beard. He had a name badge pinned to his blue blazer. Georges.

"*Bonjour.*" His voice was a whisper.

"*Bonjour*, Georges. *Parlez-vous Anglais?*" I said.

"Yes, how can I help you?"

I felt Jack and Gunner close in behind me. "Do you know the details behind the story told on this window?"

"Yes, of course." He glanced past me down to the church entrance. "I'm starting another tour in a minute if you'd care to join. The cost is ten euros per person. I will describe many of the details here—"

Jack's arm shot past my shoulder. He held up a hundred euro note. "We don't have time for the group tour, but we'll pay you extra for a private one, and all we care about is the story behind this subject."

The man's eyes fluttered, and he took the note, glanced past me again, then took a step closer to the stained glass.

"Captain d'Aire was one of the prime donors who helped fund the construction of our church." He paused. "Unfortunately, he passed long before construction was complete."

"That's an interesting portrayal," I said. "Why the tropical setting?"

"The captain had recently returned from several years at sea in the New World. His ship, *Le Griffon*, was the sole survivor amongst eleven Spanish vessels that sunk during a terrible storm."

I paused for a moment but again feared Gunner would frighten the docent by being too abrupt, so continued. "We're familiar with Captain d'Aire. I'm an archeologist and these are my colleagues. We've been in Brest and Saint-Renan researching his life."

The docent glanced quickly at Gunner, replete in his blue-mirrored glasses—and then back to me.

"Madame d'Aire down the street sent us here to see the depiction."

The man smiled. "Then you know that Captain d'Aire was a local hero for surviving the storm and returning to France with treasure that had been owed to King Philip V of Spain."

"No love lost between France and Spain after the Peace of Utrecht," I said.

"You know your history."

"And he used it to build this church?" Gunner said.

The man's eyes fluttered again. "He was very generous."

"A shame he was murdered by a former *Griffon* crewman," I said.

"Tragic."

"Was that because Captain d'Aire kept all the treasure for himself and the crew was angry?" I said.

Georges again smiled, no doubt pleased at being able to engage on history he knew well, and based on his expression, he was appreciative that we too knew the history. "The crew had been treated well by the captain, each receiving a share based on their rank."

"Then why did the crewman kill him?" Jack said.

Georges turned toward the stained glass window and pointed. "Because of this."

"I don't understand," I said.

"*Le Griffon*'s sailing companion had sunk on its return from the New World. Captain d'Aire refused to bring the crew back to the place where that occurred."

Interesting. Why wouldn't d'Aire use his former crew to return to salvage the *Farnese*?

"What was the name of the other ship?" I said. It was a rhetorical question, but I wanted to see if Ubilla's purchase of the second frigate was known here.

"That we don't know," he said. "But Captain d'Aire told family members that the commander of the Spanish fleet had placed important cargo on this other ship to keep it safe in case the main fleet was attacked." Georges shook his head. "They never considered a storm would sink them all. *Le Griffon*'s crew knew that significant treasure was on the other ship, and when d'Aire refused to take a particular crewman back, he killed him."

I glanced from Jack's to Gunner's eyes. Both were enraptured.

"Was Captain d'Aire's shipping company able to return to where the second ship had sunk to salvage it?" I said.

"No, he never returned to the New World. His trade was primarily with the British for the time he operated, but he had been planning a return voyage to the New World at the time of his death."

"Here, to this island in the Bahamas?" Jack said.

The man's eyes lit, and he lifted his chin to look at Jack. "Is that where the other ship sank? We never knew."

I interjected. "We're not sure. That may come out of the research we're doing into Captain d'Aire's history."

Georges' eyes suddenly popped open. "Are you Buck Reilly? The famous archeologist who saved our First Lady from assassins in the Caribbean last year?" His eyes shot from me to Jack and Gunner and back.

"Thanks for your help, George." Gunner mispronounced the docent's name.

"I recognize you from the news—it is you, isn't it?" Georges said. "The man who rescued Giselle Huibert."

I frowned. Recognition of losing Giselle was another turn of the knife I now had to endure thanks to Jack and Gunner dragging me to France.

"Such an honor to meet you!" He took my hand and shook it vigorously. "Will you be visiting the Palais Royal while here?"

I felt Gunner's hand land squarely in the center of my back. "No, we're returning the States toot-sweet."

I winced. "We're leaving today, I'm afraid."

"Is there anything else about Captain d'Aire you can tell us?" Jack said.

"Um, well, let's see." He scratched his beard. "Only that after his death, the d'Aire family was forced to sell off his boats and assets he'd compiled since returning from the New World."

"Why's that?" Gunner said.

"The captain had been very generous. As I said, he had donated a significant amount to help build the church. But, like many entrepreneurs, apparently he was spending money based on the expectations of future earnings." Georges nodded toward the stained glass window. "But he is buried in a place of honor in our cemetery."

Captain d'Aire never got to return to the Bahamas to salvage the *Farnese*, so his family couldn't afford to keep his estate intact. Shame.

I had originally planned to investigate whether the church kept death books—the documents detailing the division of estates of members upon their deaths, which were often held by churches or with old records at libraries or courthouses—but that line of research no longer seemed relevant. The real treasure, the queen's jewels, was still out there somewhere.

The captain had been killed for refusing to include a particular crewman as they prepared to return to Andros to salvage the *Farnese*. Whatever caused him to make that decision had cost him his life.

We thanked Georges and stepped out into the twilight of dusk.

15

"WHO WOULD HAVE THOUGHT WE'D LEARN SOME-THING AT CHURCH," Gunner said.

We stood on the cobblestone road that led back toward the main square, where we'd left our van. There was a bite in the air now that the sun had dipped below the rooftops.

"You've still got the gift, Buck," Jack said.

I wondered what Scarlet had learned while she was here and what she'd told them before demanding to go home. Had she held anything back to protect herself, or were they holding out on me? Was that why the name of d'Aire's shipping company resonated with them?

"Scarlet didn't figure any of this out when she was here?" I said.

"She was always good at finding the raw material. But it was you that polished it into diamonds," Jack said. "You were a good team."

"Except in the parenting department," Gunner said.

I spun toward him and grabbed the front of his shirt. "Don't you dare—"

Both of his arms shot up between mine—it felt like a vice had closed on my left wrist as he pushed it up and spun it hard—the stone buildings blurred—I was flung to the ground, my faced pressed into cobblestones. His knee was on the back of my neck—

"Gunner!" Jack's voice was muffled. "Get off him!"

Gunner's substantial weight pressed my face into the damp

grit of the street, a Gauloises cigarette butt just inches from my nose. His weight lifted, and he stepped back. The urge to jump back up and use my longer reach, height, and former boxing skills to bloody his nose was quickly squelched—I'd tried that in the past, unsuccessfully.

I felt hands grab me under the armpits and lift me up—I brushed Jack's hands away, stood on my own, and took a step toward Gunner.

"You need to get your goon away from Scarlet and my son, asshole."

"Or what?" He hadn't even broken a sweat, and his reflective blue sunglasses still sat squarely on his wide face.

"Or you can try and figure out what all this means without me." I held my arms wide.

"What about your brother, you gonna leave him hanging?" he said.

"That's enough," Jack said. "Scarlet and Charlie are fine, Buck. So is Ben. And we're doing well as a team." He stared daggers at Gunner for a moment. "Let's get back to the plane. We'll take it from there."

Standing between us, Jack gripped my left bicep and Gunner's right and urged us forward. I pulled my arm out of his grip. "Wait a minute. Since we're here, we might as well see d'Aire's grave."

"Wanna leave him some flowers?" Gunner said.

I shook my head and went the opposite direction up the street from the square, around the church to an arched stone gate. A small cemetery was behind the church. A chest-high stone wall was built around it, and there was a metal gate that wasn't locked. Inside were maybe fifty headstones, some crumbled and eroded to the point where inscriptions were indecipherable.

"Can't even read these things," Gunner said.

Closer to the church were larger monuments, one with a

winged angel atop an obelisk. The docent said the captain had a position of honor here. Once we were in front of the larger gravestones, one with a ship's anchor stood out. The pea gravel crunched beneath our feet as we approached.

"What do you know," Jack said. "Antoine d'Aire." He paused. "I can't read the rest."

I knelt down. "It says 'Antoine d'Aire, died June 23, 1720. *Capitaine, Patriote, Corsaire.*'"

The inscription caused a flash of mental lightning in my head. Corsair?

Captain d'Aire had served the Spanish king, been captured by the British, and released after the Peace of Utrecht. How could he have been—

"You look like you saw a ghost, Reilly," Gunner said.

"What's up?" Jack said.

I licked my lips and hesitated, not really wanting to share the cavalcade of thoughts that the word had released in my mind to these jerks, but what choice did I have?

"It says he was a corsair, which is a French term for 'privateer' going back to the Middle Ages."

"So?" Gunner said.

"Corsairs were essentially pirates sanctioned by the Crown to capture opposing vessels. If captured themselves, they were treated as prisoners of war, not hung as pirates, since they were acting on orders of the king."

Gunner and Jack stared at me with blank expressions.

"Remember that the *Griffon* was on a special assignment from King Philip V? Obviously, Captain d'Aire was too. So how could he have been a French corsair? The Spanish would have never trusted a French corsair on a special assignment to collect treasure on their behalf."

A cool wind blew through the cemetery and caused a shiver to run through me.

"Maybe he was dubbed corsair when he returned to Brest with Spanish treasure," Jack said. "The old lady and the guide at the church said he was considered a French hero."

"Maybe," I said. "But corsairs were only allowed to keep a percentage of what they captured. The king collected the lion's share."

"Mercenaries. I love it," Gunner said.

"Maybe he gamed the system somehow," Jack said.

Another thought percolated in my head. It bubbled up and I couldn't hold back. "Or, after being imprisoned by the British and released, only to immediately be sent to Veracruz on King Philip's behalf, then getting dragged in with the Plate Fleet and stranded in the Americas for two years, maybe all that pushed him over the edge." I paused. "What if d'Aire sank the mystery frigate? His first mate was forced to sail aboard the other ship, so maybe they plotted it together—and if he shared the wealth with the French king, that would make him a corsair."

"The plot thickens," Jack said.

"So what did they do with the treasure?" Gunner said. "Or the crew from the other ship? Somebody would have ratted them out. Wouldn't there have been some other history on that?"

"Unless they killed them all," I said.

I winced as Gunner smiled. "I'm liking this French captain more every minute."

"Let's say this is all true," Jack said. "Why didn't they go back for the treasure from the other ship?"

The wind now howled through the cemetery, and dead leaves from trees outside the walls swirled through the air. "Let's head to the van," I said. "My blood is too thin for this weather."

We exited the cemetery and hurried toward the square. I could see our driver standing outside the van, having a smoke and watching us.

"This has been a good trip," Jack said. "Glad to have you

with us, Buck, but time to head home."

Like I had a choice? "What home are you referring to?"

"The one I rented for us back in Vero Beach. That's our base camp until we figure out the mystery frigate's location."

Gunner slapped his hand against my back. "Home sweet home, Reilly." His smile infuriated me. "If you're a good boy, maybe we can arrange a conjugal visit for you and red—"

"Gunner, stop. Please," Jack said. "Don't poke the bear."

I bit my tongue on my response and made a silent oath to myself. He could keep poking until I turned and bit his head off. Asshole.

16

BACK ON THE GULFSTREAM, WE WERE QUICKLY AIRBORNE, and the same flight attendant had showered and put on fresh clothing. Must have napped too, as she was now bright-eyed and had already laid out another buffet and poured champagne. I stared into the black oblivion through the window as the winter winds rocked us. Pin lights of France disappeared below as we set out over the Atlantic.

I'd been so physically close to Giselle but unable to even call to say hello. I hoped she was still well, as the damn pandemic had coursed through Europe in a second wave.

There had been moments on this trip—in the Maritime Museum in Brest, at the small museum in Saint-Renan, in the cemetery—where I'd been so consumed with the mystery of the *Griffon*, I'd forgotten about Jack and Gunner's presence. Even if only for a minute, the fact that I'd been so enthralled by the hunt now sickened me. Was it the smell of gold or the thrill of discovery?

Hopefully it was the latter, especially because there was little chance of my ever seeing a dime of the treasure, and I didn't want their blood money anyway. The good news was I'd bought time by successfully whetting their greed with theories steeped in conjecture and wishful thinking. Limited facts supported fragile hypotheses, but from what I'd learned, seen with my own eyes, and deduced by reading between the lines, they felt like logical assessments, albeit subject to further confirmation. Most importantly, they needed me—not only here but also for this to go further, which meant I had leverage, for the moment.

That thought pushed me forward in the plush leather chair and led me to interrupt Jack and Gunner's dreamy conversation about finding the mystery frigate in Bahamian waters.

"Here's the deal, guys. If you want my continued help, you need to release Ben, Scarlet, and Charlie by the time we get back to Florida."

Jack and Gunner's smiles turned serious.

Gunner leaned toward me. "Don't tell us what to do—"

Jack held his hand up. "We're not holding Scarlet and Charlie, we just have someone watching them."

"So tell your goon to leave and not go back." I paused. "Same for the people holding Ben. And I want my phone back so I can speak to them."

"No problem with your phone. You've earned that," Jack said. He reached into his pocket, pulled out my phone, and laid it on the table between us. His smile twisted into a rueful grin. "But you know I have all the copies of the old e-Antiquity research material, right? We've learned a lot on this trip. Your help isn't as necessary going forward."

Gunner's smile reappeared. "That means you're becoming expendable, sport."

I didn't flinch. "Let's say we're right and the mystery frigate sank or was scuttled in the Bahamas off Andros. We have a long way to go to narrow that down to any kind of search area. Do you really think you two can figure that out?"

Jack gave me one of his slick smiles. "I'll call our man in Florida and have him discontinue watching Scarlet's house." Now he leaned toward me. "But not Ben. Not until you figure this out, partner."

I bit my tongue. Scarlet and Charlie's safety was paramount. I took the phone off the table and clutched it tightly. I realized my palm was sweaty. "Call your guy in Florida now. Once I confirm they're safe, I'll continue on." I smiled. "Partner."

"Seemed to me you were eating it up back in France," Gunner said. "What happened, your conscience finally caught up with you?"

I felt my face flush. For lack of any response, I took a gulp of champagne.

Jack took out his phone, but rather than calling anybody, he sent a text. A few moments later, his phone pinged. He read the text, then held his phone up for me to read.

His message said: "Discontinue surveillance entirely." The response was: "Understood, leaving now."

"Happy?" Jack said.

"Overjoyed."

He put his phone away. "Being with you here reminded me of when were teenagers, Buck," he said. "Whether on the football field, at parties, chasing the girls, or just hanging out. Those were good times."

"Until they weren't," I said.

"Taking e-Antiquity public was where we screwed up. The demands of investors and Wall Street was too much—"

"For you," I said.

Jack paused. "That's what I'm saying. You were out doing what you did best, and I was stuck with bankers, investors, analysts giving us quarterly financial colonoscopies. Going to Harvard sent me on that path, but I hated it—and I hated myself when I was doing it."

"That makes two of us."

"You never would have achieved what you did without my sacrifice—no, I know you'll never see it that way—and yes, I flipped out, took the money, and ran, but I did five years of hard time."

"Am I supposed to feel sorry for you?"

Jack shook his head and took a slow sip of champagne. "No, but like I said … I was just thinking back to when it was you and me against the world in our teens. I miss those days."

"Spare me the mea culpa, Jack. Too much sewage through the pipe at this point. The Jack Dodson I went to high school with is dead and gone. He was replaced with a money-hungry, pathological liar." I glanced toward Gunner. "And your choice of friends and partners went down the shitter too."

Gunner laughed. "We're not so different, Reilly."

I felt my face twist into a knot of disbelief. "You're a cold-blooded killer."

"That's right, you don't have the balls for that. But you're a helluva strategist. You got results by greasing palms, lying, manipulating. Just as dirty."

"That's bullshit."

Gunner did something I didn't recall ever seeing him do before intentionally: he removed his blue-mirrored sunglasses.

"You may not want to believe what others think about you, Reilly, but don't delude yourself into thinking you didn't deserve your reputation or that everything that went bad was Jack's fault. Sure, he took the money and ran, but you took all your maps, letters, and files—which were worth a hell of a lot more in the long run." Gunner nodded toward Jack. "You're every bit as guilty, you just didn't get caught."

I fell back in my seat—then had a sudden urge to jump up, pace the aisle, or jump out of the damn plane.

They watched me squirm.

Yeah, you struck a nerve, asshole, congratulations. Feeling like a cornered dog, I changed course.

"So how's Heather, Jack?"

Jack sat back too but kept eye contact with me. "About time you know the truth about that. I told you Heather and I were friends back at Harvard, but we were actually lovers—"

"Which you rekindled while I was hunting for treasure—"

"She wasn't at Harvard for long—left after getting discovered by a modeling agency—but we were close." Jack paused. "Real close. Then she left, I got Laurie pregnant, got married, graduated, reconnected with you, and off we went with e-Antiquity."

"So what are you trying to say? You had dibs?"

"No, I'm just saying that when I introduced you to her, I was trying to save my marriage. After you made the discovery in Guatemala and e-Antiquity was on the cover of every newspaper in the world, Heather reached out to me. She'd already been the top supermodel in the world for years by then, and she wanted to see me." He paused. "We got together in New York, and man, oh, man, I wanted to drop everything and run off with her myself, but my children meant too much to me. So I introduced her to you."

My mouth hung open.

"Given her lifestyle and being world-renowned in her own right, playing second fiddle to you or being a stay-at-home mom wasn't in the cards," he said.

"So when the shit hit the fan ..."

"She split." Jack finished the sentence for me.

A warm flash hit me. "Not long after you did."

The flight attendant appeared from behind me. "Dinner is ready, gentlemen." She proceeded to remove the platter of vegetables, fruit, and crackers, refill our champagne glasses, and give each of us a bottle of water.

I stood, turned, and went to the aft head. I didn't have to go to the bathroom, but I needed a moment to calm my racing mind. I turned on the faucet and let cold water run through my hands, then splashed some on my face. It had never occurred to me that Jack and Heather had had a relationship back at Harvard. I knew he'd met her there, but that was it. The epiphany didn't make me feel better about them later running off together. It just reinforced that they'd both lied to me from the beginning.

My reflection in the mirror showed dark circles under my eyes, wild hair, and two days of growth on my beard. Here I was at thirty thousand feet over the Atlantic in a fifty-million-dollar private jet, and I couldn't be more miserable. It wasn't just the company that made me want to puke in the gold-plated toilet … it was the truth.

The truth about Jack and Heather, what Gunner had said about us being similar, was causing my lip to quiver in self-disgust. My island lifestyle, Key West, and Last Resort Charter and Salvage felt a long, long way away.

Right now, right here, I wasn't sure if I'd ever get back to Key West again.

SECTION 3

ON THE COAST
OF SOMEWHERE
HOT

17

I SLIPPED IN AND OUT OF SLEEP FOR THE BALANCE OF THE FLIGHT. We landed at Vero Beach Municipal Airport at 9:45 in the morning. I turned my phone on with the intent of calling Scarlet, then my brother. A few new emails came through—three of which were from Director Roth of the Maritime Museum in Brest. Curiosity got the better of me, and I clicked open the first one and read the message.

"Buck, again, it was an honor to meet you. I was able to expedite the delivery of Captain d'Aire's log from *Le Griffon* and have sent scans of the pages in multiple emails due to the size of the files. But to summarize, I did find details that may interest you based on what I gleaned from your discussion with your *colleagues.*

"Captain d'Aire noted when they departed from Havana that his first mate, Jean Bart, had been seconded from *Le Griffon* to help navigate a newly acquired Spanish frigate, *Señora Nuestra Elisabeth Farnese.*"

We'd already learned about the first mate from Scarlet's research, and I had the *Farnese*'s name from Ubilla's letter, but Scarlet hadn't shared the first mate's name. Had that been an intentional omission?

Roth's email continued. "Another passage I found a couple pages later was particularly interesting. It says, 'But revenge was ours due east of Andros, off the northern tip, where the water turned to indigo,' which is most intriguing. Why he says 'revenge' is unclear, but as we discussed, relations between France and Spain were very strained at that time, and Captain d'Aire was forced to sail to Veracruz immediately after being released by the British once the Peace of Utrecht was finalized. But what he did to take revenge is a mystery. The next couple emails contain scans of the remaining pages of the log in case there is any other information that may assist your search. Again, it was a pleasure. Please let me know how you fare."

Roth's email jumpstarted my mind and had me imagining the Bahamian waters, which were largely shallow and a study in shades of turquoise. Could "indigo" refer to the Tongue of the Ocean, a particularly deep swath on the east side of Andros separating it from New Providence? The west side of Andros would make more sense, as the Windward Passage was the sailing route the ships would normally have followed—unless they were dodging a storm and sailed east around Andros, but they'd have had to cross the shallow waters of the Bahama Bank to get there.

I felt the plane come to a stop at the fixed base operations center. I typed out a quick reply:

"Thank you, Director Roth, the pleasure was all mine. Interesting information about Jean Bart. Could you check your database to see if there is any more information about him? Did he die when the *Farnese* sank? Any record of him from before this fateful journey? Thank you again, and I will indeed keep you up to speed with the results of our search."

I then texted Scarlet to ask if her keeper was gone.

"What are you reading, Reilly?" Gunner said.

"I want to confirm Scarlet is safe and speak with my brother this morning."

"I can arrange that," Jack said.

Scarlet texted back that the man watching their house was gone, but she was still scared. I told her to leave and go somewhere safe.

We were swept up into a black Escalade, and from the back seat, I saw the Beast still tied down up the flight line. Ray must have been beside himself wondering why I'd fallen off the face of the earth with Gunner. Had he realized I was being taken against my will? Would he have done anything about it? That I couldn't be sure of. Ray was a worrier but not a man of action. He did okay on the fly when he was with me, but left to his own initiative, he'd go back to his house, play video games, and wait for me to call.

We drove a few miles and arrived at a seaside mansion that looked like a Tuscan villa. The tan stucco walls were adorned with terra-cotta shutters and half-round roof tiles that contrasted brilliantly against the azure Atlantic Ocean, with a white sand beach between them. A tall stucco wall that matched the color of the house enclosed the property, and the electric gate slid shut once we'd come to a stop inside.

"Home sweet home," Gunner said.

Once outside the vehicle, I stretched my arms and legs, still stiff from the trans-Atlantic flight. "How long have you had this beauty?" I said.

"It's just a rental," Jack said. "But we've had it for a couple months, and it's been our base of operation as we've prepared for the next phase of the expedition."

"Good. I want to get this over as fast as I can," I said.

"Couldn't agree more. Given what we learned in France, thanks to you, we're going right into the physical exploration phase." Jack glanced over his shoulder at me as we walked up the wide, white staircase the led to the entrance of the home, which had been constructed on an elevated platform to protect it from storm surges.

The door opened for us as we reached the top step, and I held my breath. Would Heather be here?

My heart raced as I entered the home.

"Welcome back," a muscular man of approximately fifty years old said. I based his age on the close-cropped gray hair and facial wrinkles, but the tattoos on his arms and athletic build made him seem younger.

"This is Randy Brown," Gunner said. "He's a former sea dog and RHIB captain that got me in and out of many a tough spot in the Middle East."

"Buck Reilly," I said. We shook hands, and I imagined him with black paint on his face as he drove a rigid-hulled inflatable boat at night to drop Gunner and other mercenaries off to do their business.

"He was also the man parked in front of Scarlet's house up until last night," Gunner said.

My eyes narrowed, but I let the moment pass. I read Randy as capable of anything but also a career soldier and a man accustomed to following orders. My hope was that he wouldn't have done anything he wasn't told to do.

Jack dropped his duffel bag, walked into the kitchen—which was equipped with top-quality appliances—opened the refrigerator, and pulled out a six-pack of Heineken.

"You already have a boat lined up?" I said.

Gunner slid open a large glass door and stepped out to the back deck, followed by Jack, Randy, and finally me. The noon sun was bright. The beach wasn't crowded, but there were a few small groups of people, several in bikinis, past the patio and large rectangular pool below us. We sat on stools that overlooked it all, and Jack handed out beers. I clenched my jaw at the thought of hanging out with them, as if we were all long-lost friends and partners.

"We have a hundred-foot ship, fully equipped with a lift, generator for compressed air, four state rooms, and a twenty-six-foot deployable dive boat," Jack said. "All we needed was you."

I glanced at Randy, who didn't smile, and realized he had to know they had my brother as leverage.

"You men have a good trip?" Randy said.

"Good enough," Gunner said.

I put the beer on the wood rail, unopened, and turned to Jack. "Can you get Ben on the line?" I said.

He popped the top off the green bottle and took a long pull. The bottle had already blossomed in sweat since we'd come out from the air-conditioned interior. He swiped his mouth off with the back of his hand. Once the beer was set on the railing, he peeled his long-sleeved shirt off, and his muscular, tattooed arms and chest bulged inside his black t-shirt. "I'm going to the head, but I'll make the call."

I watched him go as Randy and Gunner kept their eyes trained on me.

"You and Jack used to be partners, huh?" Randy said.

I turned to face the beach. Grabbed my beer, popped off the top, and guzzled it. "In another life," I said.

Fifteen minutes later, while Gunner and Randy relived stories of covert operations in the Persian Gulf, Jack stepped outside with his phone to his ear. "Okay, put him on," he said. "Here's Buck." He handed me the phone. I glanced at the screen. The number on the other end had a 703 area code—Virginia—and the elapsed time of the call showed 14:42.

"Buck, are you there?" Ben sounded tired.

"I'm here, Ben." I walked to the end of the porch, as far from the others as I could, and lowered my voice. "Are you okay? Have they hurt you at all?"

"I-I'm okay. They've kept me tied up in my bedroom."

"How many? Are these some of Gunner's former mercenaries?"

"There's three, and yeah, I think that's right. Mercenaries. Said they'd kill me if—Hey! Cut the shit—I didn't say anything." There was a muffled sound and what sounded like shouting in the background.

"Ben? Ben?"

"Okay, just one more minute," he said to someone there. "I'm back, Buck. How was your trip? Did you find what they wanted so they'll let me go?"

I watched Jack and Gunner as I balled my fist. "Yeah, I found some information. Making progress here, so you should be fine—"

"How much longer are they going to—okay! Let me say goodbye!"

More muffled sound over the phone. I wanted to leap off this balcony and run down the beach screaming for help, but that wouldn't solve anything—it'd probably just make things worse for Ben.

"Ben, you still there?"

Heavy breathing sounded from the receiver. "I've got to go, Buck. Please, hurry. Do whatever they want so I can get free. Please—"

Click.

18

GUNNER AGAIN COMMANDEERED MY PHONE when I went upstairs to the room they assigned to me to take a nap. An hour later, I walked out to the balcony that overlooked the main living area of the house and found it empty. There were two other bedrooms upstairs: one door was closed and the other ajar. Nobody was inside. Downstairs was another bedroom, and the door was cracked open. Based on the junk I saw inside, I assumed it was Gunner's. The kitchen, dining, and main living rooms were all empty.

I peered outside and saw Jack lounging by the pool, with Gunner and Randy seated under the umbrella at the table. If it was as simple as me escaping, I would have walked out the door, but they'd figure it out before I got far enough to make a difference. Tempted to call Special Agent Booth of the FBI, my occasional handler who sometimes sent me to take care of business outside his jurisdiction, I reluctantly decided I was too close to learning something of value about the *Griffon* and Captain d'Aire's relationship to the *Farnese*. At least Randy was here and no longer watching Scarlet and Charlie, and after speaking with Ben, I knew he was relatively safe. I would play along long enough to learn more—a dangerous game, all things considered.

Another glance outside found all three men in their same places, so I quickly searched the house. In Gunner's room, I found three large footlockers, all with padlocks, which, based on the weight, must have held an armory of weapons. Again, tempting, but my brother's end wouldn't justify my means. Upstairs, the closed bedroom door was locked, and the other held the meager possessions of a hired gun accustomed to a lifetime on the road: a Sig Sauer P226 9 mm automatic with a full clip, three different knives in scabbards, and a desert-tan camouflage duffel bag.

Jack's room was where the information would be, but the door was closed. If it was locked or had an alarm or a nest camera inside, my breaking in would immediately eliminate whatever goodwill I'd earned so far and put me under lock and key. There was no choice but to keep playing the game. That realization gave me an idea.

Time to go on the offensive.

On the kitchen counter was my cell phone, which I pocketed, and I grabbed another six-pack of Heineken from the refrigerator and slid open the back door and walked out to the porch and down the steps to the pool deck. Gunner stopped speaking mid-sentence when he spotted me, and Randy craned around to watch me approach.

"Anybody need a beer?" I said.

There were four empties on the table where Gunner sat, so I placed the six-pack there, took one for myself and one for Jack and walked over to where he was reclined in the sun at the foot of the pool. I handed him a cold beer, and he gave me a restrained smile.

"That nap must have done you well," he said.

"I feel a lot better." I sat in a teak chair next to him.

Jack pulled the sunglasses that had been atop his head down over his eyes and sat up. He was pretty ripped, and I wondered if he'd been using steroids. The tattoos, which I'd thought were only on his arms, also covered his back and much of his chest too.

"When did you start getting all of those?"

"In prison." He pointed to a dagger with blood dripping off

the tip of the blade that ran from his forearm down to his wrist. "This was the first one, from a gang I bought my way into in Attica. Kept me alive, but when I got out, I needed to camouflage it, so I got the whole sleeve done. I liked it so kept going."

I drank my beer. On the beach, people threw Frisbees, played bocce, boogie-boarded in the surf, and lay baking under the sun. Not a cloud was in sight, and the blue sky was brilliant and clear. For most, it would be a day of escape from the pandemic, relaxation, games, and sunburned skin, but for me, it was a game of survival.

"You hear anything from the director of the museum in Brest yet?" Jack asked.

"Nah, nothing." I took another sip of the beer. I wasn't going to share anything more with Jack that might make me even more expendable. I pulled my chair closer to him and leaned forward. "So what's the deal here?"

"What do you mean?"

"Our partnership. I seem to be the only one adding value—"

"Hold on now, Buck. Who do you think is financing this operation?" I bit my tongue to refrain from reminding him *his* money was partially *my* money. "Private jets, salvage ships, muscle—"

"Muscle, exactly. That's why I'm asking. Is everybody here an equal partner?" I nodded back over my shoulder to the pair of mercenaries.

An involuntary smile creased Jack's cheeks. Greed was something he could understand. It fueled him, drove him toward his version of success, which included manipulation, kidnapping, and any other means necessary to get what he wanted.

"Randy's not a partner, if that's what you're asking. But his expenses come off the top, along with all our other expenses, plus interest. This isn't a charity project."

I shrugged. That sounded more like the Jack I remembered.

Sure, he'd fund the project, but he would be first to cash out, with a hefty bonus and interest on top. "So that means we're fifty-fifty—"

Jack sat up and spun around to face me directly. "No, no, no, Buck. There are other partners involved. Your cut is twenty percent."

"What? Twenty percent?" I intentionally raised my voice a couple decibels. I glanced back over my shoulder. Gunner was laser-focused on our backs. He wasn't smiling. "That better not be the same cut as him." I waved my thumb back over my shoulder.

I heard the screech of Gunner's chair scrape against the stone patio.

"Don't make a scene," Jack whispered.

"Why should we share our expertise with a couple mercenaries?"

Gunner cast a long shadow over me as he stood close and blocked the sun.

"Because I'll do things you wouldn't dream of, Reilly," he said. "You don't think we'll have impediments? Other treasure hunters sniffing around? Not to mention the authorities. Without me, you'd give 90% away to Florida, Spain, and anyone else who files a claim." He leaned down closer to me. "That won't happen with me in charge of security and negotiations."

A tingle ran through my arms all the way down to my fingertips. When Gunner was angry, it was like having the biggest, meanest killer pitbull on the planet zeroed in on you.

"Without me, you won't have anything to negotiate for," I said. Then back to Jack. "You need to do better than twenty."

Jack gave me that slippery smile I'd seen him use ever since we were teenagers whenever he thought he had the upper hand. "Twenty percent plus Ben's life, Buck. I'd say that's priceless, wouldn't you?"

I sat back. "Actually, I've been thinking. Ben's hated me ever since our parents got killed. He dies, I get everything I was denied in their will."

Gunner's shadow bent down, and I could feel his hot breath on my neck. "If your brother dies, that means you failed, so you'll die too, asshole."

Jack shook his head. "All right, boys. Calm down, now." Then to me. "We have other silent partners too, Buck. People who provided information, funding, equipment, and can grease wheels at a high level if needed. And I've acquired an amazing salvage vessel for us. So twenty percent is it, which, if we find the queen's jewels and Gunner does his job right, could easily be worth fifty million dollars. Let's not be greedy, okay?"

An involuntary laugh sprang from my lips. "That's like the heroin dealer telling the meth dealer not to do drugs." I glanced back over my shoulder to look up Gunner's fat head still breathing down my neck. "Mind passing me one of those other beers before they get hot, Gunner?"

He stood up, pressed his shoulders back, and glanced at Jack. In Gunner's reflective glasses I saw Jack wave toward the table. A slow burn of a smile crossed Gunner's lips. "Sure, Reilly, I'll grab you a beer."

I watched as the hulk of a man stomped back toward the table where I'd left the six-pack. He ripped a bottle from the cardboard container, and as he approached me with it, I half expected him to try and crack me over the head with it. He extended his hand with the bottle clenched between his meaty fingers and stopped it an inch from my nose.

"Thanks." I took it casually from his hand, which trembled with rage. "So tell me about this salvage vessel. Did you buy it?"

Jack smiled. "No, leased it from a friend of yours. Found his name in my copy of your old files on the 1715 fleet."

I sat back in the teak chair, trying to remember who ... then it dawned on me. I'd paid a local treasure hunter for some information on the fleet based on findings they and others had made since the 1960s when Kip Wagner first set up shop here on the Treasure Coast, so named thanks to gold and silver coins that still washed up on the beach from time to time.

"Bill Black?"

"That's right. He was thrilled to hear from me and excited we were teamed back up and on the hunt."

Fucking Jack—using my name to trick my former friends and colleagues to share information and, in this case, lease us a ship.

There was a sudden vibration in my pocket, which alerted me to an incoming email. "Beer's going right through me," I said. "Be right back." On my way up the steps, I glanced back and saw Gunner and Jack engaged in a serious discussion. Gunner waved his hands with intense animation, and I smiled to myself.

Once inside, I checked my emails. As I'd hoped, there was a new one from Director Roth in Brest. With the door locked in the bathroom, I read the email: "As it turns out, Jean Bart was on *Le Griffon* when it returned to Brest. How, I'm not sure, but perhaps something to do with the revenge noted earlier. Since this was an anomaly to what the earlier passage in the log says, I researched further. In a court record from Jean Bart's trial, I found mention of his claim that he and d'Aire had conspired before departing Havana to sink the *Farnese* and did so in the Bahamas in deep water—too deep to salvage at the time with the storm bearing down on them, but they planned to return at a later date to recover the ship's treasures."

That was the end of the message. Hoping Director Roth would still be available, I responded: "Did they ever return to salvage the *Farnese*? And why did Jean Bart have a court record? Was it because he filed a claim?"

I paced the small bathroom for a few moments, hoping Roth would respond quickly, since it would be harder to disappear yet again once I returned to the pool deck.

The phone vibrated in my sweaty palm. Roth.

"They never got the chance to return. Apparently, Jean Bart confronted d'Aire as he was preparing to embark for the Bahamas without him. D'Aire claimed that Bart had become a loudmouthed drunk and didn't want him on the voyage, so his former first mate strangled d'Aire to death in the public square. Jean Bart was hung within a week for the murder of d'Aire, who had become a local hero for his success as a corsair and for being the only ship to return."

Wow.

Greed killed, even back in the 1700s.

The phone vibrated again. "Thank you for pressing this research, Buck. The details had never been researched adequately to connect d'Aire's murder with Jean Bart's involvement and their collusion to sink the *Farnese*. Frankly, Jean Bart's only standing in history was as a murderer, so these other facts now make sense. Please let me know if you learn anymore about the *Farnese* so we can complete the history."

Crap. Director Roth had been immensely helpful, but now armed with these new discoveries, the historian would be compelled to publish the details. That meant the secrets I'd pieced together, with his help, would be made public and complicate any efforts to recover the contents of the *Farnese*, whatever they might be. Jack had a salvage ship ready to go, and I had a pretty good idea of the approximate location, but best-case scenario, it could be weeks if not months of searching. And depending on the depth, we might require even more equipment. All without a salvage permit in Bahamian waters—and they took these matters very seriously. Getting caught would mean guaranteed jail time, or worse if Gunner and Randy started shooting at the authorities.

All while, my brother Ben was being held hostage.

Now what? I peeked outside the door. Nobody was there, so I dialed Scarlet's number.

"Buck! Are you still in France?"

"No, I'm hiding in a bathroom in Jack's rented Vero Beach mansion trying to figure out what to do. I refused to help any more unless they pulled their watchman. Are you and Charlie okay? Did Gunner hurt you?"

"No and no, just threats, which got worse when I demanded to go home after finding enough to get you going—sorry I didn't have the chance to warn you."

I felt sweat bloom in my armpits. "Can you leave ASAP while I have them distracted?"

"Did you figure out the second ship?"

I couldn't help but smile. "You omitted details, didn't you? Yes, I found the second ship. It's the one noted in Ubilla's letter to his wife. It's called the *Farnese*. The letter said he instructed them to sail an easterly course toward the Bahamas. D'Aire attacked and sunk it as they fled the storm." I recalled Jack and Gunner's goofy smiles back in the church in Saint-Renan. Could they know about Ubilla's letter?

"I remember it," she said. "What about his first mate? The one they forced onto the *Farnese*?"

"They were in on it together. His name was Jean Bart. Find anything you can on him. They sank the *Farnese* in the Bahamas, apparently off Andros, but there must be more information that d'Aire squirreled away. I met his last remaining relative, a feisty old woman in the town of Saint-Renan—"

"That's where d'Aire was from!" Scarlet said. She'd left that fact out of her summary too. The realization sent a warm glow through my bloodstream. Like me, Scarlet had been providing just enough information to seem helpful.

"And where he was murdered by his old friend Jean Bart for planning to salvage the *Farnese* without him."

"Some things never change." Scarlet laughed when she spoke, clearly feeling better about hearing from me and my progress. It suddenly felt like old times. I caught my smile in the mirror.

"Charlie and I are all packed up and about to leave," she said. All mirth had left her voice.

"Good. I'll play along to help Ben."

"You're hooked now, aren't you." It wasn't a question.

My lack of response was answer enough. She knew me too well.

"What about Ben?" she said. "What will happen to him?"

I stared at my reflection in the mirror. "I'll protect him. Go—get a burner phone and text me when you're safe. Don't tell me where you are, and remove the chip so it can't be traced. Jack is very resourceful." An idea turned my scowl to a smile in the mirror. "Sign your texts Bill Black."

"The treasure hunter from Sebastian Inlet?"

"That's right. Jack rented a ship from him. Now go, Scarlet. Please."

She hesitated. "I'm scared, Buck."

"You'll be okay."

"Not for me. For you."

Gunner had said I was expendable, but they'd be Laurel and Hardy out on the water, with no ideas to go on, fancy salvage ship or not. "I'll be fine. Check in a few days from now when you're good and safe."

Her deep exhale caused static on the phone. "Be smart, Buck." She paused. "We can't lose you."

Her words caused a glow in my heart. It was the first time I'd sensed any affection from her since she ditched me at the airport on St. Thomas, just before I met Giselle … but that was another story.

"Scarlet, I have one last question for you. I'll understand if you had to, but did you tell Jack about Ubilla's letter?"

"No. Why would I have done that?" Her voice had an edge to it now.

"I just have a sense that they know about it, somehow. Jack has full copies of all our former research material, but I kept that letter separate. He should have never seen it."

"Well, he didn't get it from me."

"It wasn't an accusation. I'm just trying to stay a step ahead of them, and for some reason, it feels like they're a step ahead of me."

We said our goodbyes, and I hit the end button before I said anything more foolish, like the emotion that had caused me to momentarily forget the situation I was in—I stared in the mirror—and the situation that Ben was in, thanks to me.

19

I NEEDED TO DISRUPT THE COURSE OF ACTION Jack
and Gunner had planned, even though I wasn't entirely sure
what that was yet. A few ideas came to mind, all but one of which
were logical follow-ups to the agitation I'd begun to stir out by the
pool.

Time to stir some more.

As I trotted down the steps to the patio, I noted Gunner's cold
stare, along with Randy's deadpan gaze. I was pretty sure
Mercenary #2 would do as ordered, but Gunner was hotheaded,
to say the least, so I had to walk a tight wire to keep him off-
balance without sending him into a complete rage. Yet.

Jack looked up from his phone. "No more beer?"

I sat back down next to him. "I don't recall Bill Black having
a 100-foot ship?"

"He brokered it to us—a 110-foot custom-built salvage vessel
in pristine condition, fully loaded with everything we need."

That would be sufficient for an operation in the Bahamas.
He'd said earlier it had four staterooms and a dive boat too.

"What about field gear?"

Jack's smile grew wider. "Multiple magnetometers—fixed and
portable, compressed air onboard for nitrox, side-scan sonar, and
two dive scooters. Everything we'll need to find the mystery
frigate and her missing treasure."

"Everything except her location," I said.

Jack's smile faded. "That's why we have you, the most expensive piece of equipment of all."

I did my best to fake a smile. "That's right." I paused. "So what else did you say to Bill Black? Treasure hunters are universally curious. When he sold me that information years ago, he was plenty cagey. Asked to be included if we ever mounted a search here."

Jack studied my face. I was certain he was trying to assess if I was working an angle to double-cross him. I was, but not how he'd expect me to.

"I told him we had some information we wanted to hunt down and it might be in deeper water—"

"Which definitely would have ignited his imagination. All the 1715 wrecks have been discovered in shallow water so far, and the missing ships are still a mystery after decades, hell, centuries of searching."

Jack grimaced. "The missing queen's jewels are the biggest mystery of all."

"Exactly. And if he provided us with the search vessel we'll use to find it, he'll be looking for more than a commission on that."

"We don't need any more crew," Jack said.

"I agree, and we don't want his network to get a sense of what we know. Otherwise, it'll be a free-for-all." I hesitated. I wanted to plant a seed of doubt in Jack's head without putting Bill in danger. "What if they have a tracking device onboard?"

Gunner stepped up behind me. "I've swept it for devices," he said.

"That won't work if it's a live transmitting device," I said. "It would only activate when the GPS is on, which may not happen until we're under way."

"Gunner will scour the ship once we get under way, and we won't take a straight course," Jack said. "But that's a fair concern. Any suggestions?"

I nodded my head. "Yeah. Let me call Bill and see what he says—"

"Not happening, Reilly," Gunner said.

"Relax, Gunner. You can sit right next to me when I call him. We don't need any surprises, and you guys have Indiana Jonesed your way right into enemy—or at least competitive—territory. Better to see if he has an agenda or if he's been telling people about our effort before we get rolling." I looked back to Jack. "When are we weighing anchor?"

"Tomorrow. You get anything else from Roth yet?"

It was my turn to smile. I'd already deleted our conversation but saved the scans Director Roth had sent me. "As a matter of fact, I have."

"What did he say?" Gunner said.

"He didn't say anything, but he sent me scans of the *Griffon's* complete logbook."

"Let's see them?" Gunner stepped toward me.

"They're in Old French and handwritten. You speak French, Gunner?" It was a rhetorical question.

"No. Do you, Jack?" Gunner said.

"No, but maybe Scarlet does."

"Leave Scarlet out of this. French was always my territory anyway," I said.

"As you proved with the French First Lady," Gunner said. "So what's it say?"

A wind blew a dried palm frond across the pool deck. It made a clawing sound as it passed, like an alligator rushing toward us.

"I assume you have a computer here. Let's look at it on a bigger screen than my phone."

Jack jumped up. "Let's do it."

"But first, I'll call Bill Black and see what he says."

Jack rolled his eyes. "Fine. Give Buck his phone back."

I pulled it out of my pocket. "I found it on the kitchen counter. How do you think I knew Director Roth wrote me?"

Jack's eyes revealed nothing, but his mouth tightened in a thin smile. "Good point." For some reason, it felt like he was testing me.

Under Jack's and Gunner's watchful gazes, I scrolled through my contacts and found Bill, opened his file, and touched his cell number. Bill had been a devoted treasure hunter for several years on the Treasure Coast and had a wealth of information on the 1715 fleet. We hadn't paid much for what he gave us, which was a comprehensive history on what was known about each ship, captain, and crew; a summary of findings to date; GPS locations; and some previously assembled archival information. It would have been a good primer for us if we'd ever pursued the missing ships from the fleet, but e-Antiquity's bankruptcy had intervened.

After a few rings, the familiar voice came on the line. "This is Bill Black."

"Hey, Bill. It's Buck Reilly."

"Long time no talk to, amigo," he said. "Was happy to get the call from your partner. About time you try and do something with that information I sold you years ago."

"Yeah, well, it's been a complicated number of years."

"Tell me about it," he said. "I've got three grandchildren now."

We caught up on a personal level—Gunner waved his hand in a circle, impatient with my small talk. He had no clue on how to maintain relationships with potential information sources in this business. With him, it was wham, bam, thank you ma'am, no foreplay and no cuddling after.

"So," Bill said. "Dodson mentioned that you had some fresh leads on one of the missing ships but that it was in deeper water? Hence the need for the larger salvage ship."

"Yeah, thanks for your help with that. Jack was always the front-office guy. He doesn't have any field experience. To your earlier point, we're just sniffing around on material you sold us previously."

"Uh-huh."

Treasure hunters never believe each other. It's always exaggeration of what you found or playing down what you know. But given our past relationship and the fact that we must have paid a ton to use his friend's ship, I was emboldened. "Anything new of value been discovered since we last spoke?"

"We've found a number of things, but still no definitive location for the *Capitana* or the mother lode." He paused. "I'm assuming that's what you're after, isn't it, *King* Buck?"

"Too soon to say. We plan to search some deeper waters that haven't been studied before—or at least that haven't borne any fruit—more in a process of elimination than anything else."

"Uh-huh. I offered Dodson my assistance, but he blew me off," Bill said. "You know I'd like to be a part of whatever you have going on."

"Yeah, we have a crew—none of 'em know the coastal waters like you, so good chance I'll call you back." Gunner rolled his eyes. "So tell me about this salvage ship. Is it any good? Jack wouldn't know if he was renting a catamaran or an aircraft carrier," I said.

Jack gave me the finger but smiled.

"It's a beautiful ship. Been sitting around a while—you could probably buy it for a half-million dollars, which is cheap, given its size and condition."

"You know the old saying about leasing things that float."

Bill laughed at that. "Truer words were never spoken. Guy who owns it is a friend, but the operating costs versus the revenue generation have been out of whack, so you guys are actually helping him out."

"Okay, cool. I just wanted to check in and get your thoughts," I said.

"Seriously, Buck, you know I've spent decades on these waters, so please don't hesitate to call if you need help."

We said our goodbyes, and I clicked *End*.

"Didn't sound like anything to be concerned with," Jack said. "Thanks for the vote of confidence, Buck."

"Just playing the game, Jack. Yeah, that felt fine to me. I would have loved to ask if he'd ever heard of a thirteenth ship, but no sense in starting rumors." My earlier concern of Director Roth going public with our new findings and revelation about Jean Bart had me bite my lip. Roth wouldn't do that without writing and researching a detailed summary worthy of being published. At least, so I hoped. If that was the case, I had a couple weeks.

As if reading my mind, Jack waved me toward the house. "Let's go take a look at that logbook on my computer," he said.

We all marched up the steps. I'd debated internally whether or not to tell him I had the log, but knew neither he or Gunner spoke French, and I needed to buy time for Scarlet to disappear and for flushing out Jack's plans, as well as make them feel I was committed to our partnership, so I felt it was a safe approach. And bottom line, even though I'd been sucked in by the hunt while in France, the safety of Scarlet, Charlie, and Ben was more important than finding the *Farnese*. Besides, going to jail in the Bahamas wasn't high on my bucket list, having already done so in a number of other places.

I hadn't seen the full logbook yet, only the couple pages Scarlet had left us copies of and transcribed. From what I'd seen, the faded, flamboyant cursive the captain had used to record their voyage was nearly illegible anyway, so with any luck, I could bullshit my way through whatever we pulled up on Jack's screen.

But we'd find out soon enough.

20

I HATED TO DO IT, BUT I FORWARDED THE SAVED SCANS of the logbook to Jack, who opened the PDF on his laptop, which was connected to a 32-inch computer monitor. The image that flashed onto the screen was both blurry and faint, but the handwriting became more legible when Jack adjusted the contrast.

"What's it say?" Gunner said.

I shook my head. "Let's scroll through it first and see how many pages there are."

Jack clicked the arrow button through twenty-seven pages. "Not much for a few years at sea," he said.

"Go back to the beginning," I said.

Once there, I noticed right away that the page was dated July 24, 1715 and noted that their location was Havana. "It's short because Roth only sent us the pages from when they departed Cuba."

"Why'd he do that?" Gunner said.

"Probably to save us time. No need to read a couple years' worth of sailing notes," I said. "But it would have been worth knowing if he expressed any dissension with the Spanish leading up to their departure from Cuba."

"The second through fourth pages are the same ones Scarlet left for us in Brest," I said. "They note General Ubilla's purchase of the first additional frigate days before departure—"

"What was the name of that frigate?" Jack said.

I pointed to the screen. "*Santa Rita y Animas,* which was one of the eleven ships that sunk days later in the storm. D'Aire goes on to talk about the provisioning of the *Griffon* and notes that part of the cargo they picked up from the governor of Veracruz for the king had been loaded onto yet another frigate, but he doesn't mention its name."

"And there's no mention in any of this about that other frigate's name?" Jack said.

A sense of déjà vu hit me from when we were at the church in Saint-Renan. Did Jack and Gunner know more than they were letting on? I weighed my options in a split second as Jack's gaze remained fixed on me. He knew, I could tell.

"Not here, but I think I know the answer."

"Really?" he said. "Do tell." His singsong voice contained an edge of sarcasm.

"I know you have copies of all the research materials we had at e-Antiquity—"

"Of the originals you stole before the Feds showed up and shut us down, that's right," he said.

He always liked to remind me that I was guilty too. "Let's spare ourselves the rehash, Jack. One thing that wasn't amongst the sheaf of records in my safe was a letter I had at home."

They waited for me to continue. The high road felt like my only option.

"It was a letter from General Ubilla to his wife dated the day they departed Havana. It mentioned he'd acquired yet another frigate, the thirteenth ship, and it was called *Señora Nuestra Elisabeth Farnese.*" I paused and checked from eye to eye. "I believe the missing frigate, the one that d'Aire's first mate was forced to sail aboard and that they may have conspired to sink together, was the *Farnese.*"

Jack sat back, placed his hands together, and held them up to his lips as if he was praying. "And you're just sharing this with us now, Buck?"

"Well, I wasn't sure—"

"Bullshit. You've known all along."

Now Gunner was smiling. Not the expression I expected.

Jack leaned forward and started pressing keys on his computer. A list of files popped onto the screen. He ran the cursor down faster than I could read the file names and then clicked one. Another PDF appeared overtop of the *Griffon*'s log that Director Roth had sent. When I saw what this new file was, my eyes involuntarily bugged wide and my mouth dropped open.

It was a copy of Ubilla's letter.

"We've been waiting for you to come clean, Buck," Jack said. "We knew all along Ubilla instructed the two frigates to sail an easterly course toward the Bahamas."

That explained the giddy smiles when we learned that the name of d'Aire's company included Andros. I felt a frog in my throat as I wondered what else of mine they might have and how they had gotten it. At the moment, it didn't matter, but it was a serious concern. More imminent, however, was how to play the immediate situation. Jack leaned forward.

"My question for you now, *partner*, is aside from what you kept referring to as the 'mystery frigate,' what else have you been holding out on us?"

I stood up and walked to the refrigerator. There were two six-packs of Heineken left. I removed one, grabbed the bottle opened from the counter, opened four bottles, and handed them out. The men accepted the bottles without thanking me and continued to watch my every move until I sat back down in front of the computer. I'd done it to buy time and deflate the tension from the room as I weighed whether or not to share the additional detail Director Roth had provided. I made my decision.

"Let's not forget that I was brought here against my will and that you do have my brother hostage. That's not exactly what I call a partnership." I glanced from Jack's face to Gunner's. "But based on everything we've learned, I now believe we've got a shot at finding the *Farnese*, so I'm all in. Hopefully we'll learn some additional details in the *Griffon*'s log."

"You were just worried the name of the ship would be mentioned here," Gunner said. "Bet you figured you'd better come clean now."

"The name of the ship doesn't matter," Jack said. "Honesty does."

"Honor amongst thieves?" I said.

"That's right," Jack said.

"How about kidnappers? Why don't you let Ben go if you really want us to be partners and totally on board with each other?"

Jack took a long pull from his beer and then closed out the file containing Ubilla's letter. "Because this proves we can't trust you."

Gunner laughed, and Randy kept a poker face. That dude creeped me out.

"Nice try, Reilly," Gunner said. "Your brother isn't going anywhere. And if we learn you're holding out on us again? Brother Ben will start to have appendages removed. One by one."

"You're a sick bastard, Gunner."

"Don't you forget it."

"I'm not holding out on you, Gunner. And you wouldn't even know if I was."

His smile faded. "True enough, jerk-off. That's why your brother isn't going anywhere."

"How did you get that letter, Jack?" This was one piece of the puzzle I couldn't fit, no matter how I turned it around. "It was never with the rest of my files at work."

"We all have our secrets, Buck."

21

"IT'LL TAKE ME SOME TIME TO TRANSCRIBE THE LOG from French to English," I said.

"Why can't you just read it aloud and transcribe as you go?" Gunner said.

"I'll try, but this is French from three hundred years ago. It's not exactly conversational." I turned to Jack. "Is your computer connected to a printer?"

Jack opened the cabinet below the computer, which contained a printer.

"Great. Print a copy, and I'll sit right here and try to convert it to English."

Within a few minutes, Jack had handed me a stack of paper. As I hoped, the printed version was faint. I would have preferred to read it by myself first, but the revelation that they'd known about the *Farnese* all along put me on the spot. I had to show some good faith, even if I intended to pull the rug out from under them as soon as possible.

I started reading from the beginning, and I hadn't been exaggerating—much—when I said the language was different back then, but fortunately, the author's writing was crisp. "One of the first notes states they left ahead of the fleet—maybe a full day or half day sooner. I'm not sure."

"Is that relevant?" Jack said.

"Ubilla instructed them to take the fastest route because the king was impatient, but he didn't say why," I said.

"Maybe he wanted the treasure for his wife—the queen's dowry," Jack said.

"That's likely the case," I said.

As I read on, I realized that d'Aire was cautious in his words. Maybe he was worried about the log passages being used against him—he would have had no way to know the other ships would be sunk in the storm—so up until now, he'd refrained from any editorial or personal comments. I explained to the others that as with most ship's logs, this one primarily described weather, seas, and issues with the boat or crew. Given the lack of trust between us, they stared at me as if they weren't sure I was telling the truth.

"One of our other partners speaks French too, Buck. So just remember, whatever you tell us will get double-checked," Jack said.

What I had said so far was true. "Always better to have two sets of eyes on an ancient translation," I said.

I scanned slowly ahead through each page looking for names or words that would make a difference. It didn't take long. "This passage here—" I pointed to the page, "states that the seas and winds came up fast and a major storm approached from the northeast. That's interesting, because I would have assumed the storm came from the southeast."

"Why does it matter?" Gunner said.

"Maybe their earlier departure helped them to avoid the storm, since the treasure fleet was driven to the west and into the shallow reefs of Florida," I said.

"Timing is everything," Gunner said.

I paged forward.

"Here, the log reads, '*un ouragan a failli coulé le navire*,' which translates roughly to 'a hurricane nearly sank the ship'"—I ran my finger under the writing—"'*mais l'île d'Andros nous a protégés*'— which means the island of Andros protected them."

"That's the first mention of Andros?" Jack leaned over the

table to look at where my finger was. "Any mention of the *Farnese*?"

"Not yet."

"The guy named his company Andros," Gunner said. "We know it's there. Let's leave tomorrow and start diving."

I turned my attention to Gunner. "Have you ever spent any time in the Bahamas, Gunner? Aside from when you followed me in that private jet years ago when we were searching for the missing sailboat."

"Why would I spend time there, Reilly? I make my money in the heat of battle, not on swanky beaches."

I smiled. "Well, just so you understand, Andros is the largest of the seven hundred Bahamian islands. In fact, it's over one hundred miles long, and all of the other islands could fit inside it with room to spare, so even if we're right and the *Farnese* sunk off the coast of Andros, it's still like finding a specific grain of sand on one of those swanky beaches you referred to."

The vocabulary of the next several paragraphs was lost on me, but I did see words that noted damage and repair, which I mentioned to the others. No surprise the *Griffon* was damaged from the storm, but was the *Farnese* mortally wounded by the storm, or was it piracy? Roth mentioned revenge—I continued on.

"Looks like they anchored up close to the island to work on the ships—here! It mentions the *Farnese* for the first time. Something about the Spanish captain taking provisions from the *Griffon*—provisions—no, *la grand-voile* means the sail—the Spanish captain wanted to take the mainsail from the *Griffon*."

"That would have left d'Aire stranded," Jack said.

"He then references his friend, the navigator—Jean Bart— who was on the *Farnese*." I pointed to the name. What choice did I have? Gunner, Jack, and Randy were all craned over the table, watching every word. Jean Bart was obviously a name.

"What about him?" Gunner said.

I scanned further, trying to read between the lines of what d'Aire was saying. "He basically says they came up with a strategy to save the ship—meaning the *Griffon*."

"Now we're talking," Gunner said.

"But then he just talks about the weather, the winds, the seas being turbid from the storm."

"That's it?"

"They weren't stupid. The ship's log could implicate them in piracy if they got too descriptive." I paused while I read further—what I saw made my breath catch. It was very specific, more specific than I wanted to share with these cutthroats here and now. "D'Aire writes that Jean Bart resituated—no, relocated—the *Farnese* to the '*nord-est*' point of the island and got revenge where the water turned to indigo."

It actually said "the islands to northeast of Andros" as the specific location. I omitted the mention of "islands."

"Revenge?" Gunner said. "I like the sound of that. What's *nord-est* mean?"

Jack scrutinized my face.

"Means northeast. But also important—he said Jean Bart moved the ship, not the Spanish captain. So maybe d'Aire and Jean Bart took control and got revenge by sinking it where the water turned to indigo on the northeastern side of Andros," I said.

Jack had pulled up a Google Earth map of Andros and zoomed in. "That would make sense, because the northwestern side looks like at least fifty miles to deep water. They wouldn't even be able to see land from there."

I pointed to his screen. "On the east side, there is what's called the Tongue of the Ocean, or TOTO, and it's some of the deepest water in the West Indies," I said.

Jack zoomed in closer. "There's a little town on the northeast point called Nicholls Town, and it's not far from shore to the deeper water."

I saw smaller uninhabited islands approximately ten miles directly north of Andros. I would have loved to zoom Jack's cursor in there but wasn't going to draw attention to the location. Instead, I said, "Scroll around along the edge of the purple water and up."

Jack did as I asked. "Pretty narrow area of shallow water between Andros and TOTO," he said.

As he zoomed in and out, I caught the names of those small islands. Long Cay was tiny, and the Joulter Cays were north of them. Jack was searching to the northeast of Andros, but d'Aire's reference was that the *Farnese* had been to the northeast of these islands. To a non–French speaker, the subtle difference would be undetectable. I clenched my teeth to stifle a smile. Based on the satellite image, there appeared to be twice the amount of shoal in that area before it dropped off into TOTO, as opposed to the area due east of Andros.

"That narrows the search area, but if it washed into the deeper water, it could be unrecoverable."

Gunner pounded his palm on the table. "Nothing's unrecoverable."

"You have a submarine you haven't told me about?"

"If it means finding the queen's jewels, we'll get one," he said.

The strip of shallow water that separated Andros from TOTO was narrow, maybe a mile or two, and once there, it dropped steeply to over six thousand feet in the north end of the Tongue. The southern portion of the trench was hardly accessible from the Atlantic, so if the *Griffon* and *Farnese* had sailed into it from the south, it was a miracle they made it through. Since hurricanes swirl in a counterclockwise direction, the storm would have caused a surge of deeper water to wash over the Bahama Bank, thus making their passage possible—or possibly even forcing them in that direction. Captain d'Aire and Jean Bart certainly deserved their heroes' welcome back in France if they had navigated the frigates into the Tongue from the south during a hurricane.

We didn't scrutinize the rest of the log, as it was mostly logistical notes on the return trip to Brest. Jack and Gunner were smirking at each other again. The tight area between the northern tongue and the Andros landmass significantly reduced the search area, which now made my assistance even less important. If the *Farnese* hadn't sunk into the depths of the Tongue, it might be sitting there waiting to be plucked. The stained glass window from Notre Dame de Liesse in Saint-Renan had portrayed the mast of the *Farnese* piercing the blue water, which, if Jack and Gunner took all this as gospel, meant that even my redacted translation of the *Griffon*'s log may have been sufficient to sign Ben's death warrant and mine.

Way to go, Buck.

"Now we know where to go, partners," I said.

Their smiles and high-fiving me meant that they hadn't come to that conclusion, at least not yet.

22

NARROWING DOWN THE LOCATION OF THE WRECK led to numerous rum shots and proclamations of impending success. I continued to sense unspoken signals between Jack and Gunner that led to a subtle eyebrow pump from Gunner to Randy. I poured them more rum in response, intentionally hooted it up, slapped them on their backs, and repeatedly dumped my rum into a plant when they weren't watching.

By 10:00, the three of them were bleary-eyed and yawning. I played along and suggested we get a good night's sleep so we'd be clear-headed for the crossing to the Bahamas tomorrow. I did a quick check on my phone. "It's approximately two hundred miles from Vero Beach to the eastern side of Andros, which at 12 knots would take us over seventeen hours," I said.

"Gonna be a long day," Jack said. "But worth it. I'm hitting the sack."

We all followed along as if it was Jack's idea. Everything was happening fast now—too fast, and the undercurrent was unsettling.

Ever since I had noticed Jack and Gunner's silent body language back in France—highlighted by them telling me I was becoming unnecessary—I'd known I needed to make a move. Now that they'd caught me in the lie about the *Farnese*, and given all the goo-goo eyes between them, now was the time.

After two hours, I hadn't slept a wink. Different volumes of snoring could be heard from multiple locations in the house.

Around midnight, I crawled out of bed and slowly opened my door. I found Jack's door closed but Randy's open. He was sprawled facedown in his bed, fully clothed. I locked my bedroom door handle, pulled it shut, and slipped down the stairs toward what sounded like a lion roaring. Gunner's door was also open, but I didn't bother to peer inside.

I spotted their cell phones on the counter plugged in and charging. Inspiration struck, and I scooped them up. At the back of the house, I slid the glass door open—listened for a second to make sure an alarm hadn't sounded—and stepped outside.

Once at the bottom of the stairs, I pulled up the rideshare app on my phone, noted my location and destination. While it found me a driver, I stared at the dark windows of the house, terrified a light would come on. Nothing did, so I walked out to the pool and dropped the three phones into the deep end.

"Talk to you later, boys," I said.

I made my way along the path around the side of the house and, once to the road, walked two doors down to the house I'd noted as my pickup location.

A Toyota Camry came slowly up the street. I pointed to the driveway of the house where I stood, and the driver pulled in and rolled down his window. "Buck Reilly?"

I opened the back door, climbed inside, and closed the door as quietly as I could.

"Vero Beach Airport?"

"Private aviation terminal. Let's go."

There was little traffic at this hour, and I used the few minutes I had to create my flight plan and calculate the time and distance to my destination. Seven hundred nautical miles, which at 120 knots would take around six hours and be at the outside limit of the Beast's range. I called the FBO and thanked my stars the fixed base operations manager was available 24/7. I let them know of my impending arrival, and they confirmed that the Beast had been refueled and that I could access the flight deck through the FBO office, which was where I had the driver drop me.

Here I go again.

Another late-night flight, but this time I'd be flying into greater danger, not running from it. I reopened the flight plan I'd hastily established in the car. The route led me out over open ocean for much of the trip, which was risky in a nearly eighty-year-old airplane, but I had no choice. If I couldn't make it to Leesburg Executive Airport in Virginia before Jack and his goons woke up and broke into my room, they'd know I'd escaped and would assume I'd either gone home to Key West or flown to Virginia to try and rescue Ben.

Jack knew me well enough to realize the latter option was exactly what I'd do.

Once through the private terminal, I exited onto the flight line, where it took me a moment to adjust my eyes to the darkness punctuated by the blue runway lights. There were a few private jets at the end of the flight line—one of which was a G-IV. Upon closer inspection, it was the same one we'd flown to France and back in. I had a flashback to stabbing the tires of another G-IV several years ago when Gunner had followed me to Panama to find missing Atocha gold and the good friend of mine who'd been accused of stealing it. Since this was a rental jet, and I planned to be in and out of Virginia before they knew what hit them, I didn't bother.

The Beast was halfway down the line. She stood out like a classic car surrounded by contemporary mediocrity, at least in my eyes. I circled around the plane, removed the wheel chocks, checked the pitot tubes, lifted the elevator, and examined the engine cowlings for excessive oil leakage. Then, after climbing on top of the plane, I checked both fuel tanks. Each was filled to the top. Satisfied that all was as it should be, I popped the hatch, shimmied through the fuselage, and climbed into the left seat.

"Good to be back with you, girl. Been a long few days."

I slowly ran the yoke forward and aft, left and right, while also moving the rudders to the maximum swing in each direction. All the flight controls felt fine. With both the engine fuel cutoff valves turned on, the cross-feed valve that shared fuel between wing tanks turned off, and the port fuel tank selected, I pumped the throttles to prime the engines and hit the ignition switch on the starboard one first. The air-cooled nine-cylinder radial Pratt & Whitney Wasp engine roared to life. I repeated the process with the port engine to the same result.

"Thanks, baby."

The mixture control was set to automatic rich and both engines were idling at 550 RPM. There was no visible traffic, but I clicked the mic to check in with air traffic control, which here was handled by Miami Center.

"Vero Beach Traffic, Grumman Goose taking runway four, departure to the northeast," I said.

There was no response from any other traffic. With the RPM revved up to 900, I released the brake. The Beast jumped forward as if she sensed the urgency of our mission. Once at the head of the runway, I was given the go-ahead from ATC and added more power. At 35 knots, the tail wheel lifted off the ground and we leaned into the tarmac until we hit 65 knots, and I gently pulled back on the controls. After several seconds we achieved a positive rate of climb, and I retracted the wheels. A glance at my ancient Rolex Submariner showed 12:55. I smiled at the thought of the fearsome threesome drooling on their pillows, oblivious to my departure.

The estimated flight time was six hours, which would put me there at 7:00 a.m. and would provide no margin for error before Jack and Jerk awoke in their rented mansion. Fortunately, Leesburg Executive Airport had car rentals on-site. I reserved one on my phone so as to not waste any time when I landed.

A deep breath prepared me for a long night. The stress of my brother's life on the line had my senses discombobulated, but I planned to catnap during the flight. Once at 5,500 feet, my optimal cruising altitude for fuel efficiency, I adjusted the manifold pressure and power until we were at 1,900 RPM. The flight plan was to stay off shore in order to avoid federal airspace, so I wouldn't need to vector until I reached Norfolk. It was only 40 degrees Fahrenheit in Virginia, which meant it would be a chilly flight as we proceeded north, but the Goose had a deicing system and a heater that would prevent me from freezing. Now cruising at speed, I'd run out of activities to keep my mind off the confrontation I was headed for. Above the gyropilot panel was a T-handle control for the automatic pilot, which I pulled to activate.

I leaned back and began to imagine our parents' farm in Middleburg, Virginia. It had been Ben's now for several years, but I still couldn't quite think of our childhood home as my brother's property.

"Focus, Buck. Think of the layout of the property and how you can surprise the captors holding Ben."

Non-pilots might think of me as crazy for talking to myself out loud, but in my headset, it sounded like someone else, and it was one way to stay awake while flying alone. Before long, though, my eyes flickered, then shut, and I drifted into a deep sleep.

I was thrust immediately into a series of dreams—I tried to run toward a door—the front door at my parent's farm—but my feet were stuck as if in quicksand. Armed sentries approached me from shadows at both ends of the covered porch, and I heard the vicious growl of a dog that was closing in on my flank. I struggled to get free—my shoes came off and I could suddenly run forward.

"Bbbeeennn!" I fought to scream my brother's name, but the words would not come out—the growling dog was gaining on me!

Dark silhouettes closed in on me—I thrashed—flailing my

arms but unable to even form a fist. I'm … so … in … capable!

The growl filled my head—my eyes popped open—an orange corona of daylight had ignited on the horizon!

"Grumman! This is Giant Killer. Respond immediately!"

Shit! I'd flown into restricted naval airspace.

"Giant Killer, Grumman Goose."

"Vector to a heading of 270 degrees now! You're in Norfolk's Oceana traffic and are ten seconds from getting shot down!"

"Roger!"

I kicked down on the port pedal and added left aileron, and the Beast carved a turn west to fly south of Richmond before vectoring north toward Leesburg. Damn—I'd planned to take a nap but had slept like a baby for nearly four hours!

"Way to go, dumbass!" What a moron. I should have set an alarm. With a quick assessment of the indicators on the instrument panel, I flipped on the heat—as it had turned cold inside the Beast—rubbed my face vigorously, and sat forward.

I could see my pulse throbbing on my radial artery, which took a good fifteen minutes to settle down. With my breathing returned to a rate that wouldn't have me hyperventilate, I concentrated on the balance of the flight. My stomach growled, my mouth was dry as dirt, and I had to pee like a racehorse. I had no food or water but did have a jug to handle the latter issue.

Dawn's glow had grown in brilliance, but sunrise wasn't due for another hour, just in time for me to land at Leesburg. For the remainder of the flight, I focused on remembering details of my parent's farm. Ben had installed a gate and cameras, which meant I'd have to hike-in for four-tenths of a mile through the woods adjacent to the driveway. I didn't own a gun, but wished I had one right now.

How many captors were guarding Ben?

He said they were keeping him locked in his bedroom.

What if they'd already killed him?

That thought had me clench my teeth and add thrust to the engines. Ben and I were far from close, especially since our parents had been killed, the chasm exacerbated by Interpol and the FBI naming me as a suspect in their deaths—a theory that held no water since I was given nothing in their wills, but none of us knew that until well after the fact.

Ben would never expect me to come help him. Our relationship was distant at best, but biological or not, he was my brother and the only family I had left. And dammit, I'd risk my life to save his any time.

With one final vector, Leesburg Executive Airport was visible in the gray countryside ahead. I cracked my knuckles.

"I'll be there soon, brother."

23

ONCE ON THE GROUND IN LEESBURG and finished with the post-flight procedures, I tied the Beast down and ran empty-handed for the FBO office. A man in his thirties with a clipboard and down jacket and what looked like a student pilot—she couldn't be more than sixteen, with braces and ponytails—walked around a Cessna 172, preparing for a lesson. It hit me that I'd taken my flying classes here at Leesburg Executive Airport a lifetime ago. I glanced back at the student.

"Don't wind up like me," I said under my breath.

Inside the office, there was an envelope on the counter with my name on it and a Cadillac key inside. I'd requested an SUV, but not something fancy. I found the black Escalade parked out front, its clean skin reflecting the orange dawn glow from the east. I hopped in, fired it up, and wasted no time heading down Route 15 south toward Middleburg. The dashboard clock read 7:05. Brown leaves wafted over the two-lane road as I sped through what was once the rural countryside but now contained newer country club–styled communities that had spawned mansions along curated fields. Golf courses had spread like rashes, which brought city folk out to the country, along with traffic, turn lanes, and realtors anxious to convert cornfields to commission crops. Gone were the horse and agricultural farms, replaced by vineyards and breweries to attract even more city dwellers bent on sucking the clean air of the Virginia countryside.

Thoughts of the evolving landscape were a brief diversion

from what lay ahead, and how it might be exacerbated when Jack and company awoke this morning—if they hadn't already discovered me gone. Randy was likely an early riser, but not the type to pound on my door, I hoped. Gunner was unpredictable, and Jack would probably be the last one up, unless he'd changed drastically since we were teenagers. The loss of their phones would buy me some time, but not very much, so I'd either be walking into a trap or had very limited time to mount my offensive.

The town of Middleburg was awake, as evidenced by traffic and mask-clad people walking out of Common Grounds with lattes and caramel macchiatos. The local gun shop, however, which specialized in rare antiques, was closed. Not that I wanted to rush the house with a Civil War–era musket, but anything would help. I tried to remember what I'd left in the barn. A few items could be helpful, but since I hadn't been there in a year, it was possible Ben had grown tired of my using the place for storage and had cleaned it all out.

I turned left on Zulla Road. Anticipation had my palms sweating as I proceeded hastily down the home stretch. I drove at the speed limit past the driveway and saw the gate was closed. The copse of trees on the far side would give me an opportunity for a frontal approach, but another strategy came to mind. Past the lower field that fronted Zulla Road was an old dirt road that Mom and Dad had used to drive the horse trailer up to the barn. I braked and turned slowly onto that path. A chain blocked further passage, but there was room to park the Escalade. I climbed out into the morning cold, my breath encircling my head like a cloud of cigar smoke. Buzzards floated above in search of carrion, small birds flitted between the leafless trees, and the smell of musty leaves brought back memories of jumping into leaf piles my father had worked all day to rake.

I shook off the past and started up the dirt road, now covered with leaves, tree branches, saplings, and moss.

On top of the hill was the house: large, in redbrick Georgian style, with columns out front, a black metal roof, four chimneys, and an overgrown hedge of boxwoods on each side of the main entry. We never used the front door because the driveway led to a parking area to the far side of the house, and the door there entered a mudroom that led to the kitchen. From here I saw no movement, no guards out front, and no vehicles, since the parking area was behind the house. What if there were camouflaged mercenaries in the trees ahead? Or what if the gravel road had been booby-trapped? Nothing would surprise me, so I continued slowly but purposefully, glancing back and forth from the house to the path ahead. Sticks buried under leaves cracked beneath my boat shoes. If there *were* trained guards nearby, they'd hear my approach. With no parka, I shivered in the 36-degree air. The weather app on my phone had shown a snowflake. I needed to grab Ben and get the hell out of here before getting stuck.

I paused. Should I call the local sheriff? That would be smart but could commence a chain of events: the guards calling Jack and him issuing orders to kill Ben and shoot it out with local police, who'd be ill-equipped to do battle with hardened mercenaries. No, I'd first get a peek at what we were up against.

After I went to the barn.

At the top of the gravel road was the clearing where Mom's horse trailer used to be parked. It, along with the horses, was long gone. Still no sound from the house, and there were no tire tracks or evidence of tinkering with the barn. I searched for any new cameras Ben may have added back here but found none. He never cared for the barn, and the only things there since he had sold off the horses and equipment were the few possessions I'd stored in the tack room.

I walked across the gravel lot, the gray stone crunching under my feet. The barn needed a paintjob, as did the black metal roof. All the windows were shuttered. The door wasn't locked, so I slid it three feet to the right and peered inside. No signs of cameras here either. Once inside, I slid the door closed. My padlock on the tack room door was still there, covered in dust and cobwebs. Good. Inside the powder room to the right, I found my key where I'd left it on top of the doorframe. The key turned smoothly, and the padlock popped open.

I entered the windowless room and turned on the naked bulb that hung from the cobwebbed ceiling. My father's metal army trunk was in the center of the room with the sister lock I'd placed on the tack room door. Paintings and furniture I'd taken from the house were dusty, as was my father's gun cabinet. I popped that open and found his Krieghoff Model 32 over and under 12-gauge shotgun. I used a seasoned gun-oil rag to wipe it down, then pulled open a drawer and found a box of Remington 12-gauge #8 shells. Birdshot, but it would cut a man in half if it came to that. I checked my Submariner: 7:52 a.m.

"Don't think, just move."

I refrained from glancing around the room to prevent any semblance of sentimentality from distracting me. If I failed and Ben got killed, it would be his stuff stored in here next. Or I might get killed myself, and then it wouldn't matter anymore. With the light off, two shells in the shotgun, and the pockets of my father's hunting vest filled with more shells, I slipped back out into the cold. In the distance I could see fog hovering over the five-acre pond.

"Focus, Buck."

From the corner of the barn, I peered slowly around toward the back porch and door to the house. The corner of the driveway was visible from here—there were two vehicles in sight. The first was a white BMW X7 SUV that looked new. Ben's? The second car was a Mercedes SUV. I didn't know the model, but it was big enough to carry four to six men.

As I watched, I saw movement in the kitchen. Silhouettes blocked the inside lights as they passed by the windows. The wood shades were down but only partially closed, which was enough to make it impossible to see any detail beyond movement. There was a camera on the porch facing the door, but nothing visible near the kitchen windows.

If I went for the door, I'd have no time to hesitate: if they were monitoring the camera footage, any delay on my part would give them time to react.

I breathed in short rapid breaths, then concentrated on taking in a deep one and letting it out slowly. After three repetitions of this, I glanced at the shotgun, clicked off the safety, took one last glance toward the parking area, and moved in a crouch toward the kitchen windows fifty feet away. A stick cracked under my foot—I jumped—my heart flip-flopped, but I continued.

Glances left and right revealed nothing as I arrived at the wall. The windows here were large and tall but didn't start until about four feet above the ground. I hunkered down between the two closest to the covered porch where we used to have family dinners in the summer—concentrate!

Voices! I could hear voices inside.

"No!" A male voice shouted—Ben!

High-pitched laughing followed. Was some sick bastard torturing him?

From a prone position, I stood slowly taller until I could peer inside the lowest part of the window—

"I said no!" It was Ben, again.

Nothing was visible from this window—the kitchen island was in the way. I scooched over to the next window—

Clunk!

The gun barrel bumped into the side of the wall—Damn!

The voices fell silent.

Shit!

I peered inside the window closest to the porch. Ben was seated at the table, unrestrained …

My eyes nearly popped out of my head at what I saw next. The breath compressed from my lungs as I bent forward in shock, and the gun nearly slipped from my hands.

I caught my breath, gritted my teeth, stood and walked up the porch steps toward the door, with a tight grip on the shotgun.

24

IT WASN'T EVEN LOCKED. I pushed the door open and stepped inside without so much as an old floorboard creaking. The voices were clear now: Ben's, along with another voice I hadn't heard in a very long time—a woman I thought I knew.

A cell phone began to ring.

My heart jumped, and I walked around the corner from the mudroom into the kitchen, the gun extended out in front of me. Ben was seated at the kitchen table, where two plates showed the remnants of breakfast: eggs and avocado, by the look of it. Ben's mouth dropped open when he saw me.

"As a matter of fact, he just walked in," Heather, my ex-wife, said into the phone.

"Buck!" Ben yelled my name.

Also on the table were a bottle of half-drunk champagne, a pitcher of orange juice, and two flutes filled to the brim with mimosas. Whether on purpose or subconsciously, the shotgun was pointed at Heather, who'd turned pale but was still listening to someone on the phone—Jack, no doubt.

"I'll call you back," she said. She placed the phone on the kitchen island.

Ben was smiling. "What a surprise for you to show up."

"What the hell's going on?" I said. "You told me you'd been kidnapped—you were terrified—"

Ben wisely stayed seated. "I know, I know. I'm sorry."

"And what's she doing here?" My mind tilted as if the world

had been shifted off its axis. I glanced around but saw no weapons—only champagne and fresh raspberries.

"Buck," Heather said.

"What am I talking about?" A dry laugh sprung from my throat. "There was no kidnapping!" I shook my head and leaned the shotgun against the corner of the kitchen wall. "I've been played. And you two—"

"Whoa, whoa, whoa," Ben said.

"It's not what it looks like, Buck," Heather said. She had on no makeup and was wearing flannel pajamas, and her blonde hair was tied up in a ponytail. She was still the most beautiful woman I'd ever seen. But I didn't know her anymore, maybe never had.

"Well Heather, if it weren't for everything that's happened these past few days, it would look like I've walked into a happy couple's breakfast celebration."

Ben laughed as if that was the funniest thing he'd ever heard. He took a sip of his mimosa.

"When I was outside, I heard you yelling 'No!' What was that all about?"

Still smiling, Ben waved off the question. "Actually, this is pretty funny given the context, but I was arguing against her pouring me another mimosa—here, let me get you a glass. You look like you could use one."

Ben stood up and reached into an upper cabinet and produced another champagne flute. He also had on pajamas and looked as if he'd put on ten pounds since I last saw him. At 5'10", he was five inches shorter than me and had never been athletic or in good shape.

"Drink up, brother. You'll feel better."

The term brother never felt further from reality. Too stunned to argue, I shifted my gaze to Heather. The color had returned to her cheeks, and she offered me a slight smile—one I remembered her making when she was trying to be cute or wanted something.

I leaned back against the black soapstone countertop.

Ben's smile finally faded. "Thank you, Buck. You came to rescue me—I would never have thought you'd do that—risk your life for me."

I wanted to puke right there on his breakfast table.

"So aside from Jack and Gunner keeping Scarlet and my son under house arrest, this whole thing has been one entire con job," I said.

"You were—are—the greatest treasure hunter in the world," Ben said.

"Archeologist." My voice was a whisper.

"And Jack's just a bean counter," he said.

I glanced towards Heather at the mention of Jack's name. She looked down at the floor.

"So you're in cahoots with these snakes, Ben?"

"I never had the chance to work with you," he said. "I was always the little brother, and—"

"You and Jack hated each other!" I said. "Ever since he used to pick on you when we were in high school—you kicked him in the balls that time!"

Ben held his hands up. "We grew up. We forgave each other." He leaned forward. "And he's still super passionate about treasure hunting, Buck. You lost that passion after e-Antiquity crashed." He smiled again. "We wanted to give you a jump start."

"A *jump start*? That's what you call this? You and I are the only family we have left, and you lie to me about being *kidnapped by mercenaries* to force me to help them find fucking treasure—while my son is held hostage too?" My fists were clutched in tight balls. I'd never beaten my younger brother up when we were kids, maybe because he was four years younger and was always a pipsqueak, but right now …

"I'm so sorry, Buck," Heather said. "Jack said he had a plan to get your help, but I didn't realize—"

"Spare me, Heather." My eyes felt like laser beams that could cut her in half. "You've been lying to me as long as I've known you."

"I'm so sorry. This is awful."

"Don't you make enough money as a freaking supermodel?"

She crossed her arms and took in a deep breath. She wouldn't meet my eyes. "It's not about the money—for me, anyway—"

"It is for me!" Ben said. "That and the thrill."

"I wanted to be a part of discovery—one of your discoveries," she said. "You never took me on one of your expeditions."

I rubbed my face with both of my palms.

"Me either," Ben said. "All I ever wanted to do was tag along to see the great King Buck in action, but you never asked me. Not once."

I sat down at the kitchen table. The past days of stress and jetting across the Atlantic, concern for Ben's safety, withholding information from Jack, then skipping out, flying all night, and racing here ready to kill some people, all in the name of rescuing my brother, washed over me like a tsunami of battery acid. As if she could sense my exhaustion, Heather pulled the eggs out of the refrigerator, turned on a gas burner, and started whipping up an omelet.

I shook my head. Maybe I'd crashed the Beast while asleep en route, and this was purgatory.

"Sounds like things went well in France," she said. "I'm glad you and Jack are getting along."

"Getting along?" My sudden laugh turned her head. "More like *playing* along. Gunner reminded me repeatedly that Ben's—your—life was at stake." I pointed to him.

"But you found some great clues, right?" Ben said. "There was a thirteenth ship that nobody ever knew about until you put the pieces together. They were going to tell you when you were on the boat today, and Heather and I were going to fly down to join the search." He rubbed his hands together so fast I thought sparks would shoot out. "And we're all going to go find it! The queen's jewels!"

I shook my head. "I'm not going anywhere."

"C'mon, Buck. It'll be amazing. Seriously." Ben leaned closer to me. "I knew this would piss you off, but tell me one thing, honestly."

"Honestly?"

"Can you really say you didn't get the bug when you were at that museum digging through ancient records, connecting information to discover a truth that had been hidden for over three hundred years? I know you, brother. I know what makes you tick."

I watched the excitement on his face. Would I have cooperated with them had he made this pitch to me, with this passion? No, never.

And as much as I hated to admit it, what he said was true. I'd lost myself while I was in Brest, then again in Saint-Renan. And even back in Vero Beach, when Director Roth had sent me the information on Jean Bart, I hedged with Jack because deep down inside, I wanted to go find the *Farnese* myself. I was no better than the rest of them, and that thought again made me sick, but when Heather placed the omelet in front of me, I looked up at her.

"Three eggs, cheddar cheese, scallions, and tomato." She smiled. "Your favorite."

I picked up the plate and dropped the entire thing in the trash can next to the sink.

"No thanks."

25

"I FIGURED YOU'D RUN, BUCK," JACK SAID. "But did you have to dump our phones in the pool?"

He had called me as I was walking out of the house. I'd left Ben and Heather after telling them I had no intention of helping Jack and the rest of them. I hated nothing more than being manipulated, and given the level of deceit amongst that crew and all the ways they'd lied to me, not just now, but for years … the thought of voluntarily partnering with them was repulsive. If anything, I'd be tempted to call the Bahamian authorities and alert them to treasure hunting without a permit off Andros.

I bit my lip rather than telling Jack what he already knew damn well: that he'd turned my own brother against me.

The sun had come out; the sky was a brilliant cerulean blue; the air was crisp, fresh, and had warmed to around 40 degrees; and it was a perfect day to fly south—all the way south. I'd hesitated at the barn to see if there was anything I wanted to bring back to Key West, but at that point, I just wanted to get out of there, so I was walking down the gravel road from the barn toward the Escalade when Jack called.

"You never would have agreed to help us, and we never would've learned what we did in France without you."

"Forgive me if I don't say you're welcome."

I heard Jack exhale loudly into the phone. "We still want you to be our partner, Buck. There's hundreds of millions of dollars of gold, silver, and precious jewels sitting on the bottom of the ocean just waiting to get picked up."

He made it sound so easy.

"So Ben's a partner too? What does he bring to your sordid table?"

"Money, for one, and frankly, we knew we could twist your arm if you thought he'd been kidnapped—plus, we didn't have to break any laws."

"Unbelievable."

"Before you answer, I want to come clean on one other detail." Jack paused. "When I confiscated your phone in France, I added my email address as an automatic copy to all ingoing and outgoing emails."

I stopped halfway down the gravel road. What the…? Oh, crap. "So you saw all the correspondence with Director Roth?"

"That's right, Buck. Everything." His voice was matter of fact. He wasn't gloating, and why he was telling me this now wasn't clear, other than to let me know he had all the same information I did, once again. "And I know you withheld information and other emails he sent about Jean Bart and additional pages from the *Griffon*'s logbook. I have them all printed, and I have another partner fluent in French on the way to meet us."

Dammit. I pulled the phone away from my ear and looked at it. Even my cell phone was being used against me. I'd have to figure out how to eliminate that blind forward from my operating system. "Well, then you obviously don't need me. I'd like to wish you luck, but—"

"All of us combined can't do what you do, Buck. We still need you, and we want you to be our partner, but now it's up to you. No more lies, no more bullshit. We cast off a few hours ago, and we're making good time toward Andros."

I thought of the loose translation I'd made of d'Aire's log and how I skewed the information, telling Jack and Gunner they sank the *Farnese* closer to Andros when it was really ten miles up to the northeast of the Joulter Cays. Just because they had all the same information I had didn't mean they could piece it together. Which was probably why he'd told me they had another French-speaking partner on the way. That made me pause.

"So who is this other French-speaking partner? Anybody I know?"

Jack took in a deep breath. "It's Heather."

Shit. Of course. Given all the time she'd spent in Paris for years of Fashion Weeks and modeling gigs, Heather's French was better than mine.

"And I might as well tell you now—she's the one who found Ubilla's letter to his wife. She got it from your floor safe back in Great Falls, made a copy, and gave it to me."

I shook my head. "Wow. You win, Jack. You have every angle covered."

"That's not true. Without you, we're just a bunch of dreamers hoping to spot shiny objects peeking out of the mud." He hesitated. "I have no right to do so, but I'm asking you to let Ben and Heather hitch a ride in your Grumman to Florida—"

"Are they a couple now? … Just so the demented connections are clear?"

"No, Buck, she was just there waiting on word from me that it was time to come south." He paused. "Have an open mind. Talk to them. Think about the opportunity. Then, either keep going to Key West and forget about it or bring them out to Andros and meet us at the ship. But if you don't come, there's no cut. And like I said, based on the projections of what's still missing from the queen's jewels, your share could be fifty million dollars."

Everybody who'd ever bought a metal detector and called themselves a treasure hunter had the same big ideas. I'd learned long ago to never calculate the potential value of something you were searching for because you'd just jinx yourself. And even if they found it, they'd have the Bahamian, American, and Spanish governments after them in court for years to take the majority, if not all, of the findings.

An image of Scarlet and Charlie popped into my head. I had no doubt that if I refused to play ball, they'd have no compunction about forcing Scarlet to help them and would use Charlie as leverage against her—and me, for that matter.

Once you're in bed with thieves, you're always fighting over the blankets.

My concerns over Scarlet and Charlie put my back up against the wall. She was no pro at hiding out, so they'd find her if they really wanted to. So would it be better to be on the inside directing the operation or dragged back in under duress?

"I'll think about it," I said.

"Great. That's all I ask. If you're leaving soon, think fast," he said. "Have a safe flight, and I hope to see you in the Bahamas."

I hit the end button. "What a shit show."

Once I reached the Escalade, I climbed inside, started the engine, and sat staring up the hill toward my childhood home. Nearly the first twenty years of my life had been spent happily there, and the memories from those times were precious. The older I got, the less I remembered, though, and ever since Mom and Dad had died ten years ago, everything else that happened here had been awful. Today may have been the worst of all.

I was at an inflection point with Ben. Either I drove away and never spoke to him again, or I threw in with these criminals and pursued the *Farnese*. For the life of me, I couldn't figure out which would be worse. But if we found the queen's jewels, then at least I'd have capital to pursue what I'd recently decided all over again was my purpose in life. And Ben's and my relationship would be on totally different ground. Whether that ground would be better or worse, I had no idea.

"In for a dime, in for a dollar," I said aloud. "Or, in this case, in for the crime, in for the collar."

I glanced both ways and backed the Escalade out onto Zulla Road, facing in the direction I'd come from. I drove slowly past the lower field and stared up at my parents' beautiful old brick home.

"Shit."

I turned suddenly into the driveway, drove up to the gate, and pressed the call button. There was a camera on the call pad, and Ben's face appeared a moment later.

"Forget something?" he said.

"Yeah, you. Open the gate. We have to get to the airport and get moving so we land before dark."

"Woo-hoo!" Ben's holler caused static on the tinny speaker.

A moment later, the gate slowly opened. Flying with Ben was one thing, but I hadn't been with Heather on a plane in years. I couldn't shake the image of her in pajamas this morning, her perfect smile, the scent of lilacs in her hair, or that damned omelet she'd cooked me (which, hungry as I was, I was starting to wish I hadn't thrown in the trash). As I drove up the tree-lined driveway, I felt butterflies in my gut. Fear, anxiety, or anticipation, I wasn't sure, but whichever it was, I had a big decision to make during these next six hours of flying.

"What are you getting yourself into now, Buck Reilly?"

SECTION 4

NO REVISION
FOR A BAD
DECISION

26

BEN SAT IN THE RIGHT SEAT AS WE FLEW SOUTH. Heather was sprawled out in the back of the plane, surrounded by Louis Vuitton luggage and fashion magazines. Neither of them had flown in the Beast before. Heather had flown in Betty, my Widgeon, but not with me. After Betty, Ray, and I had had a particularly unfortunate experience in Cuba, I was forced to leave her behind in what I thought was irreparable condition. I remembered the shock when I next saw the Widgeon, restored—poorly—in St. Barths, in the possession of Jack and Gunner.

It had been yet another nail in the coffin of our collective relationships.

Still worse was that while in Jamaica, I'd discovered that Heather and Jack were together. A memory from the end of that adventure floated in my mind like faint smoke. Heather had crashed our victory celebration and come on to me, but I was otherwise involved with Professor Adou. With the gash in my heart still fresh from finding her with Jack, I had rebuffed Heather, but the recollection had me sitting up straighter in my seat now.

I glanced over my right shoulder and saw her sitting on the starboard side forward-facing seat with her feet up on the aft-facing seat across from her. She must have sensed my stare, because she looked up. Our eyes locked in a long second, then she smiled and turned her gaze back down at the magazine. I noticed an image of her in a miniskirt, midriff shirt, and knee-length boots on the cover.

"This plane is slow as hell." Ben's voice spoke in my headset and broke my momentary reverie.

"You could have flown commercial—hell, with your money, you could have chartered a G-IV like Jack did. He's going to take all his expenses off the top of whatever we find anyway. You might as well do the same," I said.

"No shit? Never thought of that."

Ben had glanced around the interior of the Beast when he first climbed on board, as if he was at an exhibition on early flight at the Air and Space Museum. Pretty close, actually. The Beast was built just forty years after the Wright brothers completed the first powered flight at Kill Devil Hills near Kitty Hawk. What Ben didn't realize was that the Beast would be a hell of a lot more effective while searching the Bahamian waters than any jet would be. It might take us three times longer to get there, but the utility of the flying boat would be well worthwhile.

I felt Ben staring at me. I glanced over at him.

"Sorry again about the charade, Buck," he said. "I truly never thought you'd risk your life to come to my rescue, and we were going to tell you the truth once we headed to the Bahamas."

"Yeah, well, not like we've been close these past several years."

He nodded. "I can't believe all your recent adventures have been aboard this old jalopy. It's bigger than I remembered."

"You're thinking of Betty, the Widgeon you helped me buy—"

"You mean that I bought for you." He laughed, and I pretended to smile. "You named it Betty? After Mom?"

"That's right."

"How sweet." His voice was a whisper. "I still support some of her charities. Hell, those fundraising people in Middleburg are relentless."

I wasn't much for small talk, even with my brother.

"You name this one after Dad?"

"No, this one I call the Beast—affectionately. Ray Floyd, my aircraft mechanic and partner in Last Resort Charter and Salvage, refers to her as the Beauty, primarily because he restored her from near-scrap condition in Pinar del Río, Cuba, where she had crashed in 1961. We joke about it …" I stopped myself short.

"Like he's a little brother?" Ben finished my sentence. "Is that what you were going to say? Lucky guy. Hope to meet him."

We flew for another hour in silence. I pulled the T-bar in the middle of the instrument panel to activate the automatic pilot, pulled off my headset, and climbed out of the left seat—

"Hey!" Ben's yell was loud enough that I didn't need my headset to hear him. "What are you doing?"

"Stretching my legs. Automatic pilot's on."

I was too tall to stand up, but it felt good to get out of the seat. Heather watched me closely, then slid her feet off the forward chair and pointed to it. After I stretched my legs, back and arms, I sat down to face her.

"Love this plane," she said.

"Not like the jets we used to fly in back in the day."

"Jets are a dime a dozen." Her smile lit the interior. "This is pretty close to one of a kind."

"Yep, not many left."

She sat forward. "I'm so happy you're coming to the Bahamas."

"Haven't made up my mind on that yet."

Her smile slid to an exaggerated pout. The familiar ploy still caused me to shake my head. Our romance had hit like a Midwestern tornado and left nearly as much damage. But when we were good, we were amazing. Enough years had gone by now since our divorce (and finding her with Jack) that the wound had healed, even if it had left a permanent scar on my soul. I'd been with a lot of women since, had felt love and a greater sense of connection with a couple of them than I had ever experienced with Heather, but I'd never felt anything close to the same physical chemistry. The memory of Heather and I making love led to a long intake of breath and equally long exhale. She raised her eyebrows and cocked her head slightly off center and smiled as if she could read my mind.

"You look good," she said. "Still in shape, still handsome."

"Well." I pointed to the magazine sitting on the fold-down table between us. "You've weathered the last ten years okay yourself. How's the modeling business?"

She rolled her eyes. "Busy as I want to be, but I'm super picky now. Like I said, I don't need the money. I just do what I like, when I want, for fun."

I held her gaze. Okay, let's dial this up a notch. "Jack doesn't like you to travel?"

She tilted her head back in a silent laugh, and then lowered her eyes back to mine. "He doesn't care. And he doesn't tell me what to do."

"No? Well, you always were the independent type."

Her lips puckered, and her eyes grew narrow. "Jack and I aren't married, Buck. In fact, we aren't even exclusive."

That pushed my back into the seat cushion. "Does he know that?"

Her lips curled into her signature Cheshire cat smile that had graced every magazine in the world. Heather had always been a lioness, and she clearly still liked to toy with her prey before attempting to devour it.

"When we were coming back from France, Jack told me about you guys being lovers at Harvard and how he had introduced us to try and save his marriage—"

"Oh, he said that, did he?" She glanced out the window at the clouds above us—we were only flying at five thousand feet of altitude over the Atlantic Ocean. "He always has had visions of grandeur, hasn't he?"

A laugh burst from my lips. "That's a fact."

She leaned forward again. "Truth is, me and Jack's relationship has run its course. We're still together, but we both know it's time to move on."

I curled my lip and nodded once.

"Or backward," she said with a lift of her eyebrows.

I laughed uncomfortably to prevent myself from choking. "Maybe whatever happens in the Bahamas will change the course of your lives."

"All of our lives," she said. "Please come. We'll have fun."

Her foot brushed my shin as she repositioned herself in the seat. Intentional? With Heather, nothing was unintentional.

"Thinking about it, but I should go fly the plane now before Ben has a heart attack—"

She leaned forward. "Buck? I wanted to tell you that I'm sorry about the situation with Giselle Huibert. I know you must have, well, cared for her deeply. And it was clear in the video footage I saw that she cares for you too, but ..."

"Yeah, thanks." I was suddenly choked up. I cleared my throat. "You know me, always lucky at love."

I sat forward, and she offered me a sad smile. Had Heather developed a heart for more than her career? Guess I'd see.

I truly hadn't decided what I would do yet, but just like I had with Gunner and Jack in Vero Beach, if I did go, I planned to do everything possible to stir dissension and confusion amongst all of them to destabilize their unified front against me. Even if it meant flirting with my darling ex-wife.

I turned toward the cockpit and stretched my arms backward once more—intentionally flaring my triceps.

The games had officially begun.

27

WE LANDED BACK IN VERO BEACH AND I still hadn't made my mind up, so I taxied the Beast to where she'd previously been tied down. Ben had slept the last couple hours of our flight but was jarred awake when we touched down.

"Where are we?" he said.

"End of the line."

"What's that supposed to mean?"

"Means this is as far as we're going. Vero Beach, Florida."

Heather had unbuckled and walked up behind us. The engines continued to rev at 500 RPM and the propellers sliced the air, making it difficult to talk.

"You mind shutting this thing off for a minute?" she said.

I cut the power, and the props gradually came to rest.

"Buck says this is the end of the line," Ben said.

Heather frowned. How could she have just sat in the back of an eighty-year-old airplane for six-plus hours and not have a hair out of place? It wasn't like there was a powder room on board.

"I got an email from Jack," she said. "He says the waters in the Bahamas are crystal clear. There's been so little boat traffic for the last year, it's like the ecosystem has stepped back in time."

"It'll make for some great diving," Ben said.

"I'm sure you guys will have an amazing vacation," I said.

"Listen," Heather said. "I know you have plenty of reasons to drop us off here, fly back down to the Conch Republic," she pronounced it Kon-ch, "and go hang out in that old hotel you call home. That would be perfectly understandable." She paused. "But I remember when I first met you—the night at the Explorer's Club after you'd found the tomb of the Serpent King in Guatemala. You were larger than life. Bigger than Indiana Jones and Superman combined."

"They're fictional characters, Heather."

"Exactly! Hollywood made them the most compelling characters anyone could imagine, but they didn't hold a candle to you! You were the real deal: a brilliant archeologist, a shrewd negotiator, a deft statesman, and a hell of a treasure hunter."

"King Buck," Ben said.

"That was all a long time ago." I stared out over the Beast's instrument panel and watched as a Falcon 8X took off and rocketed at a sixty-degree angle into the sky. It seemed like a lifetime ago when I was jetting all over the globe in search of rare and precious artifacts. What a run it had been.

"I know you went through hell, Buck. You lost your company, your parents, all your money—"

I gritted my teeth at what I knew would come next.

"And yes, I ran off too," she said. "I was too shallow in my twenties to be with a man on the decline. Your world had imploded, and I was on top of my game."

I felt Ben's eyes staring lasers into the side of my head. I hadn't anticipated this ten-year-old postmortem. Her words cut but hit home at the same time. Was it just five days ago that Reverend Willy Peebles died of COVID and my friends asked me the same question she was stirring now?

"You were the best, Buck, and that's what I fell in love with. Forget about Jack—yes, we had fun, and yes, we reconnected, but that wasn't because I fell *out* of love with you. *You* fell out of love with yourself."

I breathed in deeply. I couldn't bear to look at her face. The Falcon was now a speck in the sky. The thought of some success-

ful entrepreneur off on his or her next adventure made me
queasy.

"That was your purpose, Buck. And nobody will ever be better."

"She's right, brother," Ben said. "I used to resent the hell out
of you, but even I had to admit you were a phenomenon. I never
got the chance to go on an expedition with you back then, but
man, I dreamed about it a hundred times."

"Okay, okay, all this buttering-me-up-BS is making me nauseous," I said. "I'm going inside the FBO to use the restroom and
make a call. I'll tell you what I decide when I come out."

"I'm coming with you," Heather said. "My bladder's about to
explode."

I slid past her, which was impossible without our bodies rub-
bing together—a sensation that again brought back memories—
and I popped open the hatch, climbed out, and waited to help
her down.

"I'll go when you get back!" Ben's shout came from inside the
shaded interior.

Heather and I walked side by side down the tarmac toward
the private aviation building, something we hadn't done for a
very long time. With heels on, she was only a few inches shorter
than me. A pair of men who looked to be in their forties, decked
out in golf attire, stepped outside just before we arrived at the
door. They stopped and stared at Heather—something that I'd
gotten used to years ago but that now caused me to tense up.

The fat one leaned over to the skinnier one. I heard "Heather
Drake."

Like the sucker I was, I held the door open so she could walk
in first, then glanced at the pair of men behind me who continued
to watch us—well, Heather—enter the building. Déjà vu all over
again. I winked at them, and they hooted as the door closed
behind me. She'd vanished, so I found the men's room, and once

I took care of business, I called Ray Floyd.

"Where the hell have you been, Buck? I've been worried sick!"

"It's a long story, Ray."

"It always is." Sarcasm was steeped in his voice. "Seeing how Gunner all but kidnapped you, I've been torn on whether to call the cops or the mortuary."

"I've been to France, Vero Beach, Virginia, and now I'm back in Florida trying to figure out what to do next."

"What are the choices?"

I gave Ray the two-minute rundown on the *Griffon*, the *Farnese*, how Jack and company wanted to partner with me—us, since Ray was my partner—and that I was at a crossroads.

"That explains the phone call I got from France," he said.

"What do you mean?"

"Giselle Huibert, the first freaking lady of France! She called here looking for you—she heard you'd been in France and didn't contact her. She was worried."

I rubbed my eyes with my free palm. "Yeah, well, we were only there for a day."

"So let me guess. I'm assuming you found some quality intel there, so now the dilemma is whether or not to work with your ex-partner Jack and that creep Gunner or not, correct?"

"There's more to it than that, but that's the tip of shitberg."

"And the *Farnese* supposedly had the missing queen's jewels from the 1715 fleet?"

"That's the theory." I checked my hair in the mirror, combing it through with my fingers. I needed a shave badly. "And I'm pretty damn certain I know where it is: just off the coast of Andros in the Bahamas."

"Andros?" Ray's voice lifted. "That's where that old Chalk's Mallard is—the one I've been talking to the owners about selling us."

"Like we need another antique plane?" I said.

"This one's bigger than the Beauty and a lot newer."

"Oh, I forgot, it was built in the '50s, so it's only seventy-plus years old."

"Gunner gives me the creeps, and Dodson is scum, but if you think you have the location—and I can't believe I'm going to say this—but maybe it's worth checking out. Why let those assholes benefit from all your research?"

I paused for a minute, then said, "You say that Mallard is on Andros?"

"Damn straight." He practically yelled now. "South Andros Airport in Congo Town."

"Okay, give me until tomorrow to check out the scene, and I'll call you back."

"Holy crap!" he said. "Treasure hunting and a new airplane!"

Like a kid on Christmas morning. I wanted to tell Ray it was more complicated than that—that we didn't have a salvage permit, that my brother had lied to me about being kidnapped, and that my ex-wife was flirting with me—but I knew if I scared Ray too much, he wouldn't come when I asked for his help, which I knew I'd need if I decided to see this through.

Before we hung up, I asked Ray to research any open insurance claims on missing boats near Andros and to get back to me ASAP.

"You don't have enough on your plate already?" he said.

"Just check and I'll explain later."

We disconnected. I checked my reflection again, then stepped out of the bathroom. Heather was waiting.

"Talking to someone special?" she said.

My lips curled into a tight smile. "For sure. My partner."

"Partner?" Real surprise showed in her eyes. Was that disappointment in her voice?

"Ray Floyd, my partner at Last Resort Charter and Salvage."

She slapped my arm. "Aren't you funny. And you need to do something about the name of your company. Sounds desperate."

"We have two planes that are almost two hundred years old combined. Desperate is a pretty good description."

A teenager standing with her parents at the flight desk craned her head over to watch us. She held her phone up and took what she thought was a discreet photo. Heather still had a lot of fans out there, while I'd faded into invisibility. That was exactly what I had wanted, but …

"I talked to Jack. Everyone still wants you to come." She paused and looked away. "Especially me."

"Ray wants me to go too."

"So?"

I nodded my head. "I'll fly you and Ben to Andros and check it out—"

Heather jumped up and down—then leaned in and kissed me on the cheek. "I'm so excited! This will be amazing!"

I reached down and took her shoulders in both of my hands. "Slow down, Heather. I said I'd check it out. This whole partnership has been based on lies so far, not to mention the overflowing litterbox of our lives, so if shit gets weird, I'm gone. Got it?"

She beamed her million-watt multi-million-dollar smile. I hadn't been its recipient for a very long time—since Jamaica, anyway. That made me wonder: What would have happened back then if I hadn't blown her off? Again, more dirty water under the bridge. She grabbed my forearm and led me out of the private terminal past the teenaged girl, who was now blatantly taking our pictures.

As she hurried toward the Beast, another thought dawned on me. "I'll be right back," I said and turned back to the terminal.

"Where are you going" she said.

"To get some snacks." I didn't add that I also wanted to purchase a burner phone, since Jack had mine rigged to copy him on all incoming and outgoing communication.

As I walked away, I reminded myself I was going to assess the situation—to look for the *Farnese*. It had nothing to do with Heather.

But if I could drive a wedge between her and Jack, I'd be like John Henry swinging a sledge through solid rock.

28

THE WATERS OF THE BAHAMAS WERE INDEED
CRYSTAL CLEAR. In all the time I'd been coming here to fish,
dive, or search for missing items, I'd never seen them like this.
From a thousand feet up, the ship Jack had rented looked big and
well equipped, bright white against the turquoise sea.

"Is that them in the marina?" Heather's voice rang in my
headset. She'd sat in the co-pilot's seat on the flight over from
Vero Beach. When I nodded, she said, "I read all about that
boat. May not look like much, but it's well equipped for our
needs."

That surprised me. I had expected her to complain that it
wasn't very pretty (like the yacht I'd seen pictures of her aboard
in Monaco for the Formula One race a few years ago). Maybe
she really had matured.

"That's what Jack told me," I said.

Another glance at the ship caused me to steel myself, because
I'd soon have to face the dynamics between her and Jack. Their
chemistry would have a direct impact on my ability to concentrate. There was just no way around it. I had only been married
once in my life, and that was to Heather. That wasn't because no
other woman could surpass her—I'd met several that did in many
areas. It was more about what losing her had done to me, the
pain and scarring that had led me to the mantra "dead men don't
bleed." I was beyond that now, but that was because I'd kept
moving forward. Backward had never been an emotional option.

The first thing I'd done when getting on the plane back in Vero Beach was have Heather call Jack and then give me the phone. I told him to call Chub Cay Club Marina on Chub Cay, directly across the Tongue of the Ocean's northern spur, and see if he could dock the ship there.

"Why would we do that?" he said.

"Nothing is more obvious than a salvage ship. You anchor that off North Andros and start searching, the authorities will be on us before we ascend from the first dive. Remember, the Bahamian government has zero tolerance for people poaching wreck sites or doing salvage without a permit, so we need to be discreet. Chub Cay is twenty miles from Andros, so we'll use the dive boat to get to the search area. Then, if we find something—"

"*When* we find something, you mean," he said.

I continued, "Then we can figure out what to do next."

He agreed with my plan, thanked me for sticking with them, apologized again for how they recruited me, and promised it would all be worthwhile.

I hung up in response. Optimism wasn't a plan.

An hour later, we were flying around the east end of Chub Cay. I winced—the salvage ship stuck out like a sore thumb in the marina. Heather glanced over at me.

"Good call on getting dockage at the marina."

The airstrip was just east from the marina on the sparsely populated kite-shaped island, which was vastly more scrub than civilization. The tug of a smile pulled at my lips. Regardless of the company, nothing felt better than being in the Bahamian Out Islands armed with solid research at the start of a potential archeological find. It wasn't the promise of riches that appealed to me as much as the process of finding a thread of information and following it to find the whole fabric of missing history, revealing patterns that could be pursued. We were at that point, and while there was no shortage of obstacles, that sensation of anticipation produced endorphins that tickled my nerve endings.

"You look happy," Heather said.

I hadn't noticed her watching me as I vectored the Beast to the far eastern end of the island, followed the flight pattern, and progressed through the landing procedure. For some reason, I was suddenly choked up and just nodded my response.

She patted her left hand on my right knee, let it linger a moment, then leaned back toward her window and pointed.

"That water is amazing! So brilliant—it's like the white sand underneath it is illuminating the water above," she said. "And the sun is dazzling!" She pointed to the celestial orb that hovered four fingers over the horizon.

I glanced back at Ben, who gave me a thumb up. He had a wide grin on like nothing I'd seen from him in a decade. Deep in my mind, I wished we could freeze this moment and treasure it, because Gunner and Jack would ruin it with their binary, zero-sum-greed philosophy.

I added flaps, reduced airspeed, lined the Beast up on the center of the runway—there was no crosswind—and pointed our angle of attack onto the lone five-thousand-foot strip. The wheels touched down hard, and the smell of burnt rubber permeated the cabin. Our speed quickly slowed, and the tail wheel dropped to the bitumen surface as we continued down toward the western end, which had no facilities, no fuel, and no perks of any kind. Good thing it was only one hundred and seventy miles from Vero Beach, where we'd refueled before departing.

My phone had cell service, and there was a text from Ray. I opened it and smiled. Perfect. I pulled off my headset as Ben shouted, "This place is badass!"

To my knowledge, Ben had never been to the Bahamas, much less the Out Islands, which possessed a raw beauty formed by the stark contrast of the white-blue water, green and brown landscape, and scant signs of humanity. Once we came to a stop, the warmth quickly penetrated the Beast's fuselage.

"Mind opening that hatch, Ben?"

While he jumped up to figure that out, I went through an abbreviated post-flight checklist. I left the plane at an angle that would allow for a fast departure, since there was better than a fifty percent chance this expedition would not end well. I couldn't predict exactly where it could go sideways, aside from the obvious presence of greed, but given the mix of volatile personalities and sordid history, calamity wasn't exactly out of the question.

By the time we deplaned, a shuttle from the Chub Cay Marina Club was there waiting for us. The driver, a middle-aged man with deep black skin, had one of the most welcoming smiles I'd ever seen and had come equipped with a jug of red liquid, a cooler of ice, and plastic cups stamped with the club's logo.

"Welcome to Chub Cay," he said. The Bahamian lilt of his voice was like a tonic, and the taste of rum punch softened the edge of what had been a long and complicated day. He checked our passports, stamped them, and as the three of us climbed into the open golf cart, Heather leaned close to me.

"Reminds me of when we went to Harbour Island." Her smile was suggestive, and—based on the recollection of our spending more time inside the suite at Pink Sands rather than on the beach—I knew exactly what she was intimating.

Focus, Buck.

The ride to the resort took all of ten minutes, and the driver took us straight to the ship. Gunner and Randy stood on the ship's deck, and Jack was waiting on the dock. He was dressed in black shorts and t-shirt, tattoos resplendent on his arms. A cocky smile was on his lips, and he wore sunglasses even though the sun was almost entirely down. I tipped the driver a twenty-dollar bill, and he puttered away in the electric vehicle.

"Welcome to the Bahamas," Jack said. He gave Heather a peck on the cheek and Ben a high five. "Glad you came, Buck."

"I suggest we get down to business. The longer we're here, the more questions people will ask, and sooner or later, somebody official will want to know what we're doing," I said.

"Couldn't agree more," Jack said. "Let's go on board."

"Hey guys?" Ben said. "I'm going to head over to the bar and check this place out. You mind?"

So much for my brother being interested in the finer details of the planning effort. His investment had bought him an expensive vacation, which was fine with me, as I didn't want all of them looking over my shoulder and questioning my every move.

"Don't talk to any strangers," I said, "and if asked, you're just visiting and don't know anything about this boat or what we're doing."

Jack frowned, then turned toward the ship. "Randy?"

The mercenary stepped forward to the rail. "Yes, sir?"

"Go have a beer with Ben. Discourage inquiries," he said.

"I don't need a babysitter, Jack," Ben said.

"Just taking all precautions."

"Lead the way," Heather said.

Jack walked up the gangway followed by Heather, and me bringing up the rear. I looked down as I walked, given the incline, but couldn't keep my eyes off Heather's black high heels and tight Hermès stretch pants. Once on board, I glanced to the stern and saw a significant hydraulic lift with a twenty-six-foot ASIS rigid inflatable boat, equipped with twin 150 HP engines, all set for diving next to it. Perfect for how I imagined we'd conduct the search. However, behind them on the stern were two large deployable mailboxes.

Mailboxes—twin four-foot-wide tubes curved at ninety-degree angles—are operated by placing one end in front of the props and the other straight down toward the area of interest. Once the engines are turned on, all that thrust blasts through the mailboxes, delivered downward with great force, blasting a hole in the ocean floor.

The problem with mailboxes is they're only used by treasure hunters. It's a red flag to the authorities, which could be a problem.

Inside, the ship's salon was sparse and dated. There was a wood table fixed in the middle of the room and long gray vinyl bench seats on each side, with blue Formica cabinetry on both bulkheads. Not fancy, but it was air-conditioned and spacious, with lots of windows.

"Not exactly luxurious," Heather said. "But it looks just like it did in the pictures you sent me."

"We'll do the work, Heather," Jack said. "Maybe you should sit at the pool while we're out on the water."

His statement produced an instant frown on Heather's face.

"Good idea," Gunner said.

"Bad idea," I said. "Heather is recognized worldwide, and it wouldn't take more than a very quick internet search to connect her with you, and a slightly longer one to connect her with me. Sorry, guys, but Heather wanted to be on the expedition, and you invited her, so she stays on the ship with the rest of us."

She pursed her lips, but I could tell she had something she wanted to say to Jack.

On the table was a stack of nautical charts, and the one on top was of Andros and the Berry Islands, which Chub Cay was a part of. "We're here." I stabbed my finger on Chub Cay. "And on the other side of the Tongue of the Ocean, which I mentioned before is commonly referred to as TOTO, is North Andros." I slid my finger across the chart. "Roughly fourteen miles southwest to where we'll be searching."

"Long commute in that dive boat," Gunner said.

"Fortunately, I got some good news when we landed." Everyone turned to face me. "I asked Ray to research any insurance claims on missing vessels in the vicinity. He sent me a text listing three such claims, one of which was last seen here in TOTO's northern passage." I dropped my index finger onto what looked like a rhinoceros horn at the northwestern point of TOTO, between Chub Cay and North Andros. "He's made contact with the vessel's insurance company—it was a sixty-foot Beneteau sailboat called *Duckbill Charlie* that vanished in a tropical storm a couple months ago—and told them Last Resort Charter and Salvage was operating in the area and would search for it on the come if they sent us a letter of authorization to do so."

Gunner laughed out loud. "You make a good pirate, Reilly."

"They agreed, and we should have a letter tomorrow. Ray will file the paperwork with the Bahamian government on behalf of the insurance company, then we'll be able to pick up a local permit and have a cover to be out in TOTO."

"Nicely done," Jack said.

Heather beamed at me.

"We can head out in the morning," I said. "The papers should arrive by the time we're in position."

"Can we go get dinner now?" Heather said. "I'm famished."

Jack pressed his lips tight. He checked his watch. "I've ordered a seafood feast from the restaurant; it'll be here in an hour. Like Buck said, we need to keep a low profile."

She exhaled loudly, and I saw Jack's jaw clench. Maybe she hadn't been exaggerating when she said their relationship had run its course.

"Fine," she said. "Gunner, would you mind grabbing my luggage on the dock?" Then to Jack. "Where's my stateroom?"

Both Gunner and Jack rolled their eyes. "Staterooms would be an exaggeration," Jack said.

"On the website it said there were four—"

"Cabins," Jack said. "Each with a pair of bunks, but they're cramped and have limited storage."

Heather's face began to turn red. "I want my own space,

Jack."

He grimaced. The tension between them was thick as Bahamian conch chowder.

"Hey, Gunner, I'll give you a hand with that luggage," I said.

We stepped toward the door. I followed after him and heard Heather's next statement as I got outside: "I expect the largest room, Jack."

Now I did laugh out loud. To my surprise, Gunner looked back at me, grinning. "She's a beauty, but a serious ball buster," he said. "Dodson did you a favor, Reilly."

"No good deed goes unpunished."

His hoot of laughter made me cringe. My plan to subtly sow discord between my "partners," whether to ensure my survival or as a form of revenge, was as important to me as finding the *Farnese*.

Paybacks are hell.

29

MORNING CAME EARLY, ESPECIALLY FOR BEN, Gunner, and Randy, who'd closed down the bar last night. From my bunk, I heard them stumble in at 1:30 a.m. So much for keeping a low profile.

All but Randy and I were still asleep when we departed the marina at sunrise. I helped cast off lines while Randy ran the ship from the pilothouse. Given the ship's size, we'd been tied up at the mouth of the marina, so it was a straight shot out to open water. Nothing from the insurance company yet, but we could reposition the ship to the western side of TOTO, anchor up, and do some exploring on the dive boat while we waited.

It wasn't long after we got underway before everyone emerged from their cabins. Ben and I shared one, as did Gunner and Randy, and Jack and Heather each had their own. That was curious. Was it due to the bunks, or was it another indicator of their declining relationship? Ben and Heather made breakfast while Randy and Gunner navigated the ship to the coordinates I'd given them. Jack and I took inventory of all the equipment.

On the stern was a gear locker full of masks, fins, snorkels, spearguns, and scuba tanks. Adjacent to that was a compressor room that had a Max-Air 90 gasoline operated compressor with pre-mixed nitrox tanks of decanted gas stamped with "32%," indicating the mixture, along with a tub of water to keep the freshly pressurized tanks cool. I inspected the compressor's intake, which was through a vent on the starboard side of the ship. The exhaust went up to the ceiling, across, and exited on the port side, all best practices to ensure that we were breathing clean air.

Another closet contained handheld underwater magnetometers, a couple of metal detectors, and two underwater scooters.

"We also have side-scan sonar and a Zodiac twelve-person dinghy," Jack said.

"Bill did us right," I said.

The sun was bright, and there were very few clouds overhead. Wind was light, and it was a perfect January day for diving. There were choppy three-foot seas in TOTO, but the big ship cut through without bother.

"I haven't even looked—what's the name of this ship?" I said.

"*Global Explorer,*" Jack said.

"Lofty, but perfect." I checked my phone again and found a new text from Ray. I showed Jack. "He says he emailed me the authorization from the insurance company, along with the salvage request required for Bahamian waters. Once we fill out the forms and send them back, he'll send a copy to the insurance company, which will then confirm our request to the Bahamian authorities."

"You want to fill them out?" Jack said.

"This is your party, Jack. Whatever name you have the boat rented under should be used on the forms."

"True. SCG International it is." He then smiled. "Second Chance Gold seems more fitting than Last Resort anyway."

"Both sound like they need redemption." I sent him Ray's link, and he headed for the bridge to get that done.

Left alone, I took in the myriad hues of blue and green for a moment before shifting back to the task at hand. The *Griffon's* log had referenced "where the water turned to indigo," and based on the other clues I'd found, I was pretty certain they were referring to TOTO. Problem was that depending on how far from shore they'd scuttled the *Farnese* or what the currents were doing at the time, it could have sunk to a final resting place in up to six thousand feet of water. If that was the case, this whole deceitful endeavor would have been a waste, unless Jack had access to a deep-water submersible in his arsenal.

Andros was visible in the distance as we closed in. I'd instructed Randy to find anchorage close to Nicholls Town on its northeastern side. It was pointless to try and conceal the *Global Explorer*, so better to hide in plain sight. Our paperwork from the insurance company would buy us some time, and if we found anything, we'd figure it out then. "Another fine mess, Buck." My whisper was lost on the breeze.

Back in the salon, a breakfast buffet had been laid out. I filled a plate and took the three steps up to the bridge. We were approaching the western edge of TOTO, where the shelf would rise steeply to shallower waters. The Joulter Cays were dead ahead, but I hadn't shared my theory that the wreck was closer to there.

"Based on everything we've found so far, I believe the *Farnese* was sunk somewhere here around northern Andros." I pointed to the northernmost point of the hundred-mile-long island to our south.

Gunner rubbed his hands together. "Let's get to it."

"I sent you back the paperwork, Buck," Jack said.

I took out my phone and forwarded his email to Ray with instructions to push the insurance company as fast as possible.

"We'll use the dive boat to search around so we can leave the ship closer to Nicholls Town. We can't appear too mysterious or we'll draw attention," I said. "Jack can go to shore and present the authorities with the paperwork."

Jack nodded and stood taller. Being "in charge" appealed to his ego, and staying under the radar appealed to my desire for invisibility. If this went south, I wanted no paper trail leading back to me. Jack's thirst for attention and willingness to use SCG

International suited my interests perfectly.

Once anchored close to Nicholls Town, we set about lowering the dive boat into the water using the winch. Fittings that connected to straps had been installed on the dive boat, which was now suspended by a cradle that Randy lowered carefully into the water. Given his naval experience, he'd be handy—up until the point he was instructed to do me harm. I'd keep him close and study his mannerisms.

Next, we dropped the Zodiac in the water. Jack and Ben used it to head ashore to find the Bahamas Disaster Reconstruction Authority, which oversaw cleanup contracts after Hurricane Dorian a couple years ago. Heather appeared on deck in a tiny orange bikini that left little to the imagination. Gunner's jaw fell open, and memories swirled through my head of happier times, but I tempered those with the recollection of the endgame to our relationship, not to mention finding her with Ben in Middleburg just days ago. I couldn't afford to let my guard down.

"I say we go for a ride in the dive boat," I said.

"I'm in," Heather said.

"Good idea," Gunner said. "Should we bring any gear?"

"Just snorkeling gear for now."

With that, I climbed aboard, loaded the RIB with gear, helped Heather in, then manned the helm. Gunner climbed on the bow. He carried a go bag, which no doubt contained a gun. The Yamaha engines fired right up. Gunner cast us off, and I began a gradual approach toward the shallower water just north of Nicholls Town. The depth decreased quickly as we moved west of TOTO.

"The water's so clear!" Heather said.

The depth gauge read 55 feet, but we could see coral heads clearly below us. All the reports had been accurate: with no cruise ships and reduced tourism traffic due to the pandemic, the turbidity was vastly less than what we'd grown accustomed to over the past decades. A year of regeneration had been a blessing for the atmosphere, oceans, and sea life, which was some measure of silver lining for the hell mankind had endured.

Heather was reclined on the bow of the twenty-six-foot boat, her head tilted back, her already bronzed body soaking up the rays. What would our lives have been like had e-Antiquity not tanked? With a shake of my head, I redirected that line of thought and took a surreptitious glance at the burner phone I'd bought in Vero Beach. There was a text from a number I didn't recognize. "More info on JB." Jean Bart? Had to be from Scarlet on a burner phone. "Crude map with X to east of L and J Cays, like you thought. Be safe. Bill Black" Long and Joulter Cays. *Confirmed.*

I pressed my lips together to stifle a smile. Then I had an idea. "I need to get the Beast over here. San Andros Airport is just south of Nicholls Town. Given the water clarity, I can survey the area from the sky."

"Good idea," Gunner said. "I'll fly with you."

"Okay, I'll need a spotter." I paused. "In fact, since we're all here and working together, I'm going to have Ray Floyd bring Betty over, too. We can cover a lot of territory at low altitude and search for anomalies." I saw Gunner frown. "He's my partner, so he'll be compensated from my cut."

His frown curved upward. "Sounds like a good idea then," he said. "You're full of them, Reilly."

Heather sat up and turned around to face us standing at the helm. "How will we find anything out here? It's endless."

"No guarantee we will," I said. "But in Captain d'Aire's log-book, which was confirmed in testimony from Jean Bart—that was his navigator, the guy who was guiding the *Farnese*—there was some good description of them sinking the ship around North Andros."

"They *intentionally* sank it?" she said. "Did anybody get killed?

"The captain and most of the crew, I assume. Captain d'Aire and Jean Bart knew it carried immense treasure and intended to return to salvage it later, but then Jean Bart killed d'Aire for planning to return without him."

"Can't ever trust a thief," Gunner said.

Heather's face betrayed no reaction. "I'd like to see the documents you're talking about," she said. "It sounds fascinating."

"Sure, we can look at them when we're back on the boat."

Once we were in shallow, flat water, I pushed the throttles down to see how the RIB would handle. She was pretty light and had a shallow keel, so she bounced and slid on a light chop. We continued north toward Long Cay and the Joulter Cays. Both island systems had been declared national parks years before, so aside from the occasional flats fisherman working the low tide between the islands, there was no sign of humanity on or around the islands. Perfect.

Just before Joulter, I turned the RIB out toward TOTO and slowed once we arrived at the darker water. I checked the depth gauge here. Over the course of a couple of hundred yards, it went from 60 feet to 200 feet, then kept dropping.

"The water is a beautiful deep blue here," Heather said.

"Indigo, in fact," I said.

30

AFTER JACK AND BEN RETURNED WITH A STAMPED SALVAGE PERMIT for the missing sailboat, we pulled anchor to return to Chub Cay so I could get the Beast and relocate her to Andros.

"You should have seen Jack lie through his teeth," Ben said. "It was a thing of beauty." He held his palm up and Jack slapped him a high five.

"You did pretty well yourself—that part about recovering the family's last remains was perfect," Jack said.

It was strange to see these two so close. Ben had hated Jack when we were teenagers and told me repeatedly what a scumbag he was. When did they reconcile all of that? Had Heather intervened? She and Ben had never been close when we were married; in fact, I'm not sure they ever saw each other again after our impromptu ceremony on Peter Island in the British Virgin Islands. Finding them together in Middleburg had been astonishing. It made me realize how little I really knew any of them anymore.

Time to light a few brush fires.

"How are Laurie and the kids, Jack?"

Heather rolled her eyes as Jack's smile faded. "She's good. Dating someone seriously—so Jack Jr. tells me. He's a teenager now. Can't believe it. And Debbie's eleven. They all still live in my old place in Great Falls."

Then to Heather, "Do you see them much?"

"Me?" Her eyes went wide. "Never. Jack likes to keep things separate."

I spotted Jack's lip curl. "Just trying to keep the peace."

"You said they blamed me for your divorce and hated me," she said.

"They are pretty spoiled," Ben said.

Now my eyebrows shot up. "You see them?"

"Jack brings them out to the farm sometimes. Young Jack likes to fish, and Debbie wants a pony—"

"No horses," Jack said.

Heather rolled her eyes again and silently mouthed the words, "No horses."

"I didn't realize you were all so close. Guess I've been out of the loop for a long time. Where do you live now?" I honestly didn't know.

"I have a penthouse condo in DC," Jack said.

"I still have my co-op in the West Village," Heather said. "It's so convenient for my work I can't give it up."

"All you do is work," Jack said.

I bit my tongue. The dynamics were way different than what I'd expected, and the tension was palpable.

"I get to DC every month." Her voice took on an edge.

"Or quarter," he said.

"That's why when I want pussy, I pay for it," Gunner said.

Jack laughed, and even Ben cracked a smile.

"You're all disgusting," Heather said.

After I shared what Gunner and I had discussed about Ray flying Betty over to help us search, I stepped outside onto the bow of the ship and called him.

"Everything work out with the permit?" Ray said.

"Like a charm," I said. "Nice job. We're headed back over to get the Beast and reposition her to North Andros." Nobody else had come out to the bow, so I filled Ray in on everyone who was here. He knew all the history but was surprised to hear that Ben and Jack were friends.

"Me too. Something weird about it I haven't figured out yet," I said. "Anyway, it'll be better for you and Betty to stay down in Congo Town. If things go bad here, no need for both planes to be in jeopardy."

"That's where the Mallard is anyway."

"I need you to spend some time helping us scan the waters for signs of wreckage, though. That was the story I sold them on to get you here."

"You make it sound like you're there against your will," he said.

Since I'd put him in danger so many times in the past, Ray was always probing for trouble, so I hedged. "If it weren't for Gunner forcing me, there's no way I'd be here, but after finding all the clues that could lead to the *Farnese*, I figured you had a point. No sense in leaving it for these jackals."

"Nothing's worth getting killed over, Buck."

The bow of the *Global Explorer* rose rhythmically with the waves as Randy steered us on a straight line toward Chub Cay Club Marina, which was now visible on the horizon. I had no intention of getting killed, but as I'd said to Ray, there was something odd about the group's dynamics that I needed to get to the bottom of. Jack said Ben had invested capital but hadn't explained how they reconnected. He and Heather were clearly on the outs, so her presence made no sense. I had a plan to get the answers, though.

"You won't be able to miss our ship, the *Global Explorer*. It's the biggest one around. Once you're here, we can discuss what we'll do next."

We disconnected. I stayed on the bow and watched Chub Cay grow larger on the horizon. I sensed someone next to me and found Ben.

"Beautiful out here, isn't it?" I said.

"Unbelievable. Thanks for coming and bringing me along," he said.

A dry laugh parted my lips. "You were coming with or without me, right?"

"Better with you—hey, look!" Porpoises were jumping in the wake of the *Global Explorer*'s bow. "There's three—no, four of them!"

It may have been the most joy I'd ever seen on my brother's face, which, under different circumstances, may have made me happy. I glanced up to the bridge and didn't see anybody watching us.

"Tell me something," I said. "When did you and Jack get so friendly?"

Ben's face twisted into what I read as an exaggerated expression. "Gee, long time ago, I guess. You were gone, we rarely spoke, and Jack was freshly divorced. He lived with me until he got his place in DC."

It still didn't add up. "When I left for Key West, I seem to recall you telling me how much you hated him."

He pursed his lips. "Hate's a strong word, Buck. Let's face it, Jack's an asshole, but we've been friends our entire lives, so, you know."

"No, I don't know, that's why I'm asking."

He scowled. "Relax, man. Look around. We're in paradise, treasure hunting on a freaking yacht." He looked over his shoulder. "I'm going to grab a beer. You want one?"

I shook my head in the negative. "Nah, I've got to fly. Thanks."

With that, Ben turned and walked away. My bullshit meter was now pinging on the red line.

"What the hell's going on here?" My words were lost on the breeze.

DESPITE HEATHER'S SUGGESTION TO HAVE DINNER
at the Chub Cay Club, Gunner and I jumped off at the marina
and Randy backed the *Global Explorer* out of the mouth again
while we waited for the steward to take us to the airport.

"Kind of a weird vibe on the ship," I said.

"What do you mean?" Gunner said.

"Heather and Jack are at each other's throats. Why is she
even here?"

Gunner laughed. "We had no choice."

"What's that supposed to mean?"

He shrugged as the clunking sound of the golf cart preceded it
appearing from around a boat on a trailer. "Means she was
coming whether Jack wanted her to or not." He must have seen
the confusion on my face, because he flashed a reptilian smile.
"She's financed most of the trip, Reilly. Jack's pissed away a lot of
the money he stole from your company. That's why he's so
anxious to make this happen."

"Heather? Are you serious?"

We climbed aboard the golf cart. "You have any idea how
much money supermodels make? Shit," he said. "Who needs
treasure when you got that?"

"The plane? The boat?"

"Jack paid for the deposit, but she'll have to pay for the rest,
and she covered the plane to France." He shook his head. "And
she made us promise nothing would happen to you."

Really? I felt my mouth hanging open and snapped it shut.
Maybe that explained why she had demanded the larger cabin on

the boat.

"What about Ben?"

Gunner laughed. "Where do you think Jack got the deposit money from? That and all our pocket money."

The airport was up ahead. The golf cart rumbled along the potholed road as my mind reeled from epiphanies brought on by Gunner's revelations. Brown scrub covered the ground in the wooded areas, with pine and palm trees sprouting up haphazard-ly. There was a Beechcraft Baron tied down next to the Beast, and the contrast in their ages was remarkable.

"So how did Ben and Jack get on moneylending terms?"

Gunner grumbled. "Enough with the questions, Reilly."

"It's my brother, ex-wife, and my former business partner. I feel like I'm two steps behind on the details."

"More like a mile, trust me."

The golf cart pulled up next to the plane. My mind spun—it was a lot to digest. I did my pre-flight check but couldn't get my mind off what was going on here. We climbed aboard, and I finished the prep and lit out down the Chub Cay runway. We saw the *Global Explorer* a couple of miles offshore headed back toward Andros, and within minutes, I began the landing proce-dure and announced my descent to North Andros Airport.

The more I learned about the situation, the more shocking it was. Jack was broke, and Heather and Ben were funding all the expenses. I still didn't fully get Ben and Jack's connection, but the rest of the story was gradually coming into focus. Time to divide and conquer. Gunner had given me some matches … now I just had to figure out when to light them.

31

THE NEXT DAY BEGAN AS AN OPERATION SHOULD:
with a planning session around the breakfast table. We studied
the charts, and I marked locations around North Andros where
I'd told everyone the *Farnese* may have been scuttled. I intentionally kept the search area just below the Joulter Cays.

"Weren't you going to show me the *Griffon*'s logbook?"
Heather said.

"Oh yeah, sure." I pulled out the pages from the log we'd
printed back in Vero Beach and laid them on the table. "They're
all in Old French, so not easy to—"

"*Mais bien sûr, mon cher,*" Heather said.

I swallowed and hoped her conversational Parisian wouldn't
let her to decipher the nuances I'd spotted.

"The writing in the log was faint due to its age, but we dark-
ened it up when we printed it," Jack said.

Heather scanned the pages without comment. She stopped at
the page that first mentioned the Bahamas. I cleared my throat.

"D'Aire wrote that Jean Bart relocated the *Farnese* to the '*nord-
est*' part of Andros and sank it where the water turned to indigo,"
I said.

She read and reread that page a few times, pulling it closer to
her face. "I think it says something else," she said.

"What do you think it says?" Jack said and looked at me.

"I read '*les isles au nord-est d'Andros*' as islands to the northeast
of Andros, not around the northeast of Andros," she said.

"Keep reading," Jack said. Now Gunner turned to look at me.

"'*Où l'eau se transforme en indigo.*' Which is 'where the water turns to indigo.'"

"That's what I said," I said.

Jack's face showed no emotion. "All of TOTO is indigo. You said northeast of Andros, not *islands* northeast of Andros."

"Let me see that." I took the page from Heather and studied it closely. "French is more complicated than English." I pointed to the words '*au nord-est d'Andros*' and said, "Okay, you could be right. That may mean 'to' the northeast."

Heather nodded her head. "*Du nord-est* only a one letter difference. Easy mistake to make."

Jack's eyes narrowed. "Yeah, but the difference between 'around' or 'to' is pretty crucial when looking for a needle in a haystack."

"And what could 'the islands northeast of Andros' be?" she said.

I pointed to the Joulter Cays. "These are the next islands up."

"Again, big difference," Jack said.

Roll with the punches. I pointed back to the chart. "Good, so we can ignore this area here and concentrate a little further northeast."

Jack nodded his head. "Good idea."

Gunner studied my face, but with his blue reflective sunglasses on, I couldn't see his eyes. I held mine steady, then checked my watch. "Here's what I suggest. I take the Beast up and do some low-altitude reconnaissance, but not so much as to attract attention."

"I'll go with you," Gunner said.

"And you guys take the boat out with the magnetometers and side-scan sonar and start cruising the area, noting hits."

"How will we know if we find anything?" Ben said.

"Just mark locations on your GPS where you get hits on the magnetometer or sonar. We'll do the same from the air if we see any anomalies of merit. Then we can go diving later today or tomorrow if anything looks promising," I said. "This could take days if we're lucky, weeks or years if we're not. But given that we're doing this under the radar, we need to be lucky."

Ben rubbed his hands together. "Let's get the show on the road."

Gunner pointed to Randy. "You stay on the ship and let us know if anybody comes snooping around."

"Ben, we need you to run us to shore down near the airport in the Zodiac," I said.

With copies of the charts and the *Griffon*'s logbook, we set off toward shore. I had to show Ben how to drive the Zodiac so he could make it back to the boat.

"I can't believe I've never come down here before," he said. "It's so beautiful."

"If we get busted with salvaged treasure, you'll have years to enjoy it from inside a cell."

His smile faded.

I had the Zodiac's 50 HP motor maxed out, and we skipped across the small swells as we headed toward shore. The taste of salt in the air, the bright sunlight, and growing heat made me smile. Company aside, and second only to flying, being on the water on any kind of boat was one of my favorite things to do. I lived on an island but didn't own a boat, so I didn't get out that often unless invited by friends. My mind drifted for a moment to what kind of boat I could buy if we found the *Farnese* and recovered the treasure.

Don't go there, Buck. One thing I'd learned long ago was to not count your money before making it. Dreaming is a distraction, and focus calls for action.

Ben dropped us off at Majestic Point, and I pointed him back toward the *Global Explorer.* Gunner and I then walked almost a mile to Queen's Highway. San Andros Airport consisted of a single asphalt runway, a small one-story blue metal building for a terminal, and a large hanger in the same color. Inside was a snack bar and a waiting area with white tile floors and bright red furniture. There was no fuel here, but the Beast's tanks were still over three-quarters full. Gunner had a Kalik at the bar while I completed the pre-flight check. Once I started the engines, he came back outside, guzzled his beer, and placed the empty bottle on a table. He climbed on board, closed the hatch, shimmied into the right seat, and let out a loud belch, fouling the air in the cockpit.

With no further delay, we taxied out to runway twelve. I announced our intent to depart over the radio and proceeded to do just that. We used half the five-thousand-foot runway and ascended heading southeast. Once over the water, I banked the Beast to the north and carved a slow course out over TOTO. We flew directly over the *Global Explore* at an altitude of five hundred feet and slowed our speed to just above stall speed at 70 knots.

"I'll run a north-south pattern starting at TOTO and work our way closer to the Joulter Cays and Andros," I said. "We'll make a couple water landings too, especially if you spot anything."

"Won't that arouse suspicion?" Gunner said. He was already peering out the vent window through a pair of binoculars.

"We'll say you're a student working on your seaplane rating."

Gunner nodded once and returned to his surveillance. I positioned the Beast so I could look out the port side vent window right where the shallow water dropped off into the indigo blue of TOTO for the first run north. I knew better than to think we'd see an intact three-hundred-year-old frigate just waiting for us: if anything, perhaps there'd be a few cannons piled together to create a detectable mass. The water was gin-clear, and the bottom was sandy with coral heads and patches of turtle grass that randomly diverted my attention.

"Nothing but deep-blue water over here," Gunner's voice sounded in my headset.

Long Cay and the Joulter Cays were now due west, their beige and green landforms rising just a few feet out of the white sandy shoal that encompassed the ocean bottom to their west. A number of deeper green creeks and channels cut through the shoal. A particularly deep channel between the islands had caused a delta to form to the east of Joulter that faded into a brilliant emerald as the seafloor dropped steadily toward TOTO, where it disappeared into oblivion. Puffy clouds cast shadows on the water's surface, which repeatedly tricked my eyes as I tried to assess the darker patches.

We continued along the route until we reached the apex of Toto's rhino-horn-shaped northwestern edge. I toggled the pedals to engage a slow arcing turn to the port side.

"Nothing so far," Gunner said.

"Just try to acclimate your vision to the contours, colors, and shapes," I said. "Once we're adjusted to that, it'll be easier to spot any irregularities."

I leveled the Beast off, descended to three hundred feet of altitude, checked by radar and visually for traffic, and continued our first southerly pass. Andros dominated the horizon ahead. As the *Griffon* and *Farnese* had beat their way north into the wind, their crews must have wanted to stop on land. Jean Bart could have detained or killed the captain of the *Farnese* to take control of the ship, or maybe he just perished in the storm, but something kept them from burying their treasure on land. What would that have been?

We flew for another hour in the grid pattern and noted four anomalies that may have been wrecks. We flew over Jack, Ben, and Heather in the RIB several times. We made one water landing in the middle, away from any of the four prospects we'd marked so as to not draw attention. Once we were back in the air flying north yet again, I flew close to the Joulter Cays and saw no manmade structures. The wind-beaten and water-washed island would easily flood during storms—that would have been pretty clear after the hurricane Captain d'Aire had endured, and that was probably one reason they'd decided not to bury anything there.

The thought of d'Aire led my mind to Jean Bart and their collusion to sink the *Farnese*. I glanced at Gunner. "No honor among thieves" was about as true today as it had been hundreds of years ago.

"I've been checked out of this group too long," I said. "I didn't realize Ben and Jack had gotten so close."

Gunner's grunt was clear in my headset. "Butt buddies, always fantasizing about finding treasure."

"How many years have they been hanging out?"

Gunner shook his head. "Ben was there when Jack got out of prison. Him and Heather, that is."

"That long ago?"

Gunner partially turned toward me with his lip curled up into a smile. "They didn't want you to know they were friends. Hell, your brother's a partner in SCG International."

My mouth fell open. Ben was a partner in Dodson's company?

Gunner laughed. "He was behind the scenes in Jamaica. They knew you'd be there, and he didn't want you to find out."

I shook my head. Why would they hide that from me? I would have been appalled—not that my approval changed anything—but what the hell was Ben thinking? And why wouldn't he talk to me about it? Could his jealousy over my previous success have been that all-consuming?

I was so distracted that I flew much further north than I'd

planned. I rocked us hard to starboard and carved a tighter turn until we were facing south.

"Blowing your mind, huh, Buck?" Gunner's smile cut me to the heart. They thought it funny how little I knew, no doubt. Living my life down on Key West, taking the occasional charter or salvage project, enough to keep fuel in my planes and pay rent at La Concha. Sure, I'd had run-ins with Gunner, and yeah, I knew he'd use any means necessary to get what he—they— wanted, but Ben had been a silent partner in that too? No wonder our relationship had been so distant since Mom and Dad died. He always blamed me for their deaths, thanks to Interpol's accusations, but I never realized he was behind the scenes competing against me on these other projects.

I once again realized I didn't know my brother at all, and for the first time, I really believed the chasm between us might be too wide to bridge.

"Another heap down there," Gunner said and stabbed the GPS button mounted to the instrument panel. That shook me from the funk.

"Couple more runs back and forth, then we better call it a day before anybody gets too curious," I said.

"Good, I have to take a leak anyway."

Since Gunner had been talkative, I did want to get a sense for one more thing. "And Heather's been partnered up with Jack and Ben all along, huh?"

He snorted. "That's a bit more complicated." He paused.

"Why's that?"

"She's not a partner in SCG, but she'd been involved off and on between all her big modeling jobs … when she and Jack were getting along. But this time, she's financing most of the expenses."

Something about that didn't make sense to me. "Seems like their relationship is pretty much toast, why would she jump in to finance him now?"

"Because she knew you'd be coming along, one way or another. She wanted in on the sure thing." He paused and looked back out the vent window. "Greedy bitch."

All of this information made it impossible for me to study the waters below, my mind reeling like a runaway slinky down a hill. It was all I could to keep the Beast aloft. Calling me a "sure thing" was wishful thinking at best.

"But she's right." Gunner shifted his large girth in the seat to face me. "We wouldn't have found shit without you in France, even with Scarlet's help. And now that we're here, my money's on you to find the *Farnese*."

I managed a thin smile. "Even a blind squirrel finds a nut now and then …"

Gunner roared with laughter. "Blind squirrel." More laughter. "That's rich, Reilly. It really is."

I shrugged. I wasn't kidding.

32

BACK ABOARD THE *GLOBAL EXPLORER*, I glanced back to be sure the Beast's anchors were holding. She appeared majestic, floating in the crystal blue waters. I'd decided to keep her close to the mothership to save the time running back and forth to town. There was no way to hide out here in the open, and since we had the permit to search for the sailboat, might as well take advantage of it.

Bikini-clad Heather was reclined in a chair on the aft deck, and I wasn't sure if her scowl was because I was blocking the sun or because she was angry.

"Next time I'm going with you," she said.

"Why, what happened?

"Those two clowns can barely operate a boat, much less use the equipment we rented to find anything."

I stared through the tinted glass beyond her into the salon and spotted Jack waving his arms as he spoke to Gunner. I turned back to Heather. "I might take the boat out in a while to dive on a couple of the spots we marked if you want to come."

Her lips turned up into a smile. "Absolutely, just say when."

Inside, Ben and Gunner sat on opposite sides of the table as Jack walked around them in a circle. "I'm telling you, we'll never find anything in that rubber boat—" He saw me, stopped his pacing, and pressed his lips together tightly.

"How'd you do?" I said.

Ben rolled his eyes and Jack shook his head. "Boy genius here dropped one of the magnetometers in twenty feet of water, then refused to dive down to get it—"

"I can't hold my breath that long!" Ben said.

"So I had to dive in, then he almost ran me over with the props when I was swimming back to the boat."

"I was trying to back the ladder up to you—"

"I can swim to the ladder, okay?"

Ben folded his arms and turned away. Gunner's shoulders shook slightly with suppressed laughter as he watched them argue.

"What about Heather?" My question was a rhetorical quarter turn of an invisible knife.

"Fucking useless," Jack said. "Aside from bossing us around."

Gunner perked up. "And writing checks."

Jack glanced from Gunner to me, then back. "Shut up, Gunner."

Too late, I felt like saying.

Gunner pretended to twist a key in his mouth, then puckered and tossed the imaginary key over his shoulder, which again stopped Jack in his tracks.

"How about you guys?" Jack said. "See anything while you were flying around up there?" Gunner nodded, then pulled the handheld GPS out of his pocket and laid it on the table. "We marked eight or ten anomalies."

"Eight, that's right."

Ben sat forward. "Anything look promising?"

"Too soon to say," I said. "From the sky, they're just dark spots. I'm going to go dive a couple shortly, though."

"Good. Take your brother," Jack said.

You mean your partner? "I told Heather I'd take her."

Jack gave two thumbs up. "Even better. We'll plot your marks on the chart when you're gone so we can review them all tonight."

I wrote down a couple of the GPS coordinates on a piece of paper and placed them in my pocket. Jack started bitching at Ben again for nearly backing over him in the boat as I stepped back out to the aft deck and closed the door. From the locker on the ship's starboard side, I removed two scuba tanks, buoyancy compensation devices, and regulators.

"Can you climb in the boat so I can hand you these tanks?" I said.

"Sure." Heather jumped up, climbed over the gunwale, and accepted the BCDs and regulators. She then took the first tank I handed her and stood it up on the far side gunwale and wrapped a bungee cord around it, locking it in place. Same with the second tank. She didn't seem useless to me.

"Good job," I said. A warm smile was her response.

There were already masks, snorkels, and fins on board. I grabbed a couple two-pound weights and flashlights and climbed aboard the smaller boat.

"Anything in that cooler?" I said.

"Water, beer, and some fruit," she said. "Where are we going?"

"Gunner and I saw a number of things to check, but odds are they're just patches of turtle grass."

"We need to check everything, right?"

I smiled and started the engines. Heather cast the lines off, and we moved slowly away from the *Global Explorer*, carved a wide turn, and headed north toward the Joulter Cays.

To the best of my recollection, Heather and I hadn't been alone together since she'd left me sitting at what had been our marital home in Great Falls, Virginia, just months before the creditors foreclosed on my life. The bitterness from her abandonment had been a blanket I'd clung to for years and was a major reason I hadn't had a serious relationship since. I remembered what she'd said on the flight over from the Bahamas: that she hadn't fallen out of love with me but hadn't been able to sit by and watch my self-deterioration. I could almost swallow that, but given what Gunner had told me, I had a sense there was more going on.

I pulled the coordinates out of my pocket. "You know how to use a GPS?"

She reached over to take it from my hand, her fingers brushing mine, and I held it tight for a second, prompting a smile from her before I let go. She stood next to me at the helm so she could enter the latitude and longitude into the Garmin GPS chart plotter fixed above the center console as I drove. Her long blonde hair blew in the wind and slapped at my shoulder as I accelerated the boat north. The small, shallow-hulled boat bounced in the seas, which pushed Heather closer to lean against me, each of us hanging a butt cheek on opposite sides of the narrow bench seat. The warmth of her skin and close proximity made my knees slightly rubbery.

The chart plotter illuminated the coordinates she'd entered, which was a mile due north. I kept my eyes on the horizon and my hands on the wheel without so much as a sideways glance toward Heather. But my skin tingled as she rubbed against me— a larger wave sent us airborne—

"Woo-hoo!" she shouted—then crashed into me, laughing.

I saw my smiling reflection in her blue Costa sunglasses. As the distance closed to our destination, I reminded myself that I wanted to prod Heather for details on their partnership, as well as chip away at the widening chasm between "the partners."

As we closed in, I reduced power. "Can you get the anchor ready?"

She sprang into action, grabbed the shank of the Danforth anchor, and glanced back toward me for the signal. When had she learned to do any of this? I placed the engines in neutral and hovered until I got a read on the current, then powered to the east of the dark area below us and swung the bow toward it.

"Go ahead and drop it there."

Heather swung the anchor out and then managed the line so it wouldn't tangle as it fed out over the bow. "How deep is it?" she said.

"Depth finder says 56 feet." I waited for the line to go taut and then slowly backed the boat away with the current. She pulled the line and it held, so I killed the engine. Silence immediately followed, broken only by the seabirds that were abundant around Joulter, which was the reason it had been made a national park. The sea was nearly flat here. The *Global Explorer* was a small dot on the southern horizon, which Heather nodded toward and smiled.

"I'm dying to get wet," she said.

She'd always enjoyed double entendres, and I could have played along, but ...

"Let's go diving, then." I pulled my t-shirt over my head, and her eyes were drawn to my abs. I was in better shape than I had been in years, and her hum of admiration gave me an inner smile.

With the tanks in the BCDs, weights in their pockets, the regulators attached, and the air turned on, I spit in my mask and rinsed it with saltwater. I lifted Heather's tank onto her back, then swung mine over my shoulder, sat on the gunwale, and pulled my fins and mask on. She did the same, and as she checked her air, I had a flashback of diving with her during our honeymoon on Peter Island. The memory was bittersweet, given all that had happened since, and up until a couple of days ago, I would have bet either of my planes that something like this would have never happened again.

I rolled backward—*splash*!

Her splash followed a few seconds later, and we came face-to-face, or mask-to-mask. I gave her the okay sign—which she repeated—then we held our inflator hoses up, released air, and began to descend. I changed my angle of attack and started kicking slowly downward, neutralizing the pressure in my ears every couple of feet.

The visibility was clear all the way to the bottom and for probably a hundred feet laterally. The current was mild, and a healthy-looking reef was below us. I saw sea fans billowing, a few nice sections of staghorn coral, a multitude of fish swirling around, and a large goliath grouper. Shipwrecks often turned into reefs if they held together long enough. Old eighteenth-century wooden frigates like the *Farnese* generally decomposed in less than a hundred years, depending on the waters they were in and the presence of woodworms in their hulls. That being the case, the larger telltale signs of old shipwrecks were usually piles of ballast stones, anchors, and cannons—none of which were evident on this coral head.

While it was a beautiful reef, it wasn't why we were here, so after swimming around it once with a metal detector that hadn't picked up anything of interest, I turned back toward Heather, who'd been following close behind me.

There was a massive hammerhead shark right behind her.

My eyes must have bugged wide in my mask, because she spun around, and once she saw it, she collided into me and wrapped her arms around my left bicep.

I swung the metal detector in front of the shark's face as it approached, causing it to take a hard right and accelerate away. I gave her the okay sign, but she didn't respond. Based on her steady stream of air bubbles, it was clear she was hyperventilating, so I wrapped my left arm around her and started a controlled ascent. We'd only been down for thirty minutes, so there was no need for a safety stop, but I had to keep pulling on her as she tried to surface too quickly, which could rupture her lungs. She looked around wildly around for the shark, but I kept my attention on her. Thanks to movies like *Jaws* and shows like *Shark Week*, sharks had been unfairly branded as dangerous, but in reality, they were just as afraid of humans as most people were of them.

We broke the surface, and Heather swam hard toward the boat twenty feet away. I didn't fight her but followed close behind. She was already trying to ditch her tank and gear before she even made it to the boat, so I helped swing it off her shoulder, wrapped my arm through its shoulder strap, then helped her onto the ladder. Her body, legs, and feet disappeared quickly as she jumped inside the boat.

With a blast of air into my BCD, I floated comfortably, and with one hand on the ladder, pulled my regulator out of my mouth. "You okay up there?"

She stood up and peered over, her eyes still wide.

"Can I hand you the tanks?" I said.

She reached her arms out to me, and I lifted hers first, which she grabbed, swung around, and dropped on the deck. When she looked down again, I handed her my tank. I pulled off my fins, pushed them on top of the transom, then climbed up the ladder. She was leaning against the back of the bench seat, shaking, with her arms wrapped across her chest. When I stepped onto the deck, she jumped into my arms sobbing.

"Hey, it's okay," I said. "We weren't in danger."

Her body shook, and her skin felt cool in my arms. I led her to the bow, where we could sit on the cooler. By the time she sat, she was shaking even worse—now with laughter.

"Did you see that monster! He was bigger than me! Holy shit!" I still had my arm around her waist, and she had her hand behind my neck, her face was alive with excitement. "Good Lord, I thought he'd inhale me."

"He was just curious," I said. The shake of her ribs under my palm as she laughed caused me to drop my hand to her waist. Her nervous laughter slowed, but she kept her eyes focused on mine, then leaned up suddenly and kissed me, gently.

I froze for a second. She pulled back, her eyes now unsure. A deep breath centered me on the moment and pushed painful memories into the recesses of my mind, and I allowed myself to look closely at her face, her tanned shoulders, her wet skin glistening in the sun, the rise of her nipples in the orange suit.

I lowered my lips to hers and stepped away from the darkness of our past. We held each other in a tight embrace as we kissed until she leaned her weight into me and we lay over onto our sides in the bow of the boat.

Her hands led the way to where we were going, but I followed along without protest. Soon her bikini and my suit were in a wad on the deck, and she had rolled me onto my back and flung a leg over me. My hand cupped her buttock as I helped her mount me. As she lowered herself, her back arched and she tilted her face up toward the sky. With her eyes half-lidded, she let out a moan.

"Buck …"

She moved rhythmically up and down as my hands pulled her closer. The sun was at an angle behind her that cast her in an orange glow as I tried to watch. My mind raced from the building sensation in my loins, to the recognition that we hadn't made love in years, to the recollection of how good our lovemaking had been—and still was.

She arched suddenly—a gasp sprung from her lips—which set loose a release inside me. I firmly held onto her hips, moving her slowly, as we were both nearly paralyzed in pleasure. She hung there for a few seconds, her face silhouetted from the sun, but as she lowered herself down onto my chest, her smile was one of satisfaction and joy. When our bodies pressed together again, it was sweat, not seawater, that was hot between us.

"I've thought about this for years." Her voice was a whisper in my neck.

Her words brought me back to earth.

Mine were still caught in my throat.

33

JACK WAS WAITING FOR US ON DECK when Heather and I returned. She tossed him the bowline, and he pulled us in closer. I felt no guilt or sense of revenge at what had happened out on the water. The triangle that Jack, Heather, and I had been embroiled in for years was more complicated than I had ever realized. Their history at Harvard, had I known about it, would have caused me to be far more cautious in the breakneck speed of the relationship, but Jack's and my continued counter-rotation around life kept drawing us together in adverse situations, even now—*especially now*—as partners.

There was no smile on Jack's face as I shut the boat down and as Heather gathered the scuba gear and passed it over the bow to him. "Find anything?" he said.

I waited for Heather to respond, curious what she'd say.

She lifted a tank off the ground and caught my eye as she turned to hand it up to Jack.

"We did a sixty-foot dive on a small reef and saw nothing but a massive hammerhead that scared me senseless." She averted her eyes. "I don't even recall getting out of the water."

I bit my tongue. She'd been affectionate on the ride back and talkative. It was clear that her relationship with Jack was all but over: it just hadn't been said yet. He, apparently, kept changing the subject whenever she broached the topic. Jack had given up his wife and children, whether *for* Heather or because of her I wasn't sure, but if what Gunner had said was true—that Jack was nearly broke and Heather had financed much of this trip—losing her might just be the final straw for Jack Dodson.

Hell, it had been for me.

"We have the GPS locations you and Gunner marked earlier plotted on the chart," Jack said. "We can study them tonight. Might be faster to fly in your plane to some of them."

That reminded me—I checked my ancient Rolex Submariner. "Ray's supposed to be here with Betty soon, so that'll expedite the hunt too."

Jack gave Heather a hand out of the boat, then turned his attention on me. Maybe it was a guilty conscience—which was a ridiculous notion—but I inadvertently diverted my eyes from his. I felt as if he knew or at least suspected something had happened between Heather and me. Or maybe he was just worried that she had told me she was the money behind the operation. Jack didn't offer me a hand as I crawled over the side of the dive boat and up the transom of the *Global Explorer.*

Inside the salon, Ben and Gunner greeted me as if they were expecting good news. Heather was nowhere in sight. "How'd it go?" Ben said.

"We only dove one location and it was just a big coral head."

"Heather looked rattled," Ben said. "Went down to her cabin."

"Must have been the ten-foot hammerhead that snuck up behind her. I scared it off with the metal detector."

A familiar noise sounded from the sky: the distant rumble of twin air-cooled inverted six-cylinder engines.

"Hear that?" I walked back out to the aft deck and avoided Jack's stare as I passed.

Ben and Gunner followed me out just in time to see Ray approach from the south. We watched as he circled the anchorage once, and I knew Ray would be assessing conditions, reviewing the spacing of all our craft, and checking the current and contrasting its direction with the wind to decide upon his ideal approach. He flew north past us, as far up as the Joulter Cays, banked to the west away from Nassau traffic, and descended toward the flat water gracefully—just like a duck on a northern stream, which was what the Widgeon was named after.

When Betty touched down, water splashed up, but his timing and approach had been perfect, so he cruised on the step toward our hodgepodge flotilla.

"That is so cool," Ben said. "I want to do a water landing."

"You'll get your chance," I said. "Ray will help us search tomorrow, and we need spotters on both planes."

My fists suddenly clenched, because it still gnawed at me how Ben had not only lied about being kidnapped but had never told me he was partners with Jack in SCG International. No, we hadn't been close for a decade, and yes, he blamed me for our parents being in Switzerland when they were victims of a hit-and-run killer. But I'd never had a clue he would go as far as he had to deceive and double-cross me.

Ray idled up to near where the Beast was anchored, but two wingspans in closer to shore so the planes wouldn't collide if an anchor came loose. "I'll go help Ray set the anchors and bring him aboard," I said.

Once in the Zodiac, I started the engine, cast off the bowline, and puttered slowly toward Betty. The nose hatch was open, and Ray had already tossed the forward anchor. Once the line was taut, he disappeared back inside and pulled the hatch closed after him. A few seconds later, the port side rear hatch popped open, and Ray dropped another anchor and held onto the rope until the blades had found purchase on the bottom.

"Ahoy there!" I said.

Ray waved once, but I knew him well enough to realize his mind was focused on the post-flight checklist etched into his brain. He caught the line I threw him and tied me off at the cleat inside the hatch before disappearing back inside the plane. He'd be in the cockpit making sure everything was turned off, tied down, locked in place, and closed off. I could have climbed aboard but decided to wait out in the Zodiac instead so I could admire Betty afloat in the shimmering Bahamian water.

"Looking good, Betty." I glanced back over my shoulder. "There are some bad men you know here, the ones who reassembled you to look like Frankenstein's bride before Ray made you beautiful again—"

"Who are you talking to?" Ray had appeared in the hatch.

"Just Betty."

He panned his attention from left to right. "Beautiful spot," he said. "How's it been going?"

"That's kind of a loaded question, Ray."

He held the loose line to the Zodiac, lifted his sunglasses, and squinted toward me. "Responses like that from you tend to make me nervous."

"It's all good—well—as good as it can be under the circumstances, but there's nothing to worry about." *Yet*, I added to myself.

"So give me a few pointers before I drop into the middle of the snake pit."

I took a deep breath to buy a moment. He crossed his arms. "Okay, well, I told you about my brother's fake kidnapping, right?"

Ray shook his head slowly. "No, you didn't mention that."

"Ahh, what about my ex-wife, Heather, being here?"

His head continued to shake from side to side. "Heather Drake? That's awkward. Aren't she and your former partner a thing?"

"Maybe not so much anymore, but Gunner confided to me—"

"Gunner is confiding in you now?"

I laughed. "Yeah, believe it or not, he's been the most cooperative of all of them. Well, at least until Heather and I hooked up after diving—"

Ray held up both palms. "Whoa, hooked up? As in had sex?"

"Like I said, it's complicated. Just follow my lead, don't ask any questions, and tomorrow you'll do some reconnaissance with my brother as a spotter and make a couple water landings, that's all."

His head shook more determinedly now. "That's fine for tomorrow, but I'm scheduled to go see that Mallard at 4:00 today."

"Better reschedule that, Ray. I need you to make a good impression here this afternoon, and it's already 3:15. Sunset is at 5:10, so there's no time for both—"

"But—"

"So hop aboard, and let's get you into the middle of the operation." I gave him an exaggerated smile. "The good news is I did find some great intel in France, so I believe we're in the right place."

Ray grumbled under his breath, and I knew better than to ask what he'd said. He'd criticized me in the past for not sharing all the facts, but I rationalized it was for his own good that I spared him the finer details.

With the hatch locked, we motored back to the *Global Explorer*. "Pretty impressive ship," he said.

"All the bells and whistles."

"Including a crazed mercenary, a lying brother, an ex-con partner, and an ex-wife," he said.

"Two mercenaries, actually. Didn't I mention Randy, our captain?"

Ray turned his back to me to face the ship. Our partners were all watching from the aft deck. Suffice it to say, it was one of the more eclectic teams I'd ever partnered with, but treasure hunting can make for strange bedfellows—literally.

I saw Ray's back rise and fall sharply as he took in and exhaled a deep breath.

Sorry, old pal.

34

"THE PLEASURE IS ALL MINE, I ASSURE YOU," Ray said. "I've followed your career since long before I knew Buck."

Heather bowed and smiled. "I wouldn't have guessed you for a connoisseur of women's fashion."

"More like a connoisseur of beautiful cover girls," I said.

Heather tilted her head back for a brief, bubbly smile that I could have sworn caused a line of drool to spill off Ray's chin.

"Gunner and Jack you've met," I said. "And this is my brother, Ben."

They shook hands. "I guess I have you to thank," Ray said.

"For what?"

"For buying Buck the Widgeon." Ray nodded toward Betty.

"Yeah, that was a while ago. Can't believe he still has it—or that it still flies. But I'm looking forward to landing on the water."

"Be careful what you wish for," Jack said.

Randy stepped up from the galley with a tray of cheese and sausages. Ben opened a bottle of Margaux and poured it into seven plastic wine glasses. Outside, the horizon looked like a California wildfire as the blazing orange sun hovered over the western horizon. The lights of Nicholls Town sparkled further south, and the ship's photocell-operated deck lights popped on as the shades of light shifted toward darkness. Anybody observing the scene would think they'd come upon a dignified setting on a private yacht, complete with a pair of classic flying boats and a couple of tenders.

How wrong they would be.

While the rest of us sat on the bench seats and sipped the ruby-red wine from the Bordeaux region of southwestern France, Jack stood over the table and pointed to each spot that Gunner and I had marked this morning.

"Buck and Ray can fly to these northernmost points here and here, land, and check them out."

Jack's effort to appear as if he were in charge made me smile. I caught Heather's elfin grin—she subtly rolled her eyes—I tried to bite my lip but laughed out loud.

"Something funny, Buck?" Jack said. He followed my glance to Heather's equally guilty expression, and he grimaced. "I'm glad you two think this is humorous."

"I didn't say anything," Heather said.

"Meanwhile, the rest of us will check these southerly spots in the dive boat," Jack said.

"I'll stay with Buck," Gunner said.

"I want to fly in the Widgeon," Ben said. "I bought the damn thing."

Heather made a scowl that only I could see. "That leaves me with Jack in the boat. When do I get to go flying?"

"You can come with me next time," Ray said. His grin was huge.

Shortly after that, Randy served a dinner of rice and fresh fish that he'd caught while we were out searching this morning. His role had become clear as the boat driver, chef, and backup muscle if needed. I hoped that latter skill was never required, especially since it would most likely be used against me. During dinner, Heather rubbed the front of my shin with her toes—I jerked my leg back, which caused her to bite her lip to stifle a giggle—which caught Jack's attention.

"You talking to yourself?" he said.

She ignored him and found my other leg with her toes. I

squirmed in my seat and realized that from where Randy was seated he could see everything happening under the table. Our eyes connected, and his were hard. I had no idea what he knew about my past with Heather, but based on his expression, he thought I was messing with the boss's woman. Heather glanced from me to him, shrugged, and left me alone after that. Another sign that she'd matured—in the past, she wouldn't have cared who saw her.

I knew it had been foolish to make love to her today. I was the first to stand up after dinner, and when I turned to face the table, Gunner, Ben, and Jack all stared at me like I was sleepwalking. Jack glanced toward Heather, who was still smiling at me. His jaw rippled.

Great.

As uncomfortable as it made me, it also helped to accomplish my goal of shoving a wedge into their partnership.

THE NEXT MORNING INCLUDED A QUICK breakfast, Jack reiterating the plan for the day, and the groups splitting up to go gather the gear required. Even though I was naturally critical of Jack, it was a logical plan. As strange as it was, I was glad to have Gunner as my spotter because he was more focused than the others. Nothing was more irritating or destructive to an archeological search than a lack of diligence, and our group was the least professional one I'd ever been a part of. I thought of reminding everyone that our cover story was that we were searching for a missing sailboat, but the group all broke and went in separate directions before I could.

We took off first in the Beast, followed by Ray and Ben in Betty. They followed us for the first ten minutes, then gradually made their way west as we followed the edge of TOTO up to the horn where we'd seen and marked the northeastern-most anomaly within the search area I felt best matched d'Aire's description. There was a little more wind and resulting chop this morning, which actually made it harder to see through the water but easier to land the Beast. I then taxied to the area where we'd spotted a dark mass yesterday.

"How are we going to do this?" Gunner said.

"Go back and get the anchor out of the storage locker, open the port hatch and drop it," I said. "We're in seventy feet of water, so make sure there's enough line out before you tie it off."

"What are you going to do?" Gunner said.

"I'm going to do the same through the bow hatch once you get out of my way," I said. "Unless you'd like to get on your knees and squeeze your ass through that tiny hatch."

Gunner grunted as he stood. He had to weigh a solid 275 pounds, was pushing fifty years old now, and was not in the best shape. If we had to hike a distance, I'd be concerned, but scuba diving was a great equalizer: everyone could achieve neutral buoyancy in the water, and with limited current, you didn't have to swim hard. But still, I wasn't sure how game he was to dive.

"Do you want to stay on board and watch the plane or dive with me?" I said.

"What, and let you have all the fun? No way. I'm going."

Fifteen minutes later, Gunner stepped out of the hatch with his gear on, and the water erupted. I lowered the ladder to make our return easier and, once I was sure he was out of the way, followed him into the translucent Bahamian water. Once my angle of attack was face down, I kicked toward the bottom but quickly recognized this was just another coral reef. Having discovered and dove on multiple wrecks around the world, I had developed a familiarity with what to expect, and there was nothing here aside from teeming fish, nice coral, and a bulky, healthy reef.

After a quick inspection, I pointed to the surface and didn't wait for Gunner to begin my ascent. His air bubbles billowed up around me as if I were in some kind of vertical hot tub with the jets on full. Once to the surface, I removed my tank, handed it to Gunner, then climbed up the ladder into the Beast. He handed me the gear and joined me inside the plane.

"That was a bust," he said.

"Process of elimination."

We dried off and stowed the gear. As I climbed into the left seat after closing the bow hatch, my radio crackled to life.

"Grumman one to Grumman two—you there, Buck?"

I clicked the mic. "Roger, Grumman one. What's up, Ray?"

"Dry hole over here. We're going to do more visual reconnaissance as we head back to base."

I checked my watch. It was 12:30. "Little early, isn't it?"

"Affirmative, Grumman two, but remember, I have meeting with possible Grumman three at 4:00, and I want to check into the hotel and shower first."

Treasure hunting or not, Ray wasn't giving up on that Mallard. "Roger, Grumman one. Let me know if you spot anything on the way in."

Gunner was studying a copy of the marked-up chart. "I'll cross this one off. What did your partner say about the one they checked?"

"Cross that off too."

Gunner pointed to another mark further south on the edge of TOTO. "Let's check this one next."

Even though it was nearly ten miles away, we took off, flew, re-landed, and re-anchored in twenty minutes. The winds had

picked up more, so the plane was a bit sporty on the waves. The
dive produced the same results as the last spot—just another coral
head. We didn't waste much air there, and by the time we had
stowed the gear again and climbed into the cockpit, I found a text
from Ray.

"We marked another spot, but you might want to check it on
the way back. Definitely looks like a boat." He provided me the
coordinates. It was on our way, only a mile south. Hardly worth
taking off, but it was getting close to sunset, so we did anyway and
kept the plane at two hundred feet of altitude. We were there in a
minute, and I circled the area, dipping the port wing so I could
see out.

"I see what he was talking about," I said. I circled around to
the starboard side now and dipped that wingtip. "Use the
binoculars and see if you can make out any detail."

Gunner lifted his blue sunglasses to the top of his head and
pressed the binoculars to his eyes. I circled twice. He lowered
them and looked at me, his face deadpan. "The good news is it's
a boat, but it's not the one we're looking for."

"How do you know?"

"It's a new-looking sailboat, that's how." He pushed his sunglasses back down to the bridge of his nose.

"Like maybe a sixty-foot Beneteau? With a blue hull?"

The corner of his lips lifted. "As a matter of fact, it just might
be."

As we headed back towards the *Global Explorer*, I spotted a
strange boat next to our ship. It was a cigarette type, maybe thirty
feet long, with a blue hull, twin inboards, and blue bimini top.
When we got closer, I saw three armed men talking to one of our
people on the deck of the *Global Explorer*.

"Trouble ahead," I said.

Gunner craned over the instrument panel to see, then sat
back heavily. "Is that a police boat?"

"Royal Bahamas Defense Force, or RBDF. It's the largest defense force in the Caribbean, and they patrol the waters here."

Gunner was silent and probably worried about the same thing I was. Who were they speaking with, and what had been said?

We landed. By the time I set the anchor, Heather had come aboard the Zodiac to pick us up. "What do they want?" I said.

"We showed them the permit from the government and the letter from the insurance company, but they were waiting for you to return."

"Do they know who I am?"

Heather smiled. "Don't be vain. They knew we had a plane and wanted to speak with the pilot."

The officials were tied up on the starboard side of the *Global Explorer,* so we pulled up to the port side. I climbed aboard without waiting for the others. Ben was speaking to the dark-skinned official, who, based on the number of stripes and insignias on his uniform, must have been in charge.

"Hello, officer," I said.

"Identification, please?" His island accent made "please" sound as if it had two syllables. I handed him my passport and the cruising permit for the Beast.

"My colleagues showed you our salvage permit and letter of authorization from the insurance company, right?" I said.

The man didn't reply. He compared the picture in my pass-port to my face. "You was a lot younger then."

"It doesn't expire for another year," I said.

Ben stepped closer to me. "He says that they don't like sal-vage hunters and that we're very close to the Joulter Cays National Park and Marine Sanctuary."

"Never seen a salvage operation use seaplanes," the officer said. "Have any luck?"

I smiled. "We actually have two planes. The other one is down on South Andros now." I paused. "No luck so far, just a few coral heads. We have a few more to check before we start searching the deeper waters of TOTO."

The officer laughed. "You got a deep-sea submersible on here?"

"No. I'm afraid if the missing ship sank in TOTO, we'll never find it."

"That be for sure." He handed me back my passport and cruising permit, along with a card. "You find anything, you call this number." He then glanced at Ben. "What he said was right: we don't like salvage hunters here. What sinks in the Bahamas becomes the property of the Bahamas, insurance company or not."

Ben's eyes were wide, but Jack, Gunner, and Heather held poker faces.

"Understood, sir. The boat has been underwater for some time now, so not likely worth raising, but the crew is missing, so part of our mission is to recover any remains, if possible," I said.

The officer nodded, panned his attention slowly around the circle of us, and said, "We're based out of Nassau, just across TOTO, so can be back in thirty minutes. We'll keep an eye on you via radar. Again, call if you find anything."

"Yes, sir," Jack said.

The officer climbed back aboard their vessel, the driver put the boat in gear, and once they were about ten feet off our starboard gunwale, he gunned it straight out into the deep water of TOTO. Probably wanted to get home before dark.

"Why didn't you tell him we may have found the boat?" Gunner said.

"You found it?" Jack said.

"Because they'll kick us out once we've found it. You heard the man: they won't want us to salvage it, and I made that up about remains to recover. There were no casualties when it sank."

"Ace in the hole?" Heather said.

"More like a 'get out of jail free' card," I said.

Jack grimaced. "Do me a favor—don't mention jail, okay?"

"Agreed," Gunner said. "Nobody's arresting me." He lifted his shirt enough so we could see a Glock tucked into his waistband.

As if the situation hadn't been complicated enough, we were now on the RBDF's radar. Literally.

35

THAT EVENING WE HAD THE CHARTS, copies of the *Griffon's* log, and all the notes from our trip to Brest spread out across the table. I read the passages aloud in French, and Heather translated them for the group. All the same things we'd read before. I paged forward to the end of the section from the logbook Roth had sent, which we'd only briefly reviewed at the house in Vero Beach.

On the last page, a short sentence jumped out at me that I hadn't noticed before: "*Trouve les canons, pas le bateau.*" It meant "find the cannons, not the boat." I guessed it was a reminder d'Aire and Jean Bart had left for themselves—it was also a critical clue these three hundred years later.

Had they dumped the treasure with the cannons and sent the boat on into deep water?

I glanced up. The others were all studying different details of our notes and the maps, except for Heather, who was watching me. Her eyes grew wide, no doubt recognizing my involuntary reaction to the sentence I'd just read. She narrowed her eyes—

My phone rang and I jumped. I saw the name on the screen.

"It's Ray." I stood and headed for the door out to the aft deck.

"Tell him to get his ass back here," Gunner said.

Once outside, I sat on a deck chair and pressed the phone to my ear. "Hey," I said.

"Buck, this plane is a steal!"

My mind was still on the sentence from the *Griffon*'s log. "Yeah, she looks good?"

"Needs fresh paint and some restoration, but they've kept her in reasonably good shape. I can get her flying in a couple days."

"That's nice, Ray." My voice was like an out-of-body experience, my brain elsewhere.

Heather walked out of the salon door onto the deck and stood over me. Ray was speaking, but I didn't hear what he said, because the look on Heather's face—pursed lips, narrowed eyes, and her foot tapping on the deck—told me something was wrong. Unfortunately, I had a pretty good idea what that might be.

"Are you okay with that?" Ray said. "Buck? Buck!"

"What, Ray? Sorry, I missed what you said."

"I said we can get the Mallard for $100,000. Are you okay with that?"

I sat forward to the edge of the seat. "Shit, Ray, we don't have that much money." I glanced up at Heather again and felt my face flush at the admission.

"We have a little over $30,000 in the company account. I can pull the rest of it together," he said. "Once I'm done fixing her up, she'll be worth a half-million, easy!"

Archeologists and treasure hunters are optimists by nature. Others would describe us as dreamers, and others still would call us fools. But nobody would ever spend the time and money on archeological exploration without visions of success. That being the case, I imagined us finding the *Farnese* and me not having to worry about Last Resort pissing away $100,000 on yet another antique aircraft.

Heather put her hands—now balled into fists—on her hips.

"Okay, Ray. Sounds good. Keep me posted." I hit the end button and looked up to Heather. "Why do you look like you have a bee in your bonnet?"

"That depends," she said.

"On what?"

"I saw the look on your face back there. We may have been apart for years, but we were married, Buck. I'll bet I know you better than anyone else in the world."

I sat back and crossed my arms. "Yeah, so?"

"So I just read that last page of the log. You know, the page you were looking at when your face lit up? Must have been that last sentence, right?"

Crap. "Oh, yeah. I read that just before Ray called. I didn't get to—"

"Bullshit." She stepped closer, then put her bare foot on top of my bare foot. "You weren't going to tell anyone. I saw it on your face."

"That's not—" I drew in a deep breath and glanced down at my foot covered by hers. She started to rub it slowly over the top of mine. "What if I was still processing the information?" I said.

"I'll keep it to myself, provided you meet me out here on the deck at midnight," she said. She pumped her eyebrows.

"If Jack catches us—"

"Hang on, big boy. I meant meet me to discuss our options."

"Oh."

She pressed down on her foot. "*Then* we'll have sex."

BEN'S SNORE SOUNDED LIKE A CAT PURRING. He never budged as I crawled out of my lower bunk, pulled the covers up, and wrapped them around my pillow in case anybody checked, then pushed the hatch door slowly open. I'd checked it earlier and it didn't creak, so I'd left it cracked slightly to facilitate my late-night exit. Once in the corridor, I saw the other doors were closed, so I walked quietly up the stairs into the salon. I was in only a pair of shorts, and the night air gave me goose bumps.

Outside, a million stars shone in the sky as if I were flying over a city and looking down. A sliver moon was near the horizon, curved upward into a smile. I should come outside every night just to see—

"Psst!"

The sound came from the port side. I walked around the corner to the walkway that led to the bridge. Heather was walking away, twenty feet in front of me. She passed the hatch to the helm and continued on to the bow. She was wearing a t-shirt with no pants and moved like a leopardess, with soft, confident steps. When she got to the end of the walkway, she disappeared around the superstructure and onto the bow. The staterooms had windows, all closed and normally covered with blinds, but I couldn't be sure, because the glass was so heavily tinted on the outside that you couldn't see through them.

At the end of the superstructure, I stopped cold.

Heather was there, reclined on the deck on a blanket with a bottle of wine and a lone candle burning. She saw me, smiled, raised her index finger toward the sky, and beckoned me. My feet were suddenly numb, and the chill I'd felt was replaced with a hot flash.

"Nice setup." My whisper was lost in the breeze.

I sat down slowly and curled my legs forward, Indian style. She handed me a glass of wine, raised her own, and we gently touched them together.

"Cheers," I said.

"*Ta santé.*" Her reply, to my health, was in French.

A few minutes of small talk about the stars, the water at night, the moon—the sliver being her favorite phase, and mine too—

she got down to business.

"Find the cannons, not the boat." Her blue eyes were black and reflected the moon. "Sounds like a pretty important clue to me."

I sipped my wine. I wasn't sure whether Heather was playing me or if I could really trust her. The fact was that it didn't really matter. She spoke better French than me and could have told everyone what the passage said. Had she?

"What did Jack and the boys think about that?" I said.

She curled her lip. "I didn't tell them. Why do you think we're meeting out here in the middle of the night?"

Hmm. Good question, but given all our sordid mutual history, I was done playing games. "Frankly, I'm not sure, Heather. Why don't you spell it out for me?"

Her teeth were lit by the moon. "Because I'm just as expendable as you are."

The statement caught me off guard. If she was being honest, though, it might actually make sense.

She leaned closer. "The truth is, I'm providing most of the capital for this adventure, even though Jack and I are over, and he resents the hell out of me." She paused and peered deeply into my eyes, now just a foot from hers. "I'm afraid that if we find the treasure, his goons will kill both of us."

I inhaled a deep breath. "What about Ben?"

Her eyes grew wide. "He was keeping an eye on me."

"What?" My voice was too loud.

"Ssshh!" She put her hand on my thigh. "Once their plan came together to draft you into their treasure hunt against your will, I agreed to finance it but demanded to come because I didn't want anything to … happen to you." Her voice broke.

She hung her head. I put the wine glass down, scooted closer, and wrapped my arm around her. She trembled under my grasp. The curve of her torso fit into my cupped hand with a familiarity that still hadn't faded.

"You have no reason to trust me, and I know it sounds pre-posterous, but I *have* changed," she said. "Which is another reason Jack and I are over." She heaved a couple times, and I pulled her closer. A teardrop fell onto my leg.

"What are you suggesting, Heather?"

She shook once more, then placed a hand on the deck, arched her back, and looked up at me. "I'm suggesting we work together to save our asses."

I suddenly realized our situation was just like not telling the RBDF officer that we'd found the missing sailboat. But in this case, once we found the treasure, it wasn't that Jack, Ben, and their henchmen would make us leave: they'd bury us at sea.

Heather continued to stare into my eyes, awaiting a response. I finally nodded, which prompted a smile—she stretched up and kissed my cheek.

"I knew I could still count on you—not that I deserve it," she said. Her face then fell, and more teardrops streaked down her cheeks.

"What's wrong now?" I said.

"I'm so sorry, Buck. I was such a royal bitch for leaving you like I did—*when* I did—and then with Jack—and there's more, but …" Her whole body heaved.

I pulled her closer, afraid that if she sobbed too loud, some-one would hear us.

"Why would … you … even … want to … help—"

Her voice was breaking and getting louder. I pressed my lips on her mouth, tasting the salt of her tears—she pressed forward hard—we collapsed onto the deck. Heather was shaking, so I pulled the blanket over us, and our lips never came apart. Her hands rubbed up and down on my chest until they continued further down, sliding into my loose-fitting shorts.

My hands rubbed slowly down her back into her underwear,

drawing them off and down her legs. We made love slowly—deliberate and gentle—much different than on the boat yesterday. Whether from the emotion, her apology, or mutual fear for our lives, we climaxed simultaneously and then held each other without words for what felt like hours but was more like minutes. Emotionally spent, we stared into the sky and counted a half dozen shooting stars.

"Listen," I said. "I've got your back, but it'll be complicated."

"What do you mean?"

"We need to keep them on their heels, and they can't think we're aligned. We need to exploit the dynamics of the situation to make that happen. Jack gets emotional, which makes him erratic—"

"You're telling me?" she said.

"Help me to understand the connection between him and Ben."

Her head fell back, and she stared straight up into the sky. "They're both evil shits, far worse than I ever realized. Schemers who will stop at nothing to get what they want. And add Gunner to the mix? Hell on wheels."

"But how did they connect?"

"Years ago, as e-Antiquity was going down the tubes, they colluded against you, both for different reasons, but …" She again heaved and threw her arm over her face. "I can't talk about them, please."

What the hell? They were working together before e-Antiquity fell apart?

"If they figure out I'm helping you, then we're both dead," she said.

"I have Ray here as an emergency escape route if necessary, but …"

"But what?"

I didn't know how to say what I wanted to say without potentially upsetting—no, ruining—our unlikely and fragile alliance. She sat up, pulled the hair out of her face, then turned to face me.

"You can trust me, Buck. Please, I promise. If nothing more, I could have told everyone what it said in that log. But I didn't."

With a lungful of air, I spoke words I never thought would pass my lips again. "I trust you, Heather."

We gathered up the blanket, wine, candle, and glasses, and stood to return to our respective cabins. As we rounded the corner of the superstructure, I thought I saw movement inside the pilot house and hurried past. Was it my imagination, or was Randy spying on us?

Why did my life always have to be so complicated?

36

GUNNER SWAM AROUND THE STERN OF THE BLUE-HULLED Beneteau while I went in the other direction. This was the missing sailboat the insurance company was seeking and our excuse to have a salvage ship here in the Bahamas. The RBDF would come immediately for confirmation of the find, but that was the last thing we wanted right now.

In the year and a half since it had sunk, a colony of sea life had already begun to grow on its surface. On land, it may be ashes to ashes, but underwater, it's more like solid to salt. The boat had come to rest on its port side, with its bow pointed east toward TOTO a quarter-mile away. I swam along a teak deck that had once been smooth and shiny but was now rotting and furry with seaweed, sea anemones, tubeworms, and other organisms. The companionway hatch into the cabin was open, and I shined my light inside—

Whoa! A fat green moray sprang out toward me and slithered across the floor of the cockpit, through one of the steering wheels, and down into an open transom locker, which still held a Highfield tender. After a few deep breaths, my heart slowed back to normal. I entered the hatch and shined the light all around to determine if there would be any other surprises.

There was junk everywhere, along with a wealth of small fish and particles floating in the still water. Amongst the debris, which included lines, electronics, milk crates with weights, dive gear, books, rotted upholstery, and clothing, I found the ship's log.

Inside was confirmation of the name—*Duckbill Charlie*—along with some photos of what I assumed to be the owners. The ink on the pages was smeared, and the paper itself disintegrated when I touched it, floating around the cabin like ash off a fire.

I tucked the log back under a milk crate, and when I turned around, Gunner was staring into the hatch at me. My heart jumped as if he were a great white. In reality, he was much worse, since he could kill me on land too, and just as indiscriminately.

I gave him the okay sign with my index finger and thumb, and he moved out of the way when I swam toward the hatch.

I checked my air and depth gauge. I still had 2,000 PSI of air left, which made sense, since the ship was only in 60 feet of water. It had sunk in a place just deep enough to stay hidden, but not so deep you couldn't spot it in the clearer-than-usual Bahamian waters.

We surfaced near the Beast, and I put a blast of air into my BCD, then spit out my regulator. "I found the log. That's *Duckbill Charlie* alright."

Gunner squinted into the sun, no doubt missing his blue-mirrored sunglasses. His small teeth and his fat gray head reminded me of a porpoise waiting for a baitfish to be thrown into its gullet at SeaWorld. "Why do we care?" he said.

"I'm not sure yet, but if the RBDF gets too nosey, we'll at least have a diversion for them."

"This is a waste of time," he said. "Let's get on to the next spot."

"We're close, only a few hundred yards away toward TOTO. We can swim if you want," I said.

Even with air in his BCD, Gunner struggled to keep his bulk buoyant on the surface. "Funny, Reilly. C'mon, we'll drive the plane over."

I climbed aboard first and collected all the gear and stowed it, just like we had yesterday. He called Jack on the dive boat while I was pulling the anchors. They'd headed to the next closest mark from the mothership this morning and had two more spots they intended to check if the first one held no interest.

"Nothing but coral heads and turtle grass," Jack said. "I'm starting to think the plan to do reconnaissance from the air was a waste of time."

Gunner rolled his eyes, prompting a smile from me. Jack bitched a little more and didn't care at all when Gunner told him we'd found the sailboat. "We have one more of your likely false alarms to waste energy on, and if something doesn't happen soon based on Buck's research, I'll send Randy back to persuade Scarlet to help."

At the mention of Scarlet's name, a pang of concern made me flinch. I hadn't heard from her since Vero Beach. She was supposed to check in when she was safe, but I'd shut off my phone when I found out Jack was getting copies of my communications. I sent a quick text that said, "Hope you're safe, Jack monitoring my main number / email, this is my burner phone. Nothing so far, xo."

The guilt I felt, however, was exacerbated because even though our relationship had devolved into a semi-shared custodial one for Charlie, it was Heather who had originally come between us. When I met Heather, I dropped Scarlet like a burnt biscuit. And here I was, flirting with disaster all over again.

"Are we going to the next spot, or are you just gonna stare off into space all day?" Gunner said.

A deep breath later, I began an abbreviated pre-flight checklist—

"Why are you checking the flaps? We're not even taking off."

I rubbed my eyes. "Best practices, Gunner. I'm sure you have some procedures you follow in your line of work, right?"

He laughed. "Yeah, I make sure the clips are full in my guns."

With that, I fired up the starboard engine first, followed by the port one. Then I manipulated manifold pressure and changed the pitch of the propellers to turn the Beast out toward the deeper blue water of TOTO.

"Keep an eye on the GPS. I spotted this one on our first day when we were headed back to the ship."

"Keep going straight on this heading," Gunner said. "We'll be there in a minute."

He was close. Three minutes later, I reduced power, and the friction of the water slowed us quickly until we drifted right over the mark on the GPS. I checked the depth gauge.

"We're at 80 feet of water here," I said. "Lengthen the aft anchor line, and I'll do the same on the bow. We're right on the edge of the deeper water, which goes from 120 feet to 6,000 in a few hundred yards."

Within twenty minutes we'd secured the flying boat, broken the gear out, and set it all up, which wasn't easy, given the fact that there were nearly five hundred pounds and almost thirteen feet of large men between us operating within a narrow tube.

"Let's hope this one yields something, Reilly. All this in and out, up and down, all around is getting on my nerves, and Jack is getting impatient."

Gunner stepped forward out of the hatch. A plume of water erupted when he hit. I dropped a twenty-foot line with a weight on the end overboard and waited until Gunner wallowed out of the way to step in after him. There was still close to 2,000 PSI in my tank, which was 2/3 of the max capacity. Our surface interval had been a bit less than an hour, which was risky, but at eighty feet, we'd only have thirty minutes of bottom time, with a brief hang at fifteen feet.

Once I began my descent and my eyes adjusted to the light, the configuration of the bottom appeared totally different than the coral heads and patches of turtle grass we'd dove on so far. After twenty feet, the visibility was clear all the way to the bottom, and my eyes nearly popped out of my head. A crisscross of structures peeked out from an elevated mound, and the closer we got, the more certain I was that I recognized them.

"Cannons!" My shout was nothing but a rush of bubbles. I kicked harder out of excitement but couldn't keep the pressurization in my ears adjusted, so slowed back down. Gunner was staring straight down, so I assumed he saw them too.

The last line of the *Griffon*'s log had said to find the cannons, so maybe the mound below them was the motherlode of the queen's jewels. My heart raced, and I sucked nitrox like a chain smoker as we closed the distance. In the deeper water, there was at least a hundred feet of visibility, and I spotted another dark mound on the periphery of my vision. The familiar rush of discovery coursed through my veins in a way it hadn't in years.

Did Gunner appreciate what was happening? Was he feeling the same rush or only estimating what his cut would be? Yes, there was that, but the thrill of investing years of research to obtain the initial leads and the fieldwork in Brest to piece together a hypothesis, followed by what felt like the culmination here, caused my limbs to tingle as if my blood were carbonated.

A sudden pressure had my leg—Gunner had grabbed it with one hand and was pointing at the now very visible pair of cannons twenty feet below us. I gave him the okay sign, and he responded with two thumbs up, which is the diving signal to ascend immediately, which I ignored. As we closed the distance, the scale of the eight-thousand-pound cannons grew in immensity. They were corroded, black, and thick with growth, but they were intact.

I swam around the two cannons. I recognized them as appropriate for the era of the *Farnese* but had no information on details that might be engraved upon the guns to identify them with certainty. But the odds of another seventeenth-century ship being here was highly unlikely, since the *Griffon* and *Farnese* had only been able to cross the Great Bahama Bank due to the elevated seas caused by the hurricane that had allowed them to escape the Florida Straits.

The cannons lay on top of each other like femurs in a skull and crossbones. My gaze shifted to the mound below the cannons. Nothing shiny: no clumps of blackened silver coins or ballast were visible. The reality was that a fourth-rate frigate like the *Farnese* carried forty-plus cannons, so as much as I'd have liked this X to mark the spot, it wasn't likely ... but it did mean we were close.

Gunner now stood on the mound with the barrel of the top cannon on his shoulder and tried to lift it. Good luck.

I swam in an increasingly wider radius around the cannons and spotted additional debris, ballast, and another smaller cannon closer to TOTO. Gunner followed after me, and I pointed toward the trail. I grabbed the air gauge that hung in front of his chest and saw that he was down to 400 PSI. I pointed a thumbs-up in front of his face, and he responded again with two thumbs-up. His eyes were wide in his mask. I pointed up, started swimming, and waved for him to follow.

After twenty feet of ascent, I checked and saw him finally break free of the treasure trance. I stopped my ascent at the weighted rope and waited for Gunner—he nearly blew past me at high speed, which if it didn't burst his lungs would give him the bends—I grabbed the collar of his BCD and was nearly ripped free from the line. His eyes were wild as if he'd just snorted an eight ball. He grabbed the line but waved his arms around and snapped his fingers.

Dancing. Gunner was dancing.

Thank God we were still underwater. His excitement was contagious, though. Next thing I knew, we were slapping five, and maybe, just maybe, I swung my arms around in an imaginary dance as well. Our three-minute hang went by fast, and we repeated our exit procedure, but the second Gunner spit his regulator out he began to bellow.

"Wahoo!" He pumped a fist. "We did it, Reilly! We found the *Farnese!*"

The company and circumstances could have been better, but his words sent a chill through me. "Yes, sir!" I said.

There was still a lot of work to be done, and the debris trail leading to deeper water made me nervous, but I'd learned long ago to savor each milestone on the road to an important archeological discovery. Once we'd put the gear away, dried off, and pulled the anchors, we took our seats in the cockpit.

"Hold on a minute, Buck."

Buck? Since when were we on a first-name basis?

He pushed his sunglasses up to the top of his head. "We did it, man! You and me flying recon." He pumped his fist again. "I just want to say what an awesome fucking job you've done here," he said. "I told you back in France how impressed I was, and now this? I'm blown away, brother."

Brother? Good Lord.

If this were my tried and true e-Antiquity research team, I would have said that it had been a team effort. But it was Gunner, and his brain circuits were as binary and prehistoric as an iguana's.

"We make a good team, Gunner." Uttering those words was the verbal equivalent of sticking a finger down my throat, and I swallowed back bile.

"Damn straight. What the hell have those other losers done but follow up on our recon?" He rubbed his hands together in a circular motion as the millstone of his brain grumbled a slow circle inside his fat head.

His next words were so predictable, I was ready by the time he found them.

"I been wasting my time with Jack for too damned long. Plus, him and your brother are always whispering and planning behind my back. What, they think I don't see that? And Heather? Shit, Jack's gonna screw her over anyway, I guarantee that. He's fed up with her."

"Even though she financed this trip?" I said.

"Especially because of that. Now there's no hiding that she's loaded, while he has to grovel because he pissed his away." He shook his head. "This'll be the icing on the cake."

I let the words float in the air for a few beats.

"He's always been an asshole," I said. "How many times have you heard him mention Harvard?"

Gunner belted out a laugh. "Thousands. Freaking snob." He rubbed his palms over the sides of his head. "Always trying to make the rest of us feel stupid." He turned back to face me again, his face now deadly serious. "Him and your brother are rotten, man, the two of them together. I'm sure you think that's the pot calling the kettle black, and hey, I know I'm no angel, but those two …" He shook his head.

Heather had said much the same thing last night, which didn't exactly make me feel any easier. There had to be more to Ben and Jack's partnership than I'd learned.

These few days alone with Gunner had been an effort in tolerance, but my efforts to drive a wedge between the conspirators were finally paying off. The real twist had been Heather's foundering status in the group. Now that Gunner had just inadvertently substantiated the concerns she had voiced to me last night, I decided there would be no better time to strike.

"What should we do about it?" I said.

Gunner bared his yellowed teeth and gave me a full-frontal smile. "You just keep doing what you do best. Leave the rest to me."

A cold sensation of someone pissing on my grave caused me to squirm in my seat. I managed a nod and fired the Beast up. As we sped across the wave tops, building speed, Gunner was back to pumping his tattooed arms in front of himself as if he were a rock and roll drummer on a crazed solo.

I adjusted the dive knife still strapped to my calf. I was forced to keep my enemies close, but my gut told me to keep a weapon closer.

SECTION 5

ONE STEP
FORWARD,
TEN YEARS BACK

37

WE RADIOED THE OTHERS ON THE DIVE BOAT TO MEET US at the *Global Explorer* but refused to answer questions. We flew over them, hauling flat-out as we approached the mothership. They waved excitedly to us five hundred feet over their heads before we set down in the light chop and circled back around to anchor near the ship. While we waited for someone to pick us up in the Zodiac, Gunner ground his teeth so hard I thought he'd break a molar.

"We're just going to take them to see the cannons?" he said.

"Time is of the essence. No doubt in my mind that RBDF is monitoring our activities. It was a lucky break we found the wreck and the sailboat within a mile of each other."

"Damn good day." Gunner held his fist up for a bump, which I gave him.

The Zodiac roared toward us with Jack at the helm. He powered down too late—I jumped down and extended my legs out from the hatch—he nearly jammed the bow of the Zodiac right into the Beast's port side.

"What's the big news?" he said.

Gunner hung over my shoulder. "We found it!" He pumped his fist and howled like a Viking.

Jack slapped his hands together. "Yes!"

While I buttoned the Beast up, Gunner climbed into the Zodiac. "Buck and I spotted it on our recon trip the other day." His voice was louder than usual.

"You and Buck, huh?"

I couldn't see Jack's face, but I heard the sarcasm. They pulled closer, and I stepped on the Zodiac's bow and locked the Beast's hatch, and we set off for the stern of the *Global Explorer*. Jack had a distant smile on his face as he stared past us. I turned to see Ben watching us approach. Gunner elbowed me and nodded toward Ben.

I tossed the painter line to Heather, who was waiting on the stern.

"Good news?" she said.

"We found the missing sailboat," I said. Her smile faded. "Oh, and some cannons from the *Farnese*."

She leaped up like a cheerleader. Her and Ben's dance around the deck was premature, but so was Gunner and Jack's excitement. None of them realized that unless this was the luckiest find in my career, we still had a lot of work to do. Once on board, Jack slapped high fives with Ben, and Heather came straight for me. She flung her arms around my neck and planted a big kiss on my lips.

The hooting and hollering fell silent. When I lowered Heather down to the deck, Jack was cutting holes through us with sharp eyes. Jack stepped toward us. "I heard you two had a nice session on the bow last night." The vein on his neck pulsed.

"Don't be an ass," she said.

He took a step toward her and I moved between them. "Easy, Jack."

Heather held my bicep in a tight grip, but she kept her mouth shut.

"Randy apologized to me this morning for interrupting us last night," Jack said. "When I asked what he meant, he said he saw us wrapped up in a blanket in the middle of, 'Well, you know.'" He crossed his arms. "So it was you two, then, huh?"

"Sure it wasn't you and Ben?" Gunner said.

Jack's head spun sharply toward him. I would have laughed if the tension weren't as thick as sea salt on the ship's hull.

"Seriously," Gunner said, "can we celebrate the moment instead of squaring off over a woman you guys have passed back and forth like a bumper of beer?"

The sharp intake of breath behind me signaled further escalation, so I stepped forward.

"Guys, the *Farnese* is out there. We've found it. Let's not ruin that with this bullshit, okay? And the sailboat is in close proximity, so we can relocate our flotilla there in the morning. Now let's celebrate, dammit!"

POP!

I jumped—Ben had snuck away as tensions were rising and returned with a bottle of champagne, and he had aimed it at us, then freed the cork. Heather gravitated toward the champagne, but Jack kept his eyes focused on mine. Over his shoulder, I saw Gunner watching us.

I set my feet solid on the deck. "Heather's a grown woman, Jack," I said. "The only permission I needed was from her."

His eyes bulged—he lunged for me. Gunner grabbed him from behind and wrapped a tattooed arm around his chest, but when Jack struggled to get free, Gunner tightened his grip.

"Calm down, boss. We're close to the prize. Let's not blow it over pussy."

Jack pushed Gunner's arm off, then squared up again, now with his teeth bared. "As soon as you married her, our company went to shit! What was it, a year before you got back out on the road?"

"That's because I was set up for the murder of the scammer you forced me to do business with on Tortola," I said.

"Bullshit! You'd already peaked in Guatemala! Then poontang blindness ruined you. Now you're falling for it again, dumbass. You deserve each other!" White spittle caked in the corners of Jack's mouth.

My hands clenched in fists.

The years flashed before my eyes—the night I met Heather at the Explorer's Club in New York City—the whirlwind romance, the globetrotting power couple—apart more than together—and it all blew up when Jack absconded with e-Antiquity's money. Heather disappeared weeks later.

"Cold champagne here." Ben held the bottle of Veuve Clicquot up in one hand and a stack of plastic glasses in the other.

Just then, the roar of a boat came up behind us. I turned and saw the same go-fast RBDF speedboat that had hassled us yesterday returning. I suddenly wanted nothing to do with any of them and flung my arms wide—Jack stepped aside, and I blew past him and into the salon.

Un-fucking-believable.

Poontang blindness—could Jack be any more repulsive? I paced circles around the table in the salon until I saw the same Bahamian officer from yesterday board our ship. Right then, I realized our entire operation could implode with one foolish statement from my sterling colleagues.

Unfortunately, by the time I got outside and walked up to Jack, it was too late.

"You don't need to come check on us every day," Jack said. "We'll be happy to cut you in on the, ah, reward, once we find the sailboat."

Oh no.

The officer's face remained inscrutable.

Jack dug into his pocket and pulled out a wad of bills wrapped in a rubber band. "Here, take this—"

I rushed forward and grabbed his arm. "Very funny, Jack, but I don't think these men have a sense of humor!" I stepped between them and stared Jack down with fire in my eyes.

The officer had his hands on his holstered automatic, visibly

chomping at the bit to arrest Jack. My former partner may have
had a knack for incentivizing investors back in the day, but he
was chumming for sharks here and now, and they'd have bitten
the arm that fed them so fast Jack's head would have spun
around.

The officer glanced at each of us. "One misstep, and we'll
impound this ship and take you all back to Nassau." The officer's
gaze stopped on Jack. "You're lucky the pilot interrupted your
foolishness." With that, he climbed back onto his speedboat, and
they sped off to the east.

"Way to tip our hand," I said.

"Shut up, Buck," he said. "You do the diving and leave the
negotiations to me."

A thought hit me, and it was my turn to smile. "That's why
the boat's in your name, big shot. So they know who to arrest the
next time you ham-hand the cops."

I walked back toward the salon as Ben reached forward to
hand me a flute of champagne. I slapped it and sent the gold
liquid flying all over his shirt.

38

"THE MALLARD IS COMING TOGETHER NICELY," Ray said. "I should have it airborne tomorrow."

I was seated on the aft deck with a coffee in one hand and the phone pressed against my ear with the other. When I'd talked to Ray last night and told him we'd found cannons, he was ecstatic.

"The Mallard's good luck, I'm telling you," he said. "We need to come up with a name for her."

Gunner walked out of the salon in a hurry. "We're getting the show on the road here. Jack wants to move the *Global Explorer* over to where the cannons are."

"I'm talking to Ray. I'll be off in a minute."

"Tell him he's missing out. He ain't here, he can't claim any of your share."

I waved Gunner off, and he went back inside. "It's getting tense here, Ray."

"How so?"

I usually didn't like to worry him, but I wanted to make sure he knew where I was physically located. "Just keep an eye on your phone. I texted you the coordinates of where we found the missing sailboat and the cannons from the *Farnese*. If I go missing or quiet for longer than a few hours, call the RBDF and send them our way."

"That bad?" His voice was shrill.

"A lot of dirty laundry getting aired. We're relocating this circus up to the site now. If you take the Mallard out, give us a flyover so I can check it out, but don't land."

"Fine with me."

When the *Global Explorer*'s twin Caterpillar diesels fired up, a whoosh of black smoke belched out of their exhausts and blew back in the breeze to wash over me. Jack, Ben, and Gunner were inside finishing the feast of a breakfast Randy had prepared. My appetite hadn't returned after last night's fight with Jack, and I didn't think Heather had left her cabin since Jack confronted us about our midnight soiree on the bow, which was just as well. Heather had once again put me on the brink of self-destruction.

Time to focus, Buck.

Gunner gave me a ride to the Beast in the Zodiac, and I took off ahead of them so I could dictate the anchorage. Those clowns would telegraph our every move if I didn't stay ahead of their antics. The Beast touched down to the east of the cannon pile but heading west. We cruised on the step over that GPS mark, and I slowed our progress to a stop halfway to the sunken sailboat. When the RBDF showed up, which probably wouldn't take long, we could steer them toward the sailboat site if they got too pushy. We could stall for a couple days, say we were investigating the wreck and searching for signs of the owner and crew, but no longer.

With the Beast anchored up, I sat on the bow and watched the *Global Explorer* cruise toward us at what appeared to be max speed. Jack probably thought I was picking the *Farnese* clean and getting ready to leave them in the dust. If only it was that easy. It took them another half hour before they arrived and dropped anchor to the west of me. My stomach dropped when I saw it was Heather coming to get me in the Zodiac.

"Shit."

I crawled back inside and locked the bow hatch. My dive gear was already out and ready to be loaded, so I sat in the cockpit to wait for my ride. I sent Ray a text pinning our location as backup to the coordinates I'd given him. The engine cut out on the Zodiac when she pulled up.

"Permission to come aboard?" Heather said.

"Double shit."

At the hatch, I caught the line and hesitated. "We need to get moving," I said.

"Just give me five minutes, Buck," she said. "Please."

I tied the bowline to a cleat by the hatch and extended my hand to help her aboard. We sat in the main cabin across from each other. I waited.

"It was stupid to kiss you—"

"And to have the candlelit setup on the bow."

"For years, he's been calling you 'the booby prize' because he introduced us that night at the Explorer's Club. What I felt for you was instantaneous and genuine, and when things started to go bad, I ran."

"Uh-huh."

"I admit I was shallow and immature. I've changed—but you know how controlling Jack is. He can't stand to see me happy, especially if it's with you." A tear ran down her cheek. "I never tried to hold you back."

I exhaled slowly. Lying in my bunk last night, I'd gone through the same exercise, and in her defense, I could only remember Heather pushing me to be more successful. Ultimately it was her who had gone back to work first. But still, Jack's indictment just reiterated that his relationship with Heather preceded mine, and even if they were on the outs now, she'd gone to him after leaving me. I could never forgive her for that.

"It's fine, Heather." I paused, and her eyes lifted. "But we're here to find the queen's jewels, not rehash the past."

Her chin dropped, and she turned to look out the window on her right—did she shudder? Whatever. Now was not the time—never *would* be the time—for this conversation.

"Let's go diving, okay?" I said. "You can stick with me if you'd like. I'll show you the cannons. We need to work as a group to search where I spotted more debris. We don't have the luxury of time to set a grid and approach this methodically, especially after Jack tipped our hand to that Bahamian officer last night."

She looked up and nodded, her lips pressed tight.

I stood before I let her expression weaken my resolve. Once Gunner's and my dive gear had been loaded into the Zodiac, I had her sit on the bow as I steered us back to the mothership. The others had already loaded the dive boat with gear and were waiting for us.

"About fucking time," Jack said.

"Buck and Heather, never saw that coming," Ben said.

So Ben supported Jack. Gunner and Heather's description of their connection continued to elude me, but from what I'd seen and heard, and based on our toxic history since our parents were killed, I was beyond pining for the brotherly relationship we never had.

"Nothing to see, Ben," I said. "Now load the boat, and let's get to work."

WITH FIVE OF US DIVING AND RANDY DRIVING the boat, we had to take the Zodiac too, which Heather and I stayed on once we had our gear. Whether Jack liked it or not, I set the strategy of starting at the cannon pile, fanning out, and swimming due east toward the deeper water where I'd spotted another cannon and a pile of rubble at the far extent of yesterday's visibility. Randy would follow our bubbles in the dive boat. Fortunately, the current was running in that direction, so it would be an easy drift dive that would preserve our oxygen/nitrox mix, but I needed to keep an eye on my dive computer to make sure the overzealous rookies didn't exceed their bottom time.

"Good plan," Gunner said.

Jack scowled but didn't argue.

We splashed in to the west of the target, and the current moved us toward it as we descended. The group stuck together, as everyone wanted to see the cannons at the bottom. When we arrived, there were more fist bumps, arm pumps, and a lot of oxygen wasted on screaming. I signaled for everyone to fan out. I was in the middle with Jack on my right, Ben to his right, Heather on my left, and Gunner outside of her. We kept a steady pace until we reached the third cannon I'd found yesterday. Everyone took a look while I searched around it with a metal detector, not finding anything else. I waved my hand in a circle, and everyone fanned out again.

The visibility today was even better, and what I had thought was a ballast pile in the distance was confirmed, even though it was still seventy feet away. I didn't draw attention to the pile ahead, as I wanted everyone facedown studying the immediate area. We hovered ten feet above the bottom, which was a mix of sand, grass, different coral formations, and rock that held fish and lobster antennae sticking out of holes. My depth gauge read 97 feet, and there was a gradual but steady decline toward the dark indigo ahead, where TOTO dropped straight down to a depth equivalent to the Grand Canyon.

Jack's metal detector must have picked something up, because he dove deeper and fanned at the bottom. Something black stuck out of the sand, and I went down and helped him dig around it with my gloved hands. We kept at it until a pointed triangular object the size of a football took shape. The iron was as thick as my bicep, curved gradually, and had a wider pointed plate about a foot further down the shaft. It dawned on me that it was a fluke to an anchor. The arm was long and continued straight into the sand. Based on its angle, I swam back around Jack and fanned sand—there! The remains of an iron shackle fixed to a shaft were buried ten feet away from the fluke.

Jack continued to dig around down the shaft until I grabbed his arm. He looked up, and I again made a circular motion with my hand for everyone to again spread out. Like a dog with a bone, he didn't want to let it go. The anchor was a good find, as it continued the trail that the cannon pile had commenced, but it wasn't what we were after. It took a moment to break Jack off the spot, but he ultimately followed after us.

Our depth was now at 112', which was our max depth for nitrox.

The dive boat lagged behind us. Randy was probably having difficulty following our disbursed bubbles due to the depth. My air was at 1,000 PSI, so I swam down the line and saw that Ben's was the lowest at 600 PSI. I tapped my dive computer and held up my hand with all five fingers extended, then pointed to the surface. Five minutes until ascent. At this depth, compressed air went fast.

The ballast pile was too far away for this dive, so I popped an inflatable buoy, tied the end of the nylon rope to a five-pound weight, dropped it to the bottom, and let the buoy soar to the surface to mark our location later on my computer's GPS. Everyone's eyes were fixed down except for Heather's. She pointed to the pile ahead, and while she couldn't see my face due to the mask and regulator, I was smiling. Out of the corner of my eye, I saw Gunner waving—I swam over to see he'd found another lone cannon. It sat on flat bottom, so likely wasn't what d'Aire had referenced in his log. I gave him the okay sign, but we'd run out of time, so waved for Gunner to follow me and tapped each diver and pointed to the surface.

Our collective ascent was on a steady pace, and after a ten-minute hang on the weighted rope from the dive boat, we surfaced. It had been a good dive, and the debris trail was clear, but one question persisted in my head.

Would we find anything of value before the trail fell off into purple oblivion?

That was the two-hundred-and-fifty-million-dollar question.

39

THE NEXT DIVE REVEALED MORE DEBRIS and a massive pile of ballast rocks that stretched fifty feet long. A tight pile like that would normally lead me to conclude that was where the ship had settled. Captain d'Aire's note to "find the cannons not the ship" would lead me to conclude the ballast pile held little value, but we'd only found a half dozen cannons, and aside from the few that formed an X, the rest were singular and in a continuous line.

We recovered ceramic fragments from olive jars, a calcified chunk of wood, and a cannonball. The mantra of treasure divers was to "follow the stones," meaning the ballast, since that was usually where the heavy precious metals would also have sunk. But this case was different. That thought led to a restless night of tossing and turning alone in my bunk. By morning, it had led to an epiphany.

Maybe the first cannon pile we'd found wasn't the start of the debris trail? If it began to the west of the two cannons that made the X, the rest might be in shallower water. As fitful as my sleep had been, I jumped out of my bunk at sunup and had the boat to myself. The rest of the group had been exhausted after the second dive and had crashed early last night. I circumnavigated the perimeter of the ship's deck from end to end multiple times, drinking coffee and trying to picture the waters between the sunken sailboat and our initial cannon pile. When I smelled breakfast cooking, I reentered the cabin.

Jack, Ben, and Gunner were sitting at the table eating eggs and bacon that Randy had made. They looked up in surprise when I walked inside.

"You weren't in your bunk," Ben said. "Figured you must be, ah, busy."

"I had an idea that kept me up half the night. Caught an amazing sunrise on the bow though."

"Alone?" Gunner said.

Jack's head whipped around like his neck was spring-loaded. He glared at Gunner.

When I shared my concept about the debris trail starting in shallower water, Gunner sat forward. "That would make diving a hell of a lot easier."

"What about that ballast pile?" Jack said. "That's where I found the anchor. We need to look there, unless you're trying to distract us with a wild goose chase."

Ben frowned and cocked his head sideways toward me.

My exhale was loud. I missed the days when I was in charge of my own excavations and Jack was back in the office lying to investors. My digs were conducted in a rational, iterative, and organized manner, and I was unequivocally in charge. This was a far cry from that: no experienced team, no permit or agreement with the host country, no time to follow a logical process, and no trust. Thinking of this as an archeological effort was a misnomer anyway. We were more like corsairs or buccaneers hunting for plunder.

"I woke up with a new idea as well," Jack said.

Ben smiled and looked at me. He was starting to remind me of Charlie McCarthy, the famous ventriloquist dummy.

"What's your idea?" I said.

Jack pointed to the back of the ship. After a beat, I turned to where he was pointing. "I don't—" Then I spotted what he had to be talking about. "No, Jack, that's not a good—"

"We don't have time to screw around, Buck. One of the reasons I chartered this ship was—"

"You mean after I chartered the plane and paid all other expenses?" Heather said as she walked up the steps from her cabin below.

Jack grimaced, his lips puckered tightly as he clearly fought with himself to restrain whatever response was pressing against his better judgment. "As I was saying, we chose this ship because of its capabilities. One of which is those magnificent mailboxes on the stern that'll blast holes twenty feet into the ocean bottom."

"Bad idea, Jack."

"Why do you question everything he says?" Ben said.

"Because when those Royal Bahamian Defense Force officers who have been sniffing around find a massive silt cloud caused by those mailboxes, our cover story will be blown and we'll be arrested!"

"Bullshit," Jack said. "We'll blow that pile of ballast rocks to bits and find our treasure underneath it."

"That ballast pile is in 130 feet of water. Mailboxes don't penetrate that deep—"

"We'll see," Jack said.

"But if I'm right, we won't even need them," I said. "The treasure could be half as deep or less."

Jack stood up and flexed his tattooed arms as if he was stretching, but with him, it was like some kind of subliminal macho power play. I was bigger and in the best shape of my life. He'd made the mistake of picking a fight with me back in high school—I'd tackled him and sat on him laughing until he hyperventilated from shrieking.

"I'm not going to jail," Heather said.

"None of us are going to jail!" Jack's face had turned red.

I held my hands up. "Do what you want, Jack. I'll take my plane and search the area to the west—"

"Nope, uh-uh, we all stay together." His jaw quivered as he wrestled with his next words. "Fine, Buck. You win. We'll search west first, and to your point, if we find a pile in shallower water, the mailboxes will be more effective."

It was my turn to bite my lip. All eyes turned toward me.

"Daylight's burning. Let's move," I said.

Gunner held his fist up and pumped it slowly.

As my father taught me, it never pays to get into a pissing match with a skunk.

Randy had refilled the scuba tanks, and our gear was loaded onto the dive boat. We'd all cram on that today instead of bringing the Zodiac, since it wasn't very functional as a dive boat. We also brought the side-scan sonar, which could provide detailed images of any structures and transmit clear images to the ship's laptop. That and the magnetometers would help us quickly assess any ferrous material we found, and with any luck, we'd spot something shiny that the mags were incapable of identifying.

Once loaded up, I stood next to Randy to guide him to the west to check my hunch. Behind me, Gunner was waxing poetic about all the years of failed treasure hunting he and Jack had pursued now coming to a climax.

"Finally, it feels like we might actually get some," Gunner said.

"Been a long road," Jack said. His voice held none of Gunner's optimism.

I listened without turning around. We hadn't deployed the side-scan sonar yet. I wanted to wait and start at the initial cannon pile.

"That's for sure," Gunner said. "Switzerland seems like a lifetime ago."

Switzerland?

I thought I heard someone shush him.

I turned around slowly.

Gunner's face was now deadpan. No more smiles, excitement, or fist pumps. Jack was smiling, but Ben's face was tight, his eyes slits. Heather was on the bow avoiding everyone, oblivious to the sudden rush of adrenaline that had coursed into my bloodstream.

"What about Switzerland?" I said.

"One thing about Switzerland," Jack said. "I would have had the only copies of e-Antiquity's research if your parents hadn't already opened that account at Swiss Bank."

My sight narrowed to tunnel vision as I stared at Jack.

He shook his head slowly. "You're lucky they did that for you, or Gunner and I would be sitting in the catbird seat with the most comprehensive and detailed resources in the world—"

"I know that, Jack. What I don't understand is what you two were doing in Switzerland."

The boat suddenly came to a stop, and I turned back to Randy, who said, "We're sitting on the mark for the first pair of cannons."

Heather was now standing on the other side of Randy. "How does the sonar work?" she said.

Randy shook his head. I swallowed and turned around to face her. "We tow the transducers that are inside that tow fish torpedo-looking cylinder, and it transmits sonogram-type images to the computer there."

"So it reads directly under the boat?"

"Yes, but depending on the quality and strength, it can also read up to four hundred feet on either side of the boat."

"Really?" Ben said behind us. "Now that I want to see."

My eyes fixed on Jack, who was holding the tow fish, getting ready to drop it over the side. What he had said about my parents and whatever Gunner was referring to in Switzerland was all I could think of now.

My parents had been killed by a hit-and-run driver in Geneva, Switzerland, directly in front of Swiss Bank, moments after they'd opened that account for me. Interpol had never found the car that killed them and considered me a suspect in the murder investigation that followed. I wasn't bankrupt at that point, but Interpol's theory was that I'd had them killed for their estate, which included the proceeds from the stock they'd sold when I broke the law and told them to cash out because e-Antiquity was days away from insolvency.

If Jack and Gunner had common history in Switzerland, I wanted to know what the hell it was.

40

THE SIDE-SCAN SONAR PICKED UP A NUMBER OF HITS between the cannon pile and the sunken sailboat. The trail was nearly a straight line west away from the ballast pile near TOTO. Captain d'Aire's statement in the *Griffon*'s log played like a loop in my head: *Find the cannons, not the boat.*

If they had dumped the queen's jewels in shallower water with a load of cannons and then scuttled the *Farnese* to sink in deeper water, the ballast pile would represent the final resting place of the ship. Ships that sunk in storms often scattered wreckage over miles of reefs or in swirling quicksands that were in constant movement, making it very difficult to establish a logical pattern. But a controlled scuttle for nefarious purposes would be different. It made all the sense in the world, too: they would have left the queen's jewels in an accessible, discernible location.

By keeping focused on the debris trail, I kept my mind from dwelling on Gunner and Jack's offhand mention of Switzerland, at least for a few minutes. Even though my left brain struggled to stay focused on facts, the rudder of my right brain pulled hard toward the emotional response they'd triggered. Consequently, the new cannons we'd picked up on sonar were hard for me to concentrate on. If the concern stirring in my gut now proved accurate, there was no way I wanted to help Jack regain the wealth he'd lost. If we didn't find the queen's jewels, it just might be a knockout punch on him continuing to be a pest in the future.

Jack had annotated the paper chart with notes on the different items the side-scan sonar had picked up along the trail. I pointed to the one furthest from the cannons. "I say we start diving here and work our way west."

"Why not start with the cannons?" Ben said. "I want one for my house in Virginia. We can use the lift to get some—"

"We're not here for souvenirs, Ben," I said.

"Exactly," Gunner said. "We can't hide cannons on deck either."

"So you want to start back here?" Jack said.

I nodded. "Of the four spots we identified, it's closest to the ballast pile where the boat must have sunk."

"Fine, but if we don't see anything on the first couple spots, Randy will bring the *Global Explorer* over here and blast some holes with the mailboxes."

"That's not a good—"

"We're running out of time—you said it yourself, Buck. Good idea or not, we need to get this over with before the damn Bahamians get too nosy."

"You made that a self-fulfilling prophecy by trying to bribe them," I said.

Jack smiled. "Move the boat to the easternmost spot, Randy. Buck and Ben can dive this one quickly."

Within fifteen minutes, we found the location and dropped anchor. The image on the sonar consisted of a number of small items, none of which appeared promising. Ben and I had geared up on the way, so once the boat stopped, I fell backwards off the gunwale and didn't bother waiting for Ben before descending. The visibility was clear all the way to the bottom, seventy feet down. Ben hurried to catch up with me.

There were scattered coral heads below us, but even halfway down, I could see a scattered pile of large olive jars, several of which looked intact—Ben tugged at my arm. I expected he'd be pointing toward the ancient pottery, but it was a shark he'd spotted twenty feet away, circling a wide area just above us. It was a good-sized lemon shark, maybe six feet long, but they weren't particularly aggressive, and we weren't spearfishing—it might be curious, but it wouldn't give us any trouble. Ben, however, now swam so close to me that our legs brushed together as we kicked.

Near the bottom, Ben finally spotted the pile of jars and darted forward. Since it was unlikely they'd contain what we were after, I ignored him and hovered ten feet above the bottom, scanning the area visually for anything else. Nothing jumped out at me. Below, Ben was moving jars around and stirring up silt. The lack of appreciation for a historic wreck seriously irked me, but this group didn't care about history, preservation, or the story the debris trail would tell. They only cared about treasure—and in Ben's case, mementos.

He held an intact one up that was at least two feet long. The gray and terracotta jug appeared to be in excellent condition. I swam around, holding the magnetometer above areas where other items poked through the sand, but found nothing more than pottery shards and a chunk of metal. Ben held up the olive jar and pointed to himself.

I held my palms up and shrugged my shoulders. Sure, Ben, keep it.

I pointed toward the surface with my thumb, and he responded with a thumbs-up. We ascended at the same speed as our slowest bubbles, and given that we'd only been down for fifteen minutes, there was no need to hang and burn nitrogen.

Ben held the olive jar aloft but still had the regulator in his mouth, so he couldn't talk.

"What did you find?" Gunner said.

At the ladder, I removed my regulator. "A pile of ceramic jars, but nothing else."

Back on board, Heather gazed at Ben's souvenir, but nobody

else bothered. On the next dive site a few hundred yards west, Jack and Gunner dove in. There was nothing but dark, circular anomalies on the screen, but I was glad they'd gone together. Once they were underwater, I turned to Ben.

"What was that about Switzerland between Jack and Gunner?"

His brow furrowed. "How would I know?"

"Gunner told me you and Jack have been partnered up for years. Thought maybe you'd have heard the story of when they first started working together."

"Don't be paranoid, Buck." Ben had the olive jar in his lap and was studying it as he spoke. "Focus on the goal here."

Heather was seated on the bow, ignoring us. The boat was too small not to hear what we were talking about, but she wasn't offering any insights either.

Jack popped up fifteen minutes later. "Nothing!" His shout radiated disgust.

Gunner surfaced a moment later and held a cannonball up like a shot put. At least he didn't hoot and holler like he had when we found the cannons. Back on board, Jack handed his gear to Randy.

"This is bullshit," he said. "I say we get the *Global Explorer* to dig a continuous trench with the mailboxes up the debris line."

"You can't do that while the boat is moving, Jack," I said. "The mailboxes aim the thrust of the propellers straight down."

He cocked his head sideways. "No shit, Buck. I meant hole after hole until we find something. We'll perforate a path."

Randy took his cue from Jack and returned to the mothership.

"Ben and Heather, you go help Randy," Jack said. "The three of us will dive the holes. Start on the next GPS mark and drill down every fifty feet toward the cannons at the end."

"You got it, Jack," Ben said.

Heather grimaced at being ordered to return to the ship but held her tongue.

It took twenty minutes for Randy to reposition the behemoth on top of the next spot. One would normally set anchors to keep the ship in place, but Jack's instructions were to keep moving. Like Heather, I held my tongue about the course of action Jack had set into motion. I had no compunction against using mailboxes in many cases, but not when we were searching under the radar with authorities increasingly interested in our activities.

"So what brought you guys together in Switzerland?" I said.

Jack rolled his eyes. Behind him, Gunner shook his head.

"Let it go, Buck," Jack said. "It's ancient history."

"What year was it?" I said.

"Forget it!"

"Around the time your company went down the shitter, wasn't it?" Gunner said. He winked at me as Jack spun on him.

"I said drop it!" He walked to the front of the dive boat, stood up on the bow, and stared into the water.

My blood began a slow boil. My initial desire to continue the divisive efforts that had produced results a couple of days ago had now been elevated beyond just a measure to keep them off-balance. Gunner's dissatisfaction with Jack and Ben's secret partnership had loosened his lips, and what was now tumbling out had my mind spinning.

Ben helped Randy drop the mailboxes into place and locked them off.

Little sound other than the revving twin diesels marked the commencement of thrust, and moments later, a swirl of sand and silt turned the water milky. Randy used the bow and stern thrusters to maintain position without anchoring up.

"How are we going to see anything in that murky mess?" Gunner said.

"We won't," I said. "We have to let it settle."

By the time Randy had repositioned four times, the visibility in the first hole had improved enough to check it out. "If you guys want to go, I'll stay on board," I said.

"Gunner can man the boat," Jack said. "You and I will go check these holes out."

I grabbed my tank, checked the air, and pulled the BCD over my right shoulder and clipped the strap on the left. Jack came back and sat on the gunwale next to me and geared up too. We pulled on kneepads and put extra weights in the pockets of our BCDs to work the bottom.

Jack strapped his dive knife to his calf. "Hand me that speargun," he said.

"What do you need that for?" I said.

Gunner handed it to him.

"Just in case we run into another one of those hammerheads." Jack handed me a small shovel. "You can dig holes while I keep an eye out."

"Might as well just go by myself—"

Jack elbowed me in the chest—I fell backward into the water. The magnetometer and shovel went flying as I struggled to grab my regulator and jam it in my mouth.

What an asshole!

41

ONCE I RETRIEVED the shovel and magnetometer, I swam to the first hole. It was thirty feet wide and only two feet deep—with the water depth at sixty, the mailboxes weren't as effective as they'd be in the shallows. I heard a splash as Jack entered the water behind me but ignored him and began a sweep around the hole with the magnetometer. The mag suddenly sang out, which led me to dig in the pile of sand and coral that had blasted up around the perimeter of the crater. I found heavily corroded chunks of indiscernible metal.

Jack was now swimming around the circle. Nothing but sand was visible, but I scanned it with the magnetometer anyway. I had a couple pings and found more encrusted chunks of metal, but nothing of interest. Jack waved me toward the next hole with the speargun, a less-than-subtle way of asserting his authority.

As I swam to the next one, I saw that the *Global Explorer* had now dug more holes and, per Jack's orders, was moving methodically west. The continuous thrust had reduced visibility to half what it had been earlier, as sand and silt swirled everywhere. Sunbeams flickered through the churned particles, creating a kaleidoscope effect that was both disorienting and disconcerting.

We dove several more craters with similar results. I was doing all the work, and Jack was mostly just following after me and watching. After checking the outer limits of the next hole, I dove in, and the magnetometer pinged at something on the western wall. Resting prone with my kneepads on the sand, I fanned the side, sweeping away the sand.

A brilliant gold escudo appeared, about the size of a half dollar. I fanned around it and saw more gold underneath it. My body was blocking Jack's view. If I left the escudo and the sand continued to trickle down the crater wall, he'd spot it.

My stomach instantly knotted up. What would happen if we found the treasure here and now? All my leverage would be gone. Even Heather was worried they'd kill her if we found it—and after Gunner's mention of Switzerland, plus Jack's obvious jealousy—

I took small flag from the pocket of my BCD and placed it next to the gold, then fanned sand back over the coin. I realized my hand was shaking.

When I started to swim up the wall to go to the next hole, I felt a sudden tug and whipped around—Jack had grabbed my fin. He pointed to the flag and raised his hands as if to ask what was there. I made a casual gesture with my hand, then pointed to the next crater.

He shook his head and dove into the hole and dug into the sand next to the flag. A few gold escudos tumbled out. When he glanced back up at me, he wasn't smiling.

He pointed to my shovel and waved toward him, so I handed it over. After a couple stabs at the side, three gold ingots appeared, approximately three inches each.

My heart was racing as I studied his body language. He glanced up at me, and I made the okay sign. He shook his head and speared the shovel into the hole. Jack might be a lot of things, but he wasn't stupid. He again used the speargun and pointed it toward me, then into the hole.

The message was clear: I was going to do all the work, and I'd be lucky if he didn't kill me when I was done. If he had something to do with my parents' deaths, then he'd have no compunction against killing me too.

I used the metal detector in the balance of the hole and found one mild ping. When I dug it up, it was a remnant of wood that held a couple fine nails. It looked like the type of wood and size of nails I'd seen on intact crates the Spanish had used to box gold in that period. I held it up for Jack, knowing he'd only see it as junk. He waved me toward the next crater.

The water clarity was getting better. Randy had stopped blasting holes with the mailboxes, and we were getting close to the end of the line. I spotted a dark pile just past the next one.

Cannons. Several cannons.

Jack also saw them and waved me into the next hole. Son of a bitch—I felt like a steer being led to slaughter. The water depth was now fifty feet, and the silt had settled down completely. Before I even dove into the next crater, a glisten of gold sparkled in the sunlight penetrating the depths.

I descended slowly and saw six inches of gold chain link sticking out of the sand. As I fanned the sand around, more and more chain appeared until I grabbed it in the middle and started gently pulling at it. Two feet of gold chain, three feet … six feet, and by the time it came free, I held over eight feet of gold chain a half inch wide. My partners wouldn't care, but wealthy Spaniards had used gold chains for currency, one link at a time.

Behind me, Jack dug furiously with the shovel and uncovered a pile of gold coins, then gold bars, ingots, and before long, a clump of silver the size of a hay bale that had corroded together into a block. Emeralds and fine jewelry swirled up in the water as we dug, and no matter where we poked, more riches appeared. Soon, there was a pile of precious cargo filling the bottom of the hole.

We'd found the queen's jewels.

On the upper lip of the hole, the barrel of a cannon peeked over, with others in a pile behind it. The log had said it: the treasure was with the cannons.

The thrill of discovery had me lightheaded until I saw Jack staring at me through slit eyes. No high fives, no fist bumps.

The speargun was pointed at the center of my chest.

I ducked to my right just as he fired the spear—it sliced across my left shoulder!

I threw my arm over the tether that connected the spear to the gun and jerked it toward me—Jack came with it, holding on tight. I swiveled my body hard to the left and shoved the palm of my right hand into his face—Jack's mask flew off his head.

He crouched, the regulator still in his mouth—he planted his feet on the bottom and lunged toward me, dive knife now in his outstretched hand.

I grabbed his arm, shoved it away, then grabbed him by his BCD and swung him toward the slope of the hole—jammed him against the lip next to the cannon barrel. I had him by the chest with my head jammed into his neck as he flung his arms—the knife slashed by my head—he knocked my mask off—water sucked up my nose as I drew ragged breaths from the regulator still clenched in my mouth.

Jack fought hard as I shoved him with all my strength under the cannon with what leverage I could manage. He was crazed, but I hung on tight and pressed with all my might—he'd kill me if I let go.

You killed my parents, you son of a bitch! I know it!

Jack suddenly went still, dropped the knife, and held his arms up—I pushed him one last time into the sand, then grabbed his knife and floated back.

Even without my mask on, I froze at what I saw.

Jack's face was blue, and his eyes were opened wide. The regulator wasn't in his mouth—it must have come out as we struggled.

Jack Dodson was dead.

42

JACK LAY FACEUP IN THE BOTTOM OF THE HOLE surrounded by gold, silver, gems, and jewelry. Hyperventilating, I had to concentrate to get my breathing under control. I found my mask, put it back on, cleared it, and took stock of the situation.

Gunner was directly overhead in the dive boat, fifty feet up. The water was clear, but he wouldn't be able to see what had happened down here.

What I'd done.

A half dozen cannons marked the spot where d'Aire and Jean Bart had executed the captain of the *Farnese* and his crew in a brazen act of piracy and mutiny born of greed and revenge. France had been abandoned by the Spanish in the Peace of Utrecht and left broke for a generation—not unlike myself when Jack's greed and thievery had robbed me of my company, my wealth, my wife, my brother … and now I was damned certain he'd killed my parents, too.

A decade had passed since then, and he'd taken every opportunity to challenge me, take what little success I'd been able to grab. He'd kidnapped, lied, and ultimately tried to kill me. What had happened to him to cause all this? What broke?

Dear God.

Now what?

Gunner could easily finish me off, and probably Heather and Ben too. I couldn't let that happen. A plan lit in my head. I checked my air gauge: 800 PSI. I dove down, found Jack's mask, put it back on his head, then lifted his lifeless form off the bottom and carried him up and out of the hole. I swam back to the last hole, lowered him to the bottom, took the regulator out of his mouth, and hit the purge valve until the gauge read zero. I placed the regulator back in his mouth, which had already begun to tighten with rigor mortis.

Back in the treasure hole, I recovered Jack's dive knife and the speargun. I placed the spear back in place on the gun, dropped it next to him, then shoved the knife back into the scabbard on his calf. The slice on my shoulder was bleeding, but it wasn't deep. Had I not ducked, the spear would have gone right through my heart, exactly where he'd aimed it.

Unbelievable.

Jack lay still, faceup, with his arms to his sides. I exhaled hard and swam back to the treasure hole. I grabbed the gold chain, some emeralds, and a handful of gold coins, then jammed them into the pocket of my BCD. I found the shovel and began to cover everything else back over again. It felt like it took forever—so much had been uncovered. Once it was covered, I moved the sand around with my hands until it was mostly uniform and appeared like the other holes had after the mailboxes blasted them open.

I told myself I was doing this out of self-protection from Gunner, not greed.

Back in Jack's crater, I took the gold and emeralds from my pocket, dug a few holes, dumped them in, and covered them back over. My air was now at 600 PSI, so I free-flowed my regulator down to 200. I took a deep breath and blew into his BCD's mouthpiece until he floated off the bottom.

With a last look around, a sense of doom filled me. Jack's and my history had been destined to end violently, and to have it happen here, at the site where hundreds more had died, sent a shiver through me. The captain and crew of the *Farnese* had been cursed by a history outside their control, and we'd been drawn here by the same burning greed that had led to their demise.

With one more breath, Jack's BCD was full, and after a blast of air into mine, we began our ascent to the surface. The site below was surreal and reminiscent of an artillery-pounded battlefield. Giant round circles in a long line that led to the pile of cannons and a vast treasure that had been buried for over three hundred years.

Would the RBDF be able to see the pattern from the surface? If so, they'd immediately know what we'd been up to.

We burst through the surface twenty feet from the boat, where Gunner stood watching us expectantly. The *Global Explorer* was anchored close by, with Ben, Heather, and Randy standing at the transom watching us.

"Help! Help me!" My voice was hoarse from the compressed air and the emotion of having just killed a man, no matter how evil.

"What happened?" Gunner said.

"It's Jack! I think he's drowned."

"Oh shit," Gunner said.

43

HEATHER LET OUT A SHRIEK THAT CARRIED ACROSS THE WATER. Gunner revved the engines on the dive boat and closed the short gap between us as everyone on the mothership climbed aboard the Zodiac. I ditched Jack's gear, and with me pushing from the water, Gunner heaved him onto the deck.

Jack landed with a loud thud.

I ditched my gear too and climbed the ladder on the stern. The others simultaneously climbed aboard the dive boat from the Zodiac, and we all stood around Gunner, who was down on one knee above Jack.

He peered over his shoulder toward me. "What the hell happened?"

"I have no idea! We cleared a couple holes, then found these—" I dug into the BCD's pocket and pulled out the three escudos.

Gunner stood suddenly. "Gold! And emeralds!"

"Gold?" Ben said.

Gunner's eyes gleamed.

"Then what happened?" Heather said. She was pale as a ghost but not crying.

"Jack kept digging. He wouldn't stop. I took the magnetometer and moved on to the next hole. I dug around there for a while. Then saw I was low on air, so I went back to see what Jack was doing." I pictured Jack lying faceup in the bottom of the hole, and my body convulsed.

"And?" Ben said.

"I found him on his back on the bottom. No bubbles—"

"His BCD's full of air," Ben said. "How did that happen if he was out—"

"I blew into it to get him to the surface."

"Where are your tanks? I want to the see the air gauges!" Ben said.

"I ditched them to get out of the water—go get 'em—they're floating behind the boat."

Gunner stepped closer to me. "Did you find any more gold?"

"What happened to your shoulder, Buck?" Ben said. He pointed to the red slash that had a few drops of blood dripping down my bicep.

I glanced down at the cut, then rubbed my hand over it and looked at the blood in my palm. "I don't know. Must've happened while I was trying to get Jack to the surface."

"You're lying!" Ben said.

Heather walked to the bow and sat heavily on the seat in front of the console, her back to us.

"The hell are you talking about?" I said.

"I know you're lying! You killed him, didn't you?"

"Are you crazy?"

"Forget about Dodson, he's dead," Gunner said. "What about the gold?!"

Ben bent down and pulled the mask off Jack's face and water poured out. "His mask is full of water? What, did you put it back on after you killed him?"

"I've never killed anyone—"

Ben shook his head and white spittle foamed in the corners of his mouth. "You're lying! I've known you my entire life—it was because he mentioned Switzerland, wasn't it?" He pointed toward Gunner.

That made me freeze, and my eyes zeroed in on Ben's face.

There was a vague whimper from Heather on the bow.

"What do *you* know about Switzerland?" I said.

"Fuck you, Buck!"

I jumped over Jack, grabbed Ben by the shirt, and shoved him back against the dive boat's steering wheel. "*What do you know?*"

"Hey!" Gunner yelled. We turned back to face him. "I said, did you find any more gold? That's why we're here, goddamnit!"

Ben tried to squeeze past me in a dash for the Zodiac, where Randy sat staring at Gunner, awaiting orders. I grabbed the back of Ben's shirt—it tore in my hands, which slowed him enough for me to shove my arms under his armpits, pull up, and get him in a full nelson.

"Tell me about Switzerland! What did your buddy—your *partner*—Jack Dodson tell you?"

Gunner pushed past us and grabbed another scuba tank that was already strapped to a BCD with a regulator hanging off its valve. "Which hole did you find the gold in?"

I struggled with Ben but was looking Gunner in the eye, amazed at his laser focus and lack of concern for his partner of so many years.

"Reilly! The gold, where did you find it?" Gunner pulled the tank over his shoulder and clicked the strap on the other one to secure it in place. "The fucking Bahamians will be here sooner or later, and we need to grab what we can."

"Let me go!" Ben said.

"Tell me what you know, Ben!"

Ben hunched down to escape the full nelson—we crashed into Gunner, who collided into the center console—Heather jumped up. Once Gunner caught his balance, he lowered his shoulder and jammed it into both Ben and me. We fell backwards.

"Enough of this bullshit!" Gunner said. From the open shelf

next to the steering wheel, he grabbed his Glock and pointed it at both of us. "I'm sick of this crap—all of you—we're so close to the prize and you're whining about the past—your damned parents? Really? Fuck me." Gunner waved to Randy, who stood up, his Sig Sauer now in hand.

"I need you to focus on the treasure, Reilly, so I'll tell you about Switzerland—"

"Gunner!" Ben's shout drew my attention. "No!"

Gunner shook his head. "Dodson masterminded Switzerland. The whole thing."

I felt the blood rush from my hands.

"He had your parents killed, okay?" He waved his hand toward Ben and then toward the front of the boat. "They were all in on it." He pointed to Ben and Heather. "Your brother, your ex. All of them."

Ben's eyes were wide as he stepped backward toward the bow.

"They lied to me!" Heather said.

My breathing was shallow as I looked from Gunner to Ben to Heather.

"He's lying!" Ben was now pressed into the bow.

Heather sobbed hysterically, her cheeks flushed—she covered her face with her hands. "They told me they were going to rob them—nobody was supposed to get hurt!"

My legs buckled. I fell back to sit on the driver's bench seat.

Gunner wrapped the waist strap from the BCD around his gut. "Your punk-ass brother knew they'd changed their wills to make him the sole beneficiary—apparently they cut you out when you were rich. He was afraid they'd change it back since you were about to be broke."

I stood up.

Ben was now crying as he cowered on the bow. "It was Jack's idea! He wanted the maps ... all the ... research shit ... so he'd … have the only … copies."

The blood rushed back into my arms, and rage curled my fingers into fists. My hands felt like sledgehammers. I looked down at Heather, balled up and crying.

Gunner actually laughed. "And your darling bride, she's the one who told Jack they were heading to Switzerland on a mission for you." He paused to tighten the shoulder straps on the BCD. He glanced down at Heather and shook his head. "Pretty is as pretty does. I'm telling you, Reilly, they were all in on it."

Heather howled like a scalded dog.

I looked past her to Ben. "It's all true, isn't it?"

He jumped up, threw himself forward and jammed his finger toward me like it was a sword.

"They always liked you better! I knew for years you were adopted, and it just made me hate you more—them too! You'll never be able to prove any of it." Then he swung his finger toward Gunner. "And he drove the car that ran them over!"

Gunner was seated on the gunwale with his mask on top of his head and was pulling his fins on. He held his hands up. "I was just a gun for hire. Wasn't personal."

My lungs burned as I sucked in a breath so deep it might make them burst. As if Gunner's rationale made it acceptable that he'd killed my parents. I could strangle him, all of them. Jack's blue face stared up from the deck.

You rotten bastard.

"I'm going to find more gold." With that, Gunner rolled backward off the boat, leaving me alone with Ben and Heather. On the Zodiac, Randy had kept a straight face. He still held the Sig, but it wasn't pointed at anyone.

My world had exploded with the force of a supernova, followed by an implosion of black hole proportions.

44

I PULLED ON ANOTHER TANK AND JUMPED IN AFTER GUNNER. Being on the boat with Ben and Heather would drive me to violence, so I needed to try and clear my head and get away from them. With slow, deliberate kicks, I aimed myself toward the stream of bubbles that Gunner was producing in the middle hole that Randy had blown. He had jumped in without a magnetometer or shovel, so I wasn't particularly concerned about him finding what I'd buried, but I wanted to keep an eye on him.

My experience had always been that a project that starts bad ends bad, which is how this entire shit show had gone. Being lied to about Ben getting kidnapped and manipulated by Jack and Gunner, their using and threatening Scarlet, and all that happened since … It was a mind-blowing situation that altered my life—all our lives—beyond repair.

And Jack was dead.

As I descended, I tried to think ahead of the current challenges. How could I make these bastards pay for what they'd done and get them out of my life once and for all? That was my focus and mission, above all else. Then I could think about the *Farnese*.

Gunner dug with his bare hands in a hole I'd already searched with the magnetometer. He pulled up a chunk of the corroded metal I'd left behind. He studied it like a Neanderthal with a crude tool. When I arrived, Gunner looked up with his eyes narrowed. Knowing how his mind worked, he was no doubt assessing whether I was a threat, given all the epiphanies that had just erupted on the dive boat. Gunner had said he was just a gun for hire, and while that was an appalling thought, it was how his world worked. My just-formed plan would be to continue my strategic alliance with him by manipulating his lust for treasure. Which meant I'd have to appear to accept his rationale until I could devise the retribution that was percolating in my head.

He held his arms up, which I interpreted as an inquiry to where we'd found the gold ingots, coins, and emeralds. With no tools, we had no choice but to visually inspect the holes, but I wanted to keep Gunner away from the last one, given his proclivity to dig like a dog with his bare hands. With an eye on my air gauge, we advanced slowly around and through one hole after the other until I was down to 500 PSI of air. The way he huffed and puffed on land, I assumed he had to be down to a couple of hundred PSI, max.

So with limited time left on this dive and with the sun low in the western sky, I led Gunner to the next hole. It was the one where Jack had been laid out on the bottom, faceup toward the surface. We spiraled our way into the crater, and as he dug at the side closest to the next hole, where I'd reburied the lion's share of what I'd found earlier, I concentrated on the lowest point in the center of this one. With enough sand fanned away to reveal part of the gold chain I'd hidden here, I grabbed Gunner's arm and redirected him to the discovery.

He lunged at the chain, where he pulled, prodded, and dug. I could see his fingers were bloody from the coarse sand—the chain pulled free. He held it up over his head like a gladiator. Then he spotted a brilliant uncut emerald the size of a golf ball peeking out from another hole. My air was down to 250 PSI—he looked up quickly, his shoulders peeling back as he sucked on his regulator with all his might.

No air left, Gunner?

I could let him drown, but that wasn't part of my plan, so I jammed my backup octopus regulator in his face, which he sucked into his mouth. I pointed to the surface. The way he Hoovered air, we'd both drown if we weren't careful. He jammed the chain and emerald into his pockets, and we began a faster ascent than I would have preferred.

We surfaced seventy feet from the dive boat. The others had returned to the *Global Explorer* in the Zodiac and had to be inside the salon.

Gunner spit out my octopus and floated on his back. He pulled the mask to the top of his head, hissed out a laugh, and smiled widely, revealing his yellowed square teeth. "Goddamn, Reilly. I always knew you were the real deal."

"This is my purpose," I said.

His shrug blew water toward me. "And here I wasted all those years with a trash-talking accountant."

We were out of earshot of the mothership, but Gunner kept his voice down, and I had a pretty good sense of why. We paddled toward the dive boat, and I swam closer to him and nodded toward the *Global Explorer*.

"You want to cut them in on this?" I said.

His smile slid to a frown. "Hell no."

I nodded. "Good, me either. Those two can rot in hell as far as I'm concerned."

"Randy can make them disappear. Just say the word." He pumped his eyebrows.

"We don't want people asking questions, but we do need to get rid of Jack's body," I said. The glow of sunset had the water's surface the color of molten copper. "We should weigh it down and dump him in deeper water tonight."

Gunner winked at me. "I like how you think, Reilly." He ran a palm over his wet hair. "Guess I had you wrong all this time. You've got more balls than I thought."

"You think you know me, Gunner, but you don't." And, just to get ahead of the curve, I added, "As for Switzerland ... I get it. It was Jack calling the shots."

The old mercenary started to laugh. "Don't forget that weasel of a brother!" He laughed so loud, Heather stepped out of the salon and stood on deck, gazing out toward us.

WHEN WE RETURNED TO THE *GLOBAL EXPLORER*, Gunner dragged Jack's body on board, and I carried the empty scuba tanks to the stern locker and began to refill them. I wasn't ready to see Heather or Ben yet, so I killed time in the gear locker and let whatever conversation Gunner was going to have with them play out.

I took my time, refilled all six empty tanks, and strapped two on the aft deck starboard hull wall. When I turned around, I nearly tripped over a bundle in a blue tarp on the deck—Jack. Gunner must have wrapped him up and left him behind the chair where I sat to drink my coffee in the mornings.

I sat down and stared at the heap. My body shivered, but not from guilt. Maybe it was fear of getting caught, but he had tried to kill me, and his death was accidental—I'd been fighting to protect myself.

"Can't believe the shit you put me through, Jack." My voice was a whisper. "And that you tried to kill me. All the damage you wrought ... You destroyed my family, one person at a time." I felt no guilt, but no satisfaction, either.

"Now it's my turn to use you, old buddy." I choked up, stood, and walked inside.

Heather was seated at the table alone, as if she were waiting. She stood quickly when I entered.

"Buck, can we talk?"

I walked past her without a word and down the steps and into my stateroom. Ben was in there on his upper bunk with his back to me. I grabbed my duffel bag and walked out into the corridor as Gunner exited the stateroom he shared with Randy. His eyes dropped to my bag.

"Where you going?"

"I'm taking Jack's cabin. I can't sleep with Ben."

"To the victor goes the spoils," he said.

I stopped to look him in the eye. "After we dump the body, let's relocate the ship and plane a mile away in case the RBDF show up. We don't want them spotting the mailbox holes," I said.

"Good idea." Gunner nodded toward the galley. "Randy's making dinner. We'll do it after that."

As if anybody was hungry—except for Gunner, of course. This was all standard in his world. With that, I entered Jack's stateroom and closed and locked the door. Seeing his gear gave me a chill—especially the Glock sitting on his nightstand. A flood of memories pressed against my heart, but I forced them away. I didn't want to be here for any reason other than to have some privacy.

I pulled the cell phone from my duffel.

Ray answered after two rings. There was music in the background.

"Where are you?" I said.

"Driff's Beach Bar."

"Caerula Mar Club?"

"It's close to the airport." Ray's voice was defensive.

"I know. Good, glad you're having fun. What's the status of the Mallard?"

"Great. Took her for a checkout flight today. I flew out past your ship. You didn't see me?"

"I must've been underwater. Watertight?"

"We landed close to shore and she did great. No leaks, nothing." He paused. "I bought her, Buck. Used what money we had in Last Resort's account and my own savings to make up the difference."

I exhaled a long breath.

"You okay?" he said. "Any luck with finding that treasure to replenish our accounts?"

"Kind of, but things have gone bad here. Dodson's dead—drowned—but I also learned some other things."

"Oh my gosh! That's awful." He paused. "And what else?"

"Let's just say he had it coming."

Reggae music played in the background, and the sound of glasses and cutlery clinking gave me a vision of why I needed to get this done successfully and get out of here.

"Listen to me carefully, Ray. I need you to do something, because if what I have planned doesn't go down right, I'll be the next one dead."

"Anything. What do you need?"

When I told him, he was initially silent, then cleared his throat.

"Yeah, I can do that. You sure it'll work?"

"I'm not sure about anything anymore, but I'm counting on you, partner."

It pained me to use that term, but Ray was the only trustworthy partner I'd ever had. And my life depended on him coming through now.

45

GUNNER FINISHED HIS DINNER IN HIGH SPIRITS. He hadn't shared details of what we'd found this afternoon with anyone, and I certainly wasn't going to. It was pitch black out tonight. The waning crescent moon from the night when Heather and I met on the bow had turned to nothing.

Once he guzzled his glass of red wine, Gunner stood. "Buck and I are gonna give Dodson a burial at sea."

A sudden whimper sounded from Heather. She stood abruptly and ran down the steps toward her cabin. Ben said nothing and stared straight ahead.

Gunner and I had discussed this earlier, and it was exactly what I wanted to happen. My nerve ends were sharp, as this next hour would be one of the riskiest of my life. If Gunner caught me, then it'd be a double burial at sea.

"Randy, you want to join us?" Gunner said.

"What?" I said. Then in a whisper, "That wasn't the plan."

"It's fine. He can drive. I'm half-drunk." Then he mouthed the word "celebrating" to me and then winked. His breath reeked of bourbon mixed with wine.

Shit. That would make the sleight of hand I needed to pull off even harder. I poured Gunner more wine. "Might as well drink up then," I said.

He laughed out loud, then said to Ben, "You have KP tonight while the men take care of business." He punctuated his statement with a burp.

With Jack gone, Gunner would be unchecked, which was dangerous. But all I could think about was how I could do what I'd planned without getting caught.

The three of us walked out to the aft deck. Randy said nothing as usual, but over the past several days, he had performed his tasks without the need for further instruction, so I appreciated his silence.

Gunner carried the remainder of the bottle of Saint-Émilion Grand Cru in one hand and his cup in the other. He paused to look at the body wrapped up in the blue tarp.

"Randy, give me a hand here," I said.

I took one end—Jack's feet—and Randy grabbed the other end. Jack had been a muscular guy and weighed at least 225 pounds. The corpse had grown stiff, so it was easier to carry than it had been shortly after he'd died. Gunner moved aside, and we laid Jack on the gunwale of the *Global Explorer* and climbed inside the dive boat. We then placed the tarp down by the transom.

Randy started the motors as Gunner climbed aboard—tripped—and dumped half his glass of wine all over the deck. I caught his arm and held him up.

"Thanks, Bucky," he said.

Good grief.

THE WIND HAD PICKED UP TONIGHT, and there were whitecaps on the waves out in TOTO. I didn't want to go too deep anyway, so I used that to my advantage. "I suggest we go north of the wreck site but stay out of the heavy currents that blow through TOTO. We don't want the package floating away."

Once we were north of the Joulter Cays and parallel to TO-TO's northwestern tusk-shaped area, the depth gauge read 95 feet.

"This should be good here," I said. My sweaty right hand was in my pocket, and I was waiting for the right moment to do what I had planned.

Gunner stood up and weaved his way back to the transom. "Lift him up on the back here," he said. "And get rid of that damn tarp."

Randy and I lifted the tarp and laid it out in front of the outboard engines. Gunner undid the bungee cords and pulled the tarp open. A rancid smell curled my nostrils. Jack's skin was now marbled and gray. The lack of moonlight spared us a more vivid view.

Gunner pulled a long knife from a sheath on his belt and cut Jack's dive shirt open.

"What are you doing?" I said.

Without a word, Gunner raised the knife and plunged it into Jack's abdomen—I turned away and raised a hand to block my view.

"What the hell was that for?" I turned back and saw that Gunner was methodically sawing through Jack's stomach.

"Dead bodies sink, initially," he said. "But after time, putrefaction causes organs to swell and fill with gas. That makes them float again." He smiled as he dug open a foot-wide gash and then stabbed around to puncture internal organs to prevent that from happening.

"Gross." My voice was a whisper. I wasn't ready for what he did next, but as Randy watched with interest, I took my phone from my pocket, which was already set to the video app, and discreetly filmed Gunner's next barbaric act.

"Always loved your blue eyes," Gunner said. He then used the end of the blade to carve out one of Jack's eyeballs—I heaved, but I was able to capture the moment on video. Randy nodded in approval. I couldn't watch as he moved on to the other eyeball, so I pocketed my camera. Two subtle splashes signaled their fate.

I spotted the milk crate with dive gear on the bow and had an idea. I stepped forward, dug around, and found a weight belt. Hurrying back to the transom, I held it up.

"Let's wrap this around his waist too," I said.

Gunner peered back over his shoulder and nodded. "Good idea."

I stood back and waited and, when Gunner was done, tried to hand him the weights. His hands and forearms glistened with shiny fluid. "You do it," he said. "Wrap it around his gut."

Lovely.

I held the weight belt up and stood in the middle of the transom and forced myself to look at Gunner's workmanship—the abdominal stench burned my eyes—I held my breath but glanced back toward Gunner.

"I'll need a guzzle of that wine in a minute."

His howl of laughter sounded like a coyote's under a full moon. I shook off the sense of disgust and grabbed the end of the weight belt from under Jack's waist. I hesitated and thought I would puke.

"What are you doing?" Randy said.

"Trying to get this weight belt tight—I got bloody goop all over my hand and it's slippery."

Randy stood up. "Let me give you a hand—"

I pushed the buckle shut on the weight belt. "That was disgusting," I said as I turned around.

Gunner was standing right behind me, his eyes slits. He looked past me toward Jack. "What's wrong with this picture?" he said.

"What do you mean?"

Gunner looked from me to Randy, his face serious. "Why is Dodson still back there?"

I stepped forward as he took another swig of French wine. I again retrieved my phone, flicked on the camera, and chose video. Without looking back, Gunner pushed Jack's body over the corner of the transom. I pocketed the phone with it still recording.

"Looks like you saw a ghost, Buck—ha! You did, didn't you?" Gunner laughed at his own joke, then handed me the bottle. "Dumping Dodson in the ocean turns him into a ghost, sure as hell!"

I grabbed it with my clean hand and guzzled a mouthful.

Randy held up the hose connected to the boat's fresh water supply. "Hold your arms over the side and I'll spray the blood off."

We dried off with a towel. There was no sign of Jack floating behind the boat. Hopefully he'd sunk straight to the bottom.

"Anybody want to say a few words?" I said.

"Allow me," Gunner said. He cleared his throat. "Later, asshole." He then roared with laughter all over again.

While Gunner admired his handiwork, I stopped recording the video.

SECTION 6

UP ON
THE
TIGHTWIRE

46

BY THE TIME WE RETURNED TO THE *GLOBAL EX-PLORER*, Gunner was too drunk and didn't want to move, and I was too rattled to fly the Beast anyway, especially to take off and land in the water at night. But like the good soldier he'd turned out to be, Randy was up at dawn getting the ship ready to relocate. After I placed the two tanks I'd strapped to the aft starboard wall last night into the dinghy, Randy took me out to the Beast, and we agreed to relocate a couple of miles south. I didn't tell him, but I planned to check on the logistics I'd asked Ray to initiate for me. Before that, though, there was another call I needed to make.

I hurried through the pre-flight check, and even though the Beast had been sitting in salt water for days now, everything seemed to be functioning properly, and the bilge was dry enough. I glanced out the starboard window and cranked that engine to turn over four times, turned off the emergency ignition switch, flipped the battery and generator switches on, and made sure the carburetor air was turned to cold. I added throttle, turned the emergency ignition switch back on, and engaged the starter.

The starboard engine fired right up. If Ben and Heather had been sleeping, they'd be awake now. I repeated the process on the port engine, checked the oil pressure gauges—which were good at 70 PSI—adjusted the props to low pitch, increased manifold pressure, and increased throttle. The light chop was ideal as we I climbed onto the step, and seconds later, we were airborne.

I studied the *Global Explorer* as we flew past. Nobody had bothered to go out on deck to wave me goodbye. On my phone, I found a number I'd only ever answered and had never called. Until now.

The destination of my short flight was already coming into view, so I didn't have time for small talk. Jesse McDermitt wasn't the chatty type anyway. But he had a reputation as a man of his word who you could trust, as long as you were straight with him.

"You find what you were looking for yet?" I said.

After a brief pause, McDermitt's voice perked up. "Nothing to my liking."

"I have something for you."

"Details? Price?"

In spite of the situation, I couldn't help but smile. "It's complicated."

"I remember it being complicated last time," Jesse replied. "Is it always that way, Reilly?"

I smiled wider. "I need your help. Here's the deal …"

McDermitt exhaled heavily after I explained what I needed, and for the first time in weeks, my luck took a turn for the better. He was geographically in a position to help, and we agreed on "the price," so we planned accordingly and ended the call. I pumped my fist once, which reminded me of Gunner, so I pumped it again.

Five minutes later, I radioed Miami Center and announced my intention to land at Congo Town Airport, also known as South Andros Airport. Permission was granted based on visual flight rules. No other airplanes were in sight or within close proximity on radar, so I entered the pattern and moments later touched down on runway 28. There were limited facilities at Congo Town, but Betty and the Mallard were tied down at the end of the runway. A jeep was parked in the gravel parking lot next to the small building there. I taxied over and, once off the flight line, powered down and turned off the Beast's batteries.

By the time I opened the hatch and stepped outside, Ray was there in the jeep.

"You made it," he said.

"Temporarily. How did you do?"

"I talked to your guy. He should be on Nassau by now. Said for you to call him once you got here."

"Good."

"What happened to Jack Dodson?"

I couldn't meet his eyes. The mention of Jack's name brought me back to Gunner's informal surgery last night and my close-up view of Jack's ribcage as I attached the weight belt. I shook my head and tried to erase the image from my mind. "Better we don't talk about it."

"That bad—"

I held a hand up. "I just need to catch my breath, Ray. I'm sorry."

"You see the Mallard next to Betty? The whole fleet is here! C'mon, let me show it to you." His face was positively glowing.

I felt bad for Ray, but if all went well, his disappointment would be short-lived. "No time. I need to call our friend and get back before Gunner gets suspicious. Give me a minute."

Stuck on the *Global Explorer*, I hadn't walked more than fifty feet in days, so I walked along the taxiway in the opposite direction from the Mallard and pulled up another number on my phone. This one I'd called more times than I cared to remember, but none as important as this one.

"About time you got in touch, hotshot."

"Special Agent Booth. For once I'm calling *you* into action."

"You better not be wasting my time, Reilly. Flying to the Bahamas with no justification could get my ass into—"

"Relax, Booth. I've just solved what you've never been capable of working out, so shut up and listen."

294 JOHN H. CUNNINGHAM

His exhale had the sound of a pissed-off grizzly bear. "Tell me."

It didn't take long to explain what I'd learned, but I hedged on the details of discovering the *Farnese*. He couldn't care less about a three-hundred-year-old shipwreck, but his Bahamian counterparts would feel otherwise.

"Those other criminals don't surprise me, but your own brother? And your ex-wife, the supermodel?" He paused. "This isn't some kind of get-even scheme of yours, is it, Reilly?"

"There's no getting even for my parents getting murdered."

"What proof do you have?"

I bit the side of my lip. "They confessed to me—"

"That's it?"

"Dodson drowned and disappeared at sea, and then they were all at each other's throats."

"Disappeared at sea? That sounds highly questionable. I was looking forward to nailing his ass to the wall." Booth paused. "I'm going to need some additional explanation, hotshot."

I spun around to see Ray inspecting the Beast. There was a scum line on the fuselage where she'd sat in the water for days. He was shaking his head.

"You'll get it, but for now, we need to nail these bastards. They'll turn on each other to save their own asses, don't worry."

"You better hope so. If this blows up on me, it'll be a shit shower for you."

I changed the discussion to the next step, but Booth was already ahead of me, thank God. After telling me what he had planned, he hung up.

I stood for a long moment, staring out at the coast. The beauty of the Bahamian water had never mattered less to me than it did right now. With a glance at my ancient Rolex Submariner, I hurried back to Ray, who watched me approach with both hands on his hips.

"The Beauty's a mess, Buck. It'll take a week to clean—"

"I gotta go, Ray." I popped the Beast's hatch open.

"That's it? Just like that?"

I turned to face him. "I'm sorry." I paused. "Listen, I finally found out who killed my parents."

His eyes bugged wide.

"Exactly. I'll explain all that later, but the good news is I also found the *Farnese*."

His eyes bugged wider. "You did?! Oh my God, that's amazing! All of it? I mean, the queen's jewels? Gold, silver, jewels?"

"All of the above."

Ray jumped up and down—I'd never seen him do that before—and his red Hawaiian shirt billowed with each hop.

"But it's complicated," I said. "Remember, we're in Bahamian waters without a permit—"

"I knew you'd do it! That's why I spent all our money on the Mallard! I had faith in you!"

"Ray." He kept jumping up and down. "Ray? Ray!" My scream curtailed his excitement. "If all goes well, we can buy any plane we want, okay? So don't get all attached to the Mallard."

His smile shifted instantly to concern. "What's that supposed to mean?"

"I've got to get back to the *Global Explorer*. Gunner's probably freaking out by now. I'll call you later, after whatever happens happens."

"What if I don't hear from you?"

"Well, then things didn't go the way we wanted them to."

Without further discussion, I climbed aboard the Beast and within moments was airborne, flying north along the eastern coast before I vectored out toward TOTO, where I spotted the *Global Explorer* on the edge of the indigo abyss.

47

AFTER CIRCLING THE *GLOBAL EXPLORER* at its new anchorage south of Majestic Bay on the edge of TOTO, I landed smoothly in the turquoise waters to the west. I'd been gone longer than I'd planned, and everyone was out on the aft deck of the ship, watching the Beast taxi toward them.

My phone lit up with a call. I pulled the throttles back and removed my headset to answer it, expecting Gunner to be questioning where I'd been. "Hello?"

"We're just setting off from Nassau now." It was Booth.

I swallowed hard. "You have plenty of help?"

"Don't tell me how to do my job, Reilly."

"My ass is on the line here, Booth."

"The captain tells me we'll be there in forty-five minutes. Man up, Reilly. It's the moment you've been waiting for." With that, he hung up.

Shit.

Butterflies rumbled like water buffaloes in my empty stomach, and my hands were numb on the controls as I powered the engines down and fumbled through the post-flight checklist. My watch read 9:20 a.m., so the shit would hit the fan around 10:00. I had no idea how to play this on board the ship or what I'd do when Booth and the cavalry appeared on the horizon. There were no feelings of sympathy or regret for Ben, as he'd made his sentiment clear. He'd always resented me, maybe more so since I was adopted—something he apparently had known longer than I had. His greed to capture our parents' estate led him to conspire with Jack to kill them before they changed their wills. Jack's desire to possess the only copies of the research materials made them the perfect collaborators, each for different reasons, but both with something separate to gain.

And Heather ... I wasn't sure what to think about her involvement.

I set the bow anchor from the forward hatch, tied off the rope, and pulled the hatch closed. With a deep breath, I stumbled through the fuselage, my mind reeling. The sound of the Zodiac's outboard motor approaching caused me to pause.

"Come on, Buck. Suck it up."

I popped open the hatch and was surprised to see it was Heather who'd come to retrieve me. Her windswept blonde hair and bronzed skin would be the dream of many a man, but looking at her now, I felt only nauseous. Her red and puffy eyes were anything but cover girl material.

"Permission to come aboard?"

A glance at my watch showed 9:35. Killing some time off the ship while Booth was en route made sense, even if it had to be with Heather. I held my hand out for the painter line, which she tossed me. I tied it off on the cleat but didn't bother to move out of the hatch.

"What do you want?" I said.

She sat back down, and her chest rose as she appeared to be searching for whatever plea she intended to make. She leaned forward.

"I'm sorry I never told you what happened."

I didn't respond and concentrated on breathing steadily.

"I didn't know how to do that without ruining what was left of your world."

That prompted a dry laugh, but I bit my tongue.

"Afterwards, I was stuck with Jack—he said if I told anybody what they'd done, he'd tell *you* about my letting him know your parents were headed to Switzerland. I didn't know anything about the stupid research material! Either he guessed it or your parents had told Ben, but—"

"Jack told me you gave him a copy of a letter—the letter General Ubilla sent his wife from Havana. It was in my floor safe at home—our home—in Virginia."

"What?" She paused, then her eyebrows lifted. "When I decided to leave, I checked the safe for cash and copies of anything that may have had value in our divorce proceeding. I made copies of everything—I had no idea what any of that was. Jack must have rifled through it all later—"

"Stop, Heather. Please."

"I would have never done anything … to …"

"Hurt me? You don't think walking out on me—"

"That was different. I told you—"

"Spare me, Heather. You've been protecting my parents' murderers for years."

She hung her head, then rubbed her eyes and pushed the hair out of her face. Her cheeks were wet, and even from this distance, I could see her jaw trembling. "I know, it was wrong—terrible. I'm so, so sorry, Buck. But this is why I financed Jack's stupid trip here—to see you, to … I don't know, but I'm glad … I'm glad the truth is out. Finally."

My gut surprised me by feeling sorry for her. My head wanted to hate her, and my heart was broken all over again. Tears poured down her cheeks, and she lowered her face into her hands as her body shook with sobs. I'd never seen her cry when our marriage ended, and this reawakened the pain I'd felt back then.

No amount of deep breathing could ease the anguish that tore at my soul over this entire revelation, and contrary to Booth's snide comment, this was hardly the moment I'd waited for.

"Listen," I said.

She looked up, her eyes blinking rapidly.

"I have to make them pay for what they did, so when the time comes, tell the truth," I said.

Her eyes narrowed for a second, then widened. She nodded. "I will, I promise."

With that, I stepped into the Zodiac, closed the hatch, and sat on the bow. After a moment, Heather pulled the cord, and the engine came to life. I untied the painter, and she backed us away from the Beast. I watched the old plane as we turned slowly back toward the ship. Ben had bought me Betty, my first flying boat, but I had to trick him to do it, and his only motivation was to get me out of Virginia, which I realized now was so he could reap the rewards of his and Jack's evil deeds.

Gunner waited on the deck, his face serious. When we arrived, he held his hands up. "Where've you been? We need to go diving."

I held up my thumbs. "I went to fill up the fuel tanks."

There was no acknowledgment. If my gut intuition was correct, then Gunner's instincts had to be supernatural to have survived so many years as a mercenary in the armpits of the world. I didn't flinch from his stare. I smiled at the knowledge that Booth was on his way—however Gunner read that, it caused him to smile back.

"Let's get moving. We have a treasure to find," he said. "The dive boat is almost fully loaded."

Heather and I climbed aboard. There was no sign of Ben or Randy. I had to stall, or Gunner and I would be gone when Booth arrived. "We can get going after I grab a quick bite," I said. "I'm starving."

"You missed Randy's breakfast," Gunner said. "But he left you a plate in the galley."

I walked through the salon, down the steps, and straight ahead into Jack's cabin. I hesitated but didn't close the door. His

Glock was still on the nightstand, which, after checking over my shoulder, I placed in the back waistband of my shorts and pulled my t-shirt over.

There was a plate of dried-up scrambled eggs and cold bacon in the galley, which I put inside the microwave and turned on. With that and a glass of orange juice, I walked back up to the salon and sat on the bench seat that faced east toward TOTO, with Nassau twenty-five miles away. The best strategy now was hiding in plain sight. Again.

Outside, Randy was helping Gunner load two magnetometers and shovels onto the dive boat, which was tied off on the western side of the ship.

I poured hot sauce onto the eggs.

My heart seized at the sight of multiple boats coming in fast from the east. I guzzled the orange juice and nearly choked. Back on the deck, Randy stood tall and pointed east. Gunner climbed out of the dive boat to see what he was pointing toward. He then turned quickly and walked into the salon. I took a bite of bacon.

"Bunch of boats headed this way," he said.

"So?"

He now watched the boats approach from the salon window. "You think it's the authorities?"

"It was stupid of Jack to try and bribe the RBDF, so yeah, they're overdue at this point."

Gunner turned to face me. "Looks like four boats, not just the one this time."

I stood. "Sounds like a search party then. Crap."

"So what?" Gunner said.

"The gold ingots? All that shit—emeralds, jewelry, escudos, Ben's olive jar—all of it!" I stood. "They find that, we're going to jail."

Gunner's face was calm. He'd dealt with worse, no doubt. "We can hide it."

The boats were now maybe a half mile away and coming fast. "They've got an army," I said. "Let's just drop it all over the side. We can get it back later."

"Good idea." Gunner hurried down the steps and into his cabin. Of course he'd kept all the treasure close to him. I fully expected that once we'd found the rest, he and Randy would eliminate all of us. I adjusted the Glock in my pants.

Gunner came up the stairs two at a time, glanced to the east, and then slid open the starboard window that was facing west. He flung handfuls of gold and gems, and finally the olive jar, out the window. I watched as it all splashed into the blue water. We were anchored in seventy feet of water, so it was too deep for the RBDF boarding party to spot it from the surface, regardless of water clarity.

Randy peeked inside. "What do you want me to do?"

"Wait out there." Gunner turned toward the stairs. "Ben! Heather! Come topside. We have visitors." Then he turned to me and smiled. "Let's go, Reilly. We got this."

Gunner led the way, and before I stepped outside, I stashed the Glock under the chart on the counter. I got outside just as the four RBDF boats pulled up. Booth was on the bow of the lead boat wearing his blue blazer and khaki pants, with four men holding Heckler & Koch UMP submachine guns behind him. The other boats held four men each, and all were similarly armed.

Show time.

48

"HANDS UP, EVERYONE!" BOOTH SHOUTED.

"What the hell's going on here?" Gunner said.

I stepped back from him but kept my eyes on his hands. Was his gun under his shirt?

Four armed RBDF agents boarded the ship, one of which was the officer Jack had tried to give money to. "Arms up, now!" the officer said.

Ben, Heather, Randy, and I complied, but Gunner kept his hands on his hips—one of the agents jammed the butt of his machine gun into Gunner's stomach—he gasped and buckled in half. The officer shoved him against the starboard wall of the ship, frisked him, and found his Sig 9 mm.

"Gun!" he said.

"Turn around, hands against the wall!" Another said to the rest of us.

We complied. There was nothing to find on me, Heather, or Ben—

"Another gun!" Randy had a Sig in his belt, too. The officer cuffed Randy and pushed him onto the ground, where Gunner was already cuffed and seated. Gunner's reflective blue sunglasses had fallen to the deck, and his eyes were squinting into the morning sun.

"We have a permit to be here, dammit," Gunner said. Then to Booth: "Are you in charge here?"

Booth put his hand on his chest. "Not me. I'm just a guest.

Officer Rolle here's in charge." Then he smiled. "But you, Richard Rostenkowski, are under arrest for the murder of Charles and Betty Reilly."

Gunner's face curled into a sour expression. "The hell you talking about?"

"Same goes for Ben Reilly and Heather Drake." He glared at each of them. "You will be immediately deported to Switzerland, indicted, and tried for two counts of murder in the first degree."

Gunner's head swiveled toward me, now standing behind Booth. "You're behind this, aren't you?"

I walked forward and intentionally stepped on his sunglasses. *CRUNCH.*

"You killed my parents."

"You fucking pussy, after what we—hey—you're going to grab all that *Farnese*—"

"Ssshh." I knelt next to him and whispered. "Jack's DNA is on your knife, Gunner."

"Habeas corpus. No body, no crime." His whisper sounded like air leaking out of a slashed tire.

"Exactly why I videoed you gutting him and dumping him overboard."

Gunner's beady eyes glared at me, but he kept his lips pressed tight. Proving a ten-year-old murder would be hard, but the RBDF could search for Jack's body if I alerted them sooner than later.

"You've got no proof against me," Ben said.

I stood up and turned around to face him. It would hard to convict Ben—

"I'll testify that Ben Reilly conspired to kill his parents," Heather said. "He and Jack Dodson hired this man, Gunner, or whatever his real name is, to run them over in Geneva, Switzerland."

Booth beamed. "Tied up with a bow and a ribbon, boys. I'd

say you're fucked. So if anyone else wants to try and reduce their sentence—"

"It's true!" Ben said. "Gunner killed them! Jack paid him to—"

"You little weasel," Gunner said.

Booth clapped his hands together once. "Gentlemen, let's separate these three and return to Nassau. You can impound their ship."

My friend Bill Black wouldn't be too happy about that, but there was nothing I could do.

"What about the plane?" Officer Rolle said.

Booth turned to look at me. "That's an official vehicle belonging to my colleague here."

"*Colleague?*" Gunner said.

"Paybacks are hell, asshole," I said.

The RBDF officers separated Ben, Gunner, Randy, and Heather, and steered them toward different boats. "Can I have a minute with her?" I said.

Booth nodded. I led Heather a few feet away. My heart raced, and the tears that carved tracks down her face produced a streak of heat that poured down mine too. My breathing was ragged, and it took a moment to clear my throat.

"Thank you, Heather."

She wept, bit her lip, and glanced up at me. "I'm so sorry, Buck."

Her wrists were handcuffed behind her back, but I put my arms around her and gave her a hug. "The truth will set you free. Thank you for cooperating. I'll help, if I can."

Her body shook in my arms, and her tears flowed onto my neck. My own trickled down to blend with hers before I stepped back. Booth was grinding his jaw, no doubt to refrain from a wisecrack, but for once, he held his tongue. Another officer led Heather away, while two others went to secure the ship. Booth and I were left alone on the deck.

"When all this settles down, I'll want to know what all of you were doing here together. And what happened to Dodson."

I nodded but didn't respond. I assumed the RBDF agents would find Gunner's knife and hold it, and the DNA wasn't going anywhere. "Keep me posted on their arraignment and trial. I want to be there," I said.

Booth smiled, and I caught a whiff of his usual coffee breath. "You and me both, kid."

With that, he climbed over the gunwale and onto the speed-boat where Heather was seated, still watching me. The boat pulled forward slowly. I held a hand up, and Heather left me with a faint smile.

49

AFTER A NIGHT OF HEAVY DRINKING WITH RAY AT the Caerula Mar Club, I crashed on his couch. In the morning, he went to check out of the hotel, and I made a call.

"Bill Black."

"It's Buck Reilly."

His usual gravelly voice lifted a notch. "Have any luck?"

"You still have a subcontract to Queens Jewels, LLC there on the Treasure Coast?"

The company 1715 Fleet – Queens Jewels, LLC had held the prime salvage permit since the 1960s for the entire coastal area where the 1715 fleet had foundered. Mel Fisher's company was one of the first to salvage the 1715 wrecks in an organized fashion, and nobody had more experience in working with the State to attain permit rights than their collective partnership had. Today, Queens Jewels, LLC got 50% of any finds by any of their approved subcontractors. From my perspective, keeping 50% was better than nothing, which is what we'd get here in the Bahamas.

"Yeah, why?" Back to gravelly.

"Want to help me with a salvage operation there next week?"

"Help King Buck? Damn straight. Where specifically?"

"I'll let you know." I paused. "Do you, ah, know any spots that are not currently being salvaged within the permit area? Maybe a location in a hundred feet of deep water?"

Bill didn't respond right away, then said, "That's a weird question, why do you ask?"

"Just humor me."

Bill exhaled loudly into the phone. "There's nothing a hundred feet deep. The permit only extends three thousand yards from shore, and that averages twenty to forty feet."

"Forty feet works. You know a spot?"

"Sure, plenty of spots." He was quiet a moment. "One place is between two sites: Corrigan's to the north and Rio Mar to the south. The outward perimeter there's forty feet deep. Nobody's worked it for a while."

I felt my face tighten with a smile. "Perfect. Can you send me GPS numbers for a location? Like ASAP?"

"Yeah, I can do that." He paused, and I closed my eyes. Bill had been a treasure hunter working Florida's east coast for a long time and was as smart as any I'd known. I suspected warning bells would be ringing in his head by now. "You know, amigo, it's frowned upon to falsify provenance."

I smiled. "Just get me those numbers, Bill. I'll take care of the rest."

"Uh-huh, okay. Keep an eye on your phone. I'll clear my slate next week." His voice lifted. "By the way, how'd you like the *Global Explorer?*"

Oh crap. "Ah, worked like a charm." I needed his help, but I'd have to tell him the truth when I saw him.

We hung up, and I was satisfied that the back end of this operation should be covered. Now we just needed to make the front end work. Ray reappeared, and we caught a ride in a golf cart to the airport.

Betty and the Beast looked small compared to the Mallard, which was the next size up in the Grumman family of flying boats. The only one larger was the Albatross.

"Isn't she a beauty?" Ray said. In reality, the finish on the fuselage was pretty rough, but I knew Ray spoke of her potential. "And she runs great—better than I expected—but she'll need both engines overhauled."

I still hadn't told Ray the full plan ahead for fear that he'd rebel, but time was running out.

"You have the coordinates for the treasure site I gave you?" I said.

"Yeah. Already entered them into my GPS."

"You sure that Mallard won't sink?"

"It's fine, trust me," he said. "What are we going to do at the treasure site?"

"I have a boat meeting us later this afternoon. Before that, I need to salvage everything possible from the queen's jewels."

Ray began to shimmy again, and I put a hand on his shoulder so he wouldn't start jumping. "Keep your cool, Ray. Remember, we don't have a salvage permit."

I let him take off first so I could watch the Mallard fly. She was indeed a beauty, which was amazing after she'd sat here for so many years under a makeshift hangar. The port engine blew black smoke, but she flew true, her flaps and rudder operated smoothly, and Ray had worked miracles to get her airborne after a week's worth of intensive care.

When we approached the dive site, the circular craters Randy had blown from the *Global Explorer* were still visible on the ocean floor. I half expected to find RBDF agents here, fearing Gunner may have tried to trade knowledge about the wreck to reduce the charges against him, but if what Booth had said was true, he might already be en route to Switzerland for processing.

I circled once to watch the Mallard land in the deep-blue water and settle onto the step before it came to a stop by the last crater. The Beast followed after, and once past the Mallard, I killed the power, shut her down, and set the anchors. Ray had collected the anchors from Betty before we took off—he already had her in place and was seated in the open hatch, smiling like a proud father.

My heart again ached, but I had to remind myself of the bigger picture.

AFTER SIX HOURS OF DIVING, I'd used all the air in the two tanks I'd taken from the *Global Explorer* and two of the four I'd stored in my aft locker. The haul of treasure was impressive—more than I'd expected—so much that we'd filled the fuselages of both planes. I just hoped we hadn't exceeded their weight specs or thrown off the centers of gravity.

"I feel like King Solomon," Ray said. "I've never seen so much gold, silver, and jewels in one place! Makes the *Atocha* museum seem rinky-dink."

I checked my watch and glanced at the northern horizon, where a white trawler was headed our way, right on time. "Okay, Ray, the next phase of the operation is about to arrive."

He followed the point of my finger to the oncoming boat. "Is that someone we can trust?"

"I believe so."

"Who is it?"

"Jesse McDermitt."

"The guy from up the Keys? One with the Beaver?"

I nodded. "Don't mention anything about the treasure, got it?"

"No shit, Buck. But since you've already recovered all that, what's he here for?"

I smiled. "Camouflage."

I RIGGED THE FOURTH AND FINAL CANNON TO THE STEEL CABLE, then ascended to the surface. Jesse and his "crew" aboard the *Floridablanca* had already raised the others and secured them on deck under canvas. I hadn't expected him to have three men with him, but apparently, they'd all just come from a fishing tournament in Palm Beach and were close friends, so he trusted them implicitly. I recognized a couple of them, including Rusty Thurman, who had the physique of a red-haired human cannonball and was the owner of the Rusty Anchor up the Keys. Jimmy Saunders, Jesse's first mate, was working on the bow. The third guy was older and had a gray pallor but stood ramrod straight and wore a Marine regulation haircut and gray goatee that made his pedigree clear.

Jesse operated the lift from the raised pilot house, and Jimmy received the cannons on the foredeck, where Jesse lowered them slowly to be laid flat.

"Dude, how many more of these pirate sticks you got down there?" Jimmy said.

"Last one," I said. "Come get me at the plane once you have that one set."

I climbed the ladder back into the Beast, changed into a dry t-shirt and shorts, guzzled some water, and grabbed my cell phone. A text had come in from Bill Black that read "27.655649, -80.344705," which were latitude and longitude numbers for the spot he was suggesting I direct Jesse to.

"You're a good man, Bill."

I heard the outboard motor from the *Floridablanca*'s dinghy fire up. I sat down in the Beast's hatch as Jimmy closed the short distance to collect me.

"Cool old planes, *hermano*." He glanced from the Goose to the Mallard. "Like stepping back in time."

Jimmy took me back to the *Floridablanca*, where Jesse and Rusty stood waiting on the covered aft deck. The large transom door was open above the swim platform. After tying the dinghy's painter line to a cleat, I glanced up at Jesse, who I knew to be a stickler on marine courtesy.

"Permission to come aboard?"

He waved me forward. Jimmy stayed in the dinghy.

"Gentlemen," I said. We all shook hands.

"Reilly," Rusty said. His bushy red beard was now peppered with gray, and even though he was only 5'6", he had three hundred pounds packed onto his frame. Based on his cool reception, he must have remembered throwing me out of the Anchor a few years ago when a drunken tourist recognized me from e-Antiquity fame and picked a fight.

"Are we talking the Goose or the Mallard?" Jesse said.

"The Mallard."

We turned to look at it and saw Ray Floyd seated in the hatch watching us. He waved.

"That Ray Floyd?"

"Yeah, he's my partner at Last Resort," I said.

"Let's go check it out," Jesse said.

"Now isn't the best time," I said.

Jesse was as tall as me at 6'3" and he peered straight into my eyes. "Then when?"

"Few days. Either you can come to Key West, or I'll bring it up to Marathon." I paused and put forth a smile that earned a frown from Rusty. "Ray wants to clean it up pretty for you."

"Well, I've got your cannons, but our deal was to drop them off today, not in a few days. So you want me to drop them back in the water?"

Rusty glowered at me.

"As a matter of fact, I do." I lifted my phone and forwarded the coordinates that Bill Black had sent me to Jesse's phone. "I just sent you the numbers where I'd like you to drop them, just north of Vero Beach."

"In the water?"

I nodded. "Three thousand feet offshore in thirty feet of water. As soon as possible."

Jesse nodded slowly and glanced from me back to the Mallard. He raised a pair of binoculars and studied the old flying boat. "Okay," he said. "Vero Beach is nearly two hundred miles away, but the cannons will be dropped in a tight pile there by this time tomorrow. I'll see you to collect the Mallard next week."

We shook hands.

I noticed the older guy atop the flybridge staring down at us like a sniper ready to punch my clock if things went awry. I gave him a two-finger salute off my forehead.

"Oorah," he responded in a low voice.

"Thanks, guys," I said. "Let me know after you make the drop."

Jimmy returned me to the Beast, and after I squeezed past all the booty, pulled the anchors, and closed the hatches, I sat in the left seat and donned my headset. The *Floridablanca* was already small on the horizon, and the Mallard's twin turboprop engines roared to life in front of me.

I changed the channel to the one Ray and I used for communication and clicked the mic, cognizant that it was still an open line. "You there, Ray?"

"I'm here." Ray paused. "Why was Jesse staring at me through binoculars?"

"He was admiring the Mallard." I bit my lip. Did I tell him now, or later?

"I hope she'll take off with all this, ah, cargo on board," he said.

"You go first. I'll follow you."

"Okay, partner, see you in Key West."

"We're headed to Vero Beach. We, ah, need to plant all this cargo with the cannons he's dropping for us, but at a nine-knot cruising speed, they won't get there for twenty hours."

The Mallard had begun to move across the water, gaining speed slowly. She was an elegant old bird with more contemporary lines than the Beast or Betty and would have made a fine addition to Last Resort's fleet, but she was a necessary means to an end.

Ray's voice sounded again in my headset. "Why do I feel like there's something you're not telling me, Buck?"

I cranked up the Beast's starboard engine just as the Mallard lifted heavily off the water. She hovered at low altitude and gradually increased her rate of climb.

"Looking good, Ray. See you soon."

50

AFTER A SLEEPLESS NIGHT AT A HOTEL close to the Vero Beach airport, where I'd claimed exhaustion rather than having dinner with Ray to avoid his increasing curiosity, we returned to the airport and had a late breakfast to kill time. My nerves were shot from leaving the planes on the tarmac loaded with millions of dollars' worth of treasure, but the theme for this operation had been to hide in plain sight, which, after a quick inspection, had worked yet again.

My phone finally buzzed to announce a text. It was from Jesse McDermitt. "Deep sixed, no eyeballs, good to go."

A warm glow lit in my chest. "10-4, thanks," I responded.

"See you next week," he wrote.

"Can we get this over with?" Ray said. "I want to get the Mallard back to her new base of operation in Key West."

We flew both planes out to the coordinates four miles away and circled once. I could see the cannons as a dark anomaly in the relatively shallow water. Once we were anchored up, Ray repeatedly lowered the cargo in a basket I'd fashioned from a throw net. I placed the items in holes I'd dug near the cannons. If anyone studied the site closely, it would be clear the items had recently been placed there, but I didn't plan to take anything other than cursory photographs to document the find.

We flew back to Key West after that to drop the Mallard, then returned to Andros to get Betty. Once home, Ray and I sat in lawn chairs on the tarmac between the three planes, our eyes drooped with fatigue. Numerous well-wishers stopped by to see the Mallard, and Ray beamed as he described how he'd been able to get her airworthy in such a short period of time.

I retrieved a bottle of Pilar Dark Rum from my locker, and we each had a tumbler of the brown liquor, neat. The sky was pink with the onset of sunset. I'd been struggling with how to tell Ray about my deal with Jesse but ultimately realized there was no good way to break the news.

I cleared my throat. "That was a hell of a deal on the Mallard," I said.

"A hundred thousand dollars. Crazy, right?"

"What would you say if we could get millions for her?"

"That's silly. What are you talking about?"

A mouthful of Pilar gave me courage. "Because that's the deal," I said.

"What deal?" Ray now half-turned in his chair to face me. His brow furled, and his eyes narrowed.

"The one I made with Jesse McDermitt in exchange for him picking up the cannons and dropping them where we placed the treasure."

"What did you do?" Ray's voice now had an edge.

"Ray, the whole thing was an illegal operation Jack roped me into. He died on the site. We had no right to salvage that ship and could have easily been busted by the Bahamians. I had to improvise—"

"With my plane? What the hell—give him one of yours—"

"It's *our* plane, Ray. Last Resort Charter and Salvage's, to be precise. We're partners, and I know it hurts, but it's business. We'll get a one-hundred-time multiple on that investment."

He clenched his jaw. "Ten million dollars?" Ray was good with numbers.

"At least, after our cut with Queens Jewels, LLC and after we pay Bill Black to help us retrieve everything."

Ray leaned his head back on the top of the chair and closed his eyes.

"I wanted to tell you sooner—"

He suddenly swatted the glass of rum off his armrest—it shattered on the tarmac. Silence followed.

Crap.

I guzzled the rest of my rum, stood, folded up the chair, and hesitated. Ray's eyes were still closed and his head reclined.

"We'll meet Bill Black in a few days to collect the treasure." I paused. "It'll be a big deal. Nobody knows about the *Farnese* except me—us—so it'll be important news in archeological communities." I inhaled a deep breath and let it out slowly. "Jesse will come down next week to collect the Mallard." I winced when I said it, and Ray pressed his lips tightly closed in response. A tear formed in the corner of his closed eye.

With the chair under my arm, I returned to the hangar, replaced the rum in my locker, and leaned the chair against it. I hated myself for breaking Ray's heart. Sunken treasure and big archeological finds meant a lot to me, but restoring rare old planes was Ray's passion, *his* purpose. It didn't matter that he could buy fifty Mallards with his share of the money: he'd fallen in love with this one. I could have offered Jesse cash or a piece of the deal, but I didn't think he'd have helped us if he knew all the details, and I didn't want to put him at risk beyond the cannons.

I had an idea on how to make it up to Ray, but before I said anything to him, I needed to call the airplane broker in Tennessee and see if that Albatross was still available.

EPILOGUE

A FEW DAYS LATER, I RETURNED ALONE TO SEBAS-
TIAN INLET. Bill Black and I departed for the site on his boat,
the *Carib*, a twenty-six-foot Stamas. The *Carib* was a far cry from
the *Global Explorer* or the *Floridablanca*, but she was perfect for
today's purposes. It was a beautiful, sunny January day, but the
temperature had dropped to the low sixties. Bill told his team that
we didn't need their help today but that I'd found something
interesting in French archives related to the *Griffon* and had put
the pieces together to locate an unknown and uncharted wreck
within the 1715 Fleet – Queens Jewels, LLC permit area. He said
he'd check it out and report back if we found anything and
needed help.

To protect Bill, I shared no details other than the information
I'd learned in France, less the facts of the *Griffon* and *Farnese*
miraculously sailing across the southern Bahama Bank into
TOTO and the details of piracy that followed. Bill stayed on
board when I dove on the cannons, and his eyes were the size of
saucers when I returned with the basket of gold ingots, chain,
coins, and jewels. And that was only the first of twenty-plus loads
I sent back up to him in the basket.

The State requires items like cannons and large anchors to be
left in situ, so I dug around them, roughing up the bottom to
make it less obvious they'd just been dropped here.

Bill insisted on following protocol and called Queens Jewels to
alert them of the significant news. "We found the queen's …
jewels." His voice broke when relaying the news.

The voice on the other end shouted with excitement, then came back on and said, "Who's 'we'?"

He beamed. "Me and Buck Reilly. He hired me to take him out based on research he'd done in Brest, and damned if it wasn't spot on."

After he hung up, I told him that the RBDF had confiscated the *Global Explorer* because some of the people on board were wanted for serious crimes abroad. His smile disappeared. He stared at me for a long moment until his brow finally lifted.

"You can afford to replace it with all this loot."

THE NEXT SEVERAL DAYS were filled with fanfare, television crews, interviews, and celebrations with the team from Queens Jewels, who'd gone back out with us to dive the site and inspect the cannons. While there was no evidence of any other remnants of the *Farnese*, nobody argued with the story. The research information Scarlet had started and I had finished in France was comprehensive and convincing, aside from the information I'd omitted about the actual location.

"*Trouve les canons, pas le bateau*," was the hook that had reeled the press in, and the next day, the *Wall Street Journal*'s headline read: "KING BUCK IS BACK!" It gave me goose bumps but also made me nervous, given the details.

I refused all other interviews.

The sad reality was that we'd totally ignored appropriate archeological practices to document and preserve the location of the *Farnese*. I rationalized, telling myself it was because of Jack dying there, the pressure of the situation, and the unlikely potential of the Bahamian government cooperating with a salvage effort ... but no matter how I tried to spin it, the ends would never justify the means.

Plus, Booth had made it clear he wanted answers on why we'd been in the Bahamas and what had happened to Jack, so my greatest concern was that the truth would come out sooner or later. I did know that everyone's possessions from the *Global Explorer* had been held by the authorities, including Gunner's knife, so if pressed, I'd suggest they check that for Jack's DNA. The video of Gunner carving up Jack and dumping him overboard while laughing about it was my only insurance against him spilling the beans as part of a plea deal. But I didn't think Switzerland would care about Bahamian treasure or a request for extradition anyway. The ten-year-old case of the double murder of my parents, especially with my father as a former undersecretary of state in the State Department, would trump any other demands.

JESSE FLEW TO KEY WEST A FEW DAYS LATER in his Beaver, and while Ray hadn't spoken to me since I told him of the deal I'd made, he was very professional with Jesse during the inspection, aside from acting like a father sending his daughter off on an arranged marriage he objected to. I briefed Jesse on Ray's heartbreak and offered him an incentive to help soften the blow. He studied Ray, who was obviously not copacetic with losing the Mallard.

"You restored Buck's other planes, right?" Jesse said.

"That's right."

"Would you be interested in restoring the Mallard for me?"

Ray's face lit up. "Absolutely. I've done a lot of research on where I, er, you, could get parts and the optimal updated specs that should be included."

Jesse nodded. "I'm more interested in quality than speed, so why don't you come up with a plan and budget, then give me a call?"

Even his share of the treasure hadn't produced a smile on Ray's face comparable to the ear-to-ear one he had now. I couldn't wait to see his face when I told him we had an appointment next week in Tennessee to flight test that Albatross—his "dream plane," as he'd called it—but we needed to get all this behind us first.

Jesse reached out and shook Ray's hand. I walked him back to the Beaver, and once he climbed aboard, I glanced back and saw Ray studying the Mallard's port engine. From my pocket, I removed an eight escudos gold coin I'd taken from the *Farnese* and palmed it to Jesse when we shook hands.

"Thanks again for your help," I said. "And for hiring Ray to restore the Mallard."

"He's the best there is, so I would have done it anyway, but I appreciate the token."

I felt like saying that the token was worth $30,000, but it didn't matter, because without Jesse, I'd still be in the Bahamas trying to figure out a way home.

"You got off easy anyway, Reilly. Or, should I say, King Buck?"

THE NEWS FROM SWITZERLAND WAS ALL POSITIVE. Heather had agreed to cooperate fully, and given that she had only alerted Jack about my parents leaving for Switzerland, which Ben confirmed—as he threw Gunner and Jack under the bus while trying to cut his own deal—no charges were filed against her. The prosecutor was confident in the case against Gunner and Ben, and while Jack had met a fitting end given his attempt to kill me, I would have preferred he were alive to face the charges.

The time I'd spent with Heather in the Bahamas and her contribution to ensuring the prosecution's success in Switzerland had helped to put our past behind us. Our frequent phone calls to stay in touch while she remained in Switzerland and her encouraging me to come to be with her during Gunner and Ben's trial had me pondering the future.

In my palm sat a large pair of pearl earrings that had been destined for King Philip V's new twenty-two-year-old wife, Elisabeth Farnese, as a part of the queen's jewels.

I imagined them on Heather's ears.

We'd see how it went …

THE END

Turn the page for a sneak peek of my historical fiction novel, THE LAST RAFT!

The Last Raft

By John H. Cunningham

PROLOGUE

THE GLASS DOORS of the Palacio de la Revolución flew open with such force that one shattered. A bearded man dressed in starched green fatigues stormed out and took the stairs two at a time as he held a bucket out to his side. As he marched up toward the José Martí tower, the sound of his boots stomped loudly against the cobblestones of Flag Square where the cry of buzzards cawed overhead.

At the tower's peak was an interior observation area that overlooked the asphalt plaza and the sprawling gull-wing shaped palacio where Fidel Castro kept his office. As the highest observation point in Havana, the tower was normally crowded with visitors, but not this morning. A siege environment had permeated the country, and citizens and visitors alike were worried by the presence of troops now in place all over the city.

The uniformed man breathed heavily as he charged through Flag Square and onto the path that led to the circular deck around the tower. His calf-height boots shined black against his olive-green tunic. The liquid in the open bucket sloshed around, its fumes burning his eyes. Buzzards circled and cast intermittent shadows over him as he climbed the incline. His eyes remained focused on the tower.

A sentry slouched behind the tower was standing guard with his back to the palacio. The sound of pounding footsteps alerted him, and as he turned toward the sound his hand dropped to his holster. Recognition suddenly filled his eyes and the gun hand snapped up in salute.

The bearded man stormed past without so much as a nod, the bucket brushing against the sentry's leg and splashing gasoline on his pants. The bearded man marched onto the deck then continued toward the two-story sculpture of José Martí at the tower's base.

THE FIRST TOURISTS who had arrived at the tower were an elderly Canadian couple, determined not to allow the marshal law to ruin their vacation. They spied the wreaths on easels placed in the shadow of the gargantuan white marble sculpture of José Martí and shuffled over to read their ribbons before entering the tower. The old man held up his guidebook.

"It says diplomats leave wreathes of good tiding before visiting Castro."

"That must have been before the exodus," the woman said.

Two large arrangements sat like old Christmas decorations at the shrine. The first ribbon read: The Republic of Gambia. It was a modest composition of pine and broad leaves that paled in comparison with the large ornate wreath next to it. As they leaned forward to read the ribbon, the uniformed man burst out from behind the tower. Beads of sweat dripped from under his green cap, and his obsidian eyes appeared ready to burst from their sockets. Armed guards followed after the soldier.

The couple stepped back, their heads swiveled toward one another, and the old man mouthed a name to his wife's frozen stare.

"*Fidel Castro?*"

The uniformed man brushed past them and heaved the bucket toward the larger wreath. They watched in astonishment as he produced a box of wooden matches, lit four at once, and tossed them forward. A huge fireball swaddled in black smoke that caressed the white marble statue followed a sudden whoosh.

The man spun around and chopped the air with his palm. *"Estos hijos de puta no saban con quién están jugando!"*

He disappeared as quickly as he'd come. Only the flames remained as proof of the moment.

"What did he say?" the woman said.

"These sons of bitches don't know who they're messing with."

The Canadians shielded their faces from the pressing heat and glimpsed the last words on the blazing ribbon as it turned to ash.

'… STATES OF AMERICA.'

1

WITH ONE FOOT on shore and the other on the raft, Ernesto del Torres looked back to his '57 Chevy convertible hidden in the thicket of mangroves. Only the tail fins, trunk and chrome bumper were visible. He could just make out the Politburo designation on the license plate.

"*Coño*, man, let's get going," a voice said from behind him.

Ernesto nodded and took one last look, savoring the idea that the Policía would soon find the car and call his father. What would the great Ramon del Torres say then?

He turned and saw the anxious faces on the raft and let out a deep sigh.

Maria reached for his hand and smiled when he met her eyes. *I'll take care of you, baby, but the rest of these people are on their own.*

Ernesto looked past her to Juan, the hustler who had organized the journey. He then glanced at Manuel, a retired sugarcane worker, squatting in a pained heap next to Vilma, an equally vintage government secretary, and wondered how their ancient bodies would fare at sea.

"Whenever you're ready," Juan said. He stood in the water behind the raft and drummed his fingers on the deck.

Ernesto glanced down at the rusty oil drums beneath the eight-foot square platform and sighed again.

This thing looks like a deathtrap. "You sure this raft will actually float?"

"You think I'd risk my own life?" Juan said.

"It's not worth much."

Juan shrugged, flicked his cigarette into the water and tugged hard on the rope to pull the raft off the shore. Ernesto's foot slipped from the raft's edge and he awkwardly half-fell into the shallow water.

Asshole.

Ernesto splashed out after them, caught up quickly and pulled himself aboard. Maria squeezed his arm with a pleading look he well understood, and he pressed his teeth together. Juan was lucky she was on board, otherwise he'd gladly wring the smug *campesino's* neck right then and there. He turned and caught Manuel staring at him, a restrained smile on his lips.

"What are you looking at?" Ernesto said.

The ocean floor dropped off sharply just a few yards from shore, and once the water was up to his chest, Juan climbed on board the crowded deck.

"Next stop Florida." He winked at Maria, who nodded and returned his smile.

Ernesto put his arm around her and pulled her close.

The morning was calm, and with no wind to help launch the raft, the small waves pushed it steadily back toward shore, where the drums scraped against the coral and sand.

Vilma stopped humming and turned to Juan. "Are you going to get us out further, or are we going to spend the day at the beach?"

Juan's lips puckered as if he had just bitten into a sour lime. He turned to Ernesto and pointed.

"You. Pull us out."

"Me? Why not you?"

"Let's get something straight, okay? I'm the captain, and when I tell you to do something, you do it." The drums again scraped loudly. "And right now I'm telling you to get in the water and pull us out."

A shock of red appeared on Ernesto's neck. Nobody aside from his father had ever spoken to him that way. He felt Maria's hand tighten on his but he pulled away.

"Well I'm telling you to go fuck yourself, Captain."

Juan's face tightened and his eyes darted quickly at the others.

"Listen—" He stopped, his cheeks flushed, and let out a deep breath. "The problem is, I can't swim, and we're sitting ducks right here unless—"

"You're kidding me, right?" Ernesto said. "You were in the Guardia Frontera and you can't *swim*? What did you do, sweep the docks?"

"Come on, Ernesto," Maria said. "A patrol could show up any second. Please—"

"We paid this schemer to take us to Florida and he can't even swim!" Ernesto said. But he was already stripping to his swimsuit. He then slid into the water and began the difficult task of getting the raft out beyond the pull of the shore.

When the bottom fell away, he swam around behind the raft and pushed it out toward the liquid horizon. After several minutes the current pulled them outward, assisted by the outgoing tide.

"Ernesto was a champion swimmer," Maria told the group before she helped him back on board.

"Thank you, Señor del Torres." Manuel handed him a jug of water.

"Champion?" Juan said. "Of what?"

"His youth group."

"*Communist* youth, eh *muchacho*?"

Ernesto ignored him and focused instead on drying himself off.

Still shaking his head, Juan slowly turned to the others. "Stay quiet and keep watch for patrols. The Guardia's been shooting *balseros* on sight since the exodus."

"I read that four thousand bodies have been found in Cuban waters already," Maria said. "We need to be careful."

"Out of a hundred thousand who have fled. I don't know about being careful, but we could use some luck," Juan said.

"So many dead, how do you know?" Manuel asked.

"They keep track of the body count in *Granma*," Maria said. "They think it'll scare others from leaving."

"In the newspaper? Like a box score?"

Juan laughed. "Are you crippled *and* blind, old man?"

Maria cleared her throat. "Lots of people make it, and we will too," she said after a moment of awkward silence. Then her eyes lit up. "Just think, we're going to Florida." Her smile was big, and although her teeth were slightly crooked, her face had a natural beauty made warmer by the slight flaw.

Ernesto watched as Juan's eyes followed her legs to her stomach, then paused on her breasts. His tongue wetted his lips as he stared at her caramel skin, the planes of her high cheekbones, her amber eyes that sparkled in the sunlight.

"That's my fiancé you're drooling over, Juan."

Maria elbowed Ernesto in the ribs, and Juan let loose a belly laugh.

"So I see."

Vilma stopped her humming. "Enough of this bickering, you two."

An uncomfortable quiet settled over the raft until Vilma asked Juan how long it would take to get to Florida.

"Six days at most, four if we're lucky. The wind's pretty calm, but we'll make good time once we get into the Gulf Stream."

The raft drifted slowly from shore at the mercy of the current, the breeze, the waves and the tide. Ernesto looked back to the gray smudges of the Pinar del Río mountains that loomed above the brown sand and green mangroves. The colors changed rapidly as the morning sun made its way higher into the sky. His eyes moved down the coast toward Mariel, where the Guardia Frontera base was located. A narrow finger of shoreline stretched out from the mainland to create a point, and as they floated beyond it, Ernesto suddenly cocked his head at the sound of a rumble in the distance.

His eyes narrowed to a squint and he carefully scanned the horizon. Nothing was visible, but the low rumble grew louder. *It sounds like a—*

"Ernesto, what is it?" Maria asked.

He held up a hand but said nothing.

"Over there." Juan pointed to a dark silhouette that emerged from behind the point.

"Is it the Guardia?" Maria asked.

"More like some kind of speedboat."

"Look at all those people," Juan said. The cigarette-shaped boat rode low in the water, and Ernesto could make out the silhouettes of over two-dozen heads crammed together like bowling pins. The boat moved slowly away from the coast, a dark shape on the azure sea, with a trail of thin lines of chalky wake trailing behind.

"Smugglers," Juan said.

"I didn't think there were any boats left after the exodus," Maria said.

"That's where we should be," Ernesto said. "They'll be in Florida in hours, not days."

The boat's rumble turned into a high-pitched buzz across the water. Ernesto watched as the bow lifted high into the air, and as the whine remained steady, so did the boat's angle toward the sky. Then the noise suddenly disappeared and the bow dropped back down.

"Your speedboat's having trouble getting up to speed," Juan said. "If they're too heavy, they're screwed."

The loud screech of an air horn suddenly ripped through the

morning air.

"Oh, God." Vilma grasped the cross around her neck.

They'd been so distracted that nobody had noticed the triangular silhouette of a Guardia patrol boat steaming straight toward them. The horn sounded again.

"Everybody down," Juan said. "Lie as flat as you can."

"Can they see us?" Maria asked.

Ernesto put his arm around Maria and tried to cover her up. "I can't tell, just lay still." He pressed his body onto hers and shut his eyes tight. The buzz of the speedboat sounded again, as did the Guardia's horn, but neither could drown out Vilma's frantic prayers.

Want to keep reading? Grab your copy of THE LAST RAFT!

ABOUT THE AUTHOR

John H. Cunningham is the author of the best selling, eight book, Buck Reilly adventure series, which includes Red Right Return, Green to Go, Crystal Blue, Second Chance Gold, Maroon Rising, Free Fall to Black, Silver Goodbye and White Knight, along with the historical fiction novel, The Last Raft.

John has either lived in or visited the many locations that populate his novels, and he mixes fact with fiction and often includes real people in the cast of characters. Adhering to the old maxim, "write what you know," John's books have an authenticity and immediacy that have earned loyal followers and strong reviews. John writes stories that concern themselves with the same tensions and issues that affect all of our lives, and his choices for the places and plots that populate his stories include many settings that he loves, including Key West, Cuba, Jamaica, and multiple Caribbean locations. John splits his time between New York, Virginia and Key West.

Follow John H. Cunningham here:
Facebook: johnhcunningham
Instagram: johnhcunningham
Twitter: @jh_cunningham
Bookbub: bookbub.com/authors/john-h-cunningham
Website: www.jhcunningham.com
Newsletter: mailchi.mp/e53f65ab50a8/jhcunningham

ACKNOWLEDGEMENTS

I would like to thank several people who have assisted me with researching the history of the 1715 fleet, starting with treasure hunter Bill Black who provided me with countless details on locations, historical facts, information on equipment and operations and then pre-read the manuscript for authenticity. Thanks also to Kim Fisher and Taffi Fisher Abt for their insights and providing me with an 8 Escudos that had been recovered from one of the wrecks.

Captain Antoine D'Aire and the French frigate, *Griffon* were both real, and the only ship and crew of the twelve to survive the journey where in excess of a thousand people perished in the nameless hurricane that sank the plate fleet off the east coast of Florida. Five of the eleven sunken ships and the queen's dowry have still not been found.

Thanks to author Wayne Stinnett for asking to include Buck Reilly in his books *Rising Moon* and *Riding Tide* to help his protagonist, Jesse McDermitt, find a Grumman flying boat, which led to a pivotal scene and collaboration between Buck and Jesse at a critical point here in *Indigo Abyss*. Thanks to the beta readers, and experts including Carl Grooms on flying details, Shawn Martin on scuba terminology and Fritz Kloepfel on nautical facts. Thanks also fellow authors, Don Rich, Michael Reisig, Nick Sullivan and Nicholas Harvey for their help in fine-tuning the story.

Thank you to Ross Browne, Shannon Roberts and Julian Delfino of The Editorial Department (I missed you, Renni, on this one); Tim Harkness for artistic contributions and Aurora Publicists for their help in launching and publicizing the book.

Thank you to the fans of the Buck Reilly series for your patience and dedication to Buck's journey and the arc of his often challenged life.

Special thanks to my brothers Jim and Jay, and their wives Mary and Beth, Ron and Linda Weiner, Holly, Bailey, Cortney and Will Prendergast for their love and support.

ALSO BY JOHN H. CUNNINGHAM

RED RIGHT RETURN
GREEN TO GO
CRYSTAL BLUE
SECOND CHANCE GOLD
MAROON RISING
FREE FALL TO BLACK
SILVER GOODBYE
WHITE KNIGHT

If you'd like to subscribe to my newsletter and receive promotions, book recommendations, and updates on coming books, please sign up on my website: jhcunningham.com/news-events

MUSIC LINKS

"THE BALLAD OF BUCK REILLY"

"RUM PUNCH"
by Thom Shepherd, co-written by John H. Cunningham

"LONG VIEW OFF A SHORT PIER"
by Dave McKenney, co-written by John H. Cunningham

"HANGING OUT AT LE SELECT"
by Keith Sykes, co-written by John H. Cunningham

"SILVER GOODBYE"
by Donald James, co-written by John H. Cunningham

Made in United States
North Haven, CT
14 November 2022

26703387R00209